ALSO BY A.Z. LOUISE

Off-Time Jive

AS T.O TATE

A Concrete Crown: MacBeth Retold

BITTERBOUND

By A.Z. Louise

Robot Dinosaur Press
https://robotdinosaurpress.com/

Robot Dinosaur Press is a trademark of Chipped Cup Collective.

ISBN 978-1-949936-87-2
Ebook ISBN 978-1-949936-86-5
Cover art and design by A.Z. Louise
Interior illustrations by A.Z. Louise
Print design and typeset by A.Z. Louise
Digital Design by A.Z. Louise
Edited by Maya Evan MacGregor
Author photo by Darzy

CONTENT WARNINGS

This book contains depictions of intrusive thoughts, severe dermatillomania, emotional abuse, discussion of suicidal ideation, death of a family member (off page), violence/serious injury, and an infectious disease epidemic. Please take care of yourself when reading.

This one's just for me

CHAPTER ONE

THE LIGHT IN THE DEAD MAN'S TENT IS A DIFFUSE GOLD, lantern glow shining through waxed canvas. The space is large enough to stand in, a departure from the one- or two-person tents that dominate the war camp. The warlord who presides over this moving demesne has an even larger tent nearby, and the sound of a lute can be heard, the singer's voice reduced to notes rather than words. Lord Felver and his sons would have real furniture, unlike the dead man, whose tent contains only a blanket roll. There's nothing else there besides a pair of boots and a single saddlebag, draped in the shirt the dead man wore that day.

Kin slips her utility knife back into her sleeve, letting the flap she'd cut fall shut behind her. She draws one of the long baselards at that hang beneath her skirt, warm from contact with her skin. The knife makes the barest hiss, covered by the sound of the dead man's deep breaths and the guards softly talking outside.

Kin kneels on the lumpy ground, watching and listening. The dead man doesn't stir, his face slack, angles carved out in sickly yellow light and gray shadow. A silver collar encircles his throat, each section connected to the next with a golden link. One such link lies against the artery that runs down the right side of his neck. Easy. Kin places the point of her knife just below that link, not breathing. The dead man wakes.

His eyes are dark and clear. Fearless. Kin may have seen that look in a target's eyes before, but she can't remember it now. His eyes are too deep, unsettling in the way most people find a dark night in an abandoned place, sensing hidden watchers where there are none. Kin would rather be somewhere lonely, instead of being anywhere near the kind of man who doesn't fear her. Anyone who doesn't tremble just a little in her presence is either foolish or more dangerous than she.

Kin waits for him to speak. Sometimes the people she ends have last words to convey—and that's their right—or a little fight in them. Kin always hopes for a fight. Fights are more interesting than pleading or requests to bear messages, especially when the messages aren't even relayed as far as she knows. Though the Binders wish to know every word exchanged with her every target, she knows them, knows that they don't care one whit for anything other than themselves. Bearing those last words with no recipient wears on Kin like sand in her shoes, slowly scraping her down.

"I had always imagined a gut wound," the dead man says at last, eyes not leaving Kin's face. Kin watches him warily, the Binders' enchantments like a second pulse as they draw her toward him. Only killing him will bring relief. "I wondered what it would feel like. Do you know what if feels like, fleshbound?"

"Yes. It's a bad way to die. You're lucky. I'm merciful," Kin says.

"Can a fleshbound have mercy?" He considers her with a newly curious eye. The dead man has the kind of face that had likely been pretty once, but has settled into something more appealing over the years. Something less startling. It's a shame he has to die. Kin might have flirted with him under other circumstances.

"I do," Kin says at last. Lost looking at a target like she's newmade. This man is strange indeed.

"Will you grant a last request, then?" the dead man asks.

"Within reason." Hopefully not a message. *Please* not a message.

"Take this off." He touches the collar around his neck. "I want to die free."

An easy request to grant. This man may be a sorcerer, but she can sink her knife into his throat in an instant. Even if he gets the upper hand somehow, she can survive anything and find him anywhere.

"It will hurt. I've tried before," says the dead man. There's a rasp in his voice, and his eyes look above Kin's head at the peak of the tent. "I always faint before I can get it off. I wouldn't want you to get caught because I screamed."

Curious. The people Kin kills never care about her safety. Who would? She places one hand over the dead man's mouth, his breath warm against her hand, and fits the tip of her knife inside the golden link at his throat. A sharp twist should lever it open, but the soft gold doesn't bend or break. The dead man jerks beneath Kin's hand, breath fast and shallow against her fingers. A second attempt fails, and his throat works visibly, a guttural sound gurgling up against his lips.

Kin takes away her hand. He's something special, something far more powerful than the Binders had let on, to wear a magical item able to resist the strength of a fleshbound.

"What are you?" Kin asks.

"I'm a Carrier."

Kin sits back on her heels. When the Binders tell her to kill a sorcerer in a war camp, she expects to find a Reaper or a Healer. Both follow war like crows. But a Carrier ought to be deep in research or at his holy Wellspring, not waiting to march into battle.

The man touches the collar at his neck again, his dark eyes two wells of buried-deep pain.

"This has made me into a war machine."

Kin may be capable of mercy, but pity was taken from her years ago, leaving behind little emotion to spare for her targets. She knows utility, though, and this man can be of use to her, and she to him.

"I'll make you a deal," she said. "I'll break the collar and take you away from here. In exchange, you'll help me find my soul and destroy it."

The man's eyes search Kin's face, dance over her body as he takes her in, deciding whether she's worth trusting. If he trusts her to kill in service of his freedom once she's set her mind to it, he's smart. If he trusts her to do anything else, well . . .

"It's a deal," he says.

Kin covers his mouth again, this time noting how soft the flesh of a mortal man feels against her callused hand. She gives one last wrench to the golden link. It twists open at last, and the alive man sits up, fumbling at his throat to pull off the collar. Kin catches his wrist when he makes to throw it away. The Binders give her only a tiny stipend every month, knowing she has no need for food or shelter. This much gold and silver is worth more than she's seen in years.

"Get dressed. Get your things." Kin stands to give him room.

The man moves gingerly, like his whole body aches, to pick up his discarded shirt and pull it on. All of his clothes are dyed the same pale blue and black as the banners outside the camp, though they're far from a soldier's uniform. They're more like the clothes Kin has seen lords dress their mistresses in: pretty decorations for something they own. She can see why he wastes no time rolling his blankets up.

When he reaches for his saddlebag, Kin stops him to grab it instead, throwing it over her left shoulder. He looks like he's ridden all day for weeks. Kin is perpetually fresh, rarely needing more than an hour's rest every night unless she's badly wounded or skipped her hour for days on end. One of the few benefits of being fleshbound.

Kin shepherds him out of the tent with a rustle of canvas. Outside in the chill night, a sliver of moon is nearly outshone by the sharp, shallow pinpricks of stars. The mist of dim light leaves the small gap between the backs of the tents shadowed and safe. As they make their way away from his tent, Kin and her target have to turn sideways more than once to fit through the narrow space, or crouch to stay hidden, listening for soldiers making their rounds. The sound of heavy boots pass by as they reach the edge of the row of tents, where Kin puts out a hand to keep her new ally from stepping into the open. She can survive a fight, but the sorcerer might not, and she refuses to risk him now that she has him.

"Who here knows your face?" Kin asks.

"Most everybody this side of camp. If we make it to the far side, I don't think anyone will recognize me there. They might get suspicious if they sense my magic."

"Can you hide it?"

The sorcerer shakes his head. "It's impossible for Carriers. We're too powerful." The words sound like bragging, but his tone and posture give away no ego. He's simply stating a fact.

"Oh, well. We'll be careful."

Kin moves from shadow to shadow to avoid being seen, the darkness welcoming her as its own. The sorcerer is absorbed just the same, as if the night is willing take him as long as he's at her side. Twice soldiers pass by, their eyes sliding right past, noticing nothing. If they sense magic, they likely dismiss the feeling as the Reapers who surely lurk all around the camp. If Kin had the same sense of magic as humans, she would use it to avoid any Reapers, but that ability was taken when she was Bound.

After skirting an open area holding tethered horses and blacksmiths' tents, Kin and the sorcerer find their way to another cluster of tents, and she feels more than sees him relax as they fade back into the darkness.

"What's your name?" Kin asks. Not because she wants to know more about the not-dead man who has no fear of her. It's simply more convenient to know.

"Verias." His voice is steady but soft.

"We're almost out, Verias. My horse is waiting."

CHAPTER TWO

THE EDGE OF THE WAR CAMP IS LINED BY WAGONS. SOME belong to the army, some to camp followers of all kinds. Smiths, hoping to find work, folk selling food and drink better than army rations. People whose homes were razed to the ground by this very army and who have nowhere else to go. An army is an economy all its own, and there are always mouths to feed and things to fix in one way or another. There are always things to forget.

The assassin stops at the edge of the row of tents, perhaps given pause by the sheer mass of camp followers. Verias waits for her to plan her next move, remembering how he has often wished that taking up with a camp follower might help him forget, too. Not that he's ever been allowed time alone with anyone but his handler, Reshon. Reshon is easy on the eyes and brutal in every other way possible, so much so that Verias shudders just thinking about him.

"This should be fun. A game I haven't played in ages." The assassin unlace her blouse. Not completely, just mostly, but mostly is quite enough. She's plump—no, fat—and enough light spills over her skin from lanterns and torches and cookfires that Verias decides the prudent thing to do is look away. He knows it'll help, though: nobody will look twice at two people looking to have a little fun in the gap between battles.

"Wait here a moment." The assassin drops Verias's saddlebag and blanketroll and vanishes among the wagons and the milling bodies of pleasure seekers. Anxiety rises up in Verias as he waits, bubbling at the back of his throat like bile. He picks nervously at a scab on his neck for lack of anything else to do while he searches the wagons for her form, but her drab clothing makes her difficult to spot.

When she returns, the assassin carries two cheap earthenware cups in one hand, and somewhere along the way she's unbraided her hair, dark springy curls hanging around her shoulders. Verias has never met or even seen an assassin, but he would never have expected one to look like this fleshbound. She seems too young, even with that stern expression she continuously fixes upon Verias. It almost seems unconscious, the little frown that forms on her face when she looks at him. It makes Verias squirmy; her expression so beautiful and so intimidating that he feels like a particularly horrible bug being looked at by a queen.

"You'll have to take those." The assassin gestures at Verias's things with her mugs. As soon as he straightens, she puts her free arm around his shoulders. It might be her boots, but he's sure she's taller than him. "Play along, Verias. It's safer that way. You might even have fun."

Verias puts his arm around her waist. "You're warm," he says faintly. He expected her to be cold, like a corpse, though the warmth is welcome in the chill night. Her steadiness is even more welcome, a wall against the spidery fear creeping up and down his spine.

"I'm not dead, I just don't have a soul." Is there a laugh in her voice, or is Verias imagining things?

As she and Verias weave through the fringes of the camp, Verias casts his eyes around, looking for anyone who might recognize him. Looking for anyone with the wherewithal to sense his magic and call for Reshon. It's unlikely that an officer would be in this part of the camp, but it isn't beyond belief. The spark of anxiety begins to flame into panic. He won't go back, won't be chained to a war machine and used to kill again. He'd rather Kin just slit his throat, but every time he tries to say so, the words get caught. He's always been a coward.

"Try to look as if you're having fun," the assassin says, and even gives him a little squeeze for emphasis. "Otherwise someone will think you're being kidnapped."

It's obviously intended to be a joke, and Verias manages to force a smile, prompting her to sigh. Verias imagines she's wondering how she'll tolerate him for more than a night.

By that point, the thin edge of camp is about to give way to darkness and worse beyond, with only a few remaining stragglers. Soldiers stand watch, eyes turned to the darkness for any sign of danger. War machines powered by sorcerers loom in the night, iron claws and hammers branching into the deep blue sky. Though too far away to see more than shadows, Verias can still smell tarred wood, oiled steel, and blood, as if he's chained inside one. The ground lurches beneath him for a moment, an imitation of the thing skittering across the countryside like a bloated spider to rend earth and flesh alike. A shudder tries to come up out of Verias's guts, but the assassin leads Verias past as if the machines aren't even there. It drains almost all of Verias's strength not to dig in his heels to avoid going near those things, drowning in memories of being shoved inside.

A tongue clucks behind them, making Verias's body go stiff of its own accord. The assassin remains loose against him.

"I'm disappointed, Hartwell," a familiar voice says. Smooth, deep, it sends a shudder through Verias. The assassin lets him go, and Verias has to grit his teeth before he can turn, lest Reshon see the fear in his face.

"Who's this?" the assassin asks.

Reshon gives her a deep bow. "I am Reshon. This Carrier is

my charge." His small, smug smile that makes Verias's stomach turn over and over. The man has a capacity for incredible cruelty, and that look on his face is tension before a headache, petrichor on the wind before a storm. "As I said, I am disappointed in you." His pale eyes rest on Verias with a terrifying intensity. "I thought you were too smart to try to escape after your last attempt. I also thought you were smart enough to know that I would sense you breaking your collar."

Verias's jaw is clenched too tight to speak, but the assassin speaks up for him:

"He's mine now." She pulls one of the long knives she carries at her belt, moonlight glinting off deadly steel. The shine is nothing compared to the magic rolling off of Reshon in waves, but the assassin looks at him the way one might look at an ankle-biting puppy they mean to kick.

Reshon's smug smirk becomes a true smile when he produces a knife of his own. "I've always wanted to try my luck against a fleshbound's blade."

All the hairs on Verias's body stand on end when the assassin chuckles, almost a purr in the back of her throat. Every instinct tells him to run, but having Reshon *and* a fleshbound chasing him is the stuff of nightmares. He stands rooted to the spot, watching helplessly as the pair circle each other, the assassin still holding two mugs in her left hand like a barmaid doing a few steps of a dance during Autumn Moon on her way to deliver drinks. She moves toward Reshon so fast that Verias can barely see the strike, and Reshon leaps back, a lock of pale hair falling across his eyes. A dark, gaping hole falls open in his uniform, the chill night wind snatching at it.

Though the assassin missed, it's immediately clear that Reshon is outmatched, but worse than that, he's angry, the kind of cold, shuttered anger that scares Verias far worse than naked fury. The assassin moves like a hungry predator looking to break its prey's claws, and Verias can only pray to the Well-spring that she kills Reshon. Instead, her knife hooks Reshon's, forcing him to pull a second blade. Verias's heart clogs his throat for a heartbeat, until the assassin uses Reshon's own body weight to send him hard into the ground, coughing as the earth knocks the breath from his body.

"Move!" The assassin pelts toward Verias, giving him no choice but to follow when she grabs his arm and drags him behind her.

The assassin doesn't take the road, instead running through the scrubland that Lord Felver chose as a campsite, which rapidly turns into scraggly trees. Roots and brush grab at Verias's boots, and with his saddlebag weighing him down, it's a struggle to keep his feet.

Verias probably wouldn't have seen the horse if he wasn't looking for it; its dark, dapple coat blends in with the shadows under the sparse canopy, and it stands still, head down in sleep. It perks up when they get close, snorting at the scent of its mistress, and a dark shape in its saddle meows. For just a moment, Verias forgets how bone-tired and terrified he is, all other thoughts overwhelmed at delight that a fleshbound, terror of mortal men, would travel with a pet cat.

"We're hidden well enough for now. Might as well enjoy these, since I paid for them." The assassin hands Verias a cup. She isn't even breathing hard, and there's not a drip of wine running down the sides. Parched from their run, Verias drops his things to take a sip, thinking wine might steady his nerves, but it's terrible, sour stuff. "Ugh. Swill." The fleshbound throws her cup into a nearby tree, where it smashes to pieces. Verias thanks the Wellspring that it's dark enough to hide his flinch. "You ride."

"But—"

"You're tired, and we're going all the way to Sestera. Ride."

She picks up his saddlebag, ready to walk, so Verias puts his cup on a nearby tree stump, not knowing what else to do with it. The cat sitting in the saddle jumps down so he can scramble up, then melts into the shadows. "There's a town nearby where I've engaged an inn room, but they'll expect us to take shelter there. We'll find somewhere else."

After riding sunup to sundown every day for the past month, Verias is ready to die of exhaustion. There have been many nights he's missed his mattress at home, but never so badly as now, slumped in the saddle with the assassin trudging ahead. On the other side of the trees is a road, not the one the army marched in on. Verias is on the verge of sleep, too tired to feel lost though he has no idea where he is. He drifts, startling awake when the assassin reaches up to steady him in the saddle.

No longer afraid for his life and freedom, Verias has time to wonder at how strange it is to be touched after a year in service to Lord Felver. In that time, the only people who have touched him are the doctor who stitched him up after he was struck by an arrow, and Reshon. Verias would rather have slugs crawl over his body than be anywhere near the man again.

When Verias startles from a slimy half-nightmare, the assassin's hand is on his wrist. The lights of a town beckon up ahead, but it's so late he couldn't imagine anyone being awake, unless someone warned them that someone was coming. But the lights are only lanterns, lighting the street for a handful of guards, who eye Verias and the assassin but walk on by without comment.

"Do you think they know anything? Reshon could have sent a runner, with the way we left the road for your horse," Verias says.

"Doubtful. They're looking at my face. They know something isn't quite right about me and they're trying to put together what it is. Happens all the time." The assassin puts a hand in

Verias's stirrup, and it dawns on him how strained her voice is.

"You're hurt." When did it happen? She and Reshon had been too quick, the night too dark for Verias to recall seeing it happen.

"It's not bad."

"I can heal you."

"It can wait." Her voice is a snap, and Verias falls silent.

CHAPTER THREE

KIN PRESSES ON DESPITE HER EXHAUSTION. NOT ONLY would capture risk her new co-conspirator, but there's always a danger, however small, that she might be recognized. Stars forbid Felver himself lay eyes on her, especially injured. The man would likely explode from glee at the chance to have her in such a weakened state. Kin can't die—the Binders made sure of that —but she can suffer, and compared to that, this is nothing.

Kin tries to assess the wound, touching her side, where the knife went in between two lower ribs. Her vision goes black, and she almost collapses in the middle of the road; there's surely a shard of knife blade lodged inside. Leave it up to soldiers to carry cheap weapons that break apart inside a body.

"Please, you need to rest," says Verias.

Kin grits her teeth and walks on, cursing the road ahead. It's hard and full of holes, every wrong step sending shards of pain through her middle and making her head swim. Pressure builds, blood filling her guts, and more than once she considers sticking another hole in her abdomen to drain it.

"At least ride," Verias insists.

"It won't be far until we find a place to hide. Those coppices are a sure sign of farms nearby." Kin nods at the road ahead, and Verias leans forward in the saddle, squinting.

"I can't see anything. Your eyesight must be incredible."

"Only in the dark."

Kin is grateful when Verias falls silent. The Binders' mark is a rope around her neck, constantly reminding her of his presence, and she needs all of her faculties about her to keep conscious and listen for attack from behind.

A set of wheel ruts appear running perpendicular to the road, and Kin's long sigh sends a lance of white-hot pain through her side. Clinging to Shadow's stirrup, she holds her breath as long as she can. The ruts run for what feels like forever before giving way to a garden completely overgrown with weeds. Beyond, a rambling farmhouse stands in disrepair, a collapsed barn looming in the dark. Inside, there are signs that other travelers have rested there. Wood and kindling by the hearth, apple cores on the battered, dusty old table. Verias finds a lantern on the mantle and lights it, casting a yellow glow around the large room. The sudden light and stench of rancid oil make nausea wash over Kin.

When he looks at Kin, Verias goes white as the wall behind him. She must look bad.

"Stay here." Verias dashes off upstairs, footsteps creaking hurriedly on the floorboards above. "The beds smell moldy. It's the floor for us." He's barely done rolling out her bedroll when Kin collapses into it, lights popping in front of her eyes.

"I think there's a piece still stuck in there."

"Excuse me, what?" Verias's voice is too bland, hiding panic.

"Of knife. A piece of knife blade."

"I'm . . . not much use at Healing. I hope this isn't beyond my skill."

"You're not going to make it worse, are you?"

"No. I've been safeguarded."

Verias inspects his fingernails and frowns before rolling up his sleeves. His forearms have little scabs all over them, some picked off and raw red.

"What does that mean, safeguarded?" Kin asks.

"I'll explain later. Lie down, please," says Verias. "I'm going to the well for water to wash my hands."

Time moves on in a way that's distinctly blurrier than usual. Kin comes in and out of queasy consciousness, her little cat Chestnut butting against her elbow, until Verias returns with his bucket. Footsteps, gentle sloshes of washing hands, scent of soap.

"Do you have a knife I can use?" Verias asks. Kin swims back into full awareness, fumbling her everyday knife out of her sleeve to flip it in his direction. He doesn't try to grab it, instead stepping to one side, and it falls point-first into the tabletop with a *thunk*. Verias pulls it free and turns to clean it too, soap and water that'll strip off the oil that keeps it free of rust in its sheath.

"What are you going to do with that?"

"Dig out the knife shard. You're going to have to lie very still." Verias kneels next to Kin. "Not everyone can catch a flying knife, you know."

"I didn't think it was a good idea to try to get up."

"Lift your blouse. I don't want to hurt you."

The thought of taking off her shirt hadn't even crossed Kin's mind. She wriggles, trying to get it out of her waistband, and the room lurches.

"Stop that." Verias takes both of her hands in his, laying them at her sides. "I'll have to wash again," he says, more to himself than to her, as he unbuttons her skirt and lifts her shirt. He makes a small, displeased sound, but that's better than, say, fainting. Or vomiting on her. He would be used to such wounds, Kin supposes, after his time in the army.

"That bad?"

Verias doesn't reply, instead standing to turn and wash his hands again. All these preparations have her gritting her teeth by the time he's back with clean hands and her knife held in a white-knuckled grip.

"Ready?" he asks, earning himself a glare. "Right. I'll be as gentle as possible."

He is, at first, his fingers ice-cold against her hot, swollen flesh, but it doesn't last long. It feels exactly like someone's digging around in her guts with a knife and his fingers. What about all that magic he's supposed to have?

"I'm sorry, I'm sorry, I'm sorry," Verias chants.

"I've had worse." She has no idea why *she's* reassuring *him* when she wants to make him eat that piece of knife blade if he doesn't hurry up.

"Don't talk. I almost have it."

The exquisite shock of bone pain radiates from Kin's insides, and pressure follows as Verias presses his hand against the wound, through Kin. Heat like a red-hot poker pierces the knife hole, far worse than actually being stabbed. The agony fades just as fast as it comes, and Kin's next breath feels like her first in a year. It takes several more to realize that Verias is folded up against her. It's been ages since she's met anyone who isn't afraid of her, so long that the closeness makes her uneasy. Doesn't he know she's dangerous?

"Sorry." Verias's eyes are bleary with pain, and he blinks at Kin like he isn't sure what she was doing there. "It's the safeguard. If I hurt anyone, I feel what they feel."

"So you don't misuse your magic? Isn't that why they had that thing around your neck?" Kin props herself up on her elbows. It sounds similar to one of the enchantments the Binders used on Kin, making it impossible for her to harm her handler, Lessa.

"No. The collar was to bind me to the war machine, so I could direct the power of the Wellspring more effectively." Verias's hands are alarmingly bloody, so he wipes the sweat from his face with the bunched-up fabric of his sleeve in the inside of his elbow. "But yes, the safeguard is to keep me from causing anyone pain."

"Even emotional pain?" Kin asks. Verias briefly glances at the ceiling.

"If that were true, I would never feel anything else. Felver has many lands to keep safe."

"Tuh! Safe. Of course."

"I'm not arguing with you." Verias stands with a grunt of exertion, stumbles on his way to wash his hands. She has no intention of letting him do this ever again; he's too valuable to risk. "Most people wouldn't, not even in Solemn Gorge, and he had many supporters there for a long time."

"Middle of nowhere."

"Yes. Carriers prefer to live away from cities." Verias unrolls his blankets next to hers, setting down the stinking lantern.

"Too many people know what you are. What to look for," Kin says. Verias stops in smoothing down his blanket roll. It doesn't need it anyway.

"Yes. Anonymity is much more comfortable." Verias moves stiffly. "I need to rest," he says, and the lantern goes out, plunging them into darkness. "I'm sorry."

At least he hasn't tried to stay awake and look after her; he needs rest. Kin listens to his breathing slow, watches the anxious furrow in his brow grow shallow, his worries melting away. As exhausted as Kin is, she doesn't intend to sleep, dream, or be anything other than ready for a fight.

CHAPTER FOUR

MORNING BRINGS SLOW, STEADY RAIN, THE SORT OF freezing cold early spring drizzle that makes everything miserable. The kind of rain that freezes, leaving mud-churned roads lined with hard ruts to turn an ankle, that slowly soaks through clothes and chills to the bone. When Verias wakes, aching and exhausted, with a massive bruise spreading across his left side, the thought of traveling is unbearable

Between the pain and the anxiety that clutches him by the throat a heartbeat later, Verias can't believe he slept at all. A second wave of fear catches him off guard when he spots the assassin's empty blankets, but he shoves it down. If something was wrong, she would've woken him, not just left him alone; she needs Verias to get her soul. That thought soothes him. She needs him.

Still, he catches himself picking at the skin of his face after he's dressed, nervousness getting the better of him. He has to bite down over a sigh of relief when the assassin strolls into the farmhouse with an armload of bundled twigs. Her blood-soaked skirt and shirt are gone, replaced by a dark blouse with breeches tucked into high boots. The daylight reveals a woman completely different from the one Verias remembers coming to kill him the night before. Younger, the shadows gone from her light brown skin. Her hair, which looked black in the night, is really a reddish-brown that's surely the product of some dye. Droplets of rain rest in her hair, diamonds cradled in velvet. If he didn't know better, Verias might think her soft, and he can't help but be fascinated by her.

"Good, I don't have to wake you," she says.

"What?" Verias asks, his brain slow from sleep.

"Most people try to scream when I wake them up," she says. "It's not a nice way to start the day."

"They *try* to scream?"

"Yes." Her matter-of-factness makes Verias want to shudder, but his curiosity always overrides his sense.

"How did you know I wouldn't, when you came to kill me?" he asks. "How did you know I wouldn't fight?"

"I didn't. I just knew one of us is functionally immortal and the other isn't. Not hard to see who would win. Now hurry up, we need a head start on whoever is coming next." She breezes past, leaving behind the woody, sweet scent of her armload of twigs, which she ties to the outside of one of her saddlebags.

"Will you tell me about your soul?" Verias asks.

"There's precious little to tell. It was taken and used against me, and I won't be able to act freely until it's back in my possession," the fleshbound says.

"That's sensible, but why destroy it?"

"So it can never be used against me again. Put on your boots. We have a fair way to go."

Verias is immediately sure she's hiding something, but he doesn't press the matter. "Will we have something to eat first? I'll be of better use once I've regained my strength."

"Of course. I forgot."

"What?" When Verias looks at the assassin, she's staring off into the distance. "Forgot what?" he asks again when she doesn't answer.

"That you'll need to eat. I hope you have something in your pack, because I don't eat often. I no longer find it enjoyable."

She looks strong enough to fight a bear.

"Why not?"

"The magic that binds my soul sustains me. That's why we can't sense magic like everyone else. We're too flooded with it."

"Strange. I don't sense any magic in you." She just looks . . . normal. Uncommonly deadly, perhaps, but otherwise normal.

"The Binders make us that way on purpose. Likely so other sorcerers can't detect us. Otherwise how would I kill you?" She looks right at Verias when she says it, dark eyes boring into him.

All of her softness is purely physical, the rest hard as marble. It unsettles his stomach. People like her, people who have strength but no need to display it, are far more dangerous than people who show their teeth. He bends to tie his boots to escape her eyes.

"What's your name, anyway?" Verias asks. "You know mine, but I don't know yours."

"Kindred Jole. Most people call me Kin."

"You're from Abseris, aren't you?" With her brown skin, curly hair, and a name like Kindred, she has to be. There are fewer Abserians in Nerefin than there used to be, after the High Council of Abseris welcomed back those who had fled during their civil war, but Verias has met several visiting sorcerers from across the sea.

"Mostly. Hurry up."

"I don't understand how you're so energetic." Verias digs wearily in his saddlebag for his horrible travel rations. "I'll likely be bruised for weeks and I didn't get stabbed."

"I'm a little tender." Kin lifts her blouse, showing nothing but smooth brown skin. "Thank you, by the way. I wish you hadn't bothered if you're so sore, but thank you anyway."

Verias can't decide if he's offended or not. Kin's way of speaking makes everything sound like a command or an insult, and her eyes do bear a menacing flash as she watches him ready to leave. But on the other hand, perhaps she's simply so used to being alone that she's out of practice being nice. How long has she been fleshbound? It must be some time, judging by the not-quite-human way she moves. How many heads are turned by that efficient grace, like a heron stalking its prey, before their owners realize what she is and think better of looking? He recalls waking to find her knife at his throat, those cold dark eyes staring at him with as much emotion as Kin might regard a stone on the ground.

That coldness is comforting, in a way. Warmth would be too much of a shock after so long spent as little more than a tool. What will he do when he returns to his family, after being regarded as half an enemy by an entire army? *Can* he return to them?

"You're riding today," Kin says, and Verias isn't about to argue. He could have slept another four dreamless hours, the Wellspring's waters running beneath him, close to the surface.

The steady, cold spring rain soaks Verias to the skin within a quarter of an hour of watching the grim, gray landscape go by. The gait of Kin's horse sends driving strikes of pain through the massive bruise at his side, and Verias can't shake the fear that going home is no longer an option. His attempts at desertion were dishonor enough, but this escape might be the last straw, and who knows how far they would go to restore that honor?

"Kindred?"

"Nobody calls me that, it's Kin," she corrects him. "What is it?"

"May I ask you something?" Verias asks. Kin grunts in response, a possible affirmative. "Did my family send you?"

"I don't know." Kin glances up at him. "Only the Binders know who hires us. I'm not important enough to know, but I don't usually care to know, anyway. I try not to care about dead people's personal lives."

"Dead people?"

"That's what they are as soon as I'm assigned to kill them," Kin says flatly.

Verias's stomach clenches with retroactive fear. In the moment, her knife at his throat, he'd been perfectly content to die. Being as free as is possible for a Carrier has changed his mind significantly.

"So when you came into my tent, you didn't consider me a living person?"

"Accurate."

"I wish I hadn't asked that." He flinches as soon as the words are out if his mouth, afraid they'll offend Kin, but when he chances a look at her, she looks the same as always.

"Did you consider yourself a living person that night?" she asks.

The question settles uncomfortably on top of the tension in Verias's gut. She knows. She knows because he told her about his fantasies of being gutted. He catches himself scraping at a scab above his eyebrow and snatches his hand away.

"Why would your family want to kill you?" Kin's voice is without judgment, and for that Verias is grateful.

"Honor. I've been trying to desert."

Kin is quiet for a while, and Verias grows more and more sure that she's thinking he deserved to die for honor.

"I've spent all my life here, but I don't understand Nerefinian ways," she says.

"It's . . . more complicated than Nerefinian ways. It's Carrier ways."

"Hm. Like your safeguard."

"Yes."

"I don't understand that, either. But I suppose magic and war are both messy," Kin muses. "I wouldn't hang around long for either."

"But—" Verias stops himself. He's really at a loss for rules of etiquette. How is one supposed to be polite about murder?

"But I kill people," Kin finishes for him. "It's not the same. Assassination is far cleaner."

"I suppose you have poisons and things."

"I absolutely do not. I'm punished for failure. I have to stick around and make sure they're good and dead, and I'm not waiting around for someone to finish vomiting before they die." Kin visibly shudders at the thought. They'd come to the one thing she was squeamish about, it seemed.

"But you said that gutting is a bad way to die. I'd assume that would be much worse to watch than a poisoning," Verias says. Kin laughs.

"I didn't mean I'd gutted anyone. I'm good at my job. When I'm not busy trying to protect someone." Her eyes flick up at Verias, sharp with annoyance. "I meant it happened to me."

"And you lived? Even being fleshbound, that seems impossible." Verias remembers only smooth brown skin on Kin's stomach, no trace of the kind of gruesome scar that would be left behind by such an injury.

"I just gathered all of it up and stuffed it back inside. Bandaged it all up tight. I did have a horrible fever for a day or so, and it took almost three weeks for everything to be right again."

"But this was in a fight?"

"Yes."

"And nobody stopped you from escaping?"

"Would you stop someone running at you with their guts in one hand and a knife in the other?" Kin asks, and Verias can't help but laugh. It's such a horrible thing to imagine that it crosses the line into funny. "Anyhow, the thing about gut wounds is that they're not as messy if you have the right tool." She pulls out one of the three knives that hung at her belt, one Verias hasn't yet seen unsheathed. It's long like the others, but needle thin. "I favor the baselard because it feels better in the hand, but if you can't get to an artery, a very thin rondel will do. Scrambles up all the guts and makes the target bleed out inside, especially if you hit the liver." Kin gives the weapon a flourish before she sheathes it again.

Verias is left nauseated but intrigued. He had never been exposed to violence a day in his life before he joined Lord Felver's army, and he hadn't wanted to do that in the first place. By all rights he still hadn't actually *seen* killing. His war machine, with all its vile strength, had enclosed him almost completely in its bloated abdomen. Its joints groaned as it crossed the field of battle, the smell of lubricating oil filling Verias's nostrils, but none of it could drown out the sounds and smells of death.

As soon as Verias learned exactly what his family's promise entailed, he had fought against it in any way he could. When his enclosure broke open and a lucky arrow hit him, Verias had faked being too weak to perform magic for weeks after he healed. He tried to escape, battering his family's honor and his own, maybe even causing them to send Kin to kill him, but worse than the memories and the guilt was knowing that his brother had died in the same machine. It was easy to imagine the smell of rot inside was Lusian's blood, soaked into the boards and festering.

The silence between Verias and Kin is just as rotten, curdling as he struggles for something to say, to stop thinking about Lusian. Kin doesn't appear to be thinking about difficult things, or about anything at all, just keeping pace with her horse. For his part, Chestnut naps the day away, even sleeping draped over the horse's neck with his back up against the saddle.

Spoiled by a night under an actual roof (though in dismal repair), dread creeps over Verias as the sun sinks. Even though the rain has stopped, everything is damp, and it won't be anything other than a wet, miserable night. Kin, at least, is clearly an old hand at camping. The spot she chooses is good, and Verias senses water flowing from the Wellspring somewhere nearby. The gentle touch of magic in the air is refreshing, calming, and Kin has a fire going shortly despite the wet.

After they hang their blankets and clothes over bushes to dry, Kin tells Verias to stay put and vanishes, returning a little while later with two rabbits dressed for cooking. Perhaps the night won't be so bad after all.

"What are those for?" Verias asks as Kin picks leaves off of the morning's twigs, putting them in a kettle while she waits for the water to boil.

"They're just olive leaves from the grove behind the farm. They make a nice tea." After a long silence, Kin pours pale tea into a tin cup. "I only have one cup. You can have the first one."

This time Kin's silence doesn't bother Verias. He sips his tea and scratches behind her cat's ears, passing the time while she stares over his shoulder, head cocked slightly to one side. Listening for something. There are dark shadows under her eyes, deeper now that the light has failed almost entirely.

"Did you sleep last night?" he asks when she takes his empty cup.

"No. I don't find I enjoy it any longer. I don't need more than an hour, anyway."

Kin said she didn't enjoy eating, either. The only thing Verias has seen her consume is bad wine and now a sip of too-hot tea. There's something unspeakably cruel about taking away her ability to enjoy small things, the things that are often all that gets Verias through the day during hard times. Or were, before he'd been enlisted. Perhaps his help will free her just as she freed him.

"Tell me about the Binders," Verias says.

CHAPTER FIVE

KIN RETREATS TO THE OTHER SIDE OF THE FIRE. BEING IN such close proximity to a human has grown strange and un-comfortable, now that most people don't let her get close enough to touch. Not that Kin knows what to do when she's that close, other than to open up a vein, so she keeps her few friends at a distance. The urge to kill might overwhelm her, es-pecially now, talking about the Binders with the gentle hum of the mark always at the back of her thoughts, calling her to end Verias. His gentle, curious gaze makes her brain feel raw.

"What do you want to know?" she asks.

"Everything," he answers. "Start with the Binding itself."

"There isn't much to say about that. They gave me a sleeping potion because I fought too hard. I had dreams . . ." Severed hands chasing her, forcing their fingers into her mouth, pinch-ing, poking, prodding. She shudders just thinking about it, though the memory is old and should be scarred over.

"Go on."

"I woke, and my soul was gone. Nothing hurt. Everything felt exactly the same, except that something was . . . not missing. Faded. I can still feel my soul. I could point to it right now.

"Once you're Bound, they make you kill something to make sure that the spells to get rid of your conscience have taken." Kin tries to keep her voice flat, but the memories, just like the dreams, are just as keen as they were the day they were made.

"Taking the soul doesn't take your conscience?" Verias's gaze has grown more focused, more intense, and Kin is sure it's the longest he's ever looked right at her. "I thought that was the entire point of fleshbound."

"No. They take the soul to redefine us as inhuman. The law only applies to humans, and humans have souls. Perhaps guilt or pity might be cut off at the source if the soul was destroyed, I don't know."

"What do they make you kill?" Verias asks. There's a tiny tremble in his voice, but fear, it seems, isn't enough to override his curiosity. He's a dangerous man in his own way, a man willing to make trouble by asking too many questions. A man willing to risk himself just to heal her. He could be what undoes her plans if she isn't careful. And firm.

"A little bird. A kitten. A puppy. Something soft and undeserving."

Verias stares at Kin across the fire. "It didn't take, did it?"

"No."

"And it stayed with you, even after the spell took? Why?" Verias asks.

"I don't know. I don't think they knew, either. I don't think they really cared."

"Why not refuse?"

Incapable of guilt though she is, Kin can still hurt, still feel anger at her own failure. She can remember soft fur and stillness. The faces of Binders around her, searching her for any sign of weakness. The burning need to resist them, fight in any way she could, no matter how much suffering it caused her. They still saw through to the guilt that they had tried to excise and she had tried to hide.

"I don't know."

"What about the Binders themselves?" Verias seems to understand that Kin won't—can't—continue that line of questioning. "How are they organized? How does one become a Binder?"

"They have a school, but it never concerned me." Kin shrugs some of the tension out of her shoulders.

"So I could infiltrate the Binders?" Verias asks. "Become one of them?"

"I had pictured something a little less sneaky."Kin envisions blasting a hole in the Binders' homepalace, stealing her soul, and running as hard and far as she can. She'd miss her city, but some things can't be helped.

"That's the plan, then. I'm becoming a Binder."

It's clear that the conversation is over: Verias's gaze has turned inward, brow furrowed in thought. Visibly exhausted, he soon goes to sleep, bidding her good night before drifting off just as quickly as the night before. Good. Kin doesn't need him distracting her while she keeps watch. Out in the open, close to the road, she has the advantage of being able to hear Felver's men approaching.

It also means that Kin can gaze up at the sky. The moon is in its first quarter, hanging low among the shallow pinpoints of stars. The crescent recalls her father's knife-edge smile at his work, turning broad and true when he made up names for constellations and told Kin stories about Abseris. His home, not hers. His bright-burning magic, not hers. Her neck begins to ache, but Kin can't tear her eyes away, can't end the moment of wonder and connection. She would surely weep for the loss.

After a few hours, her ears, sharp from spending so much time alone and in silence, catch what is unmistakably a footstep. She stands, ready to fight the single person whose breath and rustling clothes and boot heels sound like they're coming from inside her head.

A shadow resolves into a man standing at the edge of the firelight, his face poorly lit by the pale yellow glow.

31

"We have unfinished business." He comes closer, the light catching a smile that Kin feels an irresistible urge to punch. She grips her knife hilts instead.

"I have unfinished business with a lot of pretty blond boys. You'll have to be more specific."

"This isn't a joke." He pulls a knife from his belt. Kin doesn't draw. There's something wrong about this man, and she isn't going to act until she's sure what it is. He surprised her in their fight back at the war camp, and she doesn't intend to let him do it again.

"Oh, you meant murder business. That narrows it down. A bit. There was Yaan, of course. And Eldereth. And sweet Hyrand."

"Where is he?" the man asks.

"Who, Hyrand? I'm afraid he tried to kill me," Kin says. "Most who try don't live to tell the tale."

"I did." He moves close, knife held low at his side as if he doesn't really plan on using it.

Kin can feel the warmth of his body through her clothes and his. It all might have been nice, under other circumstances. He's pretty, with fine-boned features and piercing eyes. He's also extraordinarily tall, half a head taller than she, and clearly brave if he thinks he can beat her, let alone menace her. But Verias is too valuable to let slip away.

"I'm sure you're very special to stand against a monster like me and live." Kin doesn't need weapons when she's this close. He's just as human as Verias, just as frail. To reach up and snap his neck would be nothing. And yet.

"Extremely." He moves to push past her, and Kin catches his wrist. He tries to pull away, just once, but her grip is too tight.

"I don't feel like killing a pretty boy tonight. Don't make me," she says.

"What is he to you? A friend? A lover? Or just money?"

"None of your business." She doesn't let him go, watching disgust slowly spread across his face.

"I can give you money, if that's what you want."

"It isn't."

His attempt to stab Kin is a fair try, but he tenses before the strike. He's so close that all Kin has to do is drop her shoulder and knock him off balance, turning like a country girl at a dance. She keeps her grip on his wrist, hooking her free arm under his elbow. With his wrist bent down at an extreme angle, he's just a breath away from broken bones and torn sinew. At least he's smart enough not to stab wildly at Kin and test her patience. She has precious little left.

"Don't feel bad about not being able to kill me," she says. "No human can."

"I might not be able to kill you, but I can wound you again, and when I do, I'm going to take that Carrier back where he belongs. And because you care about him so much, I'll make sure his caning is twice as bad, just for spite."

"Stars above, you're boring. Why not be even more predictable and threaten to put a hole in my gut and stick your cock in there? Men who think they're better than me always seem to say something like that. Now get out of here. I'm sick of you." Kin shoves him, and he almost falls.

"I'll be back for him," he says.

"Good luck."

Kin's heart is pounding fast as she watches his retreating back. This man is dangerous, perhaps more dangerous than Felver. The thought makes her shudder. Her memories of Felver are too sharp, his perfectly lordly features too easy to recall, twisting up in delight when Kin was penned in like a pig for slaughter and he smugly offered her a way out. There's no chance she'll underestimate a man like him again.

CHAPTER SIX

VERIAS SHUDDERS AWAKE, SHAKING OFF A DREAM OF . . . something. Something bright and burning, some nightmare forgotten almost as soon as he's shaken out of it. The hand is familiar, hard and callused, brutally ungentle. Her.

"It's the middle of the night," he mumbles to Kin.

"Yes, but if you don't want to be taken back to your army, you'll get up right now," Kin says.

"What?"

"That big blond boy come to bother us. I sent him on his way, but I doubt he came alone. Hurry, now."

When Verias sits up, Kin grabs him by the hands and pulls him to his feet, tosses him a fresh shirt. A shiver runs down his spine as he dresses and picks up his blanket roll, a sharp, acidic tingle of magic that settles somewhere in his stomach. He knows that feeling, has experienced it too many times in battle to ignore.

"Reaper," he croaks.

"What? Where?"

"I don't know. That's not what I was trained for. But they're nearby, or I wouldn't be able to sense them." Verias ties his things to Shadow's saddle.

"Can they sense you?"

"Without a doubt."

"And there's no way to hide your power?" Kin asks.

"Not that I know of. It isn't—"

"What you were trained for," Kin finishes for Verias. "Come along."

"Where are we going?"

"Anywhere but here. There's nothing you can do to hide yourself? Nothing at all?"

"Well, if there's water nearby, and the Reapers aren't too strong, they might not notice me," Verias says.

"What?"

"All water comes from the Wellspring. All life energy comes from the Wellspring, and anyone attuned to it can feel it when it's running nearby. It can be confusing to less powerful sorcerers. The deeper the water the better," Verias explains.

Kin dives into her bags to shove a map into Verias's hands. It's seen better days, with tears around the edges and a round stain from the bottom of a winecup. The paper has a familiar sweet smell, like an old book, that should calm Verias with its familiarity. No such luck.

"Look for a river or something." She turns to saddle Shadow.

"What's the name of the last town?"

"I don't know."

Verias looks for Sestera on the map, searching through all the dots nearby. For a few moments, the fear churning in his gut makes it impossible to focus. He isn't sure the village is even on the map, but he does see a crossroads, which he remembers seeing sometime just before the sun set. That has to be nearby. A river passes to the north, thank the Wellspring.

"Meow." Chestnut appears to weave around Verias's ankles, watching him with luminous yellow eyes.

"Found something," he says to Kin.

"Good. In the saddle."

Kin takes the map and folds it up, shoving it into her pocket, and climbs up after Verias, grabbing him around the waist as he guides Shadow back to the road. Her grip makes the bruise on Verias's ribs ache. "She's smoother at a gallop," Kin says. "We'll see if I can hold on. You'll have to lean down and lift out of the saddle a bit to tell her what—"

She's cut off by a sound like a breaking branch, and the night lights up bright yellow. Shadow dances a few steps, nervous but not yet ready to bolt.

"Hup!" Kin's shout sets Shadow to a trot. Verias leans forward in the saddle, and Shadow runs.

Verias had never ridden a day in his life before he swore to Lord Felver, and he's never ridden so fast traveling at an army's pace. It's absolutely terrifying, and he grabs Kin's wrist, afraid she'll fall off and be roasted alive. For a few moments, arrows and magic whistle past, until Shadow outpaces Reshon's soldiers and Reapers. It can't last long; Reshon will inevitably get his group horsed, and Shadow will tire faster carrying two people. They have to get to that river fast.

As urgent fear fades into a lower-simmering anxiety, Verias starts to feel his interrupted night of sleep. His body aches, the muscles in his legs and stomach growing tired from riding. His fingers hurt from clutching the reins and Kin's wrist. Her arms dig into his sides. His breath comes too fast, making him so lightheaded that the night is peppered with bright white lights around the edges of his vision. More than once, Verias is sure he hears hoofbeats behind them, but he doesn't dare turn to look.

"Can you smell that? We're close."

Verias should have noticed the water flowing nearby without Kin mentioning it. It's near the surface, bright and deep and cold to his consciousness, the most calming feeling Verias knows. Shadow's hooves thunder over a wooden bridge, and Verias thinks to draw rein. He sighs in relief when Kin slides down from Shadow's back, and the pain in his bruised side dulls.

"Come, we need to find a place to bring Shadow down the bank," she says.

"Hurry." Being close to the water won't help if Reshon sees them from the road, but Kin walks slowly, making sure the ground is even for Shadow's hooves.

"Can you attack like a Reaper can?" she asks as she walks.

"I can, but in ways that are neither as impressive nor as deadly. Those methods aren't my area of expertise."

"Verias, you weren't trained to heal, or to hide, or to attack. What *were* you trained for?"

"I'm a historian. I was trained to learn the histories of those techniques, and to revive lost ones," Verias says, and knows he sounds peevish. Kin doesn't say anything for a long time, leading Shadow by her bridle until she finds a slope shallow enough for the horse. "I'm sorry I'm not very useful."

Kin says nothing, eyes still focused on the ground. Verias's stomach somehow tightens even more around the knot in his belly. She's likely listing all of his failings in her head, measuring whether he's worth the trouble.

"I suppose it's a lie by omission, in a way," he says. "If you'd known, you likely would have killed me."

"It's possible. I'm not bothered. I did have a fantasy of you burning down their homepalace with thousands of fireballs, but you were already set on becoming a Binder. I wasn't going to see that place burn unless I held the torch myself. Ground's soft here. We have to keep moving before we stop so I can clean Shadow's hooves."

Kin can't fool Verias with the way she passed right by the subject of his abilities. She's disappointed, possibly angry. He wonders whether she'll kill him now, but a shivery twinge distracts him from becoming truly frightened of her.

"The Reapers are coming," he says. "Probably near the bridge."

"Let's hope they follow the road."

"They might know what we're doing and come after us, and I don't think it's likely that they'll search both ways. They must know we're going to Sestera by now. They'll find our tracks and follow us and kill us as soon as we try to rest."

"Verias, we're moving away from Sestera."

"What?"

"We're going east. They'll either follow the road north or go west," Kin says. Verias's face heats in the cold spring air.

"I suppose I got turned around. The dark."

"Fear does things to a person," Kin says, as though it's completely understandable.

Verias has yet to see her scared, and he probably never will. She's lived outside the reach of mortal fear for years, probably, and she likely doesn't plan on caring about him enough to fear for him.

"I won't let them take you back."

"You need me, I suppose," Verias observes.

"True. But I know what it's like to be trapped like that."

"I thought you said fleshbound couldn't feel pity."

"I don't pity you, Verias," Kin says.

Verias glances down at her. He can't see her face in the dark, but he doesn't need to. He's little more than a dog to her, short-lived, incapable of surviving in the wild, and—whatever she says—pitiable. Maybe she can't feel it now, but she was human once. She's aware of what pathetic looks like.

"I suppose what I feel is anger." Kin's voice is utterly calm. "I was always quick to anger, but after being Bound, anything similar makes me sick with it."

"This isn't like that," Verias says. "I knew I might have to do this. I was prepared."

"Did you know you'd be chained to a war machine?"

"Yes."

"But?"

"I was obligated to stand in for my brother when he died in battle. It would have been the height of dishonor not to," Verias says.

"You'll never convince me to think less of you for getting away from the war that killed your brother, so I don't know why you bother."

"I'm not trying to convince you, I'm only saying that I understand if you do think less of me. I'm a coward, and I've only made things far worse. I always do."

"Don't be silly. I've kidnapped you. That's not your fault."

Verias almost laughs, but a sickly shiver runs down his spine, and he pulls Shadow up short. Kin grabs his wrist where he holds the reins, looking around the ravine for an attack. Verias points upwards to try to indicate that the Reaper is on the bank above. She gives him a sharp nod, and vanishes into the night. Terror spikes, and he digs his nails into his arms to calm himself.

CHAPTER SEVEN

THUNDER ROARS, THE NIGHT LIT WITH A BLUE-WHITE GLOW. Pain washes over Kin like boiling water for a heartbeat, the scalded air around her thick with the scent of unbearable loss. The rare times when her father used his magic stand out in her memory as bright as the lightning itself. Once, she'd been callow enough to believe that her father's powers made her safe. Once, she'd loved the smell of lightning. Now a grimace spreads across her face as she cuts the Reaper's saddle girth, wishing she didn't have to leave a scar on the poor horse's flank.

The Reaper crashes to the ground, but he recovers fast, climbing to his feet and pulling a short sword from a scabbard on his back. One hand blazes with fire as he slashes with wild haste, heat exploding in Kin's face. He must have intended it to stagger her, but she turns his blade away so easily that it's he who takes a step back. His face, lit from below, is shocked for an instant before he recovers enough to retreat further.

"Kin!" Verias calls from behind her.

Kin doesn't react, but the Reaper does, and the instant he's distracted, she jams her baselard into his throat. In the same moment, he releases the burning orb in his hand. By the time Kin steps away from the gout of blood rushing from the wound, Verias is flat on his back, breathing hard with a high-pitched whistling sound. Kin prays it's not a lung injury as she kneels at his side.

Verias's shirt is smoldering at the edges of a long, vertical burn over his heart. Or rather, it looks like the meeting of a burn and a cut. Blood seeps from the wound, which reeks of seared flesh. His face is white as a sheet.

"What did you think you were doing, following me?" Kin tears his shirt to examine the wound more closely, and he jumps. "It's not as bad as it looks. Up."

She hauls him to his feet. From the sound of his breathing, labored and fast, the injury hurts worse than it looks. Kin has to help him back down into the ravine with much slipping and pained wincing. She peels him out of his shirt and bandages him up to stop the bleeding before shoving Verias into the saddle and starting out again, this time back toward Sestera. It's all she can do to confuse their destination once Reshon and the others eventually find their unfortunate Reaper friend.

They ride on until shortly before dawn, when they come to a village. The place looks familiar, but all little towns look similar after riding through enough of them. Kin lends Verias one of her shirts, which hangs too loose, but it's clean, black, and won't show blood.

"What about you?" Verias asks as he pulls her shirt over his head in the relative cover between two houses.

"What about me?"

"Kin, your face is burned," Verias says. She touched her cheek and finds tight, painful skin there.

"We need a lie anyway. For why we'd show up at dawn," she says.

"I meant you need me to heal you, not that people will comment on your face."

"Don't you dare, or I'll give you worse than that Reaper did. You're too valuable." Kin grabs Shadow's halter and leads her toward the inn, giving Verias no choice but to trot to keep up with her.

"Why—"

"You lied about the safeguard," Kin says.

"I didn't think you'd allow it if I told you how difficult it would be. You're my safety, Kin. I had to make sure you were well enough to fight," Verias says.

"That's practical of you." Kin can't keep the growl out of her voice. Though there's light coming from the public room of the inn, the door is locked, so she knocks. The innkeeper had better hurry up, because Kin is in no mood to be kept waiting. A plump older woman with dark skin and wavy hair, likely dyed with the same allei leaf Kin used on her hair before she was Bound, answers her knock.

"My goodness, what—"

"Bandits," Kin growls. The woman gasps at her harsh tone, but recovers quickly. "We need a room to rest."

"Of course, of course." She has a familiar accent, like someone Kin used to know in Sestera. "Just tie your horse there, someone will see to it."

She leads them to a large room just above the public room, with two beds and a window overlooking the street. Good for keeping watch. Kin passes her a few fathoms—she's not sure how many—for the trouble. The woman delivers them hot water to wash and then vanishes.

"That wound needs cleaning," Kin tells Verias. He drops his bag and obediently strips off his borrowed shirt. Good. He can be taught.

Kin clears the towels off of the washstand, leaving enough room to grab Verias and place him there to put the injury closer to her eye level. He gives a surprised grunt but allows himself to be manhandled, wincing when hot water and soap touch the wound.

"You have absolutely no bedside manner."

"My specialty is ending lives, not saving them. Hold still."

Verias obeys, but the air in the room is tense, thicker than usual. He's holding something back, not speaking until Kin dries the injury and begins bandaging it again.

"I can never go home, can I?" he asks.

Kin looks up from her work. His brown eyes lock on hers. It's the closest Kin has looked at him since she gazed down at his lantern-lit face the first night they met. In that dim light, Kin didn't notice that his right iris has a dark spot, or the occasional strands of gray in his dark hair. She ties off the gauze and takes a step back, discomfited by being so close.

"Unclear."

"But?" he can tell she's holding back, just as he had.

"I . . . have some knowledge of Felver. More than the average person who knows his work on the Nerefinian War Council. He will not give up easily."

"I know." Verias rubs a fresh scar, still red and puffy, on his upper arm. An arrow wound, by the look of it. "How do you know him?"

Kin wants to tell him it isn't his business, but at this point it is. All of her business is his, because her business is likely to get them killed. The reverse is probably true, too. She should have thought this plan through more thoroughly, but she feels as if she can't think clearly any more.

"Let's just say that he's an old enemy. Of which I have many."

"I suppose I'm not short on enemies these days, either. I wish I knew who took out the contract on my life." Verias slides down from the washstand. "May I ask you something?"

"Don't you need to sleep?"

"I'm exhausted, but this is important. Will destroying your soul kill you?" Verias asks. Kin cuts her eyes at him. "I have to know, Kin. It's not fair to expect me to have a hand in killing you without knowing it."

He's right, and Kin hates it.

She watches him turn to pull a fresh shirt from his saddlebag. He has older marks on his back, no longer puffy but still pink. The broken-open strikes of a caning, which Kin knows all too well. Many people she's known over the years are victims of a strap or cane, favorite Nerefinian punishments for petty crime. His are the product of an escape attempt, no doubt. When he turns back to her, Kin can see in those tired dark eyes that he's been party to enough death and suffering in his life. It's only fair to be honest with him.

"I don't know if it'll kill me. It's a risk I'm willing to take."

Kin can actually see Verias's heart falling to pieces in front of her. It's a strange sensation, watching his face fall while she feels almost nothing. She knows what will happen if her soul is back in her body. The unknown is better, no matter how sad that makes Verias.

"I'm sorry," he says. "I can't imagine what it's like to want to do the right thing and be made miserable for it."

"I can't, either. I didn't volunteer for this. I'm a monster, but I'm not a monster who wants to kill people with no consequences."

"But the fleshbound are—"

"They're supposed to do what humans can't, because they don't have to follow the rules. Ask yourself this, Verias: who would be attracted to being fleshbound? Maybe one or two good people who honestly think it's the right thing to do, and dozens and dozens of people who like killing." She twists a towel in her hands, which are completely dry and unpleasantly restless.

"May I touch you?" Verias asks.

"You've already touched me plenty fixing that wound," Kin says. "I think we're past that."

He hugs her. Kin isn't expecting it at all, and it takes everything she has not to stiffen in surprise, not to wrench away from him.

"I'm sorry," he says.

"Why should you be sorry? It's not your fault."

"Because I wish this hadn't happened to you."

"Oh. Thank you." Kin has no idea what to say, or whether she should hug him back, or even what she thinks of his words. She was simply there, noticing the smell of soap and dilute blood on Verias's skin and the rough stubble he hasn't bothered to shave off. Noticing how soft and strange a human body feels against hers. How fragile. Her stomach turns at the thought of how many times she'd gotten close without thinking of the damage she could do.

Still, she doesn't want him to let go. This one quiet moment feels like a blessing from the stars, a memory of something she'd forgotten she missed.

CHAPTER EIGHT

VERIAS HAS WOKEN UP TO KIN'S FACE SEVERAL TIMES NOW, and every time it startles him. She always looks deadly serious, as if whatever lives inside her mind is of grave importance and possibly nightmarish terror. It likely is, and this time he's sure she's going to kill him by the way she looks at him: brow furrowed, casting her dark, intense eyes into shadow, as she squats next to his bed with her elbows on her knees.

"Good afternoon," she says, her voice strangely light. "If we travel soon, we can be in Sestera by nightfall."

"Good afternoon?"

"Does that sound like a question because you're unsure of the time or the distance to Sestera? Or the goodness of this afternoon?"

"Because you're staring at me like you want to slit my throat," Verias says.

"I was wondering why you'd torn your face up like that."

Verias touches his cheek to find more than one crusty scab there. He hadn't even noticed he'd been picking at his skin.

"I don't know. I do it when I'm worried." He sits up, wishing Kin would stop staring at him. "Most of the time I don't even realize I'm doing it."

"You're an anxious person." Kin rises, straightening her blouse.

"I suppose so."

"I'm sorry. I can't help with that, except to keep you safe. It shouldn't be a difficult job, given that I can feel you in my head. The Binders' mark means neither of us will be truly alone unless and until they pass the mark to another Binder."

"How does that work? Is it anything like linking?" Verias leans forward, curiosity overwhelming the discomfort of knowing that Kin is tied to him that way.

"I don't know what linking is."

"A process by which two people can be tied together through magic. It's common for Carriers. A question for the Binders, I suppose." Verias shrugs.

"Be careful what questions you ask, Verias. If you get too close to their secrets, they will not hesitate to kill you. I don't want to end up splattered against some wall in the homepalace to protect you, because I will. That's what I'm good at. I think." Kin offers Verias a hand.

"You think?"

"It's been some time since I've protected anyone." Kin pulls Verias to his feet, and his wound tugs painfully. Still, he's less distracted than he has been, and has time to notice that she's remarkably strong. He isn't tall, but he isn't a small man, either, and it feels like she could snap him in half as easily as she lifted him that morning.

"How long have you been Bound?" he asks, more to distract himself from that line of thinking than to learn anything about Kin. He minds being manhandled by her much less than he should.

"What year is it?" Kin asks Verias.

"What?"

"What year? I don't remember."

"Five hundred fifty-two after Emergence." Verias can't imagine not knowing what year it is, how long it had been since the Wellspring bubbled up, releasing its power for Nerefinian sorcerers to use. That wouldn't be an important measurement for an Abserian, though. Kin's people use the magics of cosmic bodies, taking their power from above rather than below.

"Oh," Kin says after a long pause.

"Oh?"

"I'm forty this year."

"Oh," said Verias. "I thought you were younger than me by at least a decade, but it's only a few years. How long have you been . . . like this?"

Kin looks around room where they slept. Actually, though her bed is unmade, she looks tired enough that she may not have slept at all. "Thirteen years," she says.

"I didn't realize it had been so long."

"It doesn't matter. Can you sense where the Reapers are right now?" Kin asks.

Verias closes his eyes, turning his thoughts inward. Through his restless sleep, he hadn't felt the telltale shiver of a Reaper nearby, and he feels nothing now. But there's a constant hum of dread at the back of his mind, an instinct that tells him they must be close. No lord, especially not one so fond of war, gives up a Carrier easily. Felver will want him back.

"I don't know," he says.

"Were they very strong?" Kin asks. Verias opens his eyes to find her watching him intently, dark eyes locked on his. Something troubles her.

"I think so. What is it?"

"That man. Reshon. He wasn't afraid of me. At all. It concerns me."

"What do you mean? How do you know he wasn't afraid?"

"Because he was standing closer to me than you are now. The only people who are willing to get that close are Binders, fleshbound, and people who think I'm an adventure to go on," Kin says. "I truly hope he's the last. But if he is, I shouldn't have made that cock joke." A gentle tap at the door interrupts her. "Breakfast. Lunch. Whatever it is."

"Pardon me, *what*?"

Kin opens the door to a maid who must be the innkeeper's daughter. "I was taunting him and made a joke about—" Kin's eyes follow the maid as she places her tray on the tea table at the foot of Verias's bed. "Never mind."

The maid bobs her head at Kin and Verias on her way out of the room, and Kin pours herself a cup of tea before moving to the window to watch the street. With her back to him, Verias is stuck wondering what possible humor Kin could have found while facing Reshon down. She doesn't give any sign that she's going to explain, either.

Verias catches himself picking at his face more than once throughout their meal, bored and distracted as he is, and it only gets worse as they travel. By the end of the day there's blood under his fingernails. Kin doesn't say anything else about it, for which Verias is grateful; he's spent his whole life having his scars pointed out, being told that he was weak or foolish or worse for scraping at his flesh for no real reason. Being compared to Lusian, who was always stronger and braver than Verias. For whatever that was worth in the end. Lusian is dead, and Verias has ruined his remaining family's reputation.

He wishes, not for the first time, that he could heal himself. Fix the pits and scabs and scars, give the illusion of stability. But the safeguard makes it almost impossible, causing echoes of pain until he loses consciousness or snaps, whichever comes first. Likely the former, since he's always taken the coward's way out.

That's why Lusian was chosen, even though Verias is—was —the elder, the more knowledgeable. Lord Felver needed a brave man, and if Verias could have been that man, he would have. He *should* have stepped in and taken Lusian's place, and now he's here, his mind going in circles until he picks, picks, picks, watching the horizon for the first glimpse of Sestera.

Not that the relative safety of Sestera will help. Verias struggles not to shred his skin in good times and in bad, but he still glances down at Kin now and then, hoping her calm confidence might slow his mind. It does little to help.

"I can't go with you through the gates," she eventually says.

"What? Why not?" Anxiety starts to give way to panic, something wild fluttering in Verias's stomach. He looks up at the walls of Sestera, framed above by the darkening blue sky and below by the greening lands. It's huge, looming, nothing like anywhere he's ever been before. Lord Felver doesn't take cities, instead subsuming smaller towns and villages into his lands under the auspices of protecting Nerefin. Verias knows little of war except that it's consumed him like it consumed so many of the lives of camp followers, but it looks to him that Felver is testing what the councils of nobles will allow him to do for "safety's sake" before they intervene. It looks to him like torn-down towns are a good place for Felver to find strong men with nothing left to do but serve in his army. He only grows more powerful with each raid and battle.

"The city watch always monitors the gates for fleshbound. They demand to know how many of us are in Sestera at any given time, and confirm each entrance and exit with the Binders. Neither of us want anyone to know I'm here."

"So how will you get in?" Verias asks.

"I have ways. If you go to the Woolworkers' Quarter, there's a boarding house by the Indigo Bridge run by a woman named Honor. Tell her Kin wants a room, and she'll see to it."

"Where's the Indigo Bridge?" Verias asks.

"It's the only bridge that goes over the stream that runs blue. Runoff from the dye vats. You'll likely smell it before you see it. Take good care of Shadow. I'll see you shortly."

"But—" Verias begins.

Kin looks up at him with a quick wink before she leaves the road, trots down into the ditch alongside, and vanishes into a high hedgerow. Verias nudges Shadow to a trot, hurrying to the safety of a city while the muscles in his body begin to tense in Kin's absence.

The evening hour renders the gates a mess; country folk heading home from selling their wares pour out of the city in droves, and the streets aren't much better. There, everyone is on their way home from market and their trades. Verias is lucky to be on horseback, or he'd be overwhelmed by the sheer number of people. As it is, he catches himself tearing a scrap of skin off his lower lip before he can stop himself.

The market, with its wooden stalls and beige stone and mud-brick shops, gives way to a high, pale wall that separates it from a square that holds massive, ancient buildings that would intrigue Verias in the absence of shattering anxiety. A city guard points him through a long, covered wooden bridge that creaks beneath the weight of ox-drawn carts and foot traffic. The river runs lazily beneath at a shallow angle to the bridge, the sound of water drowned out by hollow hoofbeats and footsteps, but its humidity is felt in the air.

The Indigo Bridge is indeed easy to find once Verias is in the Woolworkers' Quarter, running a dark, scummy blue. A pungent, sweetish odor hangs in the air, mixing with the smell of spices and cooking meat from a large brick building with a shallow tile roof. A copper sign reading *AN HONORABLE REST* hangs above the blue-painted door, and a brown-skinned young boy comes bounding out the front door after spotting him through the open front window. He takes Shadow to the stable, leaving the door hanging open for Verias.

Inside, a dark-skinned woman with a cloud of gorgeous black hair greets Verias. She wears a high-collared, bright yellow dress that reminds him of squash flowers like the ones that grow in the garden back home in Solemn Gorge. As soon as she hears Kin's name, she sweeps Verias up to a room on the top floor. It's tiny, but there's a wardrobe, a tea table doubling as a washstand with two chairs, and a comfortable-looking bed. Supper and their belongings are delivered, and Verias sinks down at the table to eat. The food is delicious, but it stings the shredded skin of his lip. Exhausted by anxiety, Verias gives up halfway through his meal to sleep.

⊱ · ⊰

Kin slips through the kitchen door of the boarding house, avoiding the cook and her assistant. They've always been afraid of her, and Kin doesn't want to start trouble for Honor. She slinks into the front room, where Honor sits reading her son a book.

"Aunt Kin!" Amity springs up from the couch, running to grab Kin around the waist. He has a bit of a struggle getting around the knives at Kin's belt, and lets go quickly, holding on just long enough that Kin feels no fear of hurting him. Amity is a smart, sensitive child, and he knows Kin isn't much for embraces.

"Missed you, sweet boy," she says.

"There you are." Honor stands to squeeze Kin's arm gently. "Amity, go help Cook clean up."

"But *Mother*—"

"There are leftover cakes, and I doubt you'll get one if you aren't in the kitchen helping," Honor says, prompting Amity to speed off into the kitchen. Kin can't help smiling. Honor waits for Amity's footsteps to vanish down the hall before she speaks. "Are you in trouble?"

"Not yet," Kin says. "If I do get in trouble, you won't see me around here. I wouldn't put you or Amity in danger."

"I know you wouldn't. I worry about you, you know."

"It's not as if I'll die," Kin reminds her.

"You won't. But someday you'll get your soul back, and I don't think I'll see you after that."

"You're preemptively worrying about it?"

If anyone has cause to worry, it's Kin. She and Honor grew up together, but now Honor looks older by a decade. Amity grows more every time Kin sees him, and Kin could easily outlive him if she doesn't get her soul back. Everyone Kin knows, everyone in Sestera and in the world, is as fragile as spun sugar, on the verge of melting away. Kin worries about her few friends every day, worries about watching them grow old and die as she petrifies, bound in flesh and blood and mourning for all eternity.

"That's what worrying is," Honor says. She touches Kin's arm again, catching the deep melancholy that's snagged her in its net.

"Well, stop it. That's not healthy." Kin tries to keep her voice level, firm, but Honor is so close, so soft, so helpless.

"Not healthy," she says. "Beloved, to know you is to invite worry into one's life."

"Haha." Kin almost panics at the word *beloved*. That's too familiar, too near the heart.

"I'm not making a joke. I knew that poor man upstairs was a friend of yours without him even opening his mouth. Nobody else would look so harried and anxious," Honor says.

"He's always like that. Do you need my help with anything while I'm here?" Kin frequently finds people who leave the boarding house without paying to recoup Honor's money, something she's been doing since long before she was Bound.

"Not right now. But I do have a few things that need a pair of strong arms, and perhaps steady balance," Honor says. Roof tiles, of course. It's always roof tiles.

"I've got those. I'd better go see Verias."

"You'd better. Room ten."

Once, Kin would have hugged Honor. Honor has never said anything about it, and Kin is sure that the hurt wore off years ago. She squeezes Kin's arm again, making her feel safe, cared for. Honor's place is the closest thing Kin had to a home for the last thirteen years, and gratitude warms the inside of her chest.

Kin climbs to the top floor and knocks on the door of room ten, the sensation of being near a target buzzing at the back of her head like a locust. She can't just burst in on Verias and scare the life out of him. He's had a difficult enough journey as it is. She wishes she could stop caring, but she's beginning to count him as a friend, and she doesn't know how to stop.

Verias looks a complete mess when he opens the door. Hair and clothes rumpled, blood on his chin, rubbing his bandaged chest like the sensation is the only thing keeping him tethered on earth.

"Did you get in a *fight*?" Kin asks. The city guards, perhaps, or maybe a thief? Does Verias have anything worth stealing?

"No. Fell asleep." He scratches at the wound, grimacing. "Why?"

"You're bloody." When Kin brushes past him, she can smell it, sweet and metallic. Distracting. Verias slumps onto the bed, wiping his face with the back of his hand. He looks miserably at the scarlet smear across his skin, and an unwanted desire to make it better boils up inside her. "Tell me what troubles you."

"I don't want to waste your time."

"Verias, I'm fleshbound. I have nothing *but* time," Kin says. Verias favors her with a weak laugh, running his hand through his gray-flecked hair. Kin has always liked gray hair.

"I had dreams . . . I was thinking of Lusian when I fell asleep."

"Your brother?" Kin asks. When he nods, Kin almost tells him how sorry she is, but that won't fix anything. She wants to reach for him, but knows that leads nowhere good.

"Do you have any siblings?" Verias does like to fill silences.

"No. I suppose my parents had their hands full enough with just me," Kin says, and Verias laughs. "Honor had the utter *gall* to tell me that to know me is to be worried."

"She's right, I've been worried the whole time I've known you."

"Tuh! I should make you sleep in the stable with Shadow for that, but you look like you need a real rest. At least a day or two before you go to the Binders."

"What are you going to be doing while I'm there?" Verias asks.

"Keeping you safe."

"How? You can't go into their homepalace without being recognized."

"It's a secret," Kin says. "You'll just have to trust me."

"I do."

For the space of a breath, Kin is sure the statement will break her so soon after hearing Honor call her *beloved*. What gives him the right to even think about her long enough to trust her? She's supposed to be invisible, a specter of death, but here he is, looking up at her with his sad eyes like a puppy who doesn't know a kick is coming. Kin almost scolds him for the sheer foolishness of trusting a person without a conscience. She could turn on him at any time and experience no guilt whatsoever (though she might miss his company). How can a grown man live through war and mortal fear and still be so *earnest?* Kin lost that years and years ago. It's possible she never had it; she only remembers the cynicism of the master thief.

"Verias, you—" Kin stops herself. She's already ruined almost all but one of her friendships. Some fell apart the moment she was Bound, others when her friends and allies learned what she'd done afterward. But most had died when she continually pushed people away, told them she was dangerous. Told them they were better off without her. She refuses to do that to herself again. She can't. It hurts too much. "You're too kind to me."

"Maybe you're not kind enough to yourself. You look tired."

"I need rest. I haven't slept since . . ." Kin can't remember. Sometime after she met Verias, she's sure of that much. "It was more important to stand watch."

"I can do that sometimes, you know. I did learn a few things about fighting in Felver's army."

"You're not suited to it." Kin doesn't want to sleep, doesn't want to dream.

"No, I'm not." Verias gets up. "Just like you're not suited for ever resting for even a moment. Go to sleep."

Kin grudgingly kicks off her boots. She usually sleeps in her clothes at the homepalace, but she doesn't want to ruin Honor's sheets, and Verias escapes before she can start peeling her clothes off. She curls up in bed, the weight of the blankets letting her feel safe and secure enough to at least lie still for a while, even if she knows she won't sleep. Chestnut leaps up on the bed and kneads at her hip before falling asleep himself.

CHAPTER NINE

THE DAYS ARE GROWING WARMER, AND VERIAS IS delighted to walk through the streets of Sestera in his shirtsleeves. Kin doesn't so much walk as stalk beside him, one hand resting on a knife hilt. Though no passersby shy away, none look right at her. Verias finds himself walking in a protected area, where eyes slide off of him just as easily as they do Kin, his power less important than avoiding eye contact with a fleshbound as they make their way through the Golden Quarter.

There, Sestera's most expensive shops, restaurants, and taverns are scattered among the homes of the wealthy and massive houses that surely belong to nobles. Verias has little knowledge of Sesteran politics (or politics in general), but he knows that Nerefin is controlled by councils of lords and ladies, and he's itching to know more. Verias's father always considered Lusian his political heir, passing his knowledge of the greater world to his favored son. Verias was always happy to leave such concerns to someone else and lose himself in spellbooks, but now that he's here, he can't help but wonder what more there is to understand.

Visiting a silversmith certainly makes clear how little Verias really does know. Kin carries a single silver tab from Verias's collar in her pocket, the rest squirreled away at Honor's. Kin told Verias where all of them were, because she'd hidden them all over the place, including one behind a hollow brick in the stable.

When he pointed out that this tactic would make it hard to leave Sestera in a hurry, Kin hadn't been worried about it, and now he understands why: the silversmith hands over bank notes for nearly seven hundred fathoms. The whole collar must be worth more than Verias's life and Kin's combined.

"We'll need to get some of this changed," Kin remarks on their way out of the silversmith's shop. "But first you need new clothes. Wearing Felver's colors is like putting out a sign to attract Reshon."

"Wouldn't you want small trade currency for that instead of merchant money?" Verias asks.

"Not for this. We want you to be as pretty as you can be," Kin says. Verias snorts. *Pretty.* "Some raggedy-looking commoner with an ocean of magic wanders in, they'll ask questions. Someone with money and the tiniest spark of power? They'll be falling all over themselves to test you in hopes of being the one to bring in someone with influence. The Binders aren't popular in Sestera," Kin says. "It's a shame your hair is so short."

"What's wrong with my hair?" Verias is turned around by the change of subject.

"Most wealthy men wear their hair long. Really, Verias, where have you been?"

"Fighting a war? Lord Felver doesn't wear his hair long," Verias points out.

"No, he doesn't, because he fancies himself a warlord and wants to wear a helmet when his soldiers burn down villages," Kin says. "Besides, he's an out-of-fashion old man, and I'm saying that as an old spinster who never cared about all that in the first place. Anyway, I meant before that. It's been the fashion for at least three years."

"I was studying."

"Well, we'll set you right in under an hour. I only know what

I see on the street, but a good tailor will have everything you need."

Kin makes good on her promise, mostly because Verias is smart enough to keep his mouth shut and simply accept the clothing given to him. His family isn't poor by any stretch of the imagination, but their home is out in the country, where it's usual to wear trousers laced with leather thong, and shirts and dresses of undyed wool. Verias's clothes under Felver were similar in construction, though more colorful. It seems that a life of leisure doesn't require bending at the knee. Verias is subjected to tight leather chausses that Kin declares quite flattering, and tells him to stop pulling faces when he sees his reflection in the tailor's mirror (admittedly, he is making faces, because he looks like a particularly sad jester). The strangling chausses are belted over linen braies, undoubtedly the least offensive part of the whole outfit. They're loose and comfortable, as is the shirt, but a heavy doublet on top makes him resent the shirt by association.

"If your plan fails, you can always find a wealthy noblewoman to wed and live a life of ease," Kin remarks once they're crammed in back at Honor's with all her purchases.

"You're making fun."

"Nobleman, then?" she asks, as if the gender of the noble is the deciding factor and not literally everything else.

"Noble anybody would do, but that's not the point."

"Noted. What is the point?" Kin somehow sounds perfectly innocent.

"I look like I should be acting out follies!"

"Take a compliment, Verias."

He catches himself staring at her. She meets his gaze, not a hint of mockery in her expression, and tucks her thumbs behind her knife belt. Verias expected her to fuss at him, something to which he's much more accustomed. His father is a fussy man, always picking at him to stand up straight, fix his clothes, comb his hair, as if he's a child. Reshon is always looking for things to criticize, to remind him of his place. His boots aren't polished sufficiently, his magic is too slow, his heart too weak.

Being unbadgered is peaceful, and knowing that Kin is somewhere watching over him makes the walk to the Binders' homepalace almost relaxing, only a small grain of anxiety nagging at the back of his mind. Verias follows the river through the Woolworkers' Quarter with the tall houses of the Golden Quarter off to his right, and wonders whether the rich whose houses butt up against the wall bounding the quarters can smell indigo from their windows, or if the wall holds the reek at bay.

He passes over the massive covered wooden bridge that Kin calls the Riverbridge (all one word, she insists), and into the pentagonal city center. There the Council houses, built of ancient mudbrick, loom over the slow-moving waters of the Embraile, where squat river barges make their leisurely way up and downriver beneath the high, curving bridges. Verias enters the Deep Quarter through the Westgate, which Kin pointed out to him on their excursion to the Golden Quarter.

The homepalace is a huge, rambling, three-story stone structure that hunches against the smaller buildings around it. Few are homes, presumably because nobody wants to live near fleshbound. When Verias strolls around the palace, he finds a few one-story shops where the owners do not sleep, a stable for the rich to board their horses, a warehouse, and a meeting hall. Verias wonders for a moment whether Kin is hiding in one of those buildings before he heads inside.

He's not sure what he expected of the Binders, but the large entry hall isn't it. The floor is old, polished wood, with thick carpets covering the places that are worn down by countless feet since the Emergence. A few people wait in chairs along one wall, and a robed woman with short, pale hair stands before a pair of ancient wooden doors, hands clasped behind her back.

Her eyes sweep up and down Verias's body as he approaches, her power cold in his belly. Her small stature belies the depths she's capable of drawing.

"Good day," she says. "To what do we owe the pleasure of a Carrier's presence?"

"I wish to become a Binder." Verias realizes his mistake when the Binder raises an eyebrow. He oughtn't have been so open with his intent. Still, a small smile spreads across her face, and Verias has to hide his shock that for once, he hasn't been found wanting.

"I see. The Dean is a busy man, but I'm sure he will find time to speak to someone of your stature."

The killing thread of magic between Kin and Verias hums like a plucked harp string. Kin tries to ignore the distraction as she crosses rooftops in the Deep Quarter, following Verias to the homepalace. When she was young, Kin ran these routes bare-foot, to better feel the way ahead. After a broken tile once sliced her foot open and left her housebound for over a month with a festering wound, she learned her lesson. Since then she wears good boots and travels at a walk.

Still, there's danger. Another time, a single wrong step sent her to the cobblestones in the Golden Quarter, leaving her with an elbow injury that still plagues her. It also landed her in jail for a time; though the city guards couldn't find proof she'd done anything wrong, they still held her as long as they could on the grounds that nobody would be on a roof in the middle of the night unless they were up to something. It was a correct assessment. Kin had been returning from reconnaissance on her last job before she retired. The first failure of many.

Kin settles on a wooden warehouse roof—no tiles to jab her —and watches Verias enter the homepalace. There's no hint of nerves in his posture, and Kin glances up into the bright blue sky that veils the stars to pray that he can keep calm. He should be safe inside as long as he can do that. Or at least he'll be safe from his family and from Reshon. That man is turning out to be more trouble than Kin expected. She probably should have killed him that night by the campfire.

The thought is cut off by a sharp shiver up Kin's spine, like the searing path of a serrated edge.

"You look terrible," a voice says behind Kin. She whirls, pulling her baselards.

"Merit." Kin should have known. Sloppy. Too sloppy.

"Kindred Jole. I didn't expect to see you until they dragged you back in kicking and screaming."

"I have neither kicked nor screamed, and you know it."

"I have absolutely heard you scream." A smile spreads across Merit's narrow brown face.

"Keep going, Merit, I'd love to have an excuse to cut out your tongue."

"I'm sure you would, but could you? Because it seems to me like you're slipping, or I wouldn't have been able to sneak up on you," Merit's slender brown hand rests casually on one of their knives, their posture loose.

Kin feels her mouth pull into a grimace. She is *not* going soft. "I sensed your presence. I have more important things on my mind."

"So are you coming back, or are you planning on lurking around the city, hoping the rest of us conceal *your* presence?" Merit blows a stray lock of curly, chin-length black hair out of their face.

"I haven't decided yet."

"You'll come back. Everyone does." They've always fancied themself smarter than Kin, and they are, but Kin always has the upper hand on account of being meaner.

64

"Not everyone gives up the instant they're Bound," she shoots back. Merit's smile falls for just a moment.

"Some of us are smarter than that, Kin," they say. Predictably.

"Tuh! If you're so smart, then why are you still Bound?"

"Why are you?" Merit crosses their arms, and Kin relaxes as much as she can in their presence. They can't kill her, of course, but they've been in some rough fights that always end in punishment for both of them.

"I'm biding my time," she says.

"So am I."

"But you gave up on fighting in the meantime, didn't you?" Kin asks. "Go bide your time somewhere else."

"*You're* accusing *me* of giving up? I should cut out *your* tongue for that kind of gall."

"Did you climb all the way up here to remind me of all my crimes, Merit? Because I'd rather be untongued than listen to you tell me what a monster I am," Kin snaps.

"I came up here to warn you. If I noticed you up here, someone else surely will. You've always been brazen, but this is reckless even for you. What are you up to?"

"None of your business."

Kin and Merit haven't gotten along in years, but she still doesn't want Merit to get hurt because of her. If anyone at the homepalace associates them with Kin, they'll get in just as much trouble as she will.

"Dangerous, is it? Of course it is. It's you."

"Merit, please." Kin turns back to her watch of the homepalace.

"What's in there that you want so bad?" Merit persists. They've always been like this, but Kin's patience for them varies greatly. At the moment, it's wearing thin, a skim of ice on an ocean of annoyance.

"My soul, fool."

"Kin, you aren't thinking—of course you are. What am *I* thinking?"

"I wouldn't know," Kin says sourly.

"You can't do this. It's impossible. People have tried."

"Yes, well. None of them were the King of Thieves, were they?"

"Stars, you are insufferable. Dig your own grave, then, *King of Thieves*." Merit's shoes scuff as they turn away, and Kin turns too.

"Merit—"

"I know. I won't tell anyone I saw you. Just . . . please don't get me killed."

"You're fleshbound, Merit," Kin says.

"I still wouldn't put it past you."

Kin rolls her eyes and turns back to the homepalace.

CHAPTER TEN

THE SLENDER WOMAN IS STRAIGHT-BACKED AS SHE LEADS
Verias deeper into the homepalace, never sparing a glance back.
Verias fairly bubbles with the power surrounding him. Though
he can't separate one sorcerer from the other in his mind, his
guts tell him there have to be dozens of Binders filling the structure. His nerves buzz at being trapped in a hive of enemies, the
sensation threatening to overwhelm him.

"Where are all the fleshbound?" Verias asks. His voice has
blessedly gone flat, so he at least sounds calm.

"In the cellars," the woman says. "Their skin is sensitive to
sunlight, so it's important to keep them below."

"Fascinating." Verias has never heard Kin say anything
about it. Is it because she's Abserian and has darker skin than
your average Nerefinian, or had she simply not bothered to
mention it? The questions begin to overwhelm his fear, and he
focuses on them, like balancing on knifepoints.

"I assume this is a matter of scholastic curiosity rather than a
desire to serve Sestera," the woman says. She must be a least a
little familiar with Carrier ways. Verias's family promised Lusian for protection and access to resources, not out of any particular love of Nerefin.

"Do most Binders come here out of a desire to serve?" Verias
can't help remembering what Kin said about the type of people
who wish to become fleshbound. Binders are surely no different,

and he fears the answer, but asking questions keeps him calm.

"Some do. Most are here for the same reason you are. To see what a human can become given the correct enchantments," the woman says.

Verias's stomach turns over, his mind creating dozens of gruesome scenarios in an instant. It fixes on a memory of the pain in Kin's shadowed face as she recalled her Binding.

"You'll forgive me for asking, but what are your numbers in comparison to the Healers or Reapers? It seems messy work, being a Binder." Ask questions. Stay calm.

"That is certainly true. There are far fewer of us than there are Healers. More than the Reapers, however. The Reapers . . ." the robed woman makes a sound of disgust in the back of her throat. "Not a crumb of finesse in the whole lot. You may wait here for the Dean. What may I tell him to call you?"

"Everis." The name is close enough that Verias won't forget.

They've come to a carved wooden door with benches set to either side, a waiting area similar to the entrance hall. Two Binders sit on one, watching him as he settles on the other and attempts to avoid eye contact. Once his guide is gone, Verias has to actively fight the urge to pick at his fingernails or rake at his skin. He can't appear anxious in front of the Binders for fear they might suspect him of something. He thinks of Kin again, but this time the Kin he imagines watching over him, protective and hawk-eyed.

When Verias is conducted into the Dean's study by the slight Binder, she takes her place behind the Dean, waiting at his left elbow for her next order. The Dean is a tall, thin man with a severe yet remarkably porridge-bland face and gray hair, who wears a robe much like the one Verias's guide does. Not quite black, not exactly gray, but the sort of in-between color one might see behind their closed eyelids. The Dean sits behind a broad desk of pale, striated wood, and the room is lined with bookshelves. There are no windows, the light provided by oil lamps.

"Please sit," says the Dean. "It has been many years since a Carrier has wished to join us."

"That is so. Tradition is important to Carrier families." Verias has already thought his answers over for hours, trying to perfect them, to have a response for anything the Binders could think to ask.

"That is certainly true. In all my years as a Binder, I have only met a handful of Carriers. What has coaxed you away from tradition?"

"There is a limit to what can be learned in such an insular community," Verias says. "I tire of books and history."

"History?" the Dean's tone is mild, but there's a spark of something in his eyes. "What kind of history?"

"Mostly pre-Emergence and early Emergence spellbooks. Lost arts." Though they might be able to tie Verias to his family in Solemn Gorge through his work, it's imperative that he impress them, which means honest answers about his skills. He can't afford to lie and come up short.

"Then you're skilled at breaking ciphers?" The Dean leans forward.

"Yes." It feels strange to boldly say that he's good, but he is. Most sorcerers of that era—when magic was new and fresh techniques and ideas sprang up every day—wrote their journals and spellbooks in code to keep their secrets safe. Tens, if not hundreds of thousands of spells were lost, and one by one, Verias brings them back.

"Lessa, please fetch a cipher evaluation for our friend Everis." The Dean doesn't bother to look back at Lessa. Still, she inclines her head and hurries out of the room. "I'd like you to complete the exercises Lessa will bring you. We have many coded books in the library—the old ways persisted here much longer than they did in other disciplines, and I daresay some of us might still be writing in code—and we are in dire need of code breakers to retain our knowledge. I'm sure that what you find in our coded books will be of use to you in your academic pursuits."

The Dean has thus far ignored Verias's mention of being tired of books, and Verias suspects he should argue so as not to seem weak, but he's also curious to know why this man is so interested in breaking codes. His mind can't help but cycle through questions. Is this a test of Verias's curiosity? His biddability?

"I'm not sure that would interest me." Verias hopes he sounds persuadable.

"Becoming a Binder has many benefits," the Dean says. "If you are accepted, all of your needs will be seen to. If you have enough skill at controlling fleshbound, it is possible to find employment with nobility, even royalty."

"Controlling them how?"

Even saying it makes Verias break out in a cold sweat. He knew when he left Honor's that morning that he was bound to run into a question to which he did not want the answer. This is far too soon for his comfort.

"That depends upon the individual fleshbound," says the Dean. "You don't have a weak stomach, do you?"

"Not at all." Verias's stomach is on the verge of rebelling over the whole conversation.

"Good. Some are obedient on their own, which is always desirable, but many require magical persuasion, including freshening the spells that subdue conscience. The most recalcitrant fleshbound need harder forms of control. Ah. Thank you, Lessa. You may leave us."

Lessa places a sheaf of papers on the Dean's desk and leaves, futilely inclining her head once more. The Dean carefully folds the papers into a neat packet and sets them on the desk in front of Verias.

"As I was saying, corporal punishment is sometimes necessary. Some subjects recover their conscience while they are away, which leads them to give up on their mission and try to hide from us. They must be brought back and punished, their enchantments refreshed. Others need to be kept in line more actively," the Dean says. "This is why we leave them with fear when we take their conscience. The good thing is that flesh-bound are never permanently damaged, no matter what you do."

Hot, sickly angers rises alongside nausea. The cruelty of leaving pain for the specific purpose of punishment angers Verias more, somehow, than his own mistreatment. It's easier to be angry on Kin's behalf than examine his own suffering, but he has to push both sources of the feeling aside, folding and cramming them in like clothes into a too-small wardrobe.

"Something troubles you." The Dean's eyes narrow, just slightly. Verias needs a lie, fast. His throat clenches like a fist.

"Functional immortality seems like a liability," he says.

"It has its drawbacks." The Dean leans forward, a little of the sharp, analytical expression fading from his face. "It can take them a long time to accept their place, knowing that nothing we do to them is permanent. But even the brightest dye fades with repeated washings. Even a stone is worn by wind and rain. In the end, after all the work has been done, an assassin who cannot be killed is valuable."

"Then patience is surely a Binder's greatest asset."

"As long as you're talented enough to do the work."

"I am. I'll have this back to you shortly." Verias picks up the paper packet. "I want to start as soon as possible."

"Good. Lessa will be waiting outside. She will see you out. When you return, ask for her."

Verias stands, gives the Dean a shallow bow, and leaves the study. His stomach swirls with nausea at the thought of what's been done to Kin, what might be done to her if he fails. She had mentioned punishment, but he was too much of a coward to picture it until the Dean's calm, scholarly explanation. A skilled Reaper can reduce a human to a fine pink mist if they care to, and the Binders' skills seem to lean in that direction. They could cut Kin limb from limb, burn her alive, and force her to live for an eternity with the searing memories.

CHAPTER ELEVEN

THE OUTSIDE AIR, WHICH SEEMED SO PLEASANTLY WARM ON his way in, is stifling on the way out. Verias is suffocating in his foolish doublet, and sweat sticks his leather trousers to his legs and stings the tightly bandaged wound on his chest. The heat worsens the nausea at the same time shivers chase each other down his spine. He keeps having to swallow to avoid being sick in a gutter. He doesn't even notice that Kin has fallen in next to him.

"Don't look back, but you're being followed," Kin says, and Verias has to physically fight the urge to disobey.

"By whom?" Verias's voice does what it always does when he's in mortal fear, flattening out into a monotone.

"Not a fleshbound, I can tell you that much. And not Reshon. She's young, with dark hair. Nondescript, looks local."

"I don't feel any magic." Thank the Wellspring for that.

"Don't get complacent. They've learned from their mistakes because they know they can't catch us if you sense them coming. I doubt she's alone. They know what I am."

"What do we do?" Panic starts to simmer in the back of Verias's throat.

"Have a drink." Kin guides Verias toward a tavern with a hand on his elbow. As they cross the threshold, a shiver of magic runs up his spine, and Kin's grip tightens. "What's wrong?"

"I thought I felt a little flash of magic, but it's gone now." Verias sits in the chair she waves him toward, hunching down to make himself smaller as if that will help.

"Lean back, I need to be able to see the room," Kin says. Verias obeys, but Kin doesn't look directly at the large room with its scattered tables and chairs. It's fairly empty because of the hour, and bright noon sunlight streams through a stained glass window at the front, casting rainbows on the floor. There's a side door to Verias's left that he itches to escape through already.

Kin orders wine, perfectly composed. It doesn't escape Verias's notice that even though she doesn't eat, she loves tea and other drinks, holding the cool pewter mug against her jaw with a peaceful expression. The rituals must be comforting, in a life with few comforts.

"Kin, can you get drunk?" Verias asks.

"Not really. Get a little tipsy, maybe. It was explained to me that drink is a mild poison, and poisons rarely touch me." She sips her wine and says no more. Kin has a habit of revealing tiny details about herself and nothing else, leaving Verias with a thousand questions. When was she *poisoned*?

After a short time, a young woman appears and sits two tables away from them. Kin nudges Verias's foot with hers. He looks into her eyes so he won't be tempted to look directly at the spy. That would surely give away that he knows they're being followed, and that might force her hand. It feels like his wine is trapped somewhere in his chest instead of making its way into his stomach. Plausible, since it's doing nothing to calm his nerves.

Studying Kin helps a little, though none of the rainbow light from the window falls on her face. She's wholly in shadow, her red-brown hair dark as crimson blood, the gray tinge of her skin more pronounced in cool light. Though she's not a small woman —she has a double chin that's especially prominent on the rare occasions that she smiles—her face is carved out by high cheek-bones, leaving hollows in her cheeks that are vaguely ghostly.

Kin's lips quirk into a smile, and she leans in close enough that Verias catches the scents of wine and citrusy hair oil. "Be ready to get out of here. And don't lose your nerve. I'm starting a fight," she whispers. "Hey!" She barks, making Verias flinch. "Yes, you! Why are you looking at him, little girl? He's mine."

Verias doesn't dare look at Kin or Reshon's assassin. He instead shares a wary look with the man tending the casks.

"I'm not looking at anyone."

"You were staring at him. You saw her, didn't you?" Kin asks Verias.

"Uh . . ." He glances again at the owner of the tavern, as if he can help. The stout, tall man looks like he's ready to throw them all out.

"Madam, I won't have fights in my establishment. I must—"

Kin stands, nothing more. The triplet knives swing at her hips, steel glints, and the owner recoils ever so slightly. She's of a height with him, just as broad. Her face is terrifying in its calm and beauty. The tavernkeeper wisely turns his attention to the spy instead.

"I must ask you to leave."

"Me? What did I do?" the young woman asks.

"You're bothering my customers."

"Quick, go out the side door," Kin whispers while the spy continues to make a scene. "Start heading back to the boarding house and don't look back."

Verias obeys, slipping away as quickly as he can, heart lodged in his throat.

It takes little to make the whole scene worse. All Kin has to do is say a few more rude things (a skill she's been working on since she could speak) to get the spy shouting to defend herself, and watch the tavernkeeper handle her out of concern for his own neck. Kin drops a few fathoms on the table and gets out of there quick, hurrying behind Verias.

As she looks out for anyone else following him, Kin stays far enough from Verias that he won't notice her. At the same time, she searches for anyone trailing her, though she doubts they care about her. Kin is just an obstacle, and if they're smart, they'll try to go around her instead of through her. Otherwise she'll go through them.

As she tails him, Kin is glad to see that Verias obeys, never looking back. The streets aren't as crowded as they will be at dusk, when the Golden Quarter is Sestera's hub of evening revelry, but he's still hard to mark. Anxious posture notwithstanding, the number of average height men with white skin and graying dark hair in Sestera has to be in the tens of thousands.

A figure draws her eye. An exceedingly ordinary man who cuts through the streets with the deadly grace of a tigerfish hunting prey. Kin knows firsthand that it's impossible to hide that carriage. No matter how she tries, she moves like a killer. He won't be as good as her—no human is—but she won't underestimate him.

Kin clenches her teeth as she observes the assassin. Knife in his sleeve, one in his boot. She scans the street for somewhere to waylay him away from prying eyes. Especially here in the Golden Quarter, where most pickpockets fear to go, anything out of the ordinary will spark suspicion. There's a stall here, a wagon there. Alleys, shadowed but clean. Kin quickens her pace, knocking elbows with him. When he tries to shove her out of the way, she snatches his wrist, shunting him back into the side of a wagon filled with bolts of fine cloth.

"You're going to walk down this alley with me," Kin says. He flinches when their eyes meet. "And you're not going to make a single sound."

He nods. Kin puts a hand on his back, guiding him into a narrow alleyway as his muscles tense with the desire to escape. He remains still. Kin wraps her arm around his soft neck in a blood choke, bracing one hand with the other so that his brief struggles won't break the hold. For an instant, the world narrows down to the warmth of skin, the faint rustle of fabric, and flailing limbs. When he goes limp, Kin lets him slump down onto the ground, steals his knives, and makes her way back out of the alley.

Kin is immediately aware that she's lost Verias. Fear she hasn't experienced in years boils up inside her, gripping her throat tight and making her fingers cold and numb. She can still sense him skittering around in the back of her mind, alive, in danger. She hurries up the street, resisting the urge to run or call out to him. She forces herself to stay focused on finding anyone following Verias. Nobody. No spies, no killers. No Verias.

She smells the Woolworkers' Quarter before she spots Verias, strolling toward Honor's like nothing's wrong. He really does trust Kin to keep him safe, and that knowledge melts her cold fear away, leaving behind something that makes it just as hard to breathe. No time to pause and catch her breath, she dashes past Honor with a quick hello before hurrying up the stairs.

"Did you lose her?" Verias asks when Kin entered their room.

"Them. There was a second one. He's out of the way." She lets the words out in short bursts, afraid he'll hear how breathless she is. "Here." She hands him the stolen knives. "In case you need them."

"You couldn't give up one of your own?" Verias accepts the knives with a wry smile.

"The only way someone can take one of these knives from me is by running off with it still stuck in them somewhere. And

I'd probably chase them."

"Terrifying," Verias says.

"You knew I was a monster from the moment you met me."

"Having a fleshbound chase me isn't the terrifying thing. The real terror is getting between you and something you want, fleshbound or not."

"I suppose I ought to take that as a compliment." Kin can't help chuckling.

"It was meant as one." With the worry gone from his scarred face, his smile lights the whole room. It's not an entirely unpleasant shock to realize he's handsome. No, she's had that thought before. The night she met him, crouched over him, Kin had admired a face aged out of perfect pretty-boy beauty into something she liked better. This isn't new information at all.

And yet. Realizing and absorbing something are two different things. Where once she saw a target, she now sees a person. Whole.

"Is something wrong?" Verias asks.

Kin crosses to the tiny window to avoid looking at him. This kind of attraction, this pull, is a luxury she can ill afford. The people who want her aren't the kind of people she wants for more than a night—people brave and foolish enough to seek out the danger of taking a monster to bed—but who else will have her? Certainly not Verias, who's kind and tired of war and blood. There are other people like him who care to know him. A fleshbound knows only other fleshbound, but they're like leopards, rarely interacting. Merit and Kin are proof.

Kin loathes herself for being so lonely when she has Honor. Honor understands so much about Kin that Nerefinians can't, but she can't know what it's like to be fleshbound. A foolish wish builds inside her that Verias has an inkling. He's just as dangerous as she, or would be if he used his magic for anything other than reading books. She hopes he'll never have to do that again, but she knows Sestera. If the city can bring out the worst in someone, it does. It smashed her on the cobblestones and used her to its own purposes, and she'll never be whole again. She can't risk being whole again.

"Kin?"

"What?"

"I asked if something's wrong." Verias touches Kin's shoulder so tentatively that she feels the warmth of his hand more than the weight of it.

"No. Just thinking."

"Would you like me to have tea brought? You look like you need it."

"I don't need anything except my soul." Kin has to remind herself of that. She neither wants nor needs him to think she's in any way soft. She can't let any doubt in. Doubt only leads to trouble.

"Everybody needs comforting things."

"I don't." What Kin needs is for Verias to back off before she says something she regrets.

"You don't seem soulless to me. Just . . ."

"Keep that thought to yourself." Kin whirls to shoot him a glare, just in time to see Verias cringe at her snap. She's already failed in her mission not to drive anyone else away. "Have you decided you're afraid of me again?"

"Again?" Verias asks. "I don't remember being afraid of you."

"You flinched even worse than that when we rode together," she says.

"Kin, that wasn't out of fear, it was because you were mashing your arm into a massive bruise on my ribs."

"Oh. I sometimes forget that your kind heal so slowly."

Though Kin feels more than a little foolish, Verias just looks at her for a while, not making eye contact, but casting his gaze around her face.

"Do you trust Honor?" he asks at last. Why is he thinking of Honor?

"To an extent," Kin says. "Why do you ask?"

"You're more afraid *for* Honor and Amity than they are actually afraid of you. It seems to me that you don't trust her to make her own choices."

"She's human. Humans are frail. A little torture and even Honor would give me up to the Binders. Even you would."

Verias blanches, his dark eyes and deep red scabs standing out stark against his white face. "They hurt you."

"Of course they did." Her brows rise. Someone must have said something to shake him, revealed to him the many torments she's been subjected to in the dank basements beneath the homepalace.

Verias has been punished before. Even if he hadn't mentioned his escape attempt, even if she hadn't seen the marks left on his skin, it's plain as day in his eyes.

"Don't dwell on it," Kin says. "I certainly don't. There's no point in feeling bad about it any more than there's a point in feeling bad about the sun coming up."

"I wish I could remember such things so lightly."

"You shouldn't wish for it. I'm not a person, Verias, and that's the price I pay for shrugging off everything they do to me. They claim the punishments make us behave, but that's a simple lie. The truth is, the toll it takes to be separated from my soul is what keeps me going back there over and over, year after year. I'm drawn to it, or I'd be years gone."

"I'll get it back for you. I swear it, Kin. I'll do whatever it takes." His brown eyes meet hers, catching the sun from the window. The light makes the dark spot in his iris even darker by comparison. Until now, Kin has always felt most comfortable in the dark.

CHAPTER TWELVE

AS VERIAS SETS TO WORK ON THE PAPERS HE BROUGHT BACK from the homepalace, Kin finds herself spending time working for Honor. It's been a while since Kin has helped Honor, and there's much to be done. Having something good, something helpful to do with her hands is a pleasure, but with Verias in their room, Kin finds herself slow to finish tasks. She makes sure he's safe three or four times an hour, anxious about losing her one chance at freedom.

She often catches him resting, perhaps recovering from the collar that sapped his strength and funneled it into the war machine for Felver, or perhaps from healing her. Though the dark circles around his eyes have faded, he looks most fragile when sleeping, his face wiped clean of worry but still harboring fresh scabs. Kin aches to share her healing ability with him and take away the crusty, bloody spots that share his skin with old, white scars.

Almost as often, Kin catches herself with her fingers a hairsbreadth from this chewed-raw lip, his breath, his very life warm against her skin. It's so brittle and easy to snatch away with little more than a pair of strong arms. That knowledge makes Kin feverish, alternating washes of warmth and cold fear rushing through her body. She can't trust herself to touch him, to be close for a moment or two, without the fear of what she might do. She loathes herself for being such a monster. She loathes caring about Verias, yet every time she sees him at rest, it takes her ages to even look away, let alone turn to slip back out of the room. Sometimes he wakes while she watches, and she has to pretend she's come into the room for any real reason.

"Kin," he murmurs once when he wakes. "You're filling the room up with anxiety."

"What's that supposed to mean?" Kin asks.

"It means I think you must be worse than I am for worrying." He sits up and rubs his eyes. They're red, probably from staring at his own tiny handwriting. "I'm not going to die in my sleep."

Kin can't explain that it isn't disease or some other assassin she fears killing him in his sleep, it's her. She's saved from having to think of an answer by a knock on their door. It's Honor, of course, wearing a bright orange dress today. The bodice is sewn with little yellow beads, and her hair is pulled into a severe bun that emphasizes her frown

"Somebody magic is asking for him." Honor jerks her chin at Verias. "He claims to be family. I told him I was checking my books to see if there was anyone here by that name."

"Did he give you a name?" Verias asks.

"Asher."

"Oh. Oh dear." Verias's face is white as a sheet.

"Who is it?" Kin asks.

"My cousin. Tell him I'm not here. Hopefully if you have a well, he won't be able to sense my presence," he says. Honor gives him a curt nod and turns to hurry back downstairs.

"Stay here." Kin steals out of the room, staying a flight of stairs behind Honor. She creeps down to the first floor to see who they're up against. She stands with her back to the wall between two guest room doors, listening to Honor tell this Asher that there's nobody there named Verias.

"He might be with a fleshbound," they reply.

"Not in my place. This may not be the Golden Quarter, but I run a reputable house," Honor sounds so convincingly offended that a smile spreads across Kin's face.

"Apologies. I meant no offense."

"Well, I'd advise you not to ask about fleshbound anywhere else. It's likely to get you thrown out on your ear, sorcerer or no," warns Honor.

"Someone's already tried it." The cousin leaves with a soft click of a door latch. Kin leans out of the corridor just enough to peer out the window without being seen. This Asher's build is more slender than Verias's, though she can't determine his age from where she stands, and he doesn't turn to look back at the boarding house. Confident, perhaps overconfident, judging by that and his voice.

"I don't like him." Honor meets Kin's eyes.

"Me neither. He'll make trouble if we let him," Kin says. Honor nods gravely.

When Kin returns to their room, Verias is sitting on the bed, elbows on knees and face in hands, nails scraping at his skin. Kin touches his left hand, and he jumps, looking at his fingers. Her own fingers are unsteady when she thinks of how close they came to his cheek. Her hands need to stop acting on their own and start obeying her brain.

"I'm sorry. I know it's disgusting." His voice doesn't crack, but it's strained. "Did he leave?"

"Yes. Didn't ask questions, either. But we'll have to be careful leaving the boarding house from now on. Do you know why he's looking for you?"

"Any number of reasons, the least of which would be to take me home and hold me there."

"That's the least?" Kin asks.

"They could want to bundle me back to Lord Felver. Or kill me."

"No wonder you're ripping half your face off," Kin says.

"I know, it's disgusting," Verias repeats. "And now I've got blood all over my hands."

He has to brush past her to get to the basin and wash his hands, the familiar metallic-sweet odor coming off him.

"You think I'm bothered by blood?" Kin asks. He doesn't look at her. "You don't have to worry. I won't let them hurt you."

"I don't want you to hurt them, either. Besides, I'd rather they just kill me than send me back." Verias is calm now, surely recalling the night they met. She pauses now as she did then. What could a person say to that except *me too*? Kin's too smart to let him know that she's just as afraid of a cage as he is, that she'd rather die than set foot in the homepalace now that she's tasted hope. Admitting to hope is admitting to weakness.

"Why didn't you sense his presence?" she asks to change the subject.

"I'm not sure. I've been noticing spikes of magic when I don't expect them. I felt one yesterday on the way back from the homepalace, but . . ." Verias turns back to Kin, drying his hands. "I was distracted." It doesn't sound like a full lie, but it doesn't sound like the truth. He looks through her for a while, still rubbing his hands, though they look plenty dry. "I think I might be starting to sense *you*."

"That's not supposed to be possible."

"The Dean said they haven't had a Carrier in ages. It's probably just that they haven't seen it in so long that they forgot it can happen. When I have access to their libraries I can find out for sure."

"I don't care about that. I need you to get into the Vault of Souls without having to take a soul first," Kin says. Verias frowns. "I'd let you fool around at the homepalace as much as you want if I didn't think we'd eventually get caught. We'll likely have to move to another inn or boarding house at some point; given enough time, a fleshbound will come to the Woolworkers' Quarter and sense my presence. Now that your cousin is snooping around, it will probably be sooner than I thought."

"You planned to move around like that?"

"I've lived my whole adult life that way. It's instinct at this point," Kin says.

"Your whole life? I thought you said you'd been Bound for thirteen years."

Kin grits her teeth. She sometimes hates the way Verias is always asking questions. His handsome face and quiet, gentle voice make her want to indulge him with the truth. She'd love to hate him for it if she wasn't so drawn in.

"I'm a thief. Was. I was a thief," she admits.

"For your whole life?"

Verias leans forward. As his eyes lock on hers, something shatters inside her, magic breaking into thousands of pieces and sending a nearly ecstatic shiver through her body. Kin knows that feeling, recognizes the sudden silence in her head.

"What was that?" Verias's curious expression sharpens. With the intensity of his gaze, the black spot in his eye seems bigger than it did the last time she looked at it. "Some kind of magic, I can feel it."

"The mark. It's gone. Your contract has been passed on to someone else," Kin says. Verias pales. "Don't think on it." She shakes off a last shudder. "It's for me to worry about."

"I trust you," Verias says.

"Well, don't. You shouldn't hold out hope that I'll go back to being a good person if I have my soul back. I never was one to begin with."

"I wasn't thinking that way. Or I don't remember thinking that. I may have done it once or twice. I'm not a very good person, either," Verias says. Kin's eyes wants to roll back in her head. Verias is so kind and accepting that it's exhausting. One can only reveal so many secrets before they run out of energy. "They wouldn't tell me how many died when I was in that war machine. I know it was many."

Kin's heart sinks. It's easy to forget that this soft, sweet man has been in battle. Kin saw the war machines at the edge of the camp where she found Verias, and she'd known in an instant that with their crushing hammers and claws, they were monstrous constructions. More monstrous, perhaps, than she. She aches to hold him, to somehow wipe the expression of pain and exhaustion from his face. It isn't safe. She isn't safe.

"I need to work on some ciphers for the Dean. If I do well enough, he'll likely want me for the Binders," Verias says. They're both ready for a change of subject.

"Is there anything I can do to help?" Kin asks.

"Do you know anything about codebreaking?"

"Not a thing."

"Then I'm afraid not." Verias doesn't have to talk about his time in the army if he doesn't want to. Kin understands. She just wishes there was something to occupy her during the increasingly unbearable time for him to get into the Vault of Souls. She doesn't feel useless, exactly—protecting Verias is an important task—but she became a thief for a reason. Being a bodyguard is mostly anxiety and staring at walls with occasional breaks for killing. Thievery involves some waiting and plenty of anxiety, but stealing itself is exciting, people die much less frequently, and if you're good enough, you get to celebrate at the end.

Kin slips out of the room, wondering how she'll celebrate once she gets her soul back and destroys it. If she lives, maybe she'll touch Verias's face like she wants, feel softness and scars under her hands. Maybe he'll feel less fragile than he does now. Maybe Kin will, too.

CHAPTER THIRTEEN

AT ANY GIVEN TIME, VERIAS CAN BE REASONABLY SURE THAT
Kin is on the roof. She's been there for the better part of two
days as he works sunup to sundown. It's all as expected, starting with easily picked apart substitution ciphers. They increase
in difficulty as Verias works, some having almost imperceptible
grains of magic woven into the text itself like glimmering beads.
Verias is confident that he can finish, but his goal is to impress,
so speed is crucial. He also has to admit that doing one of the
things he's best at makes him feel happy and at home.

Still, there's a point at which he's done more than he should.
His eyes are dry and burning, his neck aches, and there's a
throbbing in his left temple that threatens to drive him to distraction. Verias tries to stretch out his aches and pains, but everything's knotted up. The only thing that doesn't hurt are the
scabs on his face, so he's at least grateful that he's been too busy
to do any more damage to his skin. A bath will probably soak
out some of the discomfort, so Verias climbs out on the windowsill, putting his head over the edge of the roof.

"What is it?" Kin asks. It's hard to see her face in the gathering dark.

"I'm going to go down for a bath. I didn't want you to come
back and find me missing."

"I should probably do the same. Make room, please."

Verias slides back in through the window. When she comes

into the light, he's sure she hasn't slept since the three hours on their first night in Sestera, and no matter what she says, she does need sleep. Her eyes are deeply shadowed and looking right through Verias. It's unsettling, so he picks up his clean clothes and bar of soap in hopes that even if she doesn't stop looking at him like that, he won't be able to feel her staring through his back.

Kin follows Verias downstairs in silence, her footfalls inaudible but her presence felt nonetheless. Even in the bathing rooms, with their echoing tile floors and walls, she's like a ghost: more felt than heard. At least there's nobody else there, each of the five stall doors hanging open. The air is cool, and the hearth, nestled in on the side with two stalls, is cold and dark. The floor slopes down to a large drain, and the well, tiled just like the floor, lies covered and quiet in the middle of the room.

When Kin removes the well cover, the soft sound of slow running water filters up. Like all wells in Nerefin, this water comes directly from the Wellspring, and wisps of invisible magic rise up and into Verias. For a few moments he just stands there, letting himself bask in the sensation of life force flooding him. He doesn't realize he's closed his eyes until Kin brushes past him, carrying a bucket of water on the way to the big cauldron on the cold hearth.

"Wait," Verias says. "I'll just use magic."

He and Kin fill the two tubs next to the hearth, and when they're done, Verias puts this hand into the water in the first tub, tasting the sweet power of magic. It solidifies inside him, filling the water like hot stones and causing steam to rise.

Kin gasps, and Verias turns just in time to watch the empty bucket slip out of her hands and clatter to the floor. The sound bounces off every surface in the room, making an ear-splitting racket, but Kin doesn't appear to notice.

"What's wrong?"

"I felt it. It's been so long since I felt it." Kin steps away, putting the well between them and her back to Verias. Verias picks up the dropped bucket and replaces the well cover to have something to do with his hands while Kin collects herself. She's utterly silent and still, but Verias can tell she's crying. He touches her shoulder.

"Don't."

"Tell me?" Verias lets his hand fall back to his side.

"No."

Kin goes to the stall with the hot water and shuts the door. Verias is left to warm his own water, anxiety curdling his stomach as he waits for her to react. Nothing. He shuts the stall door and undresses to wash, the heat of the water giving immediate, though marginal, relief from the tension in the air despite the way it stings his healing wound. His ears instinctively strain for any sound from her side of the divider, and when Kin speaks, her soft voice is so loud against the silence that it startles him.

"My father was a Reaper," she says.

"What?" Verias doesn't know what else to say.

"Well . . . he was what you would call a Reaper here. He wanted to be a Healer, but Abseris was caught up in a civil war. Father chose the side of his father. It was the wrong side. He came here after the war was over." Her voice wavers just a little.

"When did you lose him?" Verias's natural curiosity would rather ask why Kin's father never went back to Abseris, but he can tell that's not what she needs right now.

"It would be sixteen years ago now. I think"—she makes the smallest hiccuping sob—"I think I've been fleshbound for so long that never feeling magic made it easier to push him out of my mind. There wasn't something constantly reminding me of him, opening the wound."

"You never fully faced your grief." Verias can't say the same. For a year he's been forced not just to remember Lusian, but live his life for him. Sit in his war machine, take his beatings, commit his crimes.

"I didn't have time. I had people to take care of. I was . . . I became . . . this."

"I'm sorry." The words are inadequate, but something has to be said. He can't leave those words hanging between them, laden with pain.

Water sloshes on the other side of the divider, and Kin says nothing more. Verias can't do anything but want to help, if only she'd let him get closer to her. Someone enters the bathing room, soft shoes on tile, and almost before Verias can recognize the sound, his stall door jerks out, the latch ripping free to rattle to the floor. Verias has less than a heartbeat to take in a woman with a knife in her hand before Kin is on her, choking her with an arm around her neck. The woman takes multiple wild, vicious stabs backward at Kin. Kin lets it happen, not making a single move. Not making a single sound. Blood runs down her left thigh, her face blank as that of a corpse.

The assassin goes limp in Kin's arms. Kin dumps her in one of the tubs, closing the stall door. For a moment, she leans against the wood and lets her head fall back, closing her eyes. Even with her leg slashed and bleeding, Verias is struck by how gorgeous she is. It's enough to make him breathless. Still naked, without the hardness of her gaze, she's the softest thing he thinks he's ever seen. She's made of curves and spirals, waves and swells. Light and shadow. Though Verias healed the knife wound in Kin's side, she has other scars, dark and beautiful in their own right. Straight lines and abruptly cut off arcs that throw the rest into sharp contrast.

"Get Honor, would you?" she asks, startling Verias out of his foolish moment of adoration.

"Kin, your leg—"

"It's a flesh wound, Verias. I only need a bandage."

"Will you shut the door, then?" Verias asked. He can't reach it without showing everything. She obliges, and Verias does the same, hastily drying and dressing to step over a puddle of blood on his way out.

When Verias returns with Honor, they find Kin holding a towel against her wounds to stanch the flow of blood. There are scarlet drips and drops on the tile around her, and one great smear in the doorway of the stall where she was stabbed. Verias is glad to see that he didn't track any of it out of the bathing room, but his sorcerer's mind is always just below the surface. He can't help but wonder why the Binders let their fleshbound rely on blood for their life; though Kin can't die from blood loss, it'll be nearly impossible to retain consciousness if she loses too much. Honor pays her no mind, taking the keyring from her belt to lock the bathing room door.

"You are a menace to linens everywhere," Honor says.

"So you say." Kin watches Honor peek into the stall with the assassin still slumped in the empty tub.

"Still alive? You're getting soft in your dotage." Honor goes to the drain, which Verias hadn't noticed has three identical locks and hinges. It looks heavy, and each lock makes a loud *thunk* when Honor turns its key.

"Shut up. It was an air choke. I planned for her to be dead, but I was bleeding out. She got an artery." Kin lifts the drain one-handed. The muscles stand out in her arm, but she gives no sign of strain. Verias looks away for fear that he's staring again.

"Help me, Verias," Honor says. He's glad for something to do, until he realizes what she wants. He freezes for an instant. "Hurry."

Together they pull the assassin out of the tub. She doesn't stir at all, and by her shallow breathing, Verias can guess she won't survive without a Healer, even if Honor doesn't have a knife out. She slits the failed assassin's throat in one practiced motion.

91

He lets the body slip from his hands and into the dark hole in the floor.

An hour ago, Verias couldn't have imagined being this numbly calm watching Kin and Honor close and lock the drain and draw buckets of sacred Wellspring water to wash the blood down to the sewers. He feels as if he's above his body and a little to the left, and only returns to it when Kin tugs at his sleeve. She's fully dressed, blood soaking through her trousers.

"Come along." Kin walks briskly out of the bathing room, and Verias follows her upstairs to their room. He sits down on the bed, because he doesn't know what else to do. Chestnut perches alert on the windowsill, gazing into the night, and Kin scoops the cat up to deposit him on Verias's lap.

"Never seen someone go like that, have you?" she asks.

"No, I have. It's war. But being in that machine . . . I was lucky, I suppose. I took an arrow not long ago." He rubs the scar, palpable under his sleeve, and knows he's not getting his point across. "This feels personal."

"I suppose it is."

Kin shrugs, turning away to rifle through her saddlebags for a wad of bandages. She removes her bloody trousers and drops them in the washbasin before propping her injured right leg on a tea table chair to bandage it. For a breath, Verias's eyes are too busy following the line of her leg for his mouth to work. A wave of self-loathing hits him hard enough to bring him completely back to himself. He should help, not stare at her, but it would be folly to think he could touch her inner thigh and maintain his composure. He shifts his attention to Chestnut, scratching his little head, and the cat begins to purr.

"Also surprising to see Honor do it," Verias says.

"She used to work for my father. Her family was on the same boat coming from Abseris. Not many options in the Honey Quarter, which is where most Abserians in this country live. I think a lot of people still think they're going back." Kin pulls on a fresh pair of trousers and sits, wincing at the pain in her leg. The room is so small that her knee almost brushes Verias's.

Verias meets Kin's eyes. Her face is set, her eyes ever so slightly red from crying. If Verias reaches out to touch her, will she feel his magic? He doesn't want to subject her to any more pain.

"And you? Will you ever go back there?"

"I don't know. I haven't thought about it since I was a child and learned just how much money it costs to rebuild a life." Kin gives him a brief, dry smile that vanishes in an instant. "Verias, you must know . . . you won't be seeing me again when this is over. We have use for each other now, but it's too dangerous for you to stay for long."

"I'm not afraid of you," Verias says.

"*I'm* afraid of me. I'm afraid of what I'll do. I lost control tonight, crying in front of you like that. I will hurt you, even if I don't mean to." The pain in her voice yanks at Verias's heart.

"Kin—"

"Do you know how easy it would be for me to snap your neck, Verias?"

"You don't want to do that."

"No, I don't. But I think about it. Often." Kin's eyes well up, but she blinks the tears away. Her hands are balled into fists on her knees, her body rigid. Somehow, it's the strongest and most vulnerable Verias has ever seen her, and he isn't afraid.

Kin breaks the intense eye contact as if she can stand it no longer. She stands to walk to the window with a heavy limp, leans a shoulder against the sash. "When did you start picking at your skin?" she asks.

Verias can't imagine why. "I'm not exactly sure. I was young, though."

"Me too. When I started imagining things, I mean. I was

made for this. My head has always been full of horrible things. I've always been a monster."

"Kin, you're not—"

"When I was young, I didn't learn to cook because I couldn't be around knives. I wanted to see what was under my skin. I needed to see."

"You're wearing three knives right now," Verias says.

"Five," Kin replies. "That's because I had other, worse thoughts to plague me once I got older. Other anxieties, other distractions. When I was Bound, I stopped having those thoughts entirely."

"And they're back because of me," Verias said. "I'm so sorry, Kin."

Kin doesn't respond. Verias places Chestnut on the bed so he can cross to the window. She turns to look at him with mournful eyes cradled by dark circles. He touches her arm as carefully as he would approach an injured bird of prey, and when she doesn't protest, he puts his hands on her shoulders.

"Do you think that perhaps you're being a bit . . ." Verias searches for the right word.

"A bit what?" Kin doesn't look sad any more. She looks suspiciously like she's going to stab him.

"Overprotective."

"Of course I'm overprotective. You're my only chance at freedom."

"Kin, I'm a grown man. I can make my own terrible choices," Verias says. It actually makes her laugh.

"I suppose you can."

"So."

"So what?" Kin looks down at Verias as if suspicious he might try to make her laugh again.

"Where are the other knives?" Verias asks. He has to try.

"Ha! Wouldn't you like to know." She turns away again,

pulling away from his hands, but this time she wears a small smile.

CHAPTER FOURTEEN

CLIMBING ROOFTOPS IS A CHORE WITH A PAINFUL, INJURED leg, but Kin makes do, slowly circling the homepalace every hour while Verias is inside with his sheaf of codes. She can't help but wish she still had his contract woven into her body, and not just because some other fleshbound will no doubt come for him. It would be helpful, and perhaps calming, to have a better idea of where he is in the vast palace.

When orange dusk begins to fall over Sestera, Kin climbs down from her perch and lurks in an alley, where it'll be easier to catch Verias when he emerges from the homepalace. She isn't nervous just yet, but she isn't all that happy. Her leg hurts, she's still annoyed by Merit's taunts (they've always had that effect on her), and she could use a drink or ten. Enough to get giggly. Maybe Verias will want to join her.

He emerges from the homepalace as orange fades to red and the shadows of the Deep Quarter merge like droplets of water on a rainy window. Kin ghosts down the street ahead of him for a while, keeping a safe distance, before they're out of sight of the homepalace and she slows to let him catch up.

"How did you fare?" she asks.

"They were impressed," Verias says.

"And?"

"What?" Verias glances at her, nervously rubbing his hands on his doublet as if trying to dry his palms.

"And what else? You were in there all day."

He hesitates. "I don't know if I can do this."

"Why not?"

"That Dean . . . he's a monster, Kin. Truly." Verias's voice is so quiet that it's almost inaudible. Hot anger rises up inside Kin, anger at what the Binders have done to her, anger at herself for exposing a genuinely kind person to what lies inside that horrible place. She forces the boiling pain down, forces herself to keep her voice light.

"Good. That just means you won't feel guilty when we rob him."

"I won't. But pretending to be like that man . . ." Verias visibly shudders.

Verias clearly isn't in the mood for a drink—wine will only make him maudlin—so she keeps on toward Honor's, making sure they aren't followed. She isn't going to let Merit or anyone else sneak up on her again.

Honor isn't in the front room to greet them when they return, leaving Verias to request his supper right from the kitchen. Kin hangs back in the shadows, keeping an eye on Verias while staying far enough away that the cook won't notice her. There's something in the air, a potential for trouble that makes her skin crawl and her stomach slither, and she walks up the stairs side by side with Verias to stay as close as possible and avoid being caught off guard.

The landing is clear, its only occupants the shadows left by the candle Verias carries to light the way. Their room, too, is empty, and Verias lights the lamp with his candle, casting a warm glow all around the room. Kin checks inside the packed wardrobe and under the bed. Nothing. But something's wrong. She feels in her guts, in her vertebrae, in the palms of her hands.

"I'll check the roof. Lock the door and don't open it until I'm back." She tosses Verias the key.

Verias nods and locks the door with a satisfying click.

Kin climbs up on the roof, quickly looking over the nearby rooftops and checking behind the chimneys. The gibbous moon gazes down at her like a lover with its shuttered, waning eye, watching her every move. Her foot is on the sill when a familiar sensation knifes through her. Mortal fear rushes in its wake, and the only thing that kept her from freezing is instinct, years of practice in disastrous situations. She throws herself boots-first through the window, and Verias backs into her, knocking her hard into the windowsill. He slumps, warm wetness spilling over her hands when she catches him. Nausea skitters up her throat, rage and hopelessness and fear all warring to see which will be first to pour out.

When Kin lowers Verias to the floor, his head in her lap, she finds that the left side of his throat has been pierced. A thin, insistent stream of blood weeps from the wound with every beat of his pulse. She pushes her hand against the wound, but there's no point. It's over. Hot tears stream down her cheeks.

"No," Kin hears herself whisper. "No, Verias, please."

"I'm sorry. I'm sorry." His voice is weak.

"No, no, it's not your fault." She touches his cheek with her free hand. What more damage can she do?

"I'm sorry you won't be free."

Verias lays his hand over hers. His breath is fast and labored, his strength fading as his body struggles to keep him alive. His hand slips from Kin's, and his knuckles knock against the floor. The pulses of blood grow weak, his eyes slide shut, and soon the rise and fall of his chest stills.

"I'm sorry."

Kin doesn't raise her head. She doesn't want to see them standing there with the knife in their hand. She doesn't want to fight.

"I didn't know," Merit says. "If I'd known—"

"What would you have done? Refused the assignment?" Kin still refuses to look up. She keeps her eyes fixed on Verias's handsome, scarred face, trying to fix it in her memory, wrap it up in her heartstrings, forever safe.

"I—"

"You wouldn't have done anything." Tears keep running down Kin's face.

"I'm sorry. I'm so sorry."

Kin raises her head. Merit has put up their knife, their arms wrapped around them, long face mournful. They really are sorry, but why should Kin care? Sorry can't put the life back into a body. Sorry can't make Kin stop regretting or mourning or missing Verias. It doesn't make her any less to blame for not knowing Merit was coming.

"Get out." She turns her attention back to Verias. Even with all the blood he lost, he's still so warm. That's all Kin can think about. He's still so warm. Footsteps, a great crash and clatter. Still so warm. Running feet. So warm.

"Kindred," Honor says. Kin doesn't raise her head. She doesn't speak. She can't. Honor kneels next to her, felt more than seen though the haze of tears. She doesn't touch Kin. She's just near, filling the air around Kin with warmth and a faint scent of perfume that can't force out the reek of blood. "I could see how you cared for him, Kin. I'm sorry. I'm so sorry."

"He was the only person anything like me who didn't hate me." Kin's head hurts from crying. Her chest hurts. Her fingers ache from clutching Verias's doublet, sodden and sticky with blood. "He was my friend."

"I know. I know. It's time to let him go for now. Just for a little while."

Kin lets out a painful, shuddering sigh. She lowers Verias's head to the floor as gently as she can, though she knows he feels nothing. She makes and attempt to stand, but only makes it to her knees before she has to bend back down. Kin presses her lips against his forehead, feels the scars and scabs he scratched into his skin. Honor's hand is heavy against her back.

CHAPTER FIFTEEN

THE FIRST SOUND VERIAS HEARS UPON BEING DRAGGED back to consciousness is a shout, throaty and surprised. When he opens his eyes, the room is a dizzy blur, and he has to squeeze his eyes shut against the light and color rocking nauseously around him. There's wood floor beneath his back. The deck of a boat? The cursed war machine that bears him into battle? No. The last thing he remembers is . . .

Verias puts a hand to his head. A flame, tiny and wavering, but growing. That's all he remembers. So tired. Can't think.

". . . do you understand? Verias? Can you hear me?" The voice is familiar, but it should be colder. That's how he remembers it. Unforgiving. Something new is there. A little shivering flame.

"Yes." The word comes out hollow and broken. "Tired."

Fingers touch his throat. Warmth spreads from the spot, filling him like bright, glorious sunrise after a long night. The sensation fades as soon as the touch is gone, leaving him empty and ready to drift away. Something's wrong, something's very right. His head spins.

"No pulse," Kin says. "He's not breathing, either."

"He needs a Healer," another voice says. Pretty. Musical.

"Go, then," Kin says. Footsteps, pounding down stairs.

"What happened to me?" Something is wrong in his throat. Not a sore, raw, sick feeling. Something beyond illness.

"You died. Someone sent a fleshbound to kill you."

"Everything hurts." Verias tries to open his eyes again, but nausea rises up and threatens to drown him in stomach juices as the room whirls around him.

"Lie still," Kin says. "I know it hurts." She touches his hand, and again warmth floods Verias.

"Feels good."

"Shh." Kin takes his hand in both of hers. Her fingers are the only sharp detail in the whole world—the calluses from working with her knives, the little ridges of her knuckles, the strength of her grip. She anchors him.

Verias's senses start coming back to him at the pace of a long eternity. The smell of cooked meat, a cool breeze caressing his face. He opens his eyes to a familiar ceiling and rafters, and they stay solid and still. When he looks to his right, Kin sits on her heels beside him, her intense, dark gaze fixed on his face. She's even more beautiful than usual, almost luminous. She's covered in blood from shoulder to hip, her hands sticky scarlet. Verias's doublet is soaked through.

"What—what happened to me?"

"You already asked that." Kin's voice is somehow even more gentle than before, not so much silken as the touch of a fur-lined cloak against his face on a cold winter day.

"I meant to ask how I died. All this blood . . ."

"Stabbed. Right here." Kin lets go of Verias's hand to touch the side of his neck. She sounds more herself, now. Matter-of-fact. "Fleshbound." She draws away to fold her hands in her lap, leaving Verias cold and empty. The world fades out.

He wakes again to hands on his chest. Not Kin's. Too cold for that, sending violent shivers through his entire body.

"I've healed the wound," an unfamiliar voice says. An elderly man gets to his feet above Verias, allowing Honor to help him up. Where's Kin? "But there's no knowing how long he can survive with no life. Clearly the body and soul are strong, but that can't make up for lack of life force. I suspect that it's his magic that kept him alive; he's surely the most powerful sorcerer I've ever seen, but that means that his condition is outside my understanding. It's possible that a better Healer than I could restore him, but the only real option is to bring him to the Wellspring."

"Thank you," Honor says. "Let me show you out, and I'll see to your payment."

When Verias shifts, he feels a soft straw mattress cradling his body. Someone's removed his filthy doublet and shirt, and though he's covered in a blanket, he's freezing. He's too weak to pull the blankets tighter around him, too weak to do much at all but watch the ceiling go about its business. The mattress sinks, and he smells fresh rooftop air, tinged with the scent of indigo dye. The metallic, sickly blood stink is still there, but fainter now.

"I'm freezing," Verias says. Kin touches his face, the warmth of her hand seeping into him just as it did before. He's immediately clearer, more himself.

"You *are* cold." She doesn't take her hand away. He turns his head so his face is cupped in her hand, and their eyes meet.

"What changed?" Verias asks. She looks down at him, expression closed. It's clear she knows what he means.

"You're dead, Verias. How much more damage could I do?"

"Fair point," Verias says. Kin chuckles.

"You sound better already."

"Your hands make me feel warm again."

Kin's fingers tremble, but she doesn't take her hand away. Instead, she brushes the hair from his forehead, sending a tingle through him. Her eyes are red. She cried over him. Verias can barely believe he ever thought her hard, cold. He couldn't have been more wrong about her gentle soul.

"Thank you," he says.

"For what?"

"I know this is difficult for you."

Kin takes her hand away to smooth his blankets as the chill returns to Verias's body. He doesn't feel as if he'll drift away again, but something is missing.

"Wait."

It's a struggle to extract his hand from his blankets. His arms feel like they're made of lead, the bedclothes like an anvil, but he manages. When he takes Kin's hand with clumsy fingers, he understands. The thrill of discovery, which he's missed so much since leaving home, overcomes his exhaustion and common sense. Sitting up is even harder than getting out from under the blanket, and Kin helps Verias stuff pillows behind his back after watching him founder.

"We've formed some kind of magical link."

Kin, in the process of straightening his blankets, snatches her hands away. "What are you talking about?"

"It's feeding your life energy into me. That's why you could sense my magic," Verias says. Kin looks ill. "What's the matter? This is good news, since you were so afraid to hurt me. You can't anymore."

"Yes, I can. If I'm not there to touch you and give you my life force, will you die?"

"I don't know. It seems likely."

"I don't like magic." Kin's hands twist in the blanket.

"You let me heal you."

Kin stands and walks to the window like she always seems to do when she's upset and wants time to think. Verias can't stop her, but he's cold and miserable, wishing she'd come back.

"I don't like being reminded of my father. I don't like being reminded of the things the Binders did to me. But still. It was easier then, before I really knew you. Before your power became more . . . personal. More familiar."

"I'm sorry," Verias says.

"You apologize too much. Your last words were to say sorry."

"I don't remember that." Verias doesn't doubt it. He's always apologizing for something.

"You said you were sorry I wouldn't be free."

"Well, I lived, in a way. You'll be free."

"Will I?" Kin turns back to Verias. "Or will we be trapped forever? Will I just be handed from master to master like a dog?"

"The Healer said my best chance was to go to the Wellspring."

He feels like she jammed a knife in his chest with no warning. He has to shake the hurt out of his head, remind himself that the deep connection that's been building between them is a magical effect. It isn't real, and Kin is right to question what comes next.

"I heard that. I was outside the window listening."

"There's a chance that you won't be stuck with me forever." He can't keep the bitterness out of his voice no matter how hard he tries.

"Do you want to be tied to me like this?" Kin's voice isn't quite a snap, but her voice is taut, on the verge.

Verias can't think of anything but her touch. With Kin's back to him, stiff and unyielding, he shouldn't ask, but all he wants is for her to come back, to give him some of her warmth.

"You don't want that. You've been held captive long enough," Kin says. "And so have I."

"Kin, a year is not comparable to thirteen. I don't know . . ." Verias starts to feel woozy again, and he has pause to gather his thoughts. "I don't know what I want. I don't know anything right now."

"You should rest, Verias. You've just been dead. We can reevaluate our plans in the morning. I don't think it's likely we'll get my soul back until we fix this."

Verias is too tired to answer. The mattress sinks again as Kin sits to hold his hand in both of hers. The next time he opens his eyes, it's morning. Kin lies dead asleep next to him, holding his arm in a loose grip. Though she's often still as a statue, Verias has never seen her look so peaceful. The perpetual watchfulness is gone, the bowstring-taut tension unwound, at rest. It calms him to watch her, and though he's famished, he doesn't want to wake her. He tries to sit up without disturbing Kin, but her hand closes on his arm hard enough to bruise, and her eyes snap open.

"What's happening? How—" She sits up, looking around the room. Verias hadn't noticed until now that it isn't the room they slept in the night before. That one is likely covered in blood. "I fell asleep hours and hours ago. I haven't slept that long in—" She breaks off with a gasp.

"What? What is it?"

"I'm *hungry*. What's happening to me?" There's an edge of panic in her voice.

"You're hurting me, Kin."

"Oh." Kin lets him go, leaving a red mark on his forearm. The loss of her touch sinks into Verias, but he doesn't immediately feel as though his life has been taken with it.

"I don't think it's something to worry about," he says.

"It's the link, isn't it?"

"Yes, I would assume so. Do you want to eat?" Verias asks.

"I think so? I'll go see about breakfast." Kin stands to leave before she turns back to him. "Are you well enough for me to go?" she asks. Verias nods.

As Kin rushes out of the room, Chestnut returns from his nighttime wanderings. Kin locks the door behind her, and

Chestnut meows at it a few times, as if he didn't just come in. Verias gives him a little *psst*, and he forgets about the door, jumping up onto the bed to wash. If only Verias could have a life as simple as a cat's. It still stings that Kin reacted with such disgust at the idea of being linked to him. That sort of thing doesn't happen to cats.

Kin reappears carrying a breakfast tray herself. She sets it on the little tea table, and brings Verias a plate with fried eggs, sausages, and toast dripping with yellow butter. He's never seen a meal look so good in his life, but he stops eating after a few bites. Kin sits motionless at the tea table, staring at her plate with fork in hand, like she isn't sure what to do with it.

"What's wrong?" Verias asks.

"If we take you to the Wellspring, I'll probably lose my desire to eat again."

"Maybe. Maybe not. You should enjoy your food while you can. Preferably before it gets cold."

"I don't know if I want to enjoy it. I'll just miss it again later," Kin says.

"That's no way to live your life."

"Tuh! What life?" Kin picks up a toast quarter and gives it a tentative nibble before setting it back down. She stares back into her plate.

"Well?" Verias asks.

"Wish I had bacon instead," Kin says.

Verias doesn't know whether he should laugh, but the urge is certainly there. Things have been grim lately, and it would be nice to laugh if Kin's behavior weren't so odd and worrisome. Kin starts eating in earnest with no more conversation, and they both clean their plates. She sets the tray outside the door and locks up before sitting back at the tea table. For a very long time she stares straight ahead, barely even blinking. She slips a knife out of her sleeve.

"What are you doing?" Anxiety makes his stomach squirm. Verias is too weak to stop her from hurting herself.

Kin nicks the skin of the back of her left hand and watches the blood bead there.

"Kin, what are you doing?" Verias repeats. She wipes the blood away on her trousers and replaces her knife inside her sleeve.

"I had to know what else changed. If I'm feeling hunger, if I —" She stops, looking almost as if she's about to laugh. She holds up her hand. The skin is unmarred. "Imagine if we got into a fight and I couldn't heal."

"You do get hurt a lot," Verias says. "How's your leg?"

"Probably better in a few days."

"I never thanked you for saving my life that night."

"You don't have to. We had a deal." Kin shrugs.

"Yes, but we're friends now, aren't we?"

"I wouldn't have cried my eyes out over you if we weren't," Kin says. Verias feels a grin spread across his face. Her answering smile is subdued, but it's a smile nevertheless.

CHAPTER SIXTEEN

VERIAS STRUGGLES TO REST WHEN THERE'S WORK TO BE done. Not once in his adult life has he paused in his studies, always taking his books and lap desk to bed with him when ill. His love of translating pre-Emergence spellwork from cosmic to earthly magic subsumes everything else, and if anything, he's more determined to see this task through than he's ever been about history. Helping Kin is by far the most important thing he's ever set out to do, but Kin insists that he needs rest. She's the most stubborn person Verias has ever met, and he can do nothing but let Kin and Chestnut (who's decided Verias is his favorite bed) bully him into a few days of recuperation.

When he finally escapes the boarding house room, Verias heads back to the homepalace to meet with Lessa, the woman who greeted him in the entryway on his first anxious visit. She reports that the Dean is away for a few days, visiting with some Binder in the countryside.

"Are you coming on with us, then?" she asks. When unguarded, she has a more country way of speaking than the Dean. It's familiar, almost homey, and makes Verias far more inclined to like her than the Dean.

"I hope to. It's my goal to learn your techniques, of course, and I understand that my codebreaking skills are of use here."

"But?" Lessa asks. Verias shrugs. The entry hall isn't empty, and he isn't yet sure of Lessa. "Come," Lessa says.

Verias glances at the other people sitting in the hall, who look rather annoyed that Lessa is leaving. Lessa ignores them, leading him into the north wing, at the end of which she opens a door that lets out the smell of books. Old paper, ancient parchment and leather, dry air. It makes Verias feel completely at home, calm despite everything that's happened since coming to Sestera, and despite the fact that he's never seen a library like this one: massive, three full stories leading up to a ceiling decorated with an ancient, fading fresco of legendary sorcerers. Verias recognizes a few, in their peaked hats and robes, but the library is dimly lit to protect the knowledge kept within the books. It's difficult to make them all out.

"With the Dean gone, this is a good chance to study as you wish. He can be single-minded to a fault, as you might have noticed." Lessa's voice is dry. Verias smiles at her, though he's not sure what she wants from him. A display of his esoteric knowledge, perhaps. "What are you interested in?"

"I'm most curious about magical linking in fleshbound. It's common among Carriers not promised to the Wellspring to hire and link with Reapers for protection when traveling dangerous places, and my hypothesis is that the same could be done with fleshbound. Think of how useful it would be for Carriers to be able to hire someone undetectable by other sorcerers to accompany them when their studies take them to unfriendly places." Verias follows Lessa as she walks deeper into the library, passing shelves and tables littered with books and papers.

It should be a good enough story. Though Carriers are often the most powerful sorcerers, the safeguard—a relatively new precaution—makes people more comfortable with their abilities. Still, there are those who fear Carriers. Most places outside Nerefin consider sorcery to be unnatural, or a form of hoarding resources to which other peoples have little access due to the location of the Wellspring. More than one war has started over the waters. But at least Carriers are known to be scholars, and Healers are useful to everyone from time to time. Reapers and Binders only arrive when war or skullduggery is afoot. Verias has no doubt that she can understand wanting protection.

"Have you told the Dean?" Lessa asks.

"Not yet. He's given me a spellbook to break, but I haven't finished yet. I came today because I need to tell him that I haven't been well. It may take me longer than expected."

"I wouldn't mention it if I were you. The link, not that you haven't been well. Though lots of people *have* been sick lately."

"Why shouldn't I mention it?" Verias asks.

"It isn't a forbidden course of study, but . . . it's complicated." They've come to a clump of carrels backed against a window covered in old red curtains that only let in half the light, as if twilight has fallen inside. Lessa perches on one of the desks with her feet on its chair. "Most Binders don't think of fleshbound that way."

"What way?"

"As human enough to link with," Lessa says. "I don't know for sure, but I think if you asked, most Binders would say that's got to do with the soul, and ask how you can link with someone who doesn't have one."

"And you?" Verias asks. Lessa looks up at Verias for a moment, the dim red light turning her blonde hair orange. She shrugs, arms crossed.

"I don't know. That's not my area. But I reckon it could be possible if you had the fleshbound's soul in your possession, couldn't it? It's not that they don't *have* a soul, they just don't have it with them."

"That was the same thought I had."

"Well, you won't meet many others with that thought in their head. Which would be why it's worth studying, in my opinion," Lessa says.

"What's your area of study?" Verias asks.

"Healing. I joined hoping that I could do some good for those who want to be released by the homepalace after their term of service is up, but are afraid of the consequences." Lessa shrugs again, but this time it's resigned. Verias's world has been knocked off kilter: Kin has neither mentioned an end to her Binding, nor any dire results from leaving the Binders.

"What consequences are those?" he asks.

"Well, that's the thing. Most people stay on after their fifty years are up because of what happens when a soul goes back in. The spells that nullify conscience are broken, and the flesh-bound—former fleshbound—has everything rush back in all at once. They don't usually live long after that."

"Wellspring's waters. That sounds like . . ." Verias tenses against a shudder.

"It's a waking nightmare. Not something most Binders are willing to face. Looking into linking is the same way, but there are books if you want them. There are always books."

Kin doesn't ask Verias how his half day at the homepalace went. He looks sick, like he always does when he emerges from its doors, and his body language is stiff. It's obvious that the longer he spends there, the more he hates it. Kin can't blame him for that. *She* hates it with every last crumb of her being, and she's tougher than old leather. He's a gentle soul who'd probably be better off as a Healer than anything else.

Verias is pale by the time they got back to Honor's, in need of a meal and rest before they move to another inn or boarding house. She'll be sorry to leave Honor, but it's best for everyone involved. Kin isn't willing to risk Verias's safety, or Honor's and Amity's. Waiting long enough for Verias to recuperate has been a dangerous but calculated move: someone being carried into an inn on death's door would have made people talk. Sometimes Kin catches herself wishing they could just live in a cave and have some peace and quiet for a while.

Honor makes bacon and tomato sandwiches for lunch, and the smoky scent of meat mingling with warm, yeasty, fresh-baked bread is honestly one of the most wonderful things Kin has smelled in years. The bacon fat melts on her tongue, salt and acidic tomato juice making her mouth water. She hadn't realized how badly she missed food until now.

She sighs over the last corner of bread before she pops it in her mouth and notices that Verias is watching her.

"What are you looking at?"

"You. It's just nice to see you enjoying your food instead of staring at it like it might bite you." A small smile plays about his lips, but it gives Kin no pleasure.

"It's hard to face things I know I'm only going to lose."

"Now why do I get the feeling you're not just talking about bacon sandwiches?"

"Possibly because I literally told you I was leaving when this is over?" Kin suggests.

"Possibly. But it isn't as if you've murdered me yet. Maybe you're not so dangerous after all."

"No? Go on ahead and say more and you'll see how dangerous I am," Kin says. Verias laughs, but it's faint. Her heart lodges in her throat. "Do you need me?"

Kin offers him her hand, and he takes it. It's strange. Kin doesn't feel any different, but she can see the difference in Verias now that she knows to look for it. All of the tension bleeds out of his face, the color returning to his cheeks as he shuts his eyes with a long sigh. The urge to touch him only grows stronger, harder to resist. Perhaps a few days ago, Kin could have convinced herself that the need was just an attraction to something forbidden, but it's not. She wants to care for him, smooth away all his hurts.

"Kindred," Verias says. She looks up at him in surprise; he's called her Kin for ages now. His face is deadly serious, and he's picking doggedly at a spot on his neck. "Why didn't you tell me what would happen if you returned your soul to your body?"

For an instant, Kin can't breathe. She has to force herself to look at Verias, instead of through him, when she answers. "I didn't think you needed to know. I didn't know you then, anyway."

"No, but maybe you should have told me at some point after that."

"Maybe," Kin admits.

"And the fifty-year time limit?" Verias asks. Kin cuts her eyes at him. Does he think she can just wait for decades, when being Bound is constant fury and torment?

"I was sentenced to seventy-five years," Kin says. His eyes search her face.

"This is a punishment? For what?"

"Thievery. It's just that once you've been caught half a dozen times, they don't want to let you out into the world again. They reckon you won't stop." Kin shrugs. She's only been caught once, and it hurts her pride to lie, but Verias can't know who she really is. Who she was. He'd hate her if he knew.

"So what exactly is your plan once you have your soul?"

"Getting out of Nerefin, that's for sure." A yawn creeps up on Kin. She's full of bacon, and the spring weather is warm. "We need to move somewhere else in the city if we're staying in it."

"We should. I don't want to risk being on the road when being away from you for the space of a morning makes me this tired. More recovery time might help."

"I don't know, Verias. The Wellspring isn't far," Kin says. Verias gives up on his neck scab and starts plucking at his lip.

"Do you know when you're doing that?"

"Doing wh—" Verias snatches his hand away, and Kin takes it firmly in her own. "Sometimes. I'm fairly sure that if you had your soul back, you'd be stronger, more able to share your life with me. I apologize, that was strange wording. I meant life force. It sounded like I was asking you to marry me." Verias's laugh is strained.

"I've come to terms with the fact that you're rather strange."

"How so?" Verias asks.

"Running around with me, for one. Being dead," Kin says.

Verias laughs again, this time less nervously. "But you see why I'm anxious? Getting your soul back doesn't change the difficulty of the journey unless you actually put it back in your body. I would never ask you to do that. It would only make me more of a burden to make you so vulnerable."

Kin bites down over a sigh of relief, not because she fears that Verias might ask, but because she fears she'll be tempted to offer. Relief is followed by immediate disturbance as she realizes that she'd do it in a heartbeat. She would, without question, risk her immortal existence, her peace of mind, her very life for him. What's happening to her? When and why did she get so foolish?

"I don't consider you a burden, but perhaps it's best to have my soul now. Just in case we have no other option," Kin says, though she's well aware of the danger—that way lies temptation.

"Are you sure? I don't want you to get hurt."

"I don't want you to get hurt, either, Verias. We have to have as many options available as we can."

"You're right. I don't like it, but you're right." Verias's hands tighten on hers. What Kin thought be an argument has turned bittersweet, each of them trying to protect the other. Kin can't remember the last time someone was willing to give up so much for her. "You wouldn't be opposed to a nap before we move, would you? I'm so tired," Verias says.

Kin shakes her head. She doesn't want to sleep and face her dreams, but she can lie quietly beside him while he rests. It'll be calming to be quiet and close.

CHAPTER SEVENTEEN

VERIAS CAN TELL HE'S IN A DREAM, AND HE KNOWS IT'S NOT his own. He can't tell whose, but it's oppressive, the brutal weight of a war machine crushing his chest. He's in a dim room lit by torches, the smell of something sweet in the air, which fails to cover something fetid. Four people in hooded robes stand around a rough-hewn rock table or altar in the middle of the small, stuffy space, magic crisscrossing above them. A layer like cobblestone, one like brickwork, one like mosaic. Familiar patterns, but work Verias has never seen done before.

The sorcerers back away from their altar, and Kin's body is revealed, lying on the crude stone surface. At first Verias thinks she's dead, but her chest rises and falls beneath a rough tunic. Holes are bored through the rock table beneath her to allow rope to be threaded through to bind her. They're tied so tight that ridges stand out on her wrists and ankles. She's serene, eyes closed, giving no sign she wants to escape. As if she's accepted that it's too late to try. Verias is sick to his stomach, not wanting to see what comes next, but the dream has him trapped.

The intense nausea makes the dream flicker around Verias, and he finds himself on the other side of the room, watching the robed Binders lead Kin out. He follows, floating more than walking, in the wake of her staggering gait. The corridor ahead wavers around him, not fully corporeal, as it gives way to a new space, far smaller than the last. It's not precisely a cell, for it has no door, but it has the feel of one. The feeling of imprisonment, of claustrophobia, is suffocating.

A woman with pale Nerefinian skin and matted, dirty hair that may once have been gold sits on the bare floor. Lessa's hand rests on her head. Kin rushes toward her, and the room bursts into incoherent sound, magic suffusing the air. Verias is inside Kin's body, then out, then in, over and over as the scene boils around him, as he grips the blonde woman's throat with brown hands. Her eyes are wide, a blue so pale that they almost match her filthy, bloodless face, white as a maggot under dungeon dirt. Her eyes slip closed, her mouth gone slack, but still his fingers tighten.

Verias wakes, his stomach roiling and sick. Kin lies beside him on her belly, her face concealed by a cascade of unbound red hair. Her hand is halfway holding his, just two fingers touching his skin. Verias needs air, needs to get away from the hands that choked the life out of that frightened woman in the dungeons of the homepalace. He can still feel her pulse fading as if he did it himself.

Kin doesn't stir, thank the Wellspring. He doesn't want her to see him scared and shaken by his foray into her dreams, doesn't want to hurt her. Verias slips out of bed and grabs his boots, getting out of the room before he puts them on. He has to open the door again when Chestnut appears to be let in, pausing to rub Verias's ankles.

Verias hurries out of the boarding house. When he escapes into the warmth of the afternoon sun, the oppressive feeling lifts, and he can breathe again. He can't go far, but he needs to settle his stomach. He goes to the Indigo Bridge, surrounded by the scent of dye that has started to smell like home, and leans his forearms against the wrought-iron rail. The bite of rough metal into flesh makes him feel more as though he's in the world, instead of trapped in that horrible nightmare.

Kin was forced to throttle that woman to death. He knows this. He knows magic, understands that was no ordinary nightmare. That was a memory, maybe the worst memory of Kin's life, one forced onto him by the magical link between them. It's no wonder she's so afraid to hurt him. She wrung the life out of a person with her bare hands, watched the light leave their eyes, and she'd even said to his face how easy it would be to snap Verias's neck. He has to go back inside, comfort her, say something, do something—

"Cousin," a voice says.

Verias turns. Asher stands between him and the boarding house, unassuming in his country clothes. He looks just like Lusian, with sharp, fine features and dark hair. In many private moments, Verias has admitted to himself that the pair look like better versions of him. Though he's ten years younger than Verias, Asher has always been held up as a superior Carrier, second in the family only to Lusian himself. Blue eyes regard Verias with an icy chill that contains a gleam of superiority.

"I knew you'd come out on your own eventually."

"You've been waiting? How did you know I was here?" Verias's body tenses head to foot.

"Whatever magic you did the other day, obviously. It was stronger than anything I've ever felt from you. I'm impressed," Asher says.

"I'm not weak, Asher. You just never appreciated any of the things I'm good at. No one in the family did. Not even Lusian."

"That's not true. Your mother always saw the use in your histories and books." Asher smirks. "Old spells for an old woman. It's a shame." Whether it's a shame that she cared or that she's dead, Asher doesn't say.

"If you don't care about my work, then why are you here? Why can't you just leave me alone?" Verias asks. "Why not just tell Father I'm dead?"

"I'm not a liar, for one. For another, you've dishonored our family, Verias. I can't let you keep wandering around and doing more damage to our reputation," Asher says.

The smug tone infuriates Verias, but he keeps his own voice level. "What reputation, Asher? Nobody here has ever heard of our family."

"Wellspring's waters, you've always been a fool, but being around that fleshbound has only made you worse. The nobles talk. They always have, and they always will. If you ruin our relationship with Felver, which of them will ally with us? Come along, Verias, or I'll have to use force."

Verias glances over Asher's shoulder at An Honorable Rest. He can't get there through Asher, leaving surprise his only chance at getting away. Verias draws magic up from below, and it his him hard, making him so dizzy that he has to clutch the bridge rail to keep from falling.

"Don't be a fool." Asher grabs the front of Verias's doublet, not even bothering with magic.

Verias wheels back and punches him hard in the nose. A blast of shivering magic strikes Verias back, knocking him over the rail and into the chilly blue water. All the air goes out of his lungs, and Asher's power piles on top of him, dragging him down so that his attempts to swim down the canal are useless. Terror claws at him for an instant before darkness closes in.

Verias is first aware of a pounding headache, so bad that being dead would be preferable. As his senses slowly return, he notices pain in his shoulders and a sickly, strange taste oozing around in the back of his throat. He can't move, can't even open his eyes, pinned under an immense weight of magic stacked on his body.

"What's wrong with him?" a taut voice whispers.

"I don't know. He's always been weak, hasn't he?"

"Not like this. This is new. What did you say . . ." The voice fades out. ". . . no pulse. What did you do to him?"

"I didn't do anything! There was something strange about him when he tried to use magic, I swear." It's Asher's voice. Memory rushes back to Verias. He tries to ask where he is, but all that comes out of his mouth is slurred mumbling. The horrible taste in his mouth is infinitely worse on contact with air, and it takes every bit of his meager strength not to vomit. "He's awake."

A little bit of the pressure lifts from Verias's head and neck, taking with it a measure of his weariness. When he opens his eyes, the room is blurry.

"How do you feel?" His uncle Gavian's face swims into focus, looking as tired as Verias feels. The gray-white hair that frames his angular face is badly mussed, and Verias can't help feeling a bit sorry that he's such a mess on Verias's account. He isn't that sorry, though.

"Where am I?" Verias asks. The nausea is still swishing around in his head, and he wants to spit more than he's ever wanted anything in his life.

"I asked first."

"I feel like I fell in a creek full of dye runoff and then got kidnapped," Verias says bitterly. "Where am I?"

"Somewhere safe. What happened to your magic?" his uncle asks.

"I don't know. May I have something to drink?"

"It's stronger," Asher says. "He's done something."

"I haven't done anything. Please, Uncle, tell me where I am. If I don't get back to Kin—"

"Well, if you're not going to tell us . . ."

Gavian shrugs and leaves the room. Asher looks at Verias for a moment longer before he follows, closing the door behind him.

Verias glances around the room. It's small enough that it verges on a closet, though there's a window behind him judging by the light stretching his shadow out in front of him. There's also a faint but definite barnyard smell, which means he probably isn't in the Woolworkers' Quarter any longer. He might not be in Sestera at all, and if he doesn't get back to Kin soon, his body will run out of energy and he'll be dead for good this time.

He takes stock of his condition. All of his limbs still seem to be attached, and the headache is beginning to fade. Verias is possibly drowning in mucus, and with no other recourse—or desire to be polite, really—he just hawks it on the floor. It's tinged blue, accounting for the strange taste in his mouth and his wobbly stomach. There's no knowing how much dye and mordant-filled water he swallowed. He's filled with an equal volume of spiteful joy knowing he punched Asher.

Exhaustion is creeping in. Verias thinks he has about half a day left before he's too weak to move. At the same time, he's suffused with a warmth similar to that he feels when Kin touches him. All of the hairs on his body stand on end from the magic stacked around him. It's possible—probable even—that his body is instinctively absorbing a fraction of the energy being used to hold him.

This feels more like a problem than a solution. He isn't actively dying, but he still has to escape, and escaping will only separate him from the power that's currently keeping him alive. The only solution Verias can think of is to constantly draw energy from the Wellspring, but that comes with dangers of its own. The fragile human form isn't meant to be a conduit for that quantity of the sacred for long, and like a river bank that erodes and fails, his body would eventually degrade and die.

Panic begins to flicker its eyes open, and the only way Verias can think of to maintain his calm is to solve the problem before it gets any worse. He considers the magical construction caging him, feels around to identify the spell. He almost laughs. It's Krellim's Brace, a spell Verias himself found in the coded journals of some forgotten wizard. The sorcerer had been using the spell to hold up failing windmills in his small community, and Verias decoded and mastered the spell to teach to his uncle in hopes that it would be useful.

He can't believe the absolute gall it takes to use a spell he discovered against him. Gavian never would have done something so disrespectful to Lusian, and knowing that leaves Verias even more disgusted. He's gladder than ever that he punched Asher, and if he gets the chance, he'll punch Gavian, too. Verias almost wishes for Kin to show up, since she's far better at such things that he is. His knuckles hurt, which indicates a lack of natural talent for damaging human faces.

Verias wriggles in his magical bonds, feeling for the knife that he's worn at his belt since Kin gave it to him. It's still there, poking into his thigh when he moves the most he possibly can. He needs to break the spell to get at it, but the more he thinks about it, the more he's sure that Gavian and Asher will be expecting it. Besides, simply bursting out of the enchantment will attract too much attention that will likely result in a fight, and Verias draws the line at fisticuffs. A poorly executed punch is leagues off from stabbing.

Dismantling a spell is very much like taking down a crumbling barn. It has to begin at the top, bit by bit, if one doesn't want the whole thing to come tumbling down on one's head. Slow is what Verias wants, to time it exactly right so that Gavian —he's quite sure this is Gavian's work—doesn't notice until it's too late. Ideally, he'll be sleeping, and won't even notice at all.

As he picks apart the Brace, Verias catches himself missing Kin again. Not just for her skill at causing calculated mayhem, but for her calming presence. She always radiates confidence, and Verias feels like anxiety will shake him to pieces the second he stops concentrating on the spell, stops thinking, doing, working. If Kin could see how badly he wants to fall apart, she'd probably laugh at him. To catch her smiling is such a rare and wonderful treat that Verias would never be able to stop himself from joining in.

What would you ever do without me? she'd probably ask. Verias would laugh aloud and privately wonder the same thing. He'd wonder what in the world he'll do when she has her soul back and leaves Sestera. Would she let him go with her, now that he's sure his family can't be counted on to provide a safe place for him? The memory of his dream cascades over him like boiling oil. Kin killed that woman, someone Verias knows in his gut she cared about deeply. What had they held over her head to make her do it, and could they convince Kin to do the same to Verias? Even so, Kin seems the better option, the safer haven, if such a place still exists.

CHAPTER EIGHTEEN

KIN BOUNCES ON HER TOES, WATCHING THE STREET through the front window of An Honorable Rest. She's starving, but her stomach is full of knots and acid, and she can't even choke down a piece of toast. Not even water. Her throat is clogged up with the memory of magic burning through her when Verias used it, waking her and freezing her guts as she scrambled out of bed and sprinted toward the Indigo Bridge. Kin got there just in time to see his cousin use magic to drag Verias out of the blue-black waters and vanish into thin air. Her chest hurts thinking about Verias, alone and anxious, with no source of life energy to fuel his body. How long can he last like that?

"Meow," Chestnut says from the back of the couch.

"I don't know what's taking them so long, either," Kin lies.

"Mow," says Chestnut. Cats know grudges, which means Chestnut is probably as surprised as Kin is when she spots Merit coming toward the boarding house, their posture hesitant, as if looking for a trap. When she trots outside to meet them, they draw up short, reaching for a knife.

"I need your help," she says, and once again they stop, their jerky movements, black garb, and long limbs giving the impression of a large spider.

"What in the world is going on?" they ask.

"It's Verias. He's been taken. I need your help."

"I *knew* it! I knew he was still alive!"

"Wha—"

"I could feel the mark. It's faint, but I knew it," Merit cuts her off.

"Merit, shut up, we have to find him," Kin says, gritting her teeth to keep from snapping like a whip. "He'll die without me."

It's Merit's turn to ask. "What?"

"It doesn't matter. He'll die if I don't find him, do you understand? You owe us for killing him in the first place." Kin draws Merit into the boarding house by their sleeve.

"Why would I owe you for completing my assignment? They'd torture me if they knew he was still alive," they say. "What I *should* do is tell you to eat some horse shit while I go kill him."

"Why did you apologize if you don't owe me?" Kin asks.

"I . . . wait. What did you mean he'll die without you?" Merit's big, pretty dark eyes narrow.

"Some kind of strange magic. Verias called it a . . . a link. He needs my life energy, Merit, otherwise he'll die. Please, Merit, I'm begging you. He's . . ."

Kin doesn't want to say it, but she has to. It would be a filthy lie to tell them that all she wants Verias for is her soul, even if Merit will mock her for it. They were there. They saw her weep for Verias, they know how much he means to her, and perhaps worst of all, they know she can't stand by and do nothing. Kin glances around for Honor, not wanting her to hear and be hurt by what Kin was about to say.

"He's my closest friend. It's so hard to be close to whole humans, but he's a Carrier. He understands."

"Kin." Merit touches her arm in a rare gesture of tenderness. It almost feels like old times. "He doesn't understand."

Kin avoids Merit's gaze. They've never forgiven her for Iyara. With no conscience of her own, she has to endure their

128

constant needling, their anger, their sorrow, as if they think she'll forget. She doesn't need guilt for the memory of squeezing the life out of Iyara to make an indelible mark. She has her own grief and loneliness, eating away at her every second of every day, inescapable even in dreams, to remind her of all she's lost. Kin isn't going to let Merit talk her away from her most meaningful friendship she's had since Iyara.

"Maybe not," she says. "But that's for me to find out on my own."

"I *suppose* that's the case, but your life would be so much easier if you just listened."

"Probably. Are you going to help me or not?" Kin asks.

"*Fine.*"

"Good. Meet me at the Honey Gate in twenty minutes," Kin says.

"I can barely get back to the homepalace in that time, let alone get my horse out of the stable."

"Then you'd better run."

Merit turns away, grumbling something about beating her senseless as they go. They could lop her head off and leave it in a ditch for all she cares, as long Verias is safe. Verias can just tuck her fool head under his arm and survive. In fact, that might be a better arrangement as far as she's concerned. She won't have to worry about hurting him unless she gets angry and bites him on the finger.

Kin grits her teeth as she fetches all of their things, including Chestnut, with a new fear growing in her guts. This is her fault. She'd been having one of her intense nightmares, wishing she could wake, wishing she could scream, likely thrashing in her sleep. Verias must have left the room to get away from her.

When she hurries down the stairs, it's to find Amity doing his duty as stableboy in the front room, keeping an eye on the street for anybody coming to stay. The rest of his attention is fixed on a stick he must have gotten from a park in the Golden Quarter, which he's whittling with a small utility knife, getting wood shavings all over the floor. He looks up at her, face falling.

"You're leaving?" he asks.

"Yes. Not sure how long this time," Kin says. If she gets her way, it's entirely possible she won't see Amity again, and the thought makes her shriveled black heart crumble into dust. She kneels down and holds out her arms. He makes to fall into them. "Hey! Knife safety," Kin warns him, and he puts it up to hug her.

He's small and warm and ten times more fragile than Verias, but she holds him longer than she ever has. She was already fleshbound when he was born.

"Take care of your mama for me?" Kin breaks away, holding his shoulders.

"Of course I will."

"Oh no he won't." Honor comes out of the kitchen, today wearing a lovely light blue dress that makes her dark skin glow. "He's focusing on his studies."

"*Mother.*"

"And also *cleaning up this mess when he's done,*" Honor says in her stern mother voice. Kin can't help smiling as she folds her old friend up in her arms. Honor makes a surprised sound at how tight the embrace is. "You've changed, beloved."

The words send a spike of fear through Kin, but she holds on a little longer. When she lets go, she holds Honor's face in her hand. "I'm sorry for being so distant. I'm sorry for everything. Thank you for always being here for me, Honor. I love you."

"I love you, Kin." Tears shimmer in her eyes.

"Stay safe. I'll be back when I can. Left things in the usual hiding places."

⊢◇ · ◇⊣

The Honey Gate isn't as pleasant as it sounds: *honey* is a Nerefinian euphemism for human waste. The gate leads to the oldest and poorest part of Sestera, where there are no sewers, and the residents have no choice but to empty their chamber pots into the gutters each morning. The day is warm, and the fumes are enough to make Kin lightheaded while she waits for Merit. What's taking them so long?

Kin can get used to the smell, but the memories that dwell in the Honey Quarter are more persistent. Kin lived there for years and years, venturing out into the other areas of the city to pickpocket and burgle. She ran tiled rooftops and drank in all the little taverns, had family and friends and lovers in the ancient mudbrick houses. Kin played in these streets with Iyara and Merit when they were small, and thought she'd outgrown them when she grew older.

"Strange being back, isn't it?" Merit asks behind her. Kin hadn't noticed their horse's hoofbeats, rare though it is to hear them in the Honey Quarter. Being near them feels like being in a pot of boiling water, and Kin wonders not for the first time whether the Binders have some enchantment that makes being near another fleshbound miserable. They can't fight back if they can't be near each other.

"Strange," Kin says. "Come along."

Merit draws some odd looks as they ride through the Honey Quarter despite an Abserian face that's in no way out of place. Most in the area can't afford horses even if they have the need, so a horse not hitched to a trader's wagon is a rare sight, but it's Merit's clothes that stand out more than anything else. They've always loved clothes and fine fabrics, and their plain black garb is embroidered, probably by Merit themself, if Kin knows them. They've always had nimble fingers, which are as much an asset for sewing as for pickpocketing.

Back in their thieving days, they'd been in trouble with Kin's father constantly for wearing stolen, imported silk and cotton and making themself conspicuous. Kin's mended and re-mended clothing blends in far better.

"Emmala's place?" Merit asks when Kin leads them behind a tavern, one of the few places with a stable in the Honey Quarter. Those that had existed a hundred years ago were converted to shops or homes long ago.

"She's got that tunnel for smuggling, remember?" Kin says.

"What?"

"How do you think she gets all those good foreign drinks? She certainly can't pay the tariffs on what she makes here."

"I mean, I knew she was smuggling them in, I just didn't know there was a tunnel."

Kin and Merit go through the stable, where a false wall hides a shallow ramp large enough for a cart full of casks. She leaves Chestnut behind, not wanting to get separated from him, though he's never minded the tunnel. Horses are never keen on going down, but Shadow's been through so many times that she no longer balks, trusting Kin to lead her through the darkness with a candle or a lantern taken from the entrance. It depends on how money is for Emmala, though Kin always tries to leave her something when she uses the passage.

Merit has some trouble with their horse, but once he's in, he's in. His ears flick nervously, and he snorts and nickers to himself as they walk down the long, straight tunnel that leads to a tumbledown barn near a branch of the river where smugglers row up from the ocean. The farmer is outside his new barn a little ways from the old one, mending a fence, when Kin and Merit come out.

"Making an escape, I see," he says blandly. Kin usually passes through at night, and often wondered if he knows what she is.

"It's no more an escape than usual," she says, not slowing as she lead Shadow past him.

"What about that fever going around? Emmala said she was thinking of coming out here before the Council of Sanitation starts closing gates like they said they were looking to do when the red rose plague went through. You would have been a little baby then, of course," the farmer says. Kin had, in fact, been twelve.

"I'm sorry, I can't talk. A friend is in trouble," she says.

"Then never mind me, get on out of here."

Kin gets in her saddle and rides the rough, winding path out to a main road that runs almost parallel to the one she'd taken into the city with Verias for a short time before it curves off southeast. She almost misses the days of traveling with him, sometimes talking, sometimes in companionable silence. While she waits for Merit to choose a direction, she can't stop herself from indulging in a daydream of traveling with Verias again. She shakes it off. Whether now or after she gets her soul back, their partnership is made to end.

"Well, he's definitely within a few hours of here," Merit says. "I can feel him."

"Which way?" Kin asked. Merit jabs a thumb away from Sestera, and they start off in that direction.

"So if I owe you for killing your friend, what do you owe me for killing mine?" Merit asks.

"Now is not the time, Merit."

"It seems like exactly the time. We're alone with nothing to do, so we might as well talk."

"She was my friend, too. I was friends with her longer than you ever were," Kin says sourly.

"What, so you miss her more? It's not as if you're sorry she's gone. You can't be. Neither of us can."

"I can be sorry, Merit. I can't feel guilt that she's dead, but she's in my nightmares. She won't leave me no matter what I do. I can still miss her and I can still wish she were alive." Kin's voice grows more brittle with every word until it shatters. She has to clear her throat before she can speak again. "I can still wish I'd taken her place."

"Then why didn't you?" Merit asks.

"I don't know. They made me feel such pain, Merit. It was as if I forgot who I was. I was lost." Tears threaten, and Kin wishes she could just poke her eyes out so she won't have to cry again. With her luck, she'll cry anyway. "I'm lost now," she whispers. "For a few weeks I had a purpose that wasn't selfish, wasn't killing, and now it's gone."

"Mayhap you oughtn't wrap your purpose up in someone else," Merit suggests. Their flip tone makes her want to throttle them.

"If you're so smart, then what's your purpose?" Kin asks.

"To wait out my service. Obviously."

"I can't do that. I can't wait."

The pressure is unbearable, even worse now that she has to search and wait and wonder whether Verias is alive. No, he's still alive. He has to be, or Merit wouldn't be able to feel him. Kin is so upset that she's being completely irrational. From what she knows of Verias's family, they're either trying to coerce him into returning to Felver, or just bundling him off tied hand and foot. She can only hope that he won't give in. Stars, she's tried to make him see his worth. Let it be enough for him to fight.

Kin and Merit come across a village as the horizon turns a deep red that darkens above into purple and black, flecked with stars. The moon still wanes, and Kin wishes it would close its tired eye. She doesn't have time to think, to watch it pass, to miss what's gone. Merit says nothing, but they touch Kin's shoulder, the burn of another fleshbound's proximity suddenly so present and unbearable that she forgets the sky entirely. It must be the link confusing her senses. In thirteen years, nothing else has been able to change what the Binders have done to her.

"Kin, hurry up," Merit whispers.

Kin shakes herself and ties Shadow to a hitching post outside the village inn, where it won't be odd to see an unfamiliar animal. She follows Merit's lead in silence, revelling in the comfort of vanishing into the darkness. Kin and Merit investigate the town's dusty dirt streets and stone buildings before they make a move, safe in the comfort of darkness. She belongs in the shadows, where villagers on their way home from their daily business pass her without even realizing she's there. Merit is a soft--edged wraith moving ahead of her, leading her to Verias.

At the very outskirts of town, a lone woman is herding goats into a small barn for the night. The barn backs up almost against a rambling one-story farmhouse where light spills out of a front window. Nobody else is outside, but conversation can be heard as they pass the glowing square of orange light that shines upon dusty ground picked clean by chickens and goats. Kin creeps closer, straining her ears, but Merit tugs at her sleeve.

"That one." They point at a darkened window. Kin's breath snags in her chest. "What's the plan?"

Kin wonders what in the world Merit thought she'd been doing on the way out of Sestera, because it wasn't planning. Her mind had been full of Verias and regrets and loneliness the entire way.

With what sounds like a heated discussion going on in the house, it's possible that nobody will notice if the two of them simply steal Verias away. Kin would much rather cut a swath of vengeance through the whole place, but that could lead to innocent people getting hurt. Besides, Kin doesn't know what condition Verias is in. Either solution could end in getting caught with him near death. At least being sneaky could buy them a bit more time than, say, fleeing a pack of furious sorcerers.

"I need to get to him, see whether he's fit for an escape," she says.

"Be quick. If you don't come back in half an hour I'll assume you've been magicked to pieces."

"Fair. I'll be right back."

Kin crosses the quiet yard, listening to the goats still settling down in their barn. The dark window is open to the spring breeze, and Kin peeks in to see a figure sitting motionless on a wooden stool. She slips through the window, heart in her throat. The room stinks of indigo, sour acid, and sweat. Stale and sickly.

Verias's chin rests on his chest. Asleep. Even in the deep dusk, Kin can see the dark circles that cradle his eyes and the stain of indigo on his skin. She reaches for him, placing one hand at the back of his head and one over his mouth so he'll remain still and silent. His eyes open wide in terror before he recognizes her, and his body goes slack, his head falling back against her palm. A wash of gratitude and anxiety overwhelms Kin, like it always does when he shows he trusts her.

"Are you hurt?" Kin lets her hand fall from his lips.

"No. Please don't let go." His voice was hoarse.

"I have to go back to Merit. They're going to help me get you out of here. I just need a little time."

"I can't move. My uncle bound me with magic."

"Can you break out without him knowing?" Kin asks.

"I was trying, but I was so exhausted I couldn't stay awake. Wellspring's waters, he'll have to come back soon if he doesn't want me to piss in my pants or starve." Verias's neck muscles tighten against Kin's hand as he grows anxious. "You have to go."

"I'll come back for you. I promise."

CHAPTER NINETEEN

FOR A HANDFUL OF MINUTES AFTER KIN SLITHERS OUT THE window, Verias sits in silence, straining his ears to hear the conversation in the next room. He'd know his father's voice anywhere, and Wellspring's waters, did he wish he couldn't hear it now. As the eldest brother in the family, Severin Hartwell has always been patriarch, but Verias had almost been willing to believe that Gavian and Asher would go off on their own to fetch him. He should have known better.

The voices come closer, Gavian and Verias's father talking just outside the room. At first he can't make out the words, but soon they raise their voices.

"He deserves any punishment he gets."

"I know that, but you're not listening." Gavian is knocking his head against a stone wall if he thinks he can make his brother see reason once he's decided on something. "It isn't the punishment that might damage him, it's the collaring and the war machine. He's unstable."

"Unacceptable. We'll right it. We don't have any other choice."

The door swings open to admit Gavian alone. The spell holding Verias sloughs away in chunks, melting back into the earth. Finally allowed to relax, every muscle in his body aches, every joint creaks, and his fingers tingle so badly with the rush of blood that he sticks them in his armpits.

"Don't try anything like you did with Asher," Gavian says. "You might be able to surprise him, but I know better. I know you're wily."

"All I want to try to do is eat supper and use the privy."

"You'll be allowed to do that as long as you are civil to your father. If you hit him, I'll hit you twice in return, do you understand me?" Gavian asks. Verias nods. "Good."

Gavian leaves the room, returning a moment later with a lantern to stand in the corner at his brother's service. When he enters, he's precisely as he's always been. Verias is shocked to realize that he expected something to be different. There's not a speck of dust on his practical traveling clothes, and his jet-black hair is combed back with extreme prejudice, not a single bit of gray or a strand out of place. He looks younger than gray Gavian, though he's six years older. For a long time, he just looks down at Verias with scrutinous dark eyes.

"Verias, I am disappointed in you," he says. Verias shrugs. "You were always the most obedient, yet here we are. After all Lusian's hard work, after he gave up *everything*, now is when you fail me? When you fail *him*?"

Verias stares at him, then Gavian, then back to his father. He has no idea whether his comment about obedience is meant as a compliment. He can't remember the last time Severin opened his mouth to do anything but criticize Verias or compare him to Lusian or Asher. Perhaps he's insulting him. He certainly *feels* insulted. Verias has always tried desperately to please his father, and it's never been good enough. Having that thrown in his face leaves him angry enough that his hands begin to shake, but he says nothing.

"Did you think we wouldn't hear from Lord Felver?" his father asks. Verias doesn't answer. He won't understand—or care—that being away from those war machines is more important to him than avoiding Severin's anger, Severin's disappointment.

"If you're clever enough to turn a fleshbound against its masters, and brave enough to keep it around, why would you bring shame to our family by breaking our promise? Why would you throw away all Lusian worked for, what he *died* for? Why wouldn't you stay, for our sake? You were almost finished with your service." His voice snaps like a whip with every word of the last sentence. Verias flinches each time, and each time he grows angrier. It's no wonder he feels safer and happier around Kin than he has any other time in his life. She understands why he had to escape.

"Almost finished," he says, his head almost spinning with disbelief. "You don't know what it's like, ruining towns and villages and watching their inhabitants follow Felver's army because they have nowhere else to go. Hearing soldiers and innocent folk alike scream as they're crushed beneath a war machine. Listening to the moans of dying men in the Healers' tents."

"I served Felver's father, when I was young," he says.

"His father was not a warmonger! You're not only lying to me, you're lying to yourself if you try to tell me you wouldn't rather take your chances with a fleshbound!" Verias's voice rises and rises until he's shouting, anger making his head throb with pain. Gavian actually looks frightened, but neither he nor Verias's father have the good grace to be ashamed. Verias closes his eyes. He takes a steadying breath.

"You will be punished, Verias. You have to be," his father says. Verias opens his eyes to meet Severin's, to tell him in no uncertain terms that he'd rather die than go back, but his father gasps, grabbing his face. "What's this? What happened to your eye?"

"What?"

"It's turning black. Gavian, did you notice this when you examined him?" he snaps.

"He was out cold; I couldn't see his eyes. Let me look." Gavian holds the lantern up to Verias's face, the light dazzling his vision, and they both touch him, trying to look into his eyes. "Are you sure something changed?" Gavian asks.

"Please stop pawing at me," Verias says.

"I know my child's eyes. It's new." Magic scrabbles over Verias's skin, and he slams up a barrier without thinking, one massive slab of magic crushing the diagnostic enchantment.

"Father, *stop*. There's nothing wrong with me except that I'm on the verge of pissing my pants."

Severin slaps him, one stinging strike of his open hand, made more painful by the onyx ring he wears. His only jewelry. "Watch your mouth. You've been spending too much time with that monster. Gavian, take him to the outhouse and fetch him supper. We can finish this discussion later."

Verias's mind races as Gavian leads him through what looks like a farmhouse, with rustic wood furniture and colorful rag rugs on the floor. Does his father truly think that he somehow talked Kin out of killing him? Why insult him and belittle Verias if he thinks he's capable of that? Does he know that Kin pitied him, might still pity him? Nervous laughter forms in Verias's chest, trying to bubble up, but he crushes it down.

The lantern that Gavian shoves into Verias's hands sends an upsetting number of spiders skittering into the cracks of the outhouse, and he's glad to shamble back into the cool, spiderless darkness of night. There, his lantern casts its oily light upon Kin, Gavian, and a tall person he doesn't know but who looks familiar. Kin holds one of her knives to Gavian's throat, her other hand gripping his arm so tight that it must be cutting off blood flow.

"Should I kill him?" Her voice shakes with anger. Verias shakes his head. "You should let me. You'd be better off."

"No. Let him go." Verias makes his voice as firm as he can manage. For a long, tense moment, Kin stares at him, mouth set and eyes burning with rage. She leans close to his uncle's ear.

"Can I make him a little less pretty?" Kin's tone makes Verias feel as if he has a deadly snake cupped in his hands, and if he moves, it will surely kill him. He has to trust her. He shakes his head. "Very well. But if I catch you or any of your family looking for Verias again, I will kill you without asking permission. You tried to take my friend from me, and I'm selfish and mean. Do you understand?"

"Yes," Gavian breathes.

"Good. You're coming with us. Verias, shutter that lantern," Kin says.

"I'll scout ahead. You'll be slow and noisy with these two." The tall, slender person vanishes into the night, and when Kin harries Gavian and Verias after them, they don't reappear once.

Verias's stomach roils with anxiety and leftover nausea as he picks his way after Gavian and Kin. He's beginning to grow foggy and lightheaded, the night bending around him as exhaustion sets in without Gavian's magic to help sustain him. He can't draw from the Wellspring yet, or his father might sense that something's wrong. Of course, that's if he hasn't already noticed that he and Gavian have been gone far too long. His hands shake as he finds old scabs on his face and neck, getting them caught under his nails as he picks. His lips are already chewed raw, though he doesn't remember doing it.

They creep through the town, where sounds of people talking behind yellow-lit windows filter onto the street. The smells of supper fill the air, and Verias imagines families sitting down to eat, happy and smiling. Except for Kin, he's alienated everyone who cares about him, if they ever cared about him at all. Just thinking about it sends such despair cascading through him that he can barely put one foot in front of the other. Lusian cared about him. Lusian *loved* him, and he loved Lusian. That's something.

The icy teeth of magic sink into him before he can get ahold of himself, and Verias barely manages a wordless cry of warning before he plunges into the Wellspring's power, shielding himself and Kin from his father's snare. Magic smashes through magic, and Severin's attempt to capture them falls away. Verias instinctively throws his arms up to cover his face, which blocks most of the searing light of a shattered spell. When Verias lowers them, his father is picking himself up off the ground. Gavian stumbles toward him, unbalanced by the shards of magic cluttering the air.

Kin meets Verias's eyes, both baselards out of their sheaths now. Though her face lacks even a grain of expression, her eyes blaze with barely controlled anger. As promised, she doesn't ask whether Verias wants her to kill his father or Gavian, instead walking straight toward them with the killing posture of a stalking cat.

"Don't hurt them." Verias's voice comes out a croak.

She sheaths her knives, but continues toward the brothers at a brisk pace. Gavian slumps to the ground on his own, and fear boils up in Verias's stomach as he watches. Some stray scrap of magic must have overwhelmed Gavian, and he might be badly hurt. Verias starts forward, reaching out to the Wellspring, though he's not sure what he's planning to do. Kin gestures him back, not even turning to look at him.

His father lashes out at Kin. The instant of hesitation costs Kin as magic flails her, battering her before Verias can react and clusters of magic rebound. His head cracks like thunder. He stays on his feet, but barely, more power washing over him. His father has to be in agony, crashing through every slab of magic Verias throws between him and Kin, hurling so much power at Kin that her body lights up the night with a blue-white aura.

Verias starts forward, unable to let Kin face an enemy alone, but he's too slow, as always. Kin can't be held back by anything, not even magic. She wheels back and punches his father in the face. Blood explodes from his nose, but he straightens, trying to look Kin defiantly in the face. Like Verias, his father can't match a fleshbound for speed, and by the time he's upright, Kin is behind him. Kin's arms go around his neck, squeezing, choking, killing him just like she did the woman in the dream.

"Stop fighting," Kin says coldly. Verias's father claws at her forearm, eyes rolling back in her head.

"Kin, stop!"

"It won't do any lasting damage." It's as if she's discussing barnyard medicine. Castrating a goat, perhaps. The fight is going out of Verias's father. The fear in his guts wants to eject itself via his mouth. Calm. Keep calm.

"I said stop."

Kin lets go. Verias's father slips to the ground, and Kin steps over him, not looking down at him or Gavian. She takes Verias firmly by the arm, leading him away as he glances back, tripping over his own feet as he tries to will his family to stand, to give some indication that they aren't dead. He can't die, he can't leave, even though Verias loathes him. Not so soon after Lusian.

"What were you doing to him?" The pain in Verias's head begins to fade, warmth flooding him from Kin's touch.

"Blood choke. Cuts off the blood flow so the victim loses consciousness fast, good way to keep people out of your business if you don't want them dead. Didn't want to kill him since he's your father and all."

People are coming out of their homes, curious about the magic they could sense but not see. A wave of relief douses Verias when he recognizes Shadow tied in front of the inn. The other fleshbound—they can be nothing else—is already waiting with their reins in hand. Verias scrambles into the saddle with his new burst of energy. Kin mounts behind Verias, guiding Shadow out of town, up to a trot, a gallop, a canter. For a short time, Verias is kept alert by leftover anxiety, but before long he's consumed by blackness.

"He sick?" someone is asking when Verias wakes. Regains consciousness? Verias isn't sure.

"He's just tired. He's had a very bad injury recently and doesn't have his strength up yet," Kin says.

"I'm fine," Verias slurs. When he opens his eyes, he's in a stable, still sitting on Shadow's back. Everything hurts.

"Why are you blue, then?" the woman peering up at him asks. She has curly dark hair, pale, freckled skin, and shrewd, deep-set eyes.

"Fell off the Indigo Bridge." Verias tries to get down from Shadow's saddle and would have immediately crumpled to the ground if he didn't grab the stirrup. The woman laughs, but Verias is fairly sure it's at his fall into the dye, not his near fall onto the floor.

"I don't know how you get into such trouble, Red," she says.

"It's a talent." Kin slides down from the saddle, her hand steadying Verias.

"You can bed down in the hay if that's what you want, but there are better places to sleep."

"More comfortable, maybe, but I doubt they're safer. The people looking for us would never set foot in the Honey Quarter, and it goes double for a hayloft," says Kin. She's right.

"Well, have it your way. You want anything to eat, or . . ." The woman's face pinches, and she shrugs. She doesn't know whether a fleshbound can eat.

"We're famished. Thank you, Emmala," Kin says. Emmala goes out, and Kin lets out a long, slow sigh, her hand relaxing on Verias's arm. "Let's get you up in the loft."

Verias hasn't taken three steps before his knees buckle again, and Kin has to grab him. Rather than remark on how tired and weak he is, she lifts him over her shoulder as if he weighs less than nothing. Verias can almost hear the voices of his family, mocking him for being useless, as she climbs the ladder to the hayloft one-handed. His anxious mind tells him to feel shame, but he finds himself laughing instead, too giddy with exhaustion for anything else.

"What's so funny?" Kin asks as she heaves them both over the edge of the hayloft.

"I don't know how I get myself into these situations."

Kin chuckles and lets him down into the hay. "I think *I* get you into these situations."

"I suppose I deserve it, hanging around with thieves and the like," Verias says, trying to make her laugh. "I've been told you're a bad influence, teaching me naughty words." He can barely say it without laughing, and Kin joins in, head thrown back, their shared relief and tension working its way out until Verias has tears running down his cheeks.

As their mirth fades, Kin's hand stays on Verias's arm to fill him with warmth and life. Her body is soft against his side, her thigh pressed against him, the toe of her boot touching the heel of his. Her face is tired and wan, but at the same time more relaxed, more beautiful than Verias has ever seen it. Her rare smile and rarer laugh impart a radiance that fades out so fast that Verias might have imagined it.

"I'm sorry about your father. I thought only of protecting you."

Verias's heart seizes in his chest just remembering. "Did he hurt you?"

"Only bruises. They'll be gone by morning."

"Thank you," Verias whispers. "You saved my life. Again. I don't know how much longer I could have survived having to fight, having to be in that machine."

"I'm beginning to lose count of how many times I've saved you." Kin's smile returns. "I'll have to keep a tally so I know what I'm owed when I call in a favor."

"No need. I'd do anything you asked," Verias says. Kin makes a sudden move, her hand lighting on his shoulder as if she reached for his face and changed her mind. He needs her to know what she saved him from. Just thinking about it makes his head fill with the stench of oil and blood.

"I was only joking, Verias. I couldn't let them send you back and live with myself. You don't owe me anything, and I would-n't ask you for it even if you did. You're a gentle soul."

Verias's chest is so tight he can barely breathe, let alone speak. "Are you so sure that whatever you would ask me to do would compromise my gentleness?"

"I'm sure."

Kin's lovely smile has gone again, leaving Verias with the desperate need to protect the soft, fragile parts of her, the parts that dream of dead women and laugh with foolish men. The parts that care fiercely no matter how difficult and painful her life might be. After knowing her for only a short time, he can see that what she needs most is gentleness, someone with whom she can be wounded and not fear they'll take advantage of her pain. It feels selfish of Verias to want to be that person for her when she simply isn't ready to be so vulnerable.

"I'm sorry for getting caught. I'm sorry for worrying you."

"Don't apologize. I know nobody can drive someone from a room like I can." Kin's smile is bitter.

"It's not. The link is getting stronger, Kin. I saw your dreams," Verias says. Kin gives a sharp gasp, pulling away. She's out of Verias's reach, back to the wall and knees pulled up to her chin, before he can blink. When he rolls onto his elbow to look at her, she avoids his eye.

"Please don't do that again," Kin whispers.

"I didn't do it on purpose. I'm sorry, Kin."

"Me, too. It's no wonder you wanted to get away from me." Her voice is so harsh it makes Verias's throat ache.

"What? No, I wasn't trying to get away from you." Verias struggles to his hands and knees and crawls to sit with her. "I needed air, I needed . . ."

When he reaches for Kin, he's not sure if it's to comfort himself or her, but he stops himself as the memory of her dream rises in his chest like bile. He understands why she was so reluctant to touch him, and he can't force that pain and fear on her. He lets his hand fall, noticing for the first time that it's completely stained a mottled blue-gray. "Wellspring's waters, I am *extremely* blue." When he rolls up his dyed sleeve, his arm is no better. "Oh no."

"I'm sorry," Kin says in the strangest tone of voice. It takes Verias a moment to realize that she's trying not to laugh. "I was just . . ." She dissolves into a cascade of surprisingly girlish giggles.

"What?"

"Didn't you notice when you had your cock in your hand in the privy? You must have looked right at it!"

"You stop imagining my business this instant! I was too busy looking for spiders."

"I'm not imagining anything, I'm only saying!"

"You're imagining it!" Verias accuses.

"No, I'm not, you take that back!" Kin throws a handful of hay at Verias. When he dodges it, he's overwhelmed by a cascade of dizziness and nausea. Kin closes the gap between them in an instant, pressing her soft, warm hand against the side of his neck. Her other hand lowers him onto his back. "Is that better?"

"Much. I suppose that I got a bit dizzy trying to follow your moods." He wants her to laugh again, but she doesn't. She's even closer than before, her body pressed flush against his, one of her thighs between his. Verias's hands move of their own accord, reaching for her. Though her breath catches audibly, she doesn't pull away, her gaze soft. He can feel the warmth of her breath against his skin, smell magic caught in her clothes. He pulls her still closer, lips seeking hers, but the stable door squeals open below them. Emmala's voice calls Kin's name, and Kin slips away.

CHAPTER TWENTY

KIN AND VERIAS FIND NEW LODGINGS IN A HUGE, RAMBLING inn at the edge of the Honey Quarter. Their room looks out at the Fishers' Quarter, where muggy breezes carry the smells of fish, tar, and river mud through their window. Shouts and cries of seabirds filter in too, just distant enough to be pleasant rather than piercing. Kin watches the fishing boats glide across the calm waters of the Embraile, dressing her hair with oil, while Chestnut butts his head against her stomach in search of attention. Verias is writing something behind her, his pen scratching a birdlike rhythm.

She's been waiting to ask him about his cousin since they got back to the city, but he's so skilled at blaming himself for everything that she needs the right moment. He's busy now, distracted enough that he might just give an answer and pay it no more mind than that.

"Verias?"

"Mm?"

"How did your cousin vanish like that?" Kin asks.

"How did he what?"

"Vanish. He pulled you out of the river and just disappeared. Can you do that? Is this an escape route I should know about?"

Verias turns to her with a distant, almost confused look in his eye. "There are legends of that kind of spell, but it's not something I know how to do, and I've never seen anything in a book about it." His expression draws into a frown. "I'm the one who learned most of the spells we use these days."

"It must be something they learned while you were away," Kin says. She recognizes that look on his face, and under no circumstances does she want him to make his way to what's dawning on her right now. His father must have neglected to teach it to Verias or Lusian, maybe even hidden the existence of such a spell from them, so they couldn't do just what Verias has: escape.

Thank the stars there's a rapid rat-a-tat from their door that causes Verias to look up, his brow unknitting. Kin crosses to the door, waving Verias back into his chair as he rises. It's likely nothing, but after what had happened with Merit and with Verias's family, she has to be between Verias and practically anybody else in the world. It's remarkable the amount of trouble Verias can get in just by sitting at a writing desk.

When Kin opens the door, Merit stands in the corridor, bouncing on their toes. Suspicion immediately bubbles up inside her. "What are you doing here?"

"Because I want in," says Merit.

"What?"

"I want in. Or out, depending on what we're talking about," Merit says. "Let me in so we can talk freely, because this is getting confusing."

They're certainly right about that. Kin steps aside so Merit can enter, keeping a hand on one of her knives as she watches them pass. The room is larger than their last, but it's still cramped with three people inside. Not ideal circumstances for a fight. Merit perches on the windowsill, leaning forward, which Kin takes as a good-faith maneuver. She could easily push Merit out, and while they won't die, they certainly won't like it.

"I want my soul back, too," they say. Kin glances at Verias, hoping he won't react.

"I don't know what you're talking about," she says.

"Oh come, now, let's not play games. You're *obviously* trying to get your soul back. Creeping around Sestera instead of running for it or going back to the homepalace, hanging around with a sorcerer—they told me that much about him—who's been lurking in the Deep Quarter. When I started sensing him there, I thought it was my imagination, but now that I've seen that he's still alive, it all fits. I don't know why you'd let him come to the homepalace if you wanted to keep it a secret." Merit's gaze is sharp, watching to see if her face gives anything away.

"I assumed you'd put it down to imagination, and you did." Kin shrugs. Merit had no reason to think Verias was still alive.

"Well, I suppose it worked. Please let me join you, Kin. I want my soul back." Merit's voice strains with emotion, and a stab of sympathy cuts through her. She knows that longing, that anger, but she shoves her emotions down. There's no way to be sure of them, no way she can fully trust them.

"I thought your purpose was to wait out your punishment," Kin says. "I thought you were better than me. Less selfish."

"Are you calling me a hypocrite?" Merit looks like they're about to jump up and beat Kin. Fair enough.

"I'm not calling you anything. I'm just asking."

"You didn't ask a question. You made an accusation," Merit says.

"Maybe the both of you ought to start over with what you're each willing to offer instead of demanding things of each other." Verias is clearly annoyed by their argument interrupting his work.

"Why should I offer them anything?" Kin asks. Everyone is on her very last nerve.

"Perhaps because you owe me for helping get him back," Merit says.

"I already told you, *you* owed *me* for killing Verias, and Verias, you can—"

"What?" Verias interrupts. "*They* killed me? Why would you let them in? Why would you bring them to rescue me?"

"I had no other choice. They were the only way I could find you since they still had the mark. And *like I said*, we're even now, aren't we, Merit?" When Kin looks at Merit, they're nervously tapping their fingers against the windowsill. They stand, put their hands on their hips, shift their weight.

"I want to be free of all this," they finally say. "Please, Kin. We were friends once. I need this."

"Kin, they *killed* me," Verias says.

"Verias, *I* was literally sent to kill you." Kin's patience hasn't worn thin; it's so full of holes it could be used to catch fish. "I know what we can offer you, Merit. What are you bringing to this endeavor?"

"You can't possibly be—"

"You're the one who told us to say what we're willing to offer," Kin cuts Verias off. Verias's eyes narrow, but he keeps quiet. "Merit?"

"I have the favor of the Binders, especially the Steward. She lets me come and go as I please."

"So? I'm just as free out here," Kin says.

"You can't go back without being punished. I can move between the homepalace and the outside world as I please. I can watch over him while he's there, so you don't need to lurk on rooftops," Merit says.

"That's assuming that I trust you. I reckon you shouldn't make that assumption."

"What reason have I ever given you to mistrust me?" Merit asks. Kin can't believe them. "I thought you said we're even."

"Even doesn't mean I trust you!" she snaps, overwhelmed by annoyance. "You killed my best friend!"

"You killed mine!"

"I know that! We'll help you get your stars-cursed soul, but I swear to the moon and stars and every fucking thing in the sky, if you let this slip to the Binders, I'm going to cut your head off and use your mouth as a chamber pot."

"You have to promise. Promise me, Kin." That desperation is in their voice again, and Kin softens against her will. She looks into their large, dark eyes, searching. She *thinks* they're sincere, but there's no way to know for sure. Still, what really frightens her is that desperation makes people forget everything else, causes them to make mistakes like the ones she keeps making. Making such a promise is committing to take on their mistakes as well as her own.

"I promise I'll try," she says. It's the best she can do.

"Very well." Merit marches out, slamming the door behind them.

"You don't think they're going to get us in trouble, are they?" Verias asks.

"Probably not on purpose. The Binders will punish them just as badly as they will me," Kin says. Verias is silent for what felt like an hour, and Kin stays still as a stone. Instinct. When it's quiet in the homepalace, it's always better to be still and silent, not to draw attention.

"I didn't know you considered me your best friend," he says at last.

Kin's face grows hot. She almost kissed him in the hayloft last night, and now she's slipped and said something she didn't mean to. Even Honor says she's changed. Maybe Merit is right. Maybe she's losing her edge. She knows she's staring at Verias like she's forgotten who he is, but she can't make any words come out to make the situation less awkward.

"You're my best friend, too," he says.

Kin has to sit down. She has no idea why he'd say that after seeing what's in her past, seeing her kill, or even just sitting through her grouchy silences while sharing a room with her. She's overwhelmed with confusion, fear, but most of all gratitude. But when she opens her mouth, what comes out is "You're out of your mind."

Verias just laughs.

Verias doesn't expect Kin to give up her watch at the homepalace for one instant. She clearly doesn't trust Merit as far as she can throw them, which would be a relief if Verias wasn't fairly sure she could get a good ten paces out of them. Maybe twelve. Even knowing she's out there watching, Verias still has a cold pit in his stomach as he enters the homepalace. He doesn't know how the Binders' mark works (he should ask), but he fears that it's somehow irresistible, making Merit dangerous even if they don't mean to be.

At least Lessa smiles to see him. She may have been in Kin's terrible dream, but at this point, her good favor will be instrumental in getting Verias into the Vault of Souls. Her presence is also considerably less distasteful than the Dean's, little though that may mean.

"I've found you a few books," Lessa says in conspiratorial tones once they've passed through the doors she seems to watch day in and day out. "I'm known for being a troublemaker, so the librarian just rolled his eyes and gave them to me." She hands Verias a few slim, ancient volumes.

"Thank you, Lessa. This ought to keep me busy for some time. Is the Dean back?"

"He is, but he's extremely busy. Do you have any questions I can relay to him? It might make it easier if he can write a message for you to pick up tomorrow," Lessa says.

"I'm not sure. I'm concerned about the safeguard, as it would surely be triggered by the Binding process. I've also been wondering if the homepalace has any . . . troublesome fleshbound." Verias knows without question that Kin is such a fleshbound, and he wants to seed the idea that he has a use for her, just in case she ends up back at the homepalace. It might save her punishment. It might save her life.

"I know for certain that we can remove your safeguard. I believe that the Steward would be able to tell you anything you need to know about individual fleshbound. Are you looking for test subjects?" Lessa leans in, curiosity alight in her pale eyes. It might be the similarity of those eyes to Reshon's or the intensity of her gaze, but for the first time since he met her, Lessa puts Verias on edge. How far is she willing to go for her studies?

"I wish to explore whether linking is even possible, or if some of your enchantments prevent the process. I assume the safeguard would get in the way of that work."

"Well, I have excellent news. A Binding is happening shortly. You should watch, so that you can understand how the spellwork comes together. Come, I'll take you to the Steward and she'll take you to the Binding."

For a moment, Verias can't breathe. He isn't prepared to see a Binding, but he can't possibly say no, or at best Lessa will think him weak. At worst, she'll suspect that he's lying about his "research." He trails along in her wake, trying to think of ways to escape. Kin's dream was bad enough, but in real life it's sure to be unbearable. He can fake being sick, but with a fever going around, that could be enough to get him banned from the homepalace. No other plan comes to mind.

The Steward is a stout, pretty older woman with iron-grey hair and a spine stiff enough to match. She looks Verias up and down with an appraising gaze that leaves him sure he hasn't measured up. He's used to that. In fact, he thinks the only time anyone has given him such a look and been anything more than disappointed was when Kin decided to spare his life. There's still time, though. He can always find new and interesting ways to disappoint.

"Well, it's a good opportunity for me to do the Dean a favor by determining whether you're worth anything to him." The Steward lifts her chin, looking down her long, straight nose at him, but Verias doesn't budge. He's used to being treated like something that crawled out of a midden heap; acting as if it affects him will only make the Steward treat him worse. "He's spoken of your power, of course, but if you don't have the stomach for the work, there's no point in wasting his time with you."

"That's reasonable," Verias says. The Steward cocks an eyebrow before she sweeps him away to the cellars. Verias insists to himself that he can do this. He's seen worse things; he just can't think of any of them just now.

He knows the room, the torches and braziers, the stone table. The handful of hooded figures are different sizes and shapes than they were in Kin's dream, but everything else is so familiar that Verias feels like he might vibrate out of his skin and disappear into the cool, damp cellar air. It's heavy with a sickly sweet scent covering a rotten stink. Verias focuses on the sweet smell, anxiety roiling hot in his chest and he struggles not to pick at his face. There are rushes mixed in, perhaps lemon balm. Chamomile?

As Verias hones in on the one thing in the room that isn't completely horrible, a man is led into the room, talking to one of the Binders and laughing. Verias bites back a sigh of relief. At least the potential fleshbound appears to be there of his own free will. Watching someone be forced into a Binding would be a nightmare. This man lies down on the stone slab like it's a comfortable bed, looking up at the ceiling as his wrists and ankles are secured and the Binders surround the table. The Steward helpfully shunts Verias to one side for a better view.

Magic begins to swirl around the room, solidifying into manageable pieces. The man's face grows ever so slightly nervous as he senses the change in the air, ginger brows drawing together. The delicate stained-glass patterns that form around him are fascinating in their complexity, vicious little shards of energy being built into a brittle structure that's laid and overlaid, growing so bright that it hurts Verias's eyes.

It shatters. The red-haired man screams, a shrill sound that rakes across Verias's very soul. He makes himself watch the technique, taking in the scraps of magic setting around the screaming man's body and the shimmer rising from his chest. It coalesces into a blue light, and the nearest Binder reaches out a slender hand gloved in mail. The light settles over their palm, solidifying further, until it becomes an azure orb the size of a shelled chestnut. The Binder closes their hand around the orb and slips it into their pocket as if it's nothing more than a common marble. The image of a perfect human soul burns in Verias's vision long after it leaves his sight and the second spell begins. Still the fleshbound screams.

This work is familiar, similar to the one he saw placed over Kin, though far less complex. This must be what she was subjected to at the time of her first Binding, before the Binders learned that it didn't take, and tried again. The fleshbound's screams cease, leaving the room in total silence.

To Verias's surprise, more magic rises from the Binder who owns the fleshbound, thin sheets falling over the victim like shimmering snow, like mica. Each piece shifts, rotates in the same direction as all the others. A compass needle. The mark that would guide the fleshbound to his first target. It's remarkably like the linking enchantment, sinking into the fleshbound's skin and becoming a part of him, and at the same time, nothing like it. Verias can't suppress his natural curiosity, can't stop himself from wondering how those millions of compasses work, how long they hold, how they're broken.

The fleshbound is released, led from the room pale and shaking. Verias is sure he's expected to follow, but each step feels like climbing a mountain wearing iron shoes. He knows what comes next, and he'd much rather stay in the horrible cellar room that stinks of shit and blood than watch.

In the courtyard, a man arrives to hand a brown-and-white dove to the Binder in possession of the new fleshbound's soul. The Binder passes the bird, docile and beautiful, to the fleshbound. These people are monsters. Every last one of them, even Lessa, and Verias has never wanted anything more than to burn their filthy palace to the ground.

He forces himself to watch.

CHAPTER TWENTY-ONE

KIN HAS NEVER SEEN VERIAS ANGRY. SHAKEN, YES, OR UPSET, but never truly angry. His gentle expression is gone, leaving behind something hard and desperate that she's sensed lurking below the surface but never really seen. She can suddenly see the darkness under his eyes, the heavy brows that lend an unexpected cruelty to his usually gentle face. It's like looking into a pale mirror to watch him pace the length of their room over and over, scraping at his face, marring his flushed cheeks with vivid red marks that weep no blood. Dead men don't bleed.

"Verias." Kin's voice makes him stop pacing and turn to her, hand still on his cheek.

Something inside her wants to flinch at the set of his jaw and the blazing fire in his eyes. Something small, weak, human. Or perhaps something animal, for Chestnut fled the room at least a quarter of an hour ago.

"Come for a walk."

"What?" His pupils are blown out, merging with the dark spot in his eye, making his iris look like an ink blot. Like something has come loose and spilled out from inside him.

"Come walk. I always walk when the anger gets the better of me. Well, I go up on the rooftops, but the street is almost as good."

"Kin, I don't want to—"

"Well, I'm going—I can't stay in here and watch you pace—

and it's safer for you to come with me," Kin says. "Come. It'll be good for you."

Verias sighs heavily, but when Kin leaves the room, he follows her. The air near the river is at once better and worse than that near the Honey Gate. The stench of human waste is less strong, but muddy river smells and heavy humidity hang around the water. Kin takes off along the Embraile, which was rerouted generations ago to run straight and true through the Fishers' Quarter. Now the stone that holds the waters to their course is crumbling, completely swept away by spring rains in some places.

Once, the riverbanks were flush with people washing clothes, gathering water, and fishing, but the dyes and tanning chemicals from the Woolworkers' Quarter have long since rendered the water too dirty for any such things. The people of the Honey Quarter now rely on wells dug far enough from the watercourse to avoid being tainted by the filth.

"How do you bear it?" Verias asks as they walk the uneven stone road that runs alongside the river. He sounds slightly calmer, but the edge isn't gone from his voice. It makes Kin's stomach ache to hear the strain. "How do you live with the anger? How do you force it down?"

"I don't. I became it. I became the hope that the Binders' day will someday come. I became the hope that I might be the one to take that homepalace apart, even if I have to do it one stone at a time." Kin feels as if she's listening to someone else talk, surprised at her own matter-of-factness in the face of his pain and hers.

"I want to help you," Verias said. He's nearly vibrating with rage and anxiety.

"You are helping me."

"I don't just want to get your soul back. I want to destroy those—" He breaks off, his voice choked. Verias digs his fingernails into his forearms through the fabric of his shirt. Kin stops walking and seizes him by the shoulders.

"You are helping," Kin repeats. "I need you to keep doing exactly what you're doing, because I can't stop them if I don't have my soul back."

"But how? It feels like I'm doing nothing, just going back and forth, back and forth . . . but what else is there to do?" Verias's knuckles are white. Kin takes each of his hands in her own, and she can feel him shaking with the desire to hurt himself again. Stars, she knows that feeling all too well. Though the thoughts that scare her half to death are born of a morbid curiosity to which she already knows all the answers, she understands. It flares up in her just from holding his hands, the need to know what's inside him, the brittle bones and soft meat and . . .

"Make them trust you enough to remove the safeguard." She cuts off her own thoughts. "It might take a long time, but if they trust you that much, they'll let you do anything. I've waited years just to meet someone like you. Someone strong enough, who cares enough. I'm patient," she lies.

"What about the others?" Verias asks.

"I don't know, Verias. They never really figured into my plans."

"Why not? How could you go through that and not have some empathy for the others?" His hands squeeze hers, hard.

"It's not that simple, Verias. The ones who weren't forced are almost as bad as the Binders themselves, and it isn't easy to tell who is who." Kin walks on, holding tight to Verias's arm to keep him from picking. "Nobody wants to tell what happened to them for fear of being punished. The only person I'm sure of is Merit, because I was there to know that they didn't want this."

"We have to show people how cruel the process is, how much—"

"Show who? Everyone thinks we do this for the good of the nation. We're heroes just as much as we are monsters. Heroes have to break themselves to be any use, Verias. Seeing the breaking doesn't make that any less true."

Verias falls into a grim silence, clutching Kin's hand where she holds his arm. He's trying to stop himself from ripping off all his skin as much as she is. When Kin takes him away from the empty riverside, her eyes keep darting toward his face, taking in the painful red spots. She finds herself walking toward the herb seller who lives near the Mouth, the gate that lets out of the city. A soothing salve will at least make Verias more comfortable.

The Mouth smells like travel. Horse and ox, polished leather and wood, dirt and burlap. Peddlers stay in the cheap inns of the Mouth to save money while they buy pretty things from the other parts of the city to sell elsewhere. Once, Kin and her mother passed through the Mouth every day to gather wild herbs and bring them back for medicines. Kin tired of that quiet life at a young age, preferring the excitement of her father's profession. She wishes she'd known better.

Though Kin remembers the woman in the herb shop, she doesn't recognize Kin. Not counting her rescue mission through Emmala's stable, Kin hasn't been out in the Honey Quarter in the daylight in years, and she half expects to be recognized everywhere. People used to stop her father whenever they saw him, thrilled to meet the King of Thieves. It seems that glory wears off quickly, the thinnest coat of electrum over base metal.

Only Verias takes any notice when Kin stops in front of her childhood home, like she often does when she passes in the night, listening and watching to see if anyone's decided the abandoned house is a nice place to live. Nobody ever does. It seems unlikely that folk remember who once lived there and respect the memory. Perhaps they think it haunted.

The place looks worse in the daylight, when Kin can see all of the crumbling mortar and missing roof tiles instead of pretending it's the same as it ever was. Someone's taken a window, sash and all, likely to replace a broken one in their own home. Kin has to wonder why they didn't take the others in case something happened to the rest of their windows. It's what she would've done.

"What is this place?" Verias's hand is still on hers, gently stroking now. Returning to himself.

"My parents' home. My mother left Sestera after my father died. It's gone to ruin since."

"Why didn't you stay here?"

"I hadn't lived here for years. Mother and I didn't get along after I started working for Father. It was easier to live with him after my mother threw him out," Kin says. Her mother still loved him, still stayed in Sestera in case he gave it all up for her, but it never came to pass.

"Oh, Kin. I'm sorry."

Kin's sorry too, because after all, it was her choice. She walks on, because there's nothing left to do about it. At least Verias is less tense, his body loose against hers. Her face grows hot, remembering how she almost kissed him in the hayloft the other night, drawn to his laughter and warmth. She'd do almost anything to recapture that feeling for both of them, but the street is dead, an eerie silence falling around them. At least every other door on the street is hung with triangular, scarlet oilcloth signs painted with a crude rose.

"The red rose plague must be getting worse," Verias murmurs.

"Have you had it before?"

"No."

"Then we need to be careful. I won't get it again, but you could get sick, and that would be a serious problem." Kin picks up her pace. She doesn't reckon walking faster will help, but it might work out some of the shivery dread growing inside her.

"*A serious problem*, she says. Yes, being dead again would be a serious problem, if I can even get sick at this point."

"Are you willing to gamble?" Kin asks. She certainly isn't.

"Absolutely not. It isn't as if I can just magic my way out of it," says Verias. Then, as if sensing her questions, "Setting aside the fact that trying to heal myself with the safeguard in place would likely kill me, I couldn't do much; disease is a level of complexity I have no experience with, and it's more likely that I'd hurt than help. The same goes for helping anyone else."

Kin bites her lip, considering the fact that it might be better to leave Sestera until the plague passes. Last time, five in ten people died. Kin herself was grievously ill, in bed for weeks while her father tried to keep her fever down.

"Thank you."

"What?" Kin almost forgot Verias was there.

"I said thank you. For not trying to tell me that being angry was foolish."

"Why would I tell you that?" Kin's attention snaps back to him. It sounds so like her mother to say that anger is useless and wrong that her head spins.

"I don't know. I'm used to being told that I'm being foolish when my emotions are strong."

"By whom? Your father?" Kin asks. Verias makes a wordless sound of assent. "I don't think I like him very much."

"He's just very particular. It's not that he thinks I oughtn't have feelings, it's that he'd rather I keep my secrets."

"From him?"

"It bothers him to see me upset, especially when I pick," Verias says.

"Verias, it sounds like you're making excuses for him. It bothers me to see you like that, too. That doesn't mean I get to tell you to stop." Kin says it as gently as she can, but she can tell her voice is hard by the way he stiffens against her.

"I'm sorry. It's just so hard to stop even when it hurts, and I look down and see blood and I know I'm disgusting, and—"

"I don't think you're disgusting, you ninny, I don't like that you're suffering enough that the picking gives you relief."

"Oh."

"I'm sure you hated seeing my dream, too," Kin says softly. Since that day, Verias makes very sure not to touch her while she sleeps. It's a relief, and it also stings just a little. "You care about me just as much as I care about you."

"Kin, I . . ." He trails off. Verias pulls his arm from Kin's grip and puts it around her waist, squeezing tight for a moment, and for the space of that moment, Kin is perfectly content.

"Isn't that just precious," says someone passing by. Kin turns to tell him to eat shit, but she finds herself eye to eye with Reshon.

"You!"

"Me." He smiles at her, gorgeous and hateful as ever. Kin wants to stab him, but they've left the quarantined neighborhood, and people will see. Even in the Honey Quarter, she can't go around murdering people in broad daylight, though she's sorely tempted to fistfight. Reshon might not cross her again if she beats him senseless.

"Leave us alone, Reshon," Verias says. He's shaking with anger, his arm still around her, body tensed as if he can't decide whether to pounce or flee. Kin wraps her own arm around his shoulders.

"We killed your assassins," she says. "And we'll kill you too, if you give us the chance."

"I know you will. I don't want to waste any more money sending people after you, and I'm sure you've tired of slinking around Sestera hiding bodies. I thought I'd propose a deal," says Reshon.

"You don't have anything I want. Fuck off." Kin tries to guide Verias away from Reshon, but he stands still as stone.

"He's a Binder," Verias whispers. Kin's guts twist up with hatred, until she's holding herself back as much as she is Verias.

"The Carrier for your soul," says Reshon. His voice goes soft, his expression suspiciously sympathetic, as if she'd ever fall for that from a Binder. "You don't have to go through all this. I can walk in and take your soul with little trouble. The others won't even know; I have a good match I can replace it with. All you have to do is give him to me."

"Once again, fuck off. Come along, Verias. We don't want his help."

"We'll think about it, Reshon," Verias says. Kin, alight with fury at Reshon, doesn't bother to argue, instead pulling Reshon away.

"Don't try to run off, now," Reshon says. "I'm always watching."

CHAPTER TWENTY-TWO

"WHAT IS WRONG WITH YOU?" KIN ROUNDS ON VERIAS THE
second they're in their room. It's not that he hadn't expected her
to be upset—he felt her tense against him when spoke to Reshon
—but he's so preoccupied with the realization that Reshon is a
Binder that he's unprepared to be shouted at.

"What—"

"I would never in a thousand years—never in ten thousand
years!—trade you for my soul!" Kin cuts him off. "I know I'm a
thief, I know I'm a criminal, but you can't buy a soul with years
of someone else's life! Who the fuck do you think I am?"

"I wasn't trying to disparage you, Kin; you know I think
you're a good person." Verias is so taken aback by her logical
leap that he can't even be angry that she's yelling at him.

"Then why would you ever even consider it? You had to
know that I'd refuse." Her anger is already dying down, her expression falling and her voice pleading.

"He's a Binder, Kin. He can just tell the Dean what we're doing. They'll punish both of us, maybe even decide you're not
worth the trouble," Verias says. Kin puts her fists on her hips,
wilting even further. "We have to at least let him think we'd do
it, or I wouldn't be able to go back to the homepalace. You becoming a Binder is the only plan we have."

"How did you not know he was a Binder?" Kin asks. Verias
shrugs. Magic sense is fickle and strange.

"He doesn't feel much different from any other Reaper. The feel of magic can be wildly different between two sorcerers. Until I met other Binders, I didn't know what undercurrents were there." A shudder works its way through him. He always hated Reshon, always knew there was something off about him. Verias put that down to being a Reaper. Reapers are killers, after all. But there's something else about Binders. Even Lessa, who Verias is able to tolerate, has something foul running beneath the surface. "I don't think there's anything else we can do. We can only fight for so long before we have to leave Sestera. I've already been killed once. We don't know if I can survive another attack." To Verias's shock, Kin doesn't argue. Instead, tears begin to stream down her face. "What's wrong?"

"I know I failed. You don't need to throw it back in my face like that." She's acting so strange, taking everything more personally than usual. Kin doesn't usually seem to care one whit what anybody thinks of her. The change is worrisome.

"I'm not trying to remind you of your failure, Kin. I'm only saying that—"

A look of horror spreads across Kin's lovely face, cutting Verias off. He reaches for her, drawing magic up from the Wellspring. Something is clearly wrong with her: She presses her hand to her chest, taking short, fast breaths like she might faint at any moment, and she backs away from his hand.

"Don't. I can't . . . I feel . . . guilty. You're breaking through the spells." She dissolves into ugly, wrenching sobs. Verias touches her arm, just a tentative brush of the fingers to show he's there for her. To his shock, Kin leans into him, letting him hold her. Her whole body shakes with each heaving sob, tears soaking through his shirt in moments. Kin is taller than Verias, but holding her still somehow feels like cupping a kitten in his hands, eyes still closed and soft as anything. He guides her to sit on their straw mattress.

"You didn't fail. You saved me, Kin," he says.

"You saved yourself just as much as I did. The link is both of us together, isn't it?" Her voice is dense with tears.

"That's not what I'm talking about. I mean when we first met. I wanted to die, Kin. I'd tried to get away so many times, and there seemed to be no way to escape battle. I was relieved to find you there with your knife against my throat. I was ready. You showed me that I was worth saving. Ever since . . ." Verias has to take a few deep breaths to keep going. "Lusian left home almost five years ago now. Ever since then I've been surrounded by people who don't care about me, who talk to me like I'm nothing. Knowing there's at least one person who cares about me enough to drag me back from death makes it easier when I'm tired and afraid. Even though I'm a terrible Carrier and a nervous wreck and I still sometimes think it would make things simpler to end it all."

"I'm glad you're alive, Verias."

Kin puts her arms around Verias's neck, pressing into him so that her weight forces him to lean against the wall at the head of the bed to support her. He's shaking with relief that she didn't pull away from him, that she still wants to be near him even though he's a complete coward. Tears sting his eyes at the feel of her melting into him, her sobs softening. She's his single glimmer of light where there is none, and it breaks his heart to see her hurt. A tear escapes, running into her red-brown curls, before Verias can take hold of himself.

She grows quiet, her breathing even and calm. The warmth of her life energy is shivery where her forehead presses against his throat. He starts noticing her again, like he had in the hayloft: soft hips and hard knives pressing into his thighs, her warm belly, her breasts. The muscles of her back, tense beneath her deceptively tender flesh as Kin holds Verias tight. Giddy humor and relief at being away from his family blurred his emotions the night she rescued him, but now there's no mistaking his feelings. Verias wants her, wants to kiss her and hold her, revel in her strength, learn every curve. He's immediately disgusted with himself. It's heartless to think of such things when she is suffering so.

"I'm frightened, Verias," she says, as if to drive the point home. "I can bear physical pain, but this guilt . . ."

"If you need to spend time away from me, I understand," Verias says. Kin's head snaps up.

"Don't be ridiculous. I'm not going to leave you to fade out because I can't bear the strain." Her face is puffy from crying, but her expression is set. Wellspring's waters, all he wants to do is kiss her. "And don't you *dare* do anything foolish."

"What?" Any thoughts of intimacy flee, though Kin has her hands on the mattress to either side of his body, at her most intense and intimidating.

"No trying to leave and die under a hedge for my own good. No avoiding me."

"Die under a hedge? Why would I—"

"Verias. I know you. You're too selfless for your own good." Kin sits back on her heels. Verias barks a laugh, sure she's making a joke—he's so anxious all the time because he's at heart a selfish person, unable to see past his own fears—but Kin neither smiles nor laughs.

"What are you talking about?" He catches himself reaching up to pick at his face and stops.

"You didn't mention the safeguard to me because you knew I might stop you from healing me. You healed me even though it caused you pain." Kin grabs both his forearms, her touch making his skin tingle. "I know you'd trade yourself for my soul if you thought I'd be better off, and I'm telling you right now, I won't be, because I'll look for you day and night until I find you and slap you so hard your whole family will feel it."

"I won't die," is all Verias can say. If he's honest with himself, being slapped silly sounds like a dream, but that's nothing he could admit to her, now or ever. He has to wrap those thoughts up and put them away before he can go on. "I learned when I was with my family that magic can sustain me for a time. It can cause problems long term, but I'll survive away from you."

"That's good, but it isn't a promise not to do anything dangerous. I need you to promise, Verias."

"I can't do that," he says. "This may be the best choice we have. If something happens to you, it might be the only one we have."

"No, it'll be the only choice *I* have. It's my soul, and my choice to make, and I don't trust him. At all."

"It's my freedom," Verias says. Why can't she see that this is her way out? "The choice is mine."

"Verias, I refuse to hear anything else about it. I refuse."

"What other option is there?"

"I don't know yet. Give me time. I'll think of something." Kin's gaze has already turned inward, even as she leans back to take the pot of ointment she purchased at the Mouth out of her pocket. "Did you learn anything at the homepalace that might be of help?" She starts dabbing ointment on his scabs. It has an herbal, grassy scent with an undertone of bitterness.

"Nothing of use. They do think I'm looking for test subjects. I led them on a bit, thinking it might be a useful seed to sow for you if they found you and took you back." Thank the Wellspring she hasn't forced him to promise. It's not a promise he can make.

"A test subject for what?"

"To see if linking between a Binder and a fleshbound is possible," Verias says. "If you're of use to me, they'll treat you better."

171

"Won't the Binders know we're already linked?"

"No. That sort of connection is undetectable to outsiders once it's made. It's the perfect excuse to keep them from hurting you," Verias says. "And if they thought I was willing to experiment on you, they would assume that I was like-minded. That's why they made me watch the Binding. To make sure I had the stomach for it."

"Clever, Verias, very clever. It would also mean I might gain access to places fleshbound usually aren't allowed. But it would leave you open to attack from Reshon if I'm not able to get away from the homepalace for some reason."

"I can hold him off for a while, but I don't know how long."

Kin doesn't reply. She finishes applying the ointment to Verias's face, rubs the rest onto her hands, and puts the pot back in her pocket. She sits back, folding her legs. She's clearly lost in thought, and Verias doesn't want to bring her back from it. She's distracted from her guilt for the time being, and that's enough for him.

Verias has begun to sense Kin at a distance. It's her warmth, marking his heart as she follows him to the homepalace to keep him safe. The morning is cool, and the people of the Honey Quarter are busy, stalls popping up to serve breakfast to people walking to work. The smells of sausage and wood smoke compete with the usual morning stench of night soil as residents empty chamber pots.

Something shifts, and the daily business of the Honey Quarter leaves Verias's mind entirely. Kin is running ahead, her soft, buzzing presence getting further and further away as Verias's heart jams in his throat. Is someone waiting to kill him? He considers turning around, but he's safer near Kin. He walks faster, not wanting to look suspicious but sure he has to catch up, find out what's wrong.

A memory of their conversation from the night before rises to the front of his mind unbidden. Kin fears that he'll run off and get into trouble for her benefit, but would she do the same for him? No, that can't be it. With the Binders' enchantments, she can't harm Reshon, and turning herself in won't do either of them any good. Verias forces himself to slow, strolling the long walk to the homepalace like nothing is wrong.

She's inside, her fuzzy warmth standing still now, and if Verias bursts into the homepalace to rescue her, he'll shatter his deception and possibly get them both killed. He has to remain calm, and he clenches his hands into fists to keep from tearing at his own skin. Be calm. Breathe. Be calm. Walk. Be calm. Survive.

Tingles of magic surge through Verias as he approaches the homepalace, now more menacing than ever as it crouches over warehouses, glimmering in the morning sun. They're hurting her, punishing her for failing her mission and staying away for so long. His hand shakes as he opens the door to let himself inside, and his every instinct tells him to close his eyes against what he knows he'll see.

The entry hall is silent, the chairs along the wall empty. Kin kneels on the soft, worn carpet in front of Lessa, who looks down at her as if she's something tracked in from the gutters of the Honey Quarter. There isn't a mark on Kin's body, but her posture gives away pain. Verias crushes down the need to run to her, comfort her.

"Now, tell me why I shouldn't tear you apart," Lessa says through her teeth. Magic shivers around her, making Verias's bones creak. Kin says nothing.

"What's all this, Lessa?" Verias asks, trying to sound casual and only mildly interested.

"Good morning, Everis. This is one of our wayward creations. We've been looking for you," Lessa says to Kin. "We have wasted resources on you."

Kin hunches further into herself, not showing any of the sheer stubbornness that Verias knows and loves. She's a different person within these walls, someone Verias doesn't know. He's never hated anyone as much as he hates the Binders for doing this to her, except maybe himself. He should have found Reshon, made the deal while she slept, saved her from this. From herself.

"I'll only ask you once more: why shouldn't I destroy you and throw the pieces into your cell?" Lessa asks.

She seemed so human in the library, talking about helping fleshbound re-enter society, and Verias thought that perhaps Lessa could be turned. Become an ally. How had he been so naïve?

"They can come back even from that?" he asks, trying to divert Lessa's attention. It's all he can do at this point.

"Of course. I could reduce her to a mist and some piece would continue to grow until it became her again. But that could take weeks, months, even years, and we need useful fleshbound, not heaps of flesh sitting in a cellar."

"So how do you punish them? Tearing them apart, like you said?" Verias asks.

"Rarely. Cutting out the tongue or removing an ear is a frequent choice."

"Lessa, I thought you wanted to help these creatures. I don't understand." Verias doesn't look at Kin as he speaks, afraid to give himself away.

"They are no more than tools until their souls are restored, Everis. The ones who have served us and earned their souls back are the people I care about. A useless tool is worth nothing. This one is constantly escaping, constantly causing some kind of trouble." Lessa face twists into a grimace at the last word, and Verias tamps down a nervous laugh. Kin is the earthly embodiment of the concept of trouble.

"Perhaps it will do for my linking experiment." Verias's chest hurts and his stomach boils to speak of Kin so. How can Lessa not see how human Kin is? "If it's not useful in any other way, perhaps I can make it so."

"Perhaps," Lessa says. "But she will need to be punished first. You may speak to the Dean. I will be taking her to the Steward."

She turns away, not waiting for Kin to unfold herself and follow. Verias prays for Kin to look back, meet his eyes, but she doesn't turn. It takes all of his strength not to shout at her to run, not to break down, not to vomit. He has to find a way to end this from inside the homepalace; with the safeguard, Verias can't rescue Kin from Lessa. He has to put the thought of Kin's suffering out of his mind and do the work she's set him to. He has no other choice.

CHAPTER TWENTY-THREE

KIN ENTERS THE STEWARD'S CHAMBERS FULL OF CRACKS
and comes out with more, just as she always does. The only
thing that hasn't shattered is the surety that she's doing the right
thing. If Verias is made a Binder, they'll have to remove the safeguard, or he'll never be able to Bind or control fleshbound. Once
the safeguard is removed, Verias can fight anyone who tries to
hurt him. He'll no longer be in danger from Reshon, and even if
they're caught, no single Binder can defeat someone as powerful
as Verias. All their fooling about, stringing him along, testing
him, is to one end: to ensure that he doesn't crack under the
strain. They want him, or that bitch Lessa never would have
greeted him as a friend.

Kin's cell doesn't have a door; none of them do. She's afford-
ed only a bed, mattress flat on the floor so she can't hide anything under it, and a wardrobe with no doors for the same reason. The point isn't even that the Binders want to monitor their
fleshbound; the point is to humiliate by removing all privacy.
Even the willing fleshbound have to know their place.

The indignity of having no privacy was what first tempted
Kin to run away, even though leaving the homepalace without
permission meant crossing a barrier that caused enough pain to
send even her to her knees. She, like Verias, has never been suc-
cessful at making a true escape, but she still leaves frequently, in
part to have the freedom of wandering Sestera, in part to show

177

them that she can. She's strong enough.

It's a lie. It makes her seem tough and mean to taunt the Binders from beyond their walls, but there's only so much she can bear, and with her flesh cruelly flayed by magic, that limit is near. She can neither sit nor lie down to rest. She has no choice but to stand in her cell and wait for Verias. He's likely in the Dean's study, hopefully pleading for her use rather than the mercy that will never come.

"So you're back, are you?" Merit appears in the empty doorframe. Their posture is loose, leaning against the jamb, but their face is taut as they look Kin up and down. She can't be a pretty sight after being sent back to her cell naked and bloody. She isn't even sure how long she's been there. It may been moments or hours. Pain twists time.

"Seems so," Kin says.

"Get tired of running?"

She shakes her head. How to tell them her plan when the Binders are surely listening?

"You missed all sorts of things. The Binders are ass over tits because of some Carrier who wants to join up," Merit says.

"I don't care about any Binders except the Steward."

"And Lessa," Merit says. "She hates your guts."

"I hate her, too." Kin feels her face draw into a venomous scowl. She isn't shy about saying that in front of Lessa. Lessa knows better than anyone else.

"They Bound a new one yesterday. They're getting better at recruiting. Only a matter of time before they kill the ones who don't want to serve. You'd better be careful." Merit turns away.

"Merit?"

"Yes?" They turn back.

"How do you do it? How do you bear waiting?" Kin asked, praying to all the stars that they understand her meaning: they need to talk. They stare at her, long and hard.

"By minding my business. You should try it some time." Merit walks away, their footsteps making not a single sound on the hard stone floor.

Other heels tap along the corridor in the opposite direction. The Steward. She always wears boots with hard wooden heels to match her icy expression, and Kin would know and loathe her step anywhere. She appears in the doorway, scrutinizing Kin as usual. And as usual, Kin very much wants to punch her smug, judgmental face right off. It's a good thing for her that the enchantments will flatten Kin to the ground if she tries anything. Is that why she never could injure Reshon? Or is it something else?

"The Dean wants you," says the Steward. "Come."

A shiver of fear skitters up Kin's spine. For the Steward herself to collect Kin, either the Dean has more punishment in mind, or Verias has succeeded in his mission to convince the Binders that she can be of use to his. She believes in Verias or she'd never have let him come to the homepalace, but belief can only stretch so far before practicality takes its place to protect her from disappointment.

"What are you waiting for?" the Steward snaps.

"My clothes—"

"Have been burned. They were shabby, disintegrating. Perhaps you should have spent your stipend on that instead of whatever it is you do out there when you leave without permission. Now come." The Steward has a wad of fabric in one hand, but instead of giving it to Kin, she turns on her heel, clacking up the corridor. Kin has no choice but to follow if she doesn't want to be punished further.

The Steward leads Kin to the Dean's Hall, where fleshbound aren't allowed. The horrible woman's back is even more rigid than usual, as if this breach of the rules physically pains her. Kin hopes it does, because misery loves company, and Kin is miserable enough for a homepalace's worth of new friends. Anger is what makes her stand straight as she's led into the Dean's office, and it burns even brighter as she takes in his study. Kin is a thief. She knows the value of the rugs, the silver winecup at his elbow. She can tell by looking that the Dean's robe is worth more than Kin's stipend for the past five years, when the man won't even provide her clothing or weapons or even feed for Shadow to travel all over the country to carry out his will.

The only thing that can make Kin more furious than standing in this room is Lessa, who lurks at the Dean's elbow with her hands behind her back. Verias sits to one side, reading a thin, ancient book that Kin has seen him with before. He looks completely at ease, and for a moment, Kin's stomach tumbles over and over. He's turned on her. They've made him believe that what they were doing is right, otherwise Lessa wouldn't look so smug.

No. Lessa is always smug. She was probably born with that expression. They haven't turned Verias against her or she'd be dead already. Verias is only pretending. He has to be.

"Pitiful," the Dean says. Kin bites her tongue, a hot, fresh swell of fury bearing her pride up with it. Verias looks up at last.

"She's angry," he says flatly. They'll read his calm as the same calm with which one might assess a horse, but Kin has spent enough time with him to know that he's terrified. Her only desire in that moment isn't her soul, but to cross to him and comfort him, but she stays still. "Spirited."

"A liability," Lessa says. Kin doesn't look at her. If she does, she'll leap at the little beast and end up splattered all over the Dean's study. Funny as the mess would be, she can neither leave Verias alone and vulnerable, nor waste time in the oblivion between bodies.

"Frankly, I think Everis's idea is a good one," says the Dean.

"It's unlikely to work the way you plan, Everis, but if you should accidentally kill her in the process, it will certainly make things easier for everyone, including her."

"It's foolishness," says the Steward. She stands to Kin's right and just behind her, not bothered by the hot reek of the blood that's crusting over on the backs of Kin's legs. "Nothing will come of it."

"I think the fleshbound are more human than we give them credit for," Lessa says, without a hint of kindness. "Otherwise how would they be so hard to break? An animal would obey, but she only becomes more feral."

"A fair point, Lessa. Very fair." The Dean presses a handkerchief to his nose, clearly disgusted by Kin's state. Kin wonders how she could make herself more disgusting and not get in worse trouble. Pissing on the rug would be amusing, but get her nowhere. "I'll allow this testing."

"Dean, if I may, it might be best to remove my safeguard before I begin this work," Verias says. "Even if she remains human enough to be linked, it's possible that it will harm her irreparably. If I'm safeguarded, it could be enough to kill me in return."

"We cannot remove the safeguard until you make the Promise," says Lessa. "Are you prepared to do that?"

"I came to Sestera to become a Binder. I am prepared."

"He saw a Binding and came back," the Steward says. Verias must have impressed her, because the woman is skeptical about everything, perhaps her fellow Binders most of all. "That's good enough for me to go ahead with the Promise."

"Agreed," says the Dean. "Everis, please place both hands over your heart, and know that should you break these promises, you will be expelled from the Binders and unwelcome in this homepalace. Under some circumstances, additional punishment may be meted out."

"I understand."

181

Verias balances his open book on one knee to place both hands over his heart. For the space of a breath, the rush of emotion that overwhelms Kin is enough to make her think he's doing magic. She struggles to get hold of herself, first through a tide of jealousy that Binders are seeing Verias as she likes seeing him best: buried in a book with that little frown of concentration, only half in this world. Then comes the fear. Though he's worked so hard for this, though there's no other way she knows of to get her soul back, Kin wants to scream at him not to listen, not to swear to them. The second he makes their oath, they'll want to keep him just as much as they want to keep their fleshbound.

"I, Everis of Solemn Gorge," he says. "Do promise that I shall serve the Binders with my full heart, to create and maintain fleshbound as I am asked, to defend the souls we hold precious with my life, and to my study to the betterment of my order until my dying day."

"And he even memorized the Promise," Lessa says with delight.

"Excellent. Now if you don't mind, Steward . . ." The Dean makes a small gesture at Kin. Too important to get his hands dirty, he's unaccustomed to seeing the aftermath of a punishment.

"May I examine her before she's returned below?" Verias asks, churning fear up inside Kin's stomach again. He shouldn't avoid the cellar. They'll suspect that he's afraid. "The Binding gave me an understanding of the conscience enchantments, but I think it best to probe her in particular, to ensure that I know exactly what I'm dealing with. A little water to clean her up wouldn't go amiss, either. I wouldn't want to get blood on the books from the library."

"Do as he says." The Dean waves a dismissive hand, clearly wanting nothing more than to be rid of Kin.

When Verias stands, the Steward gives him the handful of cloth she withheld from Kin, again denying her the dignity of deciding whether she'll go naked or dress. Lessa leads Verias and Kin to another room, small, and from the view of the Deep Quarter out the window, situated above the library. Beneath the window, a broad work table takes up that half of the room, two chairs pushed up to it.

"I'll speak with the doctors about your safeguard right away. Ring if you need anything." Lessa gestures to the bell cord hanging next to the door. Kin has always suspected that the Binders have servants to cater to their whims, but she's never seen one. "And you." Lessa turns to Kin. "If you disobey him, I'll punish you twice as badly as if you disobeyed me, do you hear me? I won't have you ruining him for the Binders because you think it's funny to make him punish you."

"Let him experiment on you if you like him so much," Kin says.Lessa's response is to slap her. Everything else hurts enough that Lessa's open palm feels almost good in comparison, and Kin can't muster a single grain more anger, anyway. The horrible woman inclines her head to Verias, who gives her a nod in return, and leaves, closing the door behind her.

When Verias's eyes meets Kin's, they're brimming with tears. "Why did you do this?" He puts his hands on her shoulders, squeezing hard, as much of a hug as he dares with her injuries.

"The safeguard. I thought you'd put it together."

"I suspected, but . . . Kin, why didn't you say something? I was so worried. I thought Lessa would kill you," Verias says.

"I'm fleshbound." Kin tries to embrace him. He takes a half step back, running into the table behind him.

"You're hurt." He's interrupted by a servant with a basin, ewer and towels. Verias pauses to pour warm water for Kin, his back turned. "Is there any way I can heal you without them knowing?"

"They're already closing up." Kin puts a hand on his shoulder, and he turns to her.

"Turn round. I'll clean you up."

Kin stiffens. She doesn't need him to take care of her. She hasn't needed that from anyone since she was a child, since the last time the plague came and she was deathly ill. But Verias's sad, deep-set eyes soften her stubbornness. She obeys, the fading pain of her wounds coming back into sharp relief with the touch of a wet cloth and warm water. Kin refuses to show him that it hurts, can't bear the thought of Verias thinking he's responsible for her pain.

"Thank the Wellspring you heal so fast." His voice is choked. A trickle of water runs down her back, slides over her ass and down the back of her left leg, settles in the back of her knee. There's a soft splash of water behind her as he wets his towel again.

"It's nothing."

Verias makes a small sound in the back of his throat, as if doubting her. He says nothing more, simply works his way down her back, moving from flayed flesh to unmarred skin without pause. Gentle hands and warm water make Kin's muscles loosen in a way she hasn't experienced in months. Perhaps years. Somehow, even here in the Binders' stronghold, he makes her feel peaceful for an instant, before his washrag moves lower and Kin's breath snags in her chest. He's always so careful with her that the touch is completely unexpected, almost shocking. Verias pauses.

"I'm sorry. I should have asked."

"Don't stop."

He doesn't.

Verias wipes away all the gore, blotting her damp skin with a dry towel. The sting has mostly faded, and what remains is soothed away by the warm sensation of being cared for. He places a towel around Kin's shoulders and puts his arms around her in a hug that's too short and too gentle. When she turns to him, Verias holds out the plain brown smock left by the Steward. His face is exhausted.

Kin pulls the itchy garment over her head and reaches for his shoulders, but with his thick doublet, Kin couldn't feed her life energy into him. Instead, she takes Verias's hands to hold in hers. He smiles at her, but it's tinged with even more melancholy than usual.

"I'm sorry to make you go so long without me," Kin says.

"I'll survive. Like I said, magic can sustain me for a while. And I'll be here every day until we succeed. I promise."

Affection swells in her so strong Kin feels like she might burst. It's been years since Kin has wanted to see someone every day, just to reassure herself that they still care about her, that they're still breathing. She pulls Verias close, resting her cheek against his forehead, and his arms go around her middle. Kin loves how they fit together, the way he tucks perfectly under her chin and his arms rest just so against her hips. His fingers bunch up in her smock.

Kin wants Verias so much that it aches inside her, right next to the hollow place her soul should occupy. She wants to hike up her hideous smock and pull him inside her, fill up one of the howling voids within, scream out her anger and frustration. It's too much, all of her senses honed in on him as strong as the Binder's mark. Kin pulls away, turning her back to him. Two hands against the door, bracing her, keeping her grounded in the real world.

"I didn't mean to hurt you." Verias's fingers brush her shoulder.

"You didn't." Fighting the urge to return his touch is harder than keeping her calm in the Dean's office. "I'm not used to having someone care for me as fiercely as you do."

"I understand. I'm not used to someone who cares for me the way I am."

Verias's hand falls away. Kin turns to meet his mournful dark eyes, and for the first time wonders if he feels the change between them too. As soon as the question enters Kin's mind, his fingers move to the back of her neck, drawing her nearer. She lets her eyes slide shut, lets her desire take her where it will.

A hard rap comes at the door, and Verias breaks away. Kin keeps her back to the him and to Lessa, knowing the Binder will see how vulnerable she is and weaponize it against her, or worse, against Verias. Lessa whispers something to Verias.

"Find your way back to your cell," she says for Kin's ears. Lessa and Verias leave the room, and Kin follows them into the corridor, watching them walk away from her. She wants so desperately to go with Verias that she actually takes two steps after them before she remembers herself, and slinks back to the dungeons to rest.

CHAPTER TWENTY-FOUR

VERIAS'S STOMACH FEELS FULL OF STONES, OR PERHAPS smooth marbles, constantly rolling around and making him queasy. Safeguarding is a closely protected secret of the Carriers, and breaking a safeguard is rarely done. The way the Dean spoke of Carriers, it's likely that no Binder has broken one in years.

Kin might be an imaginary test subject, but Verias is about to become a real one. It doesn't seem likely that he'll die, but if the Binders somehow strengthen the safeguard or mangle his connection to the Wellspring, what will he do? What will Kin do? He has to fight the need to look over his shoulder as he walks away from her, wishing he'd had the courage to kiss her when he had the chance. There's nothing he can do now but accept his fate.

He takes a firm hold on himself as he follows hateful little Lessa through the corridors of the homepalace, telling himself that if something happens, at least he'll lose his power in service of something good. Better yet, he'll be useless to Reshon, unable to be stuffed in a war machine to crush people beneath a power torn from his control. Of course, it would also make him useless to Kin. That thought makes him less terrified, but more anxious, if there's a difference to be found in such circumstances. It doesn't matter to his hands, which itch to pick at his skin, and he doesn't dare touch his face. If he does, the floodgates will open and he won't be able to stop, perhaps until his nails scrape bare bone.

Lessa wordlessly leads Verias to a room in the south hall that's completely opposite the torture chamber where the Binders' victims are Bound. Though small, it's airy and bright, with whitewashed stone walls and a featherbed pushed against one wall. Verias walks to the little window, trying to seem unbothered, and sees a courtyard he recognizes: the place where the Binders made that red-haired fleshbound snap a dove's neck to test their enchantments. Kin is now below him somewhere, her presence still and silent in the cells hidden below the home-palace's beautiful exterior.

"This is the infirmary," Lessa says. "The doctors have told me that removing the safeguard can be difficult, and they expect that you'll need a few days to recuperate before you can attempt to link with the fleshbound."

"I would have preferred to have more time with her. The conscience spells felt . . . odd," Verias lies. He hadn't probed the enchantments one bit, too busy thinking about how much he wants Kin. How much he wants to protect her, how little he can do. Having seen her dreams seems like a blessing now that he needs to act like he knows anything.

"You're right to say so. She had a hard conscience to break. Everything about her is hard to break." Her voice grates ever so slightly.

"She may well be easier to control when she's linked to me," Verias says.

"Or more difficult, if she resents the connection."

"I suppose we shall have to see."

"Here are the doctors," says Lessa. "Excuse me."

The three doctors have a bedside manner that leaves even more to be desired than Kin's. By the familiar, grimy feel of their magic, they're Binders, not Healers. There's always overlap between magical disciplines—Reapers need to know how to heal on the battlefield, for example, and Binding clearly shares traits with linking—but Verias never suspected until now that the Binders had their own doctors. It makes sense, though, knowing how jealously they guard their secrets. It also makes sense that they don't explain the procedure before they instruct Verias to drink from a cup of wine. It contains some bitter medicine that makes him cough.

"For the pain," says a man with grey-flecked brown hair and piercing green eyes. "Finish it and lie down."

Verias obeys, his anxious stomach rebelling against the acrid potion so strongly that it's a struggle not to gag. The doctors shift impatiently from foot to foot while Verias stops to take off his boots before he lies down—he wasn't born in a barn—and the room starts to swirl around him by the time they're off. He's asleep the moment his head touches the pillow.

He dreams himself home to the rolling hills that turn into mountains to the west. More than once, Verias has climbed the side of the nearest mountain, the Blacktooth, to look down at Solemn Gorge when the trees have lost their leaves to bare the long, rocky gash in the earth. His father's house nestles against the base of a foothill, its back pressed into the earth as if it's trying to hide.

There, in a windowless underground room, Verias once studied and tested spells from the old books that his mother found in her travels. The light of a few ancient silver lamps lit his desk, filling the space with the smell of olive oil fragranced with bitter orange.

Though the workroom has no fireplace in life, in Verias's dream a hearth blazes near his desk. His skin is tight and uncomfortable, and when he looks into the flames, they're too bright, sharp enough to cut. Verias stands from his chair to start the process of putting out the fire, but when he reaches for the poker, a hand closes around his. When he looks up, it's into Lusian's dark eyes.

"You're dead," Verias blurts. Lusian takes the poker from his hand. He hefts it like a weapon, reminding Verias of Kin testing the balance of a knife.

"So are you." Lusian wheels back and slams the sharp end of the poker into Verias's chest. He staggers back, his body and brain numb with shock. "Father won't forgive you."

And with that, he turns and folds himself into the smoky air. He's gone.

Verias's chest begins to crumble around the poker, shards of flesh vanishing into worn carpet. He's on his knees, picking up pieces, putting them back inside.

"This pain is temporary," a familiar voice says. Verias looks to his right, hands still full of bits, to see Kin watching him from her knees. They're in the entry hall of the homepalace. "All pain is temporary, because life is temporary." Tears of blood begin to sheet down her cheeks, and Kin is on fire, tongues of orange flame licking at him from her sizzling skin and ruined clothing. *"Are you not a sorcerer?"* Her shout turns to a high, agonized keen at the last, as she collapses, a column of searing-hot ash covering Verias from head to foot. It fills his mouth, his nose, his eyes, blots out the room.

Kin's face swims in the darkness, whispering something inaudible, sometimes smiling and laughing, others crying or bloody or worse. The faces coalesce as Kin's voice grows louder.

"Use it. Show them. Show them all."

Power floods the hole in Verias's chest, charring his insides as his flesh is mortified by Kin's searing ashes. He's left the shelter of darkness for the fury of dazzling daylight, and all he wants in the world is to go back to his little hole in Solemn Gorge to hide. His chest aches, his skin burns, and when the struggle to open his eyes is finally over, Kin stands over him in a halo of raging orange light. He sucks in a breath to tell her how glad he is to see her, and it sets him off coughing.

When Verias regains his breath, Kin and her light are gone. His infirmary room is dark save for a single candle, and a doctor stands over him, her hand on his chest. Though there's magic all around him, he can't see it, the afterimage of Kin's form blazing purple before his eyes.

"I can prepare another sleeping draught, if the pain is too bad," the doctor says, her voice as distant as if it were on the other side of the homepalace.

"It's not." The burn in his flesh has dulled to a furious tingle, like his whole body is being pricked by pins and needles, but it's bearable.

"Call if you need anything. Try to rest." She leaves the room, the flicker of her candle vanishing behind the closed door.

A hand closes around Verias's, and when he looks up, Kin is there again.

"How did you find me? There are a thousand rooms in this place," Verias whispers.

"I followed your magic," Kin says. "I could feel it break free. Like the whole palace was underwater. Like drowning."

"I thought you were on fire, you were glowing so bright," Verias says. "My dreams . . ." His head begins to swim, the room blurring around him.

"Shh." Kin sits on the edge of the bed, reaching for his hand. Her touch is no longer warming but a hot iron against his skin, filling him with power that threatens to wrench itself out of his control. "Shh. Breathe."

Kin brushes the hair from Verias's forehead, the touch half agony and half giddy joy that leaves him craving more despite how dangerous it feels.

"Will you stay with me for a while?" he asks.

"As long as you like."

Verias has never heard Kin sound so gentle. She curls around him, combing strong fingers through his hair. Nobody in this place is what they seem; Kin's defiance melts for him, and Lessa's mask falls away to hurt the person Verias cares for most. What inner face will the homepalace reveal for Verias? His cowardice? His pathetic desire to impress Kin, to show her what he's worth?

He rolls onto his side, burying his face in the curve of Kin's throat as if he can hide there forever. She rests her cheek against his forehead, warm against his sweaty, clammy skin. He drifts for a time, too tired to stay awake for long. The dream of Kin burning returns over and over, until he can smell smoke in the waking world, see her aura of searing light again.

"Shh. You have to be quiet or the doctors will come back," Kin whispers, her breath against his ear sending a down his spine.

"I was dreaming. You're so bright. So beautiful." Verias looks up at her, touches her cheek. She's silent for a time, avoiding his eye, before she looks at him again.

"Verias?"

"Yes?"

"Do you need me the way I need you?" Kin asks. There's such naked desire in her eyes that Verias can barely see the otherworldly glow that emanates from her very skin.

"Yes," he whispers.

Kin's lips seek his, at once gentle and hungry. The anxious part of Verias's brain is acutely aware of the bitter medicinal taste in his mouth, the sweat on his face, before it goes silent. He should have known that Kin, soft at heart, would kiss him so tenderly, but it surprises him anyway. His body is light as a feather, his head somewhere in the sky above, weighed down only by Kin's arms.

Verias's hands get lost in Kin's curly hair, her thick thigh draped over his, her hand lying at his throat. The only sounds are their breath, quickening, skin upon skin, the whisper of fabric. When the long, slow kisses end and Kin draws away, her fingers still rest against his pulse. He's acutely aware that she could end him then and there, if it's still possible for him to die, and he doesn't care. All he wants is her, any way he can have her.

"It's nearly dawn," Kin whispers. "I have to go."

"Will you come back tonight?" Verias asks.

"Will you be strong enough?" A wicked smile spreads across Kin's lovely face.

"For company, Kin," Verias says.

Kin kisses him again, this time a fierce, fast press of her open lips. A promise. She slips out of his bed and out of the room, not making a single sound. Verias lies awake, the sunrise creeping pink over his little whitewashed room, and misses her, though she can't be more than a thousand paces away. As he falls asleep, he can still feel her searing kiss upon his lips, drawing him back into burning dreams.

CHAPTER TWENTY-FIVE

AS DAWN BREAKS, KIN SLIPS OUT INTO THE STABLEYARD. There she can enter the kitchens, where preparations are already underway for breakfast. Even if she hadn't already greased every palm in the kitchen, everyone is too busy to pay attention to her as she ghosts past. She leaves through the entrance for food deliveries, passing through the barrier that's meant to keep her from leaving without permission. It's an interesting trick, nausea and stomach pain that hits her hard and grows worse with every step away from the homepalace and into the alleys of the Deep Quarter.

Kin is halfway to the Honey Quarter before the misery drops out from beneath her, leaving her light, free. Exhausted. She's only been back at the homepalace for a day, and it feels like years piled on her back. She's glad to be out, but what's important is to make sure the innkeeper sees her and doesn't think that she and Verias have abandoned the room, otherwise he'll sell Shadow and their things to settle their bill. She also needs to eat and sleep where the Binders won't notice her sudden need for human comforts. If she's punished for leaving, it's worth it to ensure that nobody suspects the connection between Kin and Verias.

But when Kin lies down in the bed they shared at the inn, she can't fall asleep. The bedclothes smell like Verias, bergamot soap and clean skin and paper. Her mind keeps returning to him, lying helpless in the infirmary, body wracked by magic that Kin can feel in her bones even now. Distant, true, but there, trembling, as his fingers did when they tangled in her hair close to the scalp, holding her fast despite their gentle touch. She goes over the memory of those stolen kisses dozens of times, heat rising inside her, until she's too exhausted to think and finally drifts off.

There's no peace in sleep. Kin dreams of Verias, is utterly tormented by his constant presence in her mind. She wakes to the sun blazing through the window, her senses full of his memory and the scent of him on her pillow. She can rest no longer, though Chestnut is in the crook of her elbow purring, and she can't bear the thought of moving him. It's late afternoon, and she's famished. She has to get up and see Verias

"Hurry up," a familiar voice says. Kin shrieks in surprise, scaring Chestnut so bad that he claws her arm up making his escape. There's a knife in her hand, pulled from beneath the pillow, but it's only Merit.

"Don't you have any respect for my privacy?" she asks.

"Not when you're taking forever to get up. Why are you sleeping, anyway?"

"That's not your business." Kin scrambles out of bed and takes off her smock. She throws it in Merit's face.

"Stars, where did you find this thing, under a saddle?" They toss it into a corner wearing an expression of disgust.

"Probably. The Steward gave it to me to save Verias's sensibilities." Kin surveys her wounds over her shoulder in the small washstand mirror. They've closed, and hurt far less than they did. "Lessa even let him give me a *bath*. She's trying to get her claws in him, I can tell."

"What? Like . . ." Merit's reflection helpfully inserts one finger into their other fist in a rude pantomime.

"Don't be disgusting. She told me not to ruin him for the

Binders. They want him as bad as I thought they would."

"Doesn't that scare you? What if they turn him against you?" Merit asks.

Kin covers her shudder by turning to wash her face and rinse her mouth in the stale water in the washbasin. She tried to push those thoughts from her mind in the Dean's study, but there's no escaping them with Merit there to ask questions. They always have questions, always want to theorize about the next steps before they make a move, which is well enough for them. Kin has no idea what to do, because she has no idea what she's doing. She doesn't even know what Verias is to her. They're friends, but they're also something else now. Maybe. It's been so long since Kin has felt such a connection to someone that it's hard to know.

What if Verias does turn on her? Kin is an expert at driving people away. Her mother, who never approved of her choice to join her father. Iyara, who never approved of her choice to join the fleshbound. Merit, who disagreed so strongly with her life-or-death choice to kill Iyara that they've physically fought on more than one occasion. What disastrous decision will be the one to make Verias hate her?

Regret and more than a little guilt wells up inside Kin, and she clutches her towel in her hand so tightly that her fingers ache. She slams the towel down on the washstand.

"Not now, you stupid cunt," Kin tells herself in the mirror. "You don't have time for this."

"Put on some clothes, you maniac. We have plans to make," Merit says.

Kin's ears are hot, but she dresses. She's even less willing to dwell on embarrassment than she is to feel sorry for herself. She marches out of the room—*of course* Merit picked the lock instead of just knocking—and to the tavern down the street for something to eat. Merit watches her as she shovels in her food, not caring about the taste. Not caring about anything, really. Caring about things does nothing but make her feel worse.

"You've gotten even stranger," they say at last. "Are you sure you're up to this?"

"Of course I am. I'm just worried. Same jitters as you get before any big job," Kin says. It's only half a lie—she *is* worried about their final push to get back their souls—she's just worried about Verias, too. Merit gives her a crooked smile.

"You were *impossible*." Their voice drops low. "Remember that time you ran off before we went to Lovrain for the Hands? I thought we'd never find you."

"I didn't *run off*, I was finding brandy for the journey," Kin grumbles.

After being—rightfully—horrible to her for over a decade, now they're going to start making jokes and reminiscing about the past? She wants to feel less guilty, not more.

"I'm aware. How could I have missed it? You vomited on my nice boots after one little tot because of the waves," Merit says.

"Don't remind me." The memory unsettles Kin's meal.

"I'll remind you as much as I want if you don't pull yourself together. What's your plan?"

Kin doesn't want to admit that her plan has been vague from the start. Once, she'd been considered a genius at working through the problems of thieving, but now her mind just skips over all of the details. She doesn't *want* to think through solutions because it means she has to face down so many horrible memories to do it. Before her link with Verias, it was only the pain of loss keeping her from facing down the most difficult problems of the process. Now there's guilt, too, cold and shuddering and trying to tear her apart.

"Verias would be allowed in the Vault if he binds someone, but I can't ask him to do that. I've seen how he reacted to just witnessing a Binding," Kin whispers. Her eyes sting with tears and her throat is tight as a sailor's knot. "The guilt would shatter him."

"Oh, no. Oh, Kin. You're in love with the poor fellow."

"*Shut up.*" Kin glances around the tavern to make sure nobody can hear them talking about breaking into the Vault. The tavern has grown busier as people finish the day's work, and the noise is steadily increasing. Nobody can hear. "He might be able to get in if he tells them that he needs my soul in hand to link with me," Kin says. "But that leaves yours out."

"He can't steal mine while he's inside?" Merit asks.

"There's no way to know until he scopes it out. It's not like either of us have seen inside, but I feel like they'd keep better track of souls than that," Kin says.

"Likely."

"I think it would take a diversion. And it would have to be *quite* a diversion," says Kin.

Merit's smile is more sincere than the last one. They love to cause a scene, and they're excellent at it, fading into the background exactly when necessary. A familiar rush of excitement fills Kin's head, washing away her guilt for a few moments; it's almost like old times.

"Well, we're known to hate each other," Merit says. Unnecessarily. "A good fight nearby could do the trick."

"True, but that doesn't allow for a dry run, does it? It's too likely that someone would notice that a fight between the two of us has happened twice while Verias was in the Vault," Kin says.

"Then the practice will need to be only for him. He can ask to see the Vault, find where my soul is, and then the next time he can grab it."

"Do you trust him to do that?" Kin asks.

"You do."

"So? Since when do you trust me?"

"I don't trust that you won't betray me like you did Iyara. I *do* trust that you would never allow yourself to be betrayed," Merit says. There's no accusation in their voice, but it still makes Kin's simmering guilt boil over. She tries to say something rude, to play it off as a joke, but it's too much.

"I'm sorry, Merit. I'm so sorry." Tears sheet down her cheeks. "I loved her like a sister, but I was afraid. The things they said they would do . . ."

The memory is sharp, as unwelcome as a nail in her foot or a knife in her guts. Lessa, standing over her, calmly telling her about her mother's home in the countryside. Every detail, every crumb of brick and mortar. Lessa outlining her mother's daily routine, explaining how vulnerable she was when she walked alone looking for herbs. Fury bubbling up as she strained against her bonds. The whip crack of magic like a switch striking Kin's back as punishment.

"Please restrain yourself," Lessa said, her voice toneless. "You have already been troublesome, and if you remain so, there's no telling what will happen to your mother before she's snuffed out. There's no telling what will happen to your friend." Lessa's hand settled on the crown of Iyara's head, smoothing ratty golden hair. "There's no telling what might happen to your precious Honey Quarter on a dry summer day. All that thatch . . . it would be a shame for all those people to suffer because of you."

Iyara's face was dirty that day after her month in a dungeon. Tears cut streaks through the filth, and her eyes remained locked on Kin's as Kin debated with herself. She didn't look away when Kin's hands went to her throat, found the soft places that would make her lose consciousness before she felt any pain. The light left Iyara's eyes before they slid shut, just as if she were falling asleep on one of those giggly nights sharing a bed as girls.

Kin held tight until she no longer felt Iyara's pulse, and then a little bit longer to be sure. She'd been empty that day, only able to feel a hollow relief, knowing that at least Iyara would suffer no more. Who knew what tortures the Binders could imagine for her?

"They would have hurt my mother. They would have hurt Iyara. They would have burned the Honey Quarter. I had to stop it." Kin tried to find some of the surety she'd felt that day, but it's gone. Perhaps it had never been there at all, and she'd been so distraught that she imagined it. Or, more likely, Kin spent so many years being sure that stealing and giving away the profits was right, being sure that breaking the law and occasionally hurting people for the greater good was a decision that she alone could make, that being responsible for something truly terrible had shattered her.

She's so surprised when Merit touches her hand that she can't suppress a flinch. Their fingers are callused just like hers, worn down by knives and soft bare throats.

"Are you sure you want this?" Kin asks. "I don't feel the guilt all the time. I don't understand how the link works. But it hurts, Merit. I wouldn't wish it on anyone, not even Lessa."

"I'm sure," Merit says. "Are you?"

"I'm going to destroy it, Merit. I don't want these feelings."

"You don't know if that will even help with the guilt," Merit says. "It might outright kill you, and if you really do love Verias, it would be cruel of you to hurt him like that."

"Shut up," Kin says again. The words crack and break on her tongue.

CHAPTER TWENTY-SIX

IT TAKES TWO LONG DAYS OF BED REST FOR VERIAS TO FEEL anything like himself. Kin visits him the first night, hollow-eyed and subdued, to explain the plan she's made with Merit. She's plagued by something unspoken, and she doesn't kiss him again. She instead perches stiffly on the corner of his sickbed, allowing him to hold her hand, but her fingers are like a doll's. It's as if Verias's touch numbs Kin as much as hers flames his every sensation to life. The second night she doesn't visit at all, and Verias's bright-burning dreams are haunted by her shadow.

When at last the doctors allow Verias to rise from his bed, he's restless. There's too much magic and pent-up energy inside him, and he walks to the inn against the doctors' advice. He'd never want to sleep in a feather bed in the homepalace when he can be in the Honey Quarter with Kin instead. He'd rather be anywhere, honestly, except in one of Lord Felver's miserable war machines.

Verias expects to find Kin waiting there for him, but he washes, dresses, and eats alone, wondering what's gone wrong. There was such passion in her lips, her surprisingly tender touch, and now she's gone as cold as she was when they met. Verias wants her more fiercely than he could have imagined on that chill night, and it frightens him. He hasn't been acting like himself, hasn't been thinking things through, and he's liable to do worse if he isn't careful.

Verias can think of little else to do but read to distract him-self, going back over the books from the homepalace library he's already read. He finds as little on the second read as the first; it seems Lessa is right. Nobody thinks of fleshbound as human enough to link with, and thus there's not even theory on the subject. He's forced to give up and give in to the exhaustion that's still constantly at the edges of his consciousness, trying to drag him down. At least sleep comes more easily than he ex-pects, until he wakes in the middle of the night to a presence in the room. When Verias sits up, a tall figure is silhouetted by the vague light coming through the window.

"This is where you're staying?" Reshon's voice says. "Do you like having fleas?"

"There were more fleas in Felver's camp," Verias says. Reshon chuckles softly. "What do you want?"

"Your answer, of course. Did you forget about me? I'm hurt."

"I wish I could." The words come out before Verias can stop them: Kin is definitely a bad influence on him. If he keeps talk-ing like that he'll get himself killed. "I don't have an answer yet. I need more time."

Verias just wants Reshon to leave so he can sleep. If he's go-ing to try to steal Kin's soul, he has to be sharp, well-rested.

"You'll give me an answer now, or you'll die. I've been more than patient with you," Reshon says. He steps toward Verias's bedside, and perhaps because he knows he can never beat Ve-rias magic for magic, presses a blade against Verias's throat. Fear doesn't touch Verias, nor does the relief he remembers from the night Kin did came to kill him. Anger swells up in-stead, magic straining at its bonds. Reshon has pushed him around enough, hurt him enough, and taken far, far too much.

"And I have been exceedingly patient with you," Verias replies through his teeth. "I don't want to hurt you, Reshon. Leave me alone."

"You don't have the guts to do anything to me." Reshon's face is in shadow, but his voice is twisted by disgust.

Memories unfurl in Verias's brain: Reshon shoving him into the war machine, Reshon spitting, laughing at Verias's attempts to escape, Reshon's careless backhand sending Verias to the ground, the taste of blood in his mouth.

Power surges through Verias unbidden. Reshon hurtles up toward the ceiling, his knife tracing a hot line across Verias's throat. He slams into the rafters above, all of the air leaving his lungs in a choking grunt. Verias's heart suddenly wakes from its slumber, hammering against his sternum as it struggles to push so much magic through his body. His hands and feet are completely numb, and his head feels detached, drifting.

Giddiness races through him. With the safeguard gone, he can do anything he wants. He can heal his own wounds, slough off the last scabs of the burn he suffered on the journey to Sestera. He can hurt or kill Reshon if he cares to. He can make everything easy with the merest thought. He can make this deal with Reshon and leave Sestera with Kin and her soul. Reshon can't force him to do anything. Nobody can force him to do anything ever again.

Verias lets Reshon go, his heart slowing as soon as the magic passes out of him. The Binder falls to the floor with a thud and a loud groan. Someone in the room below shouts a curse.

"I'll take your deal, Reshon, but I'll take it because I say so, not because you held a knife at my throat."

Reshon gets to his feet, looking at Verias with an expression like a thunderhead. Verias knows that face; Reshon looked at him that way when Verias tried to destroy his war machine from within, swelling the wood and iron and steel until it was fit to pop, and Reshon stopped Verias by choking him half to death. The bruises lasted weeks, the nightmares months.

"Verias," a soft voice whispers.

Verias looks away from Reshon, from the fear in his ghost-white face. Kin stands in the open doorway, her face brightly lit by . . . Verias's hands glow bright, searing orange. They're two embers fashioned into shapes that only vaguely make sense to his magic-addled brain. Too many fingers, too few, none, heat and light.

"Your family might find you if you use too much." Kin's voice sounds as distant as Verias feels, but the words make sense. He lowers his hands into his lap, willing the lights to go out. Kin looks away from him. "I knew you'd be a problem," she says to Reshon.

With the light gone, Verias can only listen to the click of the door latch. Kin's feet are silent, but the warmth of her body is like a beacon as she passes Verias, shunting Reshon away from the bed. She's a lantern to a moth, a well to a man dying of thirst. The flame of a lamp jumps to life, but Kin doesn't spare a glance at Verias. Her full attention is on Reshon. Magic simmers inside the Binder, and Verias prays Kin won't do anything she can't take back.

Verias doesn't expect any less than the brutal kick Kin aims at Reshon's knees, knocking the Binder to the floor. She's thrown backward with equal force, striking the wall, but she's tougher than Reshon, and she keeps her feet. Kin rolls him over with the toe of her boot in his ribs, and he reaches for his knife, but he dropped it somewhere between the floor and the ceiling. Magic builds up around Reshon, doing something horrible to Kin's insides, scrambling them up like a deer unlucky enough to tumble down a mountainside scree. Before Verias can help her, Kin presses her foot against Reshon's throat, but doesn't bear down hard enough to set off the enchantments. With no reaction to his magic, Reshon struggles, his nails leaving long scrapes in the leather of her boots.

"Quit ruining my shoes. I'm not going to kill you." Kin eases the pressure against Reshon's neck. "Even if I could, if I wanted you dead, I would let Verias do it. He has every right to, the way you've dogged him ever since he bought his freedom."

"He didn't buy anything," Reshon chokes.

"Not from you. From me." Kin takes her foot off his throat, bending to drag him up by his collar. "Leave. Leave Sestera right now, and tell Lord Felver that if he sends anyone else—a soldier, an assassin, a fleshbound—I will find him and have his skin for a new saddle blanket. Tell him Kindred Jole is still in the business of thievery, but she steals lives now."

"I don't care about Felver, and he doesn't give a fuck about you." Reshon pulls away and wrenches open the door. "But I get what I want."

Kin slams the door behind him, and the downstairs person curses again, getting profanity from Kin in return. She turns to Verias, hands on her hips. Verias wants to tell her what he'd done, but the words won't come. He can only think of how he'll be punished for Kin's actions when Reshon takes him back to Lord Felver. Fresh anger wells up, a hot, bilious, unwelcome tide. If he's too cowardly to tell her what he's done, he has to accept the consequences.

"You need to be careful, Verias," Kin says. "I know what's happening to you right now. You've become so strong that everything feels easy. People seem like insects. You could pull their little legs off and watch them squirm. Feel nothing."

Hearing those words spoken aloud sends a shudder through Verias. If Kin had arrived a few moments later, he might have killed Reshon without a second thought. He chokes back acid.

"Kin" is all he can say.

"I'm only just starting to see humans as anything more than fragile objects again. And it's more than likely that I'll lose that and more once I've destroyed my soul. It's hard. Knowing you won't matter to me anymore."

"No." Something brittle shatters inside Verias. He sounds like a trained raven, grating out words the meaning of which he doesn't know.

"I won't do it until you get your life energy back at the Wellspring. I don't know what will happen to our link if my soul is just . . . gone. I suspect it won't be nice, and I wouldn't risk you dying like that. But it's likely that I won't be the same. It's likely I might seem even less human than I do now." Kin's voice is hoarse. The thought of losing her like that, watching her destroy herself so she can never be controlled again, makes Verias ill, fills him with dread and grief for something he hasn't yet experienced.

"I can't . . ." Verias has to clear his throat. It doesn't dislodge the lump that's trying to choke him. "I can't stop you from doing this. It wouldn't be right to try. But just . . . just know that no matter what, you're still my friend." He wants to scream at her how much he wants her, needs her, but he can't bring himself to say anything else.

"This link . . . this guilt . . ." Kin presses both hands to her chest. "I would bear it for you. If you asked."

Verias can never do that. He can never ask her to suffer for him. He has to get her soul back and destroy it. He shakes his head, and she lets out a shuddering breath that sounds painful.

"Go back to sleep," she says. Verias can't help but think that he gave the wrong answer. "We'll have to move inns at dawn and pray Reshon found you because of your magic and not because Merit led him here."

"Will that even matter? At this point I must be like a beacon for the homepalace. I won't be surprised if Lord Felver shows up down in the public room," Verias says. Kin opens her mouth to answer, but he cuts her off with a question before she can say anything. "Kin, wait. Why would Lord Felver know your name?"

"Because I stole from him, of course. Or tried to. It was the job that got me Bound." Kin sits down at the washstand, stretching her long legs out and crossing them at the ankle. For a moment, he doesn't speak, too surprised that she'd offer so much information.

"What happened?"

"I was looking to make a cartload of fathoms fast." She shrugs. "Someone needed help. Someone always needs help, you know? Anyway, Felver was in Sestera, head of the Security Council at the time. Naturally."

"Of course," Verias says.

"Now he has this brooch. Cloak pin. Whatever they call it when a very masculine and tough man who owns many swords wears a brooch," Kin goes on. Verias laughs. "Worth tens of thousands of fathoms. Enough money to keep every shopkeeper in the Honey Quarter secure as long as I could find someone to sell it to. It was meant to be the last time I stole anything. After a while, you pay someone else to do it for you. That's how you know you've made it.

"Anyhow, he's having a big ball at his house here in the city, so we get an invitation and get dressed up like fancy little nobles. I'm tipsy on imported mead. Not drunk, somehow, but I had enough in me that I wasn't about to be sick from nerves or drink. That's a fine line I've walked wrong a lot of times. I'm waiting for my chance to get into Felver's chambers and steal the thing, while Iyara keeps an eye on him. She was beautiful, you know? For years I was always falling in and out of love with her, but that just wasn't meant to be. Some friendships can't change that way.

"So this fancy fucking house is just filled to the brim with nobles and music and the most expensive things you've ever seen, and at first I'm thinking to myself that I just want to live like that. Have everything. It's not like I was raised on nothing. I had much more than most people in the Honey Quarter, but when you see how much these people have, you can't help but feel some envy."

Verias nods, watching her grave, beautiful face, the gray cast to her fleshbound skin warmed by the steady golden lamplight. He doesn't dare speak. If she needs to talk, he has to listen.

"I'm thinking about finding a nice noble to seduce, live a life of ease and stop risking my neck stealing. Lots of pretty ones. They're bred to be pretty. But then I start thinking of how I would feel if I were to marry one of these people for all those fathoms while others were still suffering, and well, that made me angry. And at this point Merit is creating a diversion for the guests, Iyara is regaling Felver with one of her stories, and I'm stalking the corridors on the way to Felver's chambers.

"I get there, and damned if there aren't two men in Felver's sitting room, taking sips off something in a crystal bottle, and I'm thinking I'm caught before I realize these two fellows are Felver's grown sons and they think *they're* caught. So now it's funny, they're half begging me not to tell their father, half trying to offer me some drink, half talking about how their father only cares about them when they do something bad. That's three halves, but you get the idea." Kin looks at Verias expectantly, and he nods. He never met Felver's sons, only seen them from afar, but he almost feels sympathy for them. Almost. "So I tell these two beautiful twits that I like trouble, and maybe we should hide something of his so he thinks it's stolen. Tee-hee, giggling and hijinks, and now the brooch is down my tits, I'm drunker than I thought, and everyone is getting carried away."

"Oh dear."

"Oh dear indeed. You don't need to hear the rest. You know what happened," Kin says. Her casual posture melts into despair. "I suppose that when you don't have to follow any laws, you don't really have to grow up until you're seven-and-twenty and something goes wrong inside you. Good thing I grew up before I met you or we might have been pretty well fucked," Kin says. Verias snorts.

"Sounds like it," he says.

"Oh, shut up and go back to sleep."

Verias obeys, but Kin's story has left him with far more questions than it answers. She never mentioned how the whole bedchamber scene had gotten Iyara and Merit in trouble. He hopes at least a little of it is true.

CHAPTER TWENTY-SEVEN

VERIAS IS EXHAUSTED BY MORNING. THE LAST FEW HOURS before dawn offer little rest, his body aching with tension and desire to draw from the Wellspring, and he's acutely aware of Kin's presence in the room, awake and watching. She says little, tired and hollow-eyed. Verias can't help but worry. On the way to the homepalace, he catches himself picking at his arms under his sleeves as he walks. Though can't risk the Binders noticing how anxious he is, feeling scabs come off cleanly under his nails makes some of the anxiety fall away for as long as it takes to find another one to dig at.

Lessa is waiting for him, always waiting. Always watching with those keen eyes. Verias almost thinks he sees something in them, some knowledge of his secret, but she greets him like nothing has changed.

"The Dean wishes me to show you the Vault of Souls today," she says once the usual pleasantries are done. "The doctors were quite upset that you insisted on leaving last night, and he doesn't want you overextending yourself by fooling about with fleshbound."

"Fair. He wouldn't want to lose his investment." Verias bites the inside of his lip to keep from picking. This is suspiciously convenient.

"Indeed. So the Vault it is. Come."

It doesn't surprise Verias that the Vault is on the top floor of the Dean's Hall. It makes sense that the Binders want to keep the souls as far from their owners as possible, and there's nowhere in the homepalace further from the cellars than this. If it were up to him, he'd keep them in a secure location away from the homepalace, perhaps, but nobody outside the small circle of the Binders talks about fleshbound wanting their souls back. Just like he once had, they live in ignorance of what happens within these pale stone walls, and the Binders surely don't want Sesterans to know that anything is amiss in the homepalace.

The door of the Vault appears to be made entirely of steel, no doubt constructed with magic. Verias can think of no other way to make anything five paces square out of metal, though it has no lock or key. It's held shut by enchantments, so many and so complex that the whole corridor is lit with magic. It scratches across his skin as they draw closer, and Lessa performs some enchantment so small and so fast that Verias nearly misses it. The door swings open, though everything around them remains layered with power. He'll either need to practice the spell or somehow compel Lessa to let him into the Vault. Ideally, he'll open it at night, with Kin at his side, and they'll escape as soon as the deed is done.

Verias feels the souls as soon as the heavy door is open. Torches, not lamps, light shelf after narrow shelf of glimmering orbs, each vibrating with an energy all its own. The inner surface of the door is lined with the telltale dull gray tarnish of lead, which explains why Verias didn't notice the souls the first time he walked into the homepalace. Each orb, too, is nestled into a small ring of the dark metal so it won't roll away.

Paper labels mark each orb with two names, presumably those of the fleshbound themself and the Binder who Bound them. There are many more spaces for souls than there are orbs themselves, and Verias comforts himself knowing that at least the Vault isn't filled.

"Beautiful, isn't it?" Lessa asks.

"Beautiful," Verias murmurs. He supposes the sight is pretty in the same way shelves of gold-plated and bejeweled human skins might be: visually stunning, but at the same time grotesque.

"We never touch them with our bare hands," Lessa says. "Such contact can leave traces of soul energy, which may make a Binder more sympathetic to their fleshbound."

"Would that be so wrong?" Verias asks. He's distracted, the feel of Kin's soul pulling him in as inexorably as iron filings to a lodestone. The light and heat that make him feel like his own soul is on fire is almost unbearable this close to her physical soul.

"In most cases, no. But troublesome fleshbound . . ." She trails off ominously.

"Lessa, can a Binder transfer ownership of a fleshbound?" Just saying the words makes Verias feel ill.

"Of course. What would we do when a Binder died if we had no way to pass control to someone else? Sometimes we trade. Speaking of troublesome fleshbound, I have often tried to trade Kindred Jole away to other Binders. With a few of my good ones to sweeten the deal, of course. None of them wanted her, so if you're thinking of taking her on, don't ask me to give her to you. You're too kind-hearted to handle a fleshbound like her right now. Perhaps in time your skin will thicken. Or perhaps this process will kill her, and she will be nobody's problem."

"Perhaps. Would I be allowed to borrow her soul if I need it for my work?" Verias asks. He walks along the shelves, trying to appear to survey the orbs without much interest. He doesn't want Lessa to notice how sick he is, the anger her words jar loose. How had he considered her a possible ally? He hates her with every fiber of his being.

"Of course. But I wouldn't recommend getting anywhere near her with it. She'll kill you if she sees a chance to steal it," Lessa warns.

"With the safeguard gone, she doesn't have much of a chance."

"I know. The whole homepalace felt your power expand. I've never been near an unguarded Carrier before. I don't think anyone here has, except maybe the Dean. You're valuable, Everis, which means you'd be a very good hostage for Jole. Remember that."

"I will." That explains why it was so easy for Reshon to find him. No point in moving inns at this juncture.

Verias's eyes fall on an opaque crystalline orb the color of carnelian. Below, the paper holds one name that Verias doesn't know, and one he does: *Merit Morthai*. It rests right next to a clear, lovely sapphire sphere with a single gold inclusion, off center. He doesn't need to read the label to know the names written there in fading blue ink. He can barely breathe. The desire to take Kin's soul and run as hard and fast as he can is almost irresistible, but Verias turns back to Lessa, instead.

"Here she is. What is the flaw in her soul?" Verias asks. "The little gold fleck, I mean."

"I don't know, but if I could drill it out I might have a full month of peace in my life. It would make her easier to control, I'm sure of it. Honestly, the best time I've had in ages was while she was off hiding after failing her assignment." Lessa says, and Verias has to suppress a vicious smile. She deserves all the trouble Kin is so expert at causing. "I do hope the link works. That might help just as much as getting rid of that flaw."

"It may well. Is she healed from her punishment?" Verias asks. Kin's soul buzzes at him from its place just above his left shoulder.

"She should be by now, but remember what I said about

overextending yourself. It wouldn't do to put yourself back on bed rest."

"That's true. Thank you, Lessa. Perhaps I'll return to my inn to rest."

"Perhaps. But you are a Binder now, Everis. You can live at the homepalace for convenience," Lessa says. "All your needs would be taken care of."

The thought of sleeping in the homepalace again makes Verias ill. Every night he spent in the infirmary was plagued by nightmares, and all he wants is to get one decent night of sleep. He mumbles some response, some excuse about not feeling well enough to see to bringing his things back. Lessa suggests the infirmary as she pulls the vault door closed, shutting out the shivering energy of dozens of souls. Verias would rather admit to everything and throw himself on Lessa's meager mercy than sleep in the infirmary again.

He begins to shamble back to the inn, thinking of how he misses An Honorable Rest. The inn isn't as bad as everyone seems to think it is, but Honor went out of her way to make Kin —and by extension, Verias—feel welcome. Verias understands the need. Kin pushes people away because she has as much fear in her heart as Verias does. She just shows it in a different way, and it's tempting to try to ease that fear in the likely vain hope of quelling her instinct to run.

When Verias finally enters the inn, his eyes are drawn to a familiar figure in the public room: Gavian. Instinct tears away the gossamer bonds holding back Verias's magic, allowing power to surge to the surface. The public room goes silent at the sudden wave of energy filling the space, and all of the patrons turn to look at him.

"Verias." Gavian stands. "I've come to talk to you. Just talk."

"I have nothing to say to you." Verias tamps his magic back down. Eyes linger on him for a few moments, watching for signs of sorcery. He holds himself in check, angry that he slipped enough to allow power to shake loose. He just wants to talk to Kin, tell her what he's learned, and Gavian is standing between them. Verias walks past him toward the stairs that lead to the room he shares with Kin.

"Wait!" Gavian hurries after him, catching his sleeve. "Your father—"

"If Father has anything to say to me, he can come here himself. Tell him I wish him luck dealing with Kin."

"I intended to bring Severin to you once I found you, but this is no place for a man of his stature," Gavian says, following Verias up the stairs. "It's no place for men of our stature either, if I'm honest."

"Then leave."

"It's important, Verias. We felt it. From leagues away, we felt you break free of the safeguard. This isn't right, what you're doing. It's dangerous."

"I'm doing what I have to do," Verias said. He made a deal, and what's more, he cares about Kin. He can't let her fend for herself with the Binders.

The door to their room opens before Verias can even reach for the handle. Kin must have sensed his flare of magic and sat in wait to hear his step in the corridor. Her lovely face is as tired as ever, if carefully blank in his uncle's presence. Her right hand is on the hilt of one of her daggers. Verias touches her elbow as he passes, trying to forestall any murders.

When Verias sits in the only chair—the stool before the washstand—Gavian has little choice but to stand. He won't sit on the bed without asking, and he's in no position to ask for anything. Kin stands just behind Gavian, not touching, but close enough that if he takes a deep breath, he'll feel her knife hilts in his back. Verias, Wellspring save him, suffers from a stab of jealousy at the thought. He'd been glad to see her last night, as he's glad to see her now, but Wellspring's waters, how he wishes she'd returned his touch.

"Verias, I recall telling your uncle that if I saw him again, I'd kill him whether I had your permission or not," Kin says. Gavian stiffens. "He seems to have forgotten."

"I just want to talk." Gavian's voice isn't as sure as it was. "As I said, performing magic without the safeguard is dangerous, Verias. Someone is going to get hurt, and it will likely be you."

"I told you—"

"Why do you care?" Kin asks, cutting Verias off. "He almost died being away from me, and I know he told you we were linked. He had to have."

"What—linked—"

"He didn't give me the chance," Verias says. "He refused to listen."

"How could this have happened? A fleshbound . . . Verias, that shouldn't be possible. She's a monster, not capable of—" Gavian stops mid-sentence again, perhaps thinking better of the words coming out of his mouth. Kin doesn't react, but Verias knows her well enough by now to see that she's holding back fury. It's in the set of her shoulders, the way her jaw cants ever so slightly to one side as she bites the inside of her lip. His own anger feels like a pot boiling over while hers is a house fire.

"I died." The words feel alien coming out of Verias's mouth, though he's been dead long enough to forget whether it's been days, weeks, or months. He touches the scar at his throat, watching his uncle's reaction. "The link saved me. Kin saved me."

Kin's face softens over Gavian's shoulder. Her mistakes haunt her, but he can see in her face that this thing, this one thing, is a precious good she's done. It feels cruel for Verias to mention it and not draw her in close and tell her that without her, he'd be lost.

"She saved me the night she was sent to kill me and had mercy on me," Verias says. "I know that carrying this amount of magic is dangerous, but I owe her." He can't say aloud that he loves her, that the only way she can be free to love him too is to steal her soul back. If only he could steal it from her, too, hide it away somewhere safe where nobody could ever find it.

"Verias, I need to talk to you alone," Gavian says.

"I trust Kin. You can say anything you want to in front of her. I'll only tell her later."

"Yes, but I'd rather be as far from her as possible when she hears it."

Kin's brown skin goes gray. Before Verias can stop her, she grabs Gavian's shoulder, her fingers digging in hard enough that he cries out in pain.

"You're the one who sent me to kill him," she says through her teeth.

"Not me," Gavian gasps. "His father."

"I don't like that bastard." Kin's expression could curdle milk.

"Please . . . you're hurting me," Gavian says. Kin lets go, and he rubs his shoulder with a noisy sigh of relief. Verias can't bring himself to feel bad about it after all the worry Gavian has put Kin through. "We just want you to come back. We won't make you go back to Felver. Just come back before you get hurt."

If Verias ever felt any temptation to go back, it's gone now. He always knew, felt it in his guts since the moment he met Kin, and he can't even find it in him to be angry. He's just tired and disappointed. Disappointed in his father for hiring the Binders, disappointed in Gavian for not stopping him, but most of all disappointed in himself. His father has shown time and again that he doesn't respect Verias, his power, his decisions, his life. And Verias hadn't believed Severin until he resorted to this.

"No." Verias says.

"But—"

"Why should I? I'll just end up serving some lord who wants to wreak as much evil on the world as Felver, or I'll sit at home hoarding spells like we've always done. Out here . . ." He glances at Kin. "Out here I have a chance to do good. Help the people who have been hurt by other magic users. There are dozens and dozens of fleshbound whose fate is to suffer, perhaps die, because of what has been done to them."

"You can't fix a broken mind," Gavian says.

"Broken is a hard word, Uncle." Verias's voice comes out harsh, shredded. He has to believe Kin can be saved.

"It's true, Verias. I can't be healed from this," Kin says. Her expression is unbearably sad.

"Perhaps not. But I can take some of the pain away. I know it."

Kin looks away, and Gavian shakes his head sadly.

"You're lost to reason. The safeguard exists for a purpose, and you know that, or you did. We won't bother you any further; there isn't any point. Goodbye, Verias." And with that, Verias's uncle leaves, the door closing behind him with a gentle click.

"You could have been free," Kin whispers. She doesn't look up at him.

"No. Even if they'd let me live my own life, I can't be free while you're a hostage to the Binders."

"I wish, just once, you'd put yourself first."

Verias stares at her, though she still doesn't meet his eyes. He'd been selfish, running away from his duty because he was too much of a coward to think of what it would do to his family. He almost ran away from his promise to Kin because the thought of setting foot in the homepalace made him sick. Over and over, fear had bested him until Kin convinced him to be braver than a garden slug. The only good thing he'd ever done was refuse when Kin said she'd bear all the pain of ending her Binding for him. Even he can't be that self-serving.

"I felt it," Kin says, surprising Verias out of his self-loathing thoughts. She still doesn't meet his eye. "When you were near my soul. I felt it. Will you do it?"

"What?"

"Will you destroy it for me? I want to feel that again before it's gone forever."

"Kin," Verias says. She looks up at him at last, and he extends a hand. For a few long moments, she looks at him warily, but she crosses to take his hand. Her touch is fire in his veins, but at the same time it's control. It strengthens the bonds around the magic that wants to break free. "Tell me what it felt like."

"Relief. Just like feeling you come to life again. Like when they took away the safeguard."

"But you said that felt like the homepalace was underwater."

"It was. Have you ever gone swimming in a very clear lake? One where the water is just cooler than your body?" Kin asks. Verias nodded. "It was like that. Peaceful."

Verias has to swallow hard to clear the huge lump that settles in his throat. When was the last time Kin had felt peaceful, if ever? That she had felt it because of him . . . he could weep over it. He wants to be able to give her that forever, because she makes him feel safe like he never has before. Like he could merely exist and be enough for her. He brushes a kiss against her knuckles, and she smiles down at him. Her mouth is taut, not quite relaxed, but it's a smile. He turns her hand over, kisses her palm, watches her expression, presses his lips to the tender skin of her wrist. Kin brushes a featherlight touch over Verias's jaw, betraying her hidden gentleness.

"Sometimes I see such softness in you," Verias whispers. Her smile is true this time. Radiant. "Sometimes I want to kiss you until you're soft the whole way through."

"We can't both be so yielding," Kin says. "Besides, you might like a little roughness if you try it."

Her hand slides across his throat until her thumb presses against the thin scar on the left side. The relief, the peace that rushes over him is an echo of the first night they met, blurred out by all that's happened between them. Kin can do anything she likes to him, not because death remains the least painful option, but because he trusts her. He needs her

"Why do you trust me like this?" Kin asks. "I don't deserve it. I told you to your face that I was afraid to touch you for fear I would hurt you."

"Are you afraid now?" Verias asks. Her grip tightens slightly.

"Yes." Kin's voice is steady, but her hand trembles against his throat. To see her scared and staring that fear in the face makes him love her even more fiercely.

"I'm not."

Kin looks away, but Verias has already seen the tears forming in her eyes. Her fingers slide down, catching in the half-buttoned neck of his doublet. She takes a few long breaths before she looks back at him, and when she does, she bends to kiss him, her lips parting for his tongue, her grip tightening on his doublet. The kiss ends too soon, and she lets him go breathless and flushed.

"I have to get back to the homepalace."

CHAPTER TWENTY-EIGHT

IF HER FIRST ROUND OF KISSES WITH VERIAS LEFT KIN shaken, the second is even worse. Kin flees to the Deep Quarter to avoid him, but doesn't go back to the homepalace. Instead she wanders as the day winds down into evening, in desperate need of time to think without the distraction of his presence, his voice, his touch. No amount of distance can excise him from her mind, the way he looked at her with those dark eyes like a little fawn too innocent to be afraid. The way he leaned into her hand at his throat instead of pulling away. Stars, she should have stayed with him. What is she doing, running off right after Verias learned his family tried to kill him?

"Fucking ridiculous question," Kin growls at her herself before she can stop herself. There are few passersby on this side of the Deep Quarter, where many of the warehouses are abandoned, and nobody heard her talking to herself. "You know the answer."

Even if she weren't alone, Kin doesn't want to say aloud that once her soul is destroyed, she won't be able to control the dark thoughts within. Fear rears up in her chest. She'd put her hand on his throat without thinking, driven by her desire and his eyes and his softness and his gentle soul and she could have killed him. Even as the thought forms in her head, she pictures herself throttling him, his eyes slipping shut as he goes limp in her arms. Kin's stomach heaves, but she can't remember her last meal. She can't go back to Verias that night. She's on crumbling ground, and if she returns to their room, she'll hurt more than his feelings.

Kin misses Chestnut. He's probably back at the inn, purring in Verias's arms, and she doesn't know which of them she envies more. Stars, to be a cat instead of a fleshbound, to kill mice and feel no guilt, to nap in a little square of sunshine cast by a window instead of being watched, always watched by the moon. It hangs waxing above Sestera as she wanders, the judgmental cosmic eye of a parent disappointed that she lied to Verias rather than admitting that she'd let some rich boy get the better of her and run to tell his father.

She has to tell Verias the truth. Kin has done very few good things since becoming a fleshbound. She spared Verias, somehow got close enough to him to anchor him in this world instead of letting him spiral out, but she also lied to him, and when she didn't, withheld all she could. Maybe if she can do another good thing, it'll cancel out the thoughts she can't banish from her head.

The idea is enough to calm Kin long enough to catch her breath. Her throat hurts and her chest is tight, but she's enough in control to scout places to regroup after they've completed their mission. Once she meets with Merit to make sure they're ready, everything is in place. She just needs to talk to Verias and pack her things.

The sun is coming up earlier and earlier as midsummer creeps up on Sestera, and the gulls are arguing about this and that in a bright blue sky. Shouts come from the merchant docks as riverboats that arrived the night before are unloaded. Kin pauses on the broad bridge that crosses the slow-moving Embraile, watching boats get underway and sail toward the sea. Some will be on the way to Abseris, and Kin can't help but wonder how different her life would be if her father had stayed there. Perhaps she wouldn't have existed.

Kin feels a desperate pull toward Abseris, but for the time being, it's out of the question. That's the first place the Binders will look, if they seek to bring her back. She plans to go further west and north, to the chilly white stone islands of Lubria for a few weeks or months, and then reassess and move on. She just has to carry on to the Honey Quarter and ask Verias if that suits him, provided he accepts her apology for lying.

She recites her planned apology a few times in her head, but the words crumble when she crosses the bridge to the Honey Gate. The massive brick arch, with its close-barred wrought iron gate, is closed, city guards standing at attention before them. Raised voices can be heard on the other side, and Kin pauses to watch and listen. It's all cross-talk, and she can't understand any of it.

"What's this?" she asks one of the guards.

"Sanitary cordon," the woman says. "Red rose plague."

"The whole quarter?" Even during the plague that killed half the Honey Quarter during Kin's childhood, there was never such a quarantine. There were rumors, but the disease had run its course before the Sanitary Council came to a decision. According to Kin's mother, they'd feared riots, and it looks like they have at least half of one right now on the other side of the Honey Gate. Last night's panic surges up again, making Kin's hands tingle and her head feel like it's rising off her body. It's over. Her plans are ruined.

"The whole quarter, as far as I know. You'll have to ask at the Sanitary Council if you want to know anything else, but I reckon it'll be busy." The guard is clearly trying to get rid of Kin, looking at her as if she's afraid Kin will get angry and decide to slit her throat.

Kin doesn't consider murder, but she does consider a disabling blow before a climb over the Honey Gate. It certainly has enough handholds. But her better judgment overrides panic; once she's in, getting out will be even more difficult if she's already attacked city guards. Besides, the story will get back to the homepalace, and Kin is currently the only Abserian fleshbound besides Merit. She'll get a punishment from Lessa, and that will only slow things more.

Instead of the Sanitary Council, Kin's feet carry her back to the homepalace, where she searches out Merit. There's nothing for it but to go through Emmala's secret passage and quietly fetch Verias, and Merit will want to help if for no other reason than to keep an eye on Kin and Verias. Kin's horse is at the inn in the Honey Quarter, so she and Merit have to ride double out of the city.

"I wish you'd just taken my horse and gone by yourself," Merit whines, their arms locked around Kin's waist. Their daggers jam into her back, making her wish the same. Combined with the uncomfortable, anxious thud of her heart, she feels like she's under attack from the inside as well as out.

"I might need you. Besides, you need us, don't you?" Kin asks. Merit grumbles something too low to hear, but Kin's sure it isn't complimentary. To be fair, if they hadn't agreed to come, Kin wouldn't be above *borrowing* their horse.

As it is, the pair leaves Merit's horse tied to a gate in the farmer's yard, not wanting to manage a nervous mount, especially when there might be a fight. Human corpses are bad enough; stars help them if they end up with a massive horse carcass, too. Kin knows horses are relatively good eating, but if the farmer has any use for a dead horse, he isn't around to say. There aren't any animals out, either, and Kin wonders whether the farmer has decided to leave the area for a while until the plague ends. Stars, don't let him get sick.

"Wait." Merit grabs Kin's arm as she starts toward the barn. "Do you hear that?" they whisper.

Kin listens. Silence. An eerie one, now that she pauses to think about it. The country is quieter than the city, but farms are always full of noise, chickens clucking, goats bleating and hooves thudding in packed dirt. She stays close to the fence as she moves, using gnarled fruit trees to hide her approach to the barn. Merit follows close at her heels, only the soft hiss of their knives disturbing the silence.

Kin points up at the hayloft, where the hatch is open, the block and tackle hanging above them. It's a long way up, but Kin is strong. She squats with her back to the barn and laces her fingers together. Merit makes a great show of sighing when they take off their boots and put one foot into her hands. They hold up three fingers. Even years on, they're both instantly back into the habits of thievery. On Merit's count of three, they leap and Kin heaves, sending them up to grab the bottom of the hatch.

Merit's stockinged toes are silent against the weathered wood of the barn as they pull themself inside. No sound comes from inside the barn for some time, and Kin's heart begins to pound faster and faster. She takes deep breaths, grits her teeth, but the anxiety is too great to conquer. She has to get to Verias, and Merit is . . . messing about? Getting themself chopped up into little bits Kin will have to stuff in a sack and carry back to Sestera? Either way, she's furious with them for it.

Merit's head pops out of the hatch. They hold up their index and middle fingers, signaling two plus four people inside, and Kin bites down on a groan. If the passage is guarded, someone must have gotten to the farmer or Emmala and made them reveal the tunnel's location. Slowly, painfully, Merit begins to lower the block and tackle. It doesn't squeak, but the rough rope brushes against the blocks, hissing its way down the side of the barn. Kin grabs Merit's boots with one hand and the hook with the other, and they draw her up into the empty loft.

Kin goes to the edge of the hayloft while Merit puts on their boots. The six guards Merit counted are waiting below, backs to the trapdoor and the loft. Her choices are to kill the guards or to sneak past them, and neither seems like a very good plan. Merit looks at Kin and draws a finger along their throat. Kin nods, but it takes all the strength she has. She's so tired of killing.

There's no ladder down from the loft, likely taken by the farmer for his new barn. No matter. Kin flies, daggers singing out of their sheaths, bodies falling beneath her. Merit is an instant behind, two down, four, six. They drag the bodies into the tunnel and hurry past, meaning to get into Sestera and back before a new shift can discover the corpses. Deep shame and guilt bubble up inside Kin as she trots along behind Merit, but she shoves them down as deep as she can. She doesn't have time to feel sorry for herself, or anyone else.

The tunnel is pleasant after the rapidly heating day outside; the air is cool and moist as always, the scent of dirt and questing roots thick in Kin's nose. She half wants to take a nap down here, where things are more peaceful than in the world above. Maybe the roots will grow through her, and the worms will eat her, and she'll never have to worry about anything ever again.

On the other side of the tunnel, Emmala's tavern is quieter than usual, but there are no guards waiting there. Money has likely changed hands, and Kin will have to make sure Emmala has fathoms to make up for that, but she doesn't have time for that now. The street she and Merit pass onto is similarly empty; folk have likely decided to stay in their homes as the news of the quarantine spreads. Makeshift flags have sprung up since the last time Kin was in this part of the Honey Quarter. Most are rags with blobs intended to be roses, but others are pieces of red cloth, often winter scarves, hung from windows. If Kin knew the plague had gotten so bad, she never would have left Verias alone in the Honey Quarter.

CHAPTER TWENTY-NINE

VERIAS CAN SENSE KIN LONG BEFORE SHE REACHES THE INN. It feels like ages since he last touched her, and his energy has been flagging since he woke that morning. Still, he drags himself out of the room to meet her on the street. Verias needs both fresh air and to see Kin's face; he's been on edge ever since she ran off the night before. That kiss had shaken her and left him with a weight of guilt in his stomach. It felt as if Verias lied, like she never would have kissed him if she knew what he had done.

"Good morning, Hartwell." Reshon leans against the outside of the inn, looking smug as always. "You always look so surprised to see me. One would think you'd be on your guard."

"I think I showed just how dangerous you are to me, Reshon. I'm more on my guard for moths eating my doublets. What do you want?" Verias has little patience for Reshon this morning. Or any morning, for that matter.

"I thought we'd speak alone while we have the chance. The Honey Gate is sealed, you see. I assume your Kindred and her little friend will be along eventually—she has an uncanny knack for being in the way—but for now, we're alone." Reshon reaches into his blue doublet to retrieve a leather pouch.

When he pulls it open to reveal two shining souls within, Verias's whole body sings out with sudden relief and joy. He instinctively reaches for Kin's soul, but Reshon snatches it away.

"Not yet. We need to discuss the terms of your return."

"We have. You give her the soul, I come back with you."

"You think it'll be that easy, do you? That bitch had the gall to attack me, and you're going to teach her a lesson."

"I'm stronger than you, Reshon." Verias is poised on the razor's edge, ready to strike.

"Of course you are. But you're also leaking magic everywhere, and this city is full of Binders. How long do you think you can avoid them once you've stolen a soul, Verias? How long can you protect her once she has it back?" Reshon asks.

Verias tenses against the flutter of hope in his stomach. Reshon has no idea that Kin means to destroy her soul. Verias has the upper hand, and Reshon doesn't even know. Verias has to play this right, though he wants nothing more than to blast a current of energy right through Reshon's smug smile.

"What do you mean I'm leaking magic?" Verias asks. Perhaps if he can keep Reshon talking, it can buy enough time to think of a plan.

"I could feel your signature all over the homepalace. Perhaps it has something to do with your safeguard being broken. I don't know, and it's likely nobody does, or ever will. Ah. Here she is."

Verias turns to follow Reshon's gaze.

Kin and Merit are walking up the street, Kin wearing a glower that could cut through steel. The magic in Verias's veins surges in her presence, straining to break through. He needs to touch her, regain control, because it would be too easy to just vaporize Reshon along with her soul. He *might* be able to stand by and let her destroy it (that remains to be seen), but he can't do it himself, let alone through negligently throwing power around.

"Verias." Kin's eyes turn to him, the accusation in her expression enough to make him take a half-step backward. She knows exactly what he's done, her eyes narrowed in what he's quite sure is disgust.

Reshon's magic flares, chunks falling around Verias in his moment of surprise. He acts as quickly as he can to piece together a barrier, pushing back against Reshon hard enough that the Binder grunts in pain. Cruel satisfaction bubbles up inside Verias as he opens a gap in his shoddily constructed cage, just large enough for his hand to fit through and grab the pouch that contains the souls.

A strange pressure builds in Verias's ribs, breaking his connection to the Wellspring. He looks down to see the blade of a long knife sticking out of his chest. It hurts. A lot. Verias struggles to draw in magic, to build anything. It takes every scrap of concentration he has, and by the time he connects to the Wellspring, the dagger is ripped free, fresher, sharper pain breaking the thread again.

Reshon grabs Verias, whirling him to slam him against the inn wall. He snugs his forearm across Verias's throat. With his free hand, Reshon plucks the souls from Verias's grasp. Kin and Merit are fighting behind him, moving so quickly and fluidly that Verias can barely follow them with his eyes.

"That's enough, Merit," Reshon says softly. Merit backs away from Kin, knives still held at the ready. "We had a deal, Verias. It's time to pay up." Reshon kicks out Verias's knee, sending him into the dirt. He touches his chest, finds no hot blood rushing from the wound. That's right. He's dead already. Verias senses the waters of the Wellspring flowing beneath the earth, lets it slowly seep into him. His flesh doesn't matter. The pain doesn't even exist. He isn't safeguarded. He can do anything.

Reshon offers the lead-lined pouch to Kin. Kin's arms fall to her sides, both baselards clattering to the street. She doesn't speak, instead staring, transfixed, hands opening and closing as if missing her knives. Verias's heart falls to pieces at the look in her eyes. Shaken, as though she can't believe she's so close, can't believe she can even hope.

"Take it, Kin," Verias says as gently as he can. Kin flinches. She shakes herself and looks down at him, the determination returning to her eyes. Take it. Wellspring's waters, please take it.

"Yes. It's mine, and I want it. It's *mine*," Kin says. Verias thanks the Wellspring that she's seen reason. All she has to do is take it, and he can fix it all. He can.

Kin reaches for the pouch with her right hand. Her left moves like a striking snake, pulling her rondel as she lunges toward Reshon. Magic surges, crumbles, there's a flash of searing light, and Kin grunts as if she'd been struck in the gut. For an instant she's frozen, and Reshon smiles a sickly smirk as his outstretched hand shoves her away.

Kin staggers back, hands pressed to her chest. Her breathing is labored, painful. "No," she whispers. "No, no, no, *no!*" Kin claws at her breast, tearing her shirt as if she can rip her soul back out with her bare hands.

Verias scrambles to his feet, ignoring Reshon and Merit and everything else in the world, but Reshon grabs his arm.

"We had a deal, Hartwell."

"You are a sad, sorry little man, aren't you?" Verias can't conceal the disgust in his voice. "Go ahead and take me back if you think you can beat me down again. Try it. I dare you."

Reshon draws in power, but Verias slams a barrier up, so hard and strong that Reshon stumbles back. Reshon tries to reach for Kin instead, and Verias lets go, lets all the Wellspring's magic rush out and through him. Reshon sails back ten paces, smashing into the packed dirt street, and rolls. All Verias has to do is glance at Merit and they run, more afraid of him than Reshon.

Verias kneels next to Kin. Tears pour down her face, and blood has beaded in the furrows she's scratched in her skin. Verias reaches for her, saying her name.

"No!" She shoves him hard, still strong as ever, and he smashes into the inn wall, hitting his head so hard that a few moments are lost to blackness. When he regains consciousness, Kin is weeping, head in her hands. Her soul still sings to him, buzzing in his ears like an insistent cicada. Head spinning, it takes what feels like an eternity to gather enough energy to heal himself, clearing his mind and knitting together the knife wound and the damage to his scalp. Thank the Wellspring Reshon is already long gone.

"Kin . . ." Verias starts to crawl toward her, to heal the damaged flesh of her chest.

"Don't touch me! I was right. I never should have listened to you. In the end, I hurt you, and it wasn't even because I was Bound. It's because this is who I am." Her eyes are wild, already bloodshot with crying.

"Kin, I'm not hurt."

"There's blood on the wall." Kin looks up at the sky, visibly trying to hold back more tears.

"It's healed. It's nothing. I forgive you." It hasn't even crossed Verias's mind to be angry. He's too worried about her to care. "You were upset."

"That doesn't make it right."

"So? I forgive you anyway. Let's get you inside," Verias says. Standing takes an enormous effort, but the power of the Wellspring keeps him on his feet. "Eventually someone will get curious enough to see what's happening out here, sanitary cordon or no." There's a small puddle of blood on the packed-dirt street, drops trailing away in the direction Reshon and Merit fled.

Kin doesn't take Verias's offered hand, but she still picks up her knives and shambles after him into the inn. The public room is empty, thank the Wellspring, and they get to their room without seeing anyone. Kin goes to the window, but Verias calls her name before she can climb out. The thought of her bearing her misery alone makes him ill. This is his fault, and he has to make it right.

"Let me heal you, Kin. I don't like seeing you in pain." Verias's stomach is sour, watching her bleed. She turns to meet his eyes, the grief on her face unbearable, and he wishes he can heal that too.

"What if I lose control again? I'm trying so hard, but . . . Verias, I can't promise I won't hurt you."

"Shh. I'm willing to take the risk. May I?" Verias reaches out as slow and gentle as he would trying to catch an injured bird. Kin nods, trembling, and Verias recognizes more than just grief in her eyes. It's the sort of panic that would either make him shut down or start screaming and never stop if he couldn't get relief from picking at his skin. "Don't think about this. Remember . . ." Verias doesn't want to tell her to think of something happier. He doesn't know what happy memories remain after being Bound and Unbound. "Remember laughing together in the hayloft, after you saved me from my family?" Verias asks. His hand is still raised, halfway to her tear-stained cheek.

"Yes," she breathes.

"That was the happiest I've ever seen you. It was the happiest I've been in a long time."

"Me too."

"I felt safe that night, Kin. You make me feel safe."

Verias brushes a stray curl from her eyes. She gasps, eyes widening, but she doesn't pull away. Wellspring's waters, he knew she was scared, knew the fear had to surface sometime, but he never expected it to be this bad. He prays to the Wellspring as fervently as he ever has that he can make her feel safe just long enough to at least take away her physical pain.

He just barely grazes Kin's jaw with his fingertips, and she closes her eyes, breathing fast. Healing her is easier than anything he's ever done, because he knows her very soul. Verias has memorized every bit of her, down to the last hair on her head, and the flesh she scratched open binds itself back together as if nothing happened. But his questing magic catches scraps of something rough and painful, a flow that judders and reverses and curls and leaves him dizzy. It's as if everything within her is churning against the weight of her soul, a still pond into which a millstone has been dropped.

Verias layers magic on top of what he's already done, trying to calm the storm, but it only makes things worse, and Kin pulls away so fast that her back hits the wall behind her.

"What were you doing?" There's accusation in her voice.

"I was trying to take the hurt away."

"It felt like you were . . . flattening me out. Making me not me."

"I'm sorry. I was just trying to help." Verias's stomach churns. What did he nearly do?

"Don't. I don't want help."

"We had a deal, didn't we?"

"Not anymore." Kin stares at Verias with empty eyes for a few long moments, watching her words sink into his chest like a knife. She stands, peeling off her shirt, and wipes the blood from her chest. She throws the soiled garment on the floor and takes off her boots to lie down in bed, pulling the blanket over her head.

Verias sits down on the stool at the washstand. He fears Kin will leave if he gives her the chance. He might be able to hear the sound of her soul when they're this close, but if Kin runs far and fast enough—or worse—Verias won't be able to follow.

Kin needs time. Maybe the rest of her life. Verias knows that the pain never fades, but for him, it can be attenuated. When waves try to drag him under, having a purpose and someone to care about, gives him something to cling to. Not always, but it helps. He won't dare presume to be that purpose for Kin, nor does he think that would be healthy, but the wish is still nestled in the back of his head.

Kin needs time. He gives her an hour.

CHAPTER THIRTY

WHILE VERIAS PACKS THEIR THINGS, KIN DRESSES AND SITS at the washstand, sharpening her knives as if nothing is wrong. Though it's not the first time he's seen her without her knife belt on—he's seen her nude—she still looks strange without them, more naked than naked. She sleeps with the weapons most nights, now that she regularly sleeps. Otherwise Kin looks normal, no sadder than usual. Her hair is pulled back from her face in a tight braid, her expression set, and she's wearing her usual shabby clothes. Rain patters against the window behind her, adding percussion to the constant *shh shh shh* of whetstone against steel.

"Kin, I'm sorry. I shouldn't have tried to fix you without your permission."

"It's nothing."

"It's very much something, Kin," Verias says.

She must be furious with him for making the deal with Reshon, but it's clear that she doesn't want to talk any longer. She's drawn the forbidding mantle from their first meeting back around her, shutting him out more completely than she has the last few days, and he's too tired for an argument.

"Where will we go?" Verias asks. She says nothing.

Verias lets the Wellspring's energy stream into him as he follows Kin out of the room, giving back a prayer that she won't tell him to get out of her sight. They pay the innkeeper, take

Shadow out of the stable, and start out. The streets are even emptier than they were before, Shadow's hoofbeats echoing hollowly off homes and storefronts and splashing through deep puddles. The rain persists, picking up as they walk toward the Mouth, where Kin puts Shadow in one of the many stables where peddlers and merchants hitch their wagons. The stable hand wears a handkerchief over his mouth, afraid to catch the plague. He stinks of vinegar and clove oil, and Verias is as relieved to escape his presence as he is to see their backs.

Kin first leads Verias to a few shops, buying candles and food and other supplies that Verias helps her carry into an alley, which lets him breathe easier for the length of their walk. At least he's useful for a while, until they stop behind a row of homes he recognizes. When Kin opens the back door of her family's abandoned house, Verias trails behind. He's sure this will be an emotional experience, but isn't sure whether Kin will appreciate his presence. It's better to be safe, to hang back and wait for her to ask if she needs him.

Inside, the tile floors are thick with dust, unmarred by even a mouse's pawprints. A broad kitchen table still stands in the kitchen, old and battered and filthy, but someone has taken all the chairs. There isn't a single mark in the dirt from a cup or a bowl, just a few dead beetles lying on their backs. Everything else but cobwebs are gone.

The place is filled to the eaves with wistfulness, people and dreams Verias will never know, filled with potential wasted, but Kin doesn't appear to notice. She goes to the fireplace that would have once warmed the kitchen and the front room beyond, and opens the flue. She crawls in to stand in the chimney, vanishing for a moment in a snow of ash. When she returns, it's with a key in hand, soot, ash, and creosote stuck to her wet clothes and hair. For a while, she just looks around, taking in her old home before passing back out into the rain.

The cellar doors, chained and locked, open with Kin's key, and she heads inside with Chestnut at her heels. Kin begins lighting candles and sticking them in little nooks in the brick foundation. The unsteady golden light reveals what's essentially a bedroom. There's a bed, a tall cabinet, and a plain washstand with a chipped basin and ewer but no mirror. A camp stove is set near the stairs leading into the cellar, its pipe leading up and out. In the Sesteran summer, they won't need it except for boiling water.

"What is this place?"

"I put it together it in case I got my soul back and needed to hide," Kin says.

"Won't people know that your parents lived here?"

"Maybe. That was decades ago." Kin goes to the slanted doors and locks the handles together from the inside. She turns to him, meeting his eyes, and from the desperation in their depths he knows what she's going to ask. He shakes his head before she can speak. "We're in grave danger, Verias. You must know that. I need to be Bound again or we'll be dead in days."

"I'll heal you," Verias says. "But I won't Bind you."

"Verias, I might freeze up, now that I have a conscience. If I can't fight, we'll both die."

"I can't, Kin. I can't hurt you like that." Verias's memory of the Binding he saw is still vivid, the agonized cries of the new fleshbound echoing in his ears. Soft brown and white feathers and meat in uncaring hands.

"You have to. It hurts less than being Unbound." Her voice remains level, but her beautiful dark eyes are troubled. Hollow. Her pain aches in Verias's chest, a millstone crushing him. All he wants is to ease her suffering, so he has to refuse, for destroying her soul can only hurt her more.

"I know you're scared, but you'll survive; you said it yourself. I can't help you destroy your soul."

241

"You can't or you won't?" Kin asks.

"I won't," he says stubbornly. Kin's empty gaze becomes a look of smoldering anger.

"After all we've been through, after what you did, you can't give me the one thing I want most?" she asks.

Verias's stomach swoops. This argument had to come, but no amount of dreading could prepare him for it. "I'm sorry, Kin. For making the deal with Reshon, and for this. But some lines I refuse to cross, even for you."

"Because you're a coward," she says.

"What?"

It's like being slapped in the face. Kin always denies his flaws, too kind to agree when he criticizes himself, and he's always privately hated it, because he neither wants to tell her she's wrong nor accept that she might be right. It would be too painful to question everything he's ever been told about himself. Somehow, hearing Kin agree with everyone else hurts even worse. He doesn't even have Lusian to fall back on like he used to.

"You heard me," Kin says with dogged determination, as if she'd been thinking it all along and has to get it all out before it poisons her. "You're a coward. You're too afraid of what would happen if I destroy my soul."

"Obviously I am! I care about you, and I don't want you to die. You said yourself that you don't know what will happen if you destroy it, and I won't help you hurt yourself. Ever." Anger and guilt battle inside Verias, making his stomach boil and his face hot and feverish.

"That's not fair. It's not your choice to make!" Kin's eyes bore into him, searing his very soul.

"Is it fair for you to force me to do something I can never take back? I'd rather have your anger than watch you destroy yourself."

"Then you'll have it," Kin snaps. "I didn't want to take my fate back from Lessa just to hand it over to you. If you stop me, you're no better than she is!"

Wellspring's waters, the blows keep coming. Kin is just jamming the knife in, twisting it until Verias's eyes sting and his throat is tight. He's too dead to take a calming breath, so he clenches and unclenches his fists, desperately trying to steady himself. He knew she'd eventually try to push him away, but he never imagined she'd be so *good* at it. He wants to be angry. He *is* angry. But he can't let her turn away from him. He loves her, and he won't let her go without a fight.

"Do you want this because you're suffering, or do you really think we won't survive unless you're Bound?" Verias speaks gently, though his voice is worn down to grit from holding back anger. Kin looks away, and without her eyes boring into his skull, Verias feels less cornered.

"I don't know. I'm too tired to know."

"Then maybe you're a little too tired to make such a huge choice," Verias says. "I won't pretend I'm happy about it, but I won't take Binding you again off the table, as long as you wait for a little while. Can you do that?"

"Maybe." Her voice breaks, like the answer is so grudging that it shatters over her teeth. "How long do I have to wait?"

"A week. Give me a week to convince you." Verias says a prayer to the Wellspring as he waits for her answer. Just let her say yes. He'll give up all his power if she just says yes. He'll go back to being safeguarded. He'll go back home. Anything.

"Five days. You have five days from right now. Then you have to take my soul and let me destroy it."

"It's a deal. And Kin?"

"What?"

"I'm sorry. I'm sorry about your soul; I'm sorry I disappointed you. I'm so sorry." Verias has always been good at apologizing, because he always has so much to be sorry for. He always disappoints. He'll likely disappoint when he fails to show her that her soul is worth keeping, because he has no idea how to do it. The knowledge aches fiercely.

"Me too," Kin says.

Once, when Verias lay recovering on his deathbed, Kin said he apologized too much. Now, his apologies will never be enough. He can only hope that she'll pity him enough to keep allowing him to use her energy to survive. Even now, he's tired and wants to reach out for her, if nothing else but to comfort her. To comfort himself. Instead, he draws in more magic. It will have to do for now.

CHAPTER THIRTY-ONE

EVEN CHESTNUT IS TENSE WHILE KIN AND VERIAS SIT IN HER secret hole and try not to look at each other. The rain is absolutely bucketing down outside, and while the cellar isn't leaky, it's the kind of damp that gets into the bones and makes the heart feel soggy and tired. Still, Kin begins thinking of reasons to go back out in the pouring rain, just to get away from Verias. Though he isn't even looking at her, Kin can't stand his sad eyes or his hurt feelings. She hates that despite how angry she is, it hurts her to seem him so upset. She hates that she cares about him and wants him. She loathes how much he needs her.

She's gritting her teeth when she steps back into the rain and locks the cellar behind her. She hopes Verias isn't claustrophobic, but she wants to get some water from the well nearby, and she doesn't trust anybody in the Honey Quarter not to try to see what's behind an open door in an abandoned house. She doesn't trust herself not to.

When Kin returns to the cellar, drenched and grouchy and so desperate for a cup of tea that she'd burn anything in place of firewood, Verias is still sitting on the bed. He's just as wet and bedraggled as she left him, not having taken the time alone to change his clothes, staring past her like he doesn't even know she's there.

"Verias?" Her heart jams in her throat. He keeps staring off into the middle distance, not looking at her. "Verias!"

"What?"

"Verias, what is it?"

"Hmm?" Verias has already lost the thread of their simple conversation. An icy knot of fear ties her guts up, wondering what's wrong with him.

"Why are you acting so strange?" Kin asks.

"I was getting tired, so I needed magic. It's quite a lot for me today. Distracting."

"Then stop drawing it. I'll hold your hand when I'm dry."

"That's not necessary."

Kin plans on ignoring him. If he needs her life energy, he's going to get it. She isn't going to let him die when she can help it. She especially isn't going to let him abandon her when she still has so much to be angry with him about. In fact, Kin is even more angry, now that he has the gall to be kind to her when she's trying to be mad at him.

Though Kin has never in her life been shy, it feels strange stripping down to hang her clothes around the cellar and dress in dry clothes. Verias *is* shy, but he stares at her the whole time. Or stares through her, which is even worse. There's something very off about him, not just exhaustion, and her body is tense, almost vibrating with the desire to make him better. Eventually he lies down on the bed, nowhere near the pillow and with his wet boots still on the ground. Crumpled up like a ragdoll.

"Verias, are you ill?" Kin pulls her shirt over her head.

"I felt lightheaded," Verias says.

"Can you get up? You should change out of those wet clothes." Kin offers him her hand. Verias straightens with a grunt and let her pull him to his feet. He leans against her for a moment before moving away.

"I'm sorry."

Kin is struck by another wave of guilt, and it only gets worse when he almost tips over trying to take off his boots. He's too weak for her to be shouting him down about her soul. She offers Verias her arm to brace himself, but he doesn't take it, instead fumbling with the sodden, tangled laces swollen with rainwater.

"Will you stop that? Let me do it."

"No!" Verias snaps. "I'm done being useless." He sits right down on the floor and starts picking apart the snarl. Kin decides it better not to say anything, so she sits on the stairs and watches him work out his frustration by taking his doublet off with an aggression she would never have thought possible for anyone, least of all him.

After removing his boots and stockings, Verias manages to get up on his own, but he immediately loses his balance, and Kin has to jump to keep him from falling.

"I'm being ridiculous." The exhaustion makes him sound almost drunk.

"Yes, you are. Once again I'm here to save you," Kin says. He snorts.

Kin pulls the laces of his shirt, lifts it over his head. Though Verias has healed the wound left by Merit's knife, a red, angry scar had been left behind, overlapping the burn scar from what feels like a lifetime ago. When Kin touches the mark, his skin, though damp, feels feverish.

"Your hands are cold," Verias murmurs. He rests his forehead against her shoulder, all the stubbornness drained out of him.

"No they're not, you're hot." Kin unlaces his trousers, takes them down. He'll have to take care of the rest on his own. "How long have you been holding magic?" Kin asks him, turning away to give him some privacy. He said something about problems from keeping magic inside him too long.

"I don't know. At least since I tried to heal you. What time is it? Noon? Just a few hours." He rustles with fabric behind her.

"Verias, that was yesterday."

"What? I thought . . . I thought I let you sleep for an hour. Maybe a little more."

"I slept through the night, and you woke me a little before mid-morning. I thought you slept, too."

"No, I was just worrying, just thinking." He touches her shoulder, and it's clear that he was worrying about her. "That's so long to hold magic. Far too long." Verias's fingers tighten.

Last night's fear surges back up, pushing bile up the back of her throat as it goes. She swallows hard, but that doesn't force back the anger that's rekindled in her belly. Stars, she wishes she could just vomit it all out and forget everything Verias has said and done. Kin touches his hand, turns to look at him. He's only gotten as far as fresh braies, but that's enough.

"Rest for a while. Sit down."

Verias falls more than sits, putting his head down on the pillow this time. Stars, she hates seeing him like this, hates being angry with him, hates being in a hole in the ground with her soul skittering around inside her chest like a parasite she could rip out with a knife and her fingernails and enough gumption. Instead she sits and holds his hand, watching him drift into sleep. It's uncanny, even when his eyes are closed, to see him lie completely still, no breath in his body, no pulse at his throat. It takes a great deal of self-control not to shake him and make sure he's still in there, not being swept away by the Wellspring, or whatever happens when Carriers die.

Kin never realized how much gray is in Verias's beard, because he's never had so much beard before. It makes him look older, more tired, though he's still handsome. He's perhaps more so, in Kin's eyes. She's glad that shaving must have fallen by the wayside in all the excitement, though she can't say the same for herself. Kin's hair is already a wreck from one night of sleeping on it without magic setting her body back to rights every morning. It's dry from the wool pillow at their last inn (even the memory of a silk scarf is distant now), and before it was rained on, it was so frizzy Kin wondered if it was possible to feel pain in one's hair.

Kin is foolish to think about her *hair* with everything else that's gone wrong, but her hair is a part of it. Suddenly she has a thousand things to take care of, none of which have been important for over a decade. She doesn't know how to be a person any longer, and maybe that's why she's so upset with Verias. He's a paragon of humanity, flawed and beautiful and frightened and brave and everything Kin doesn't know how to be. Being with him makes her *want* to be human, even though everything inside her screams to be Bound again.

"May I try to heal you again?" Verias asks. Kin sucks in a breath.

"I thought you were sleeping," she says.

"I'm in and out. May I heal you?"

"No. You've already done too much. Besides, there's no healing a mind, Verias."

"It's a body part, isn't it? Your brain, I mean. I could feel your emotions pulsing through you, just like blood does. Maybe if I can reroute something . . ."

"Verias, you said red rose plague was too complex. Why would a brain be any less so?"

"I'm stronger now than I was then. Magic is easier," Verias says.

"Well, you're not any better at healing. You almost squashed my brain." Kin might have worded it better, but it's true.

"I am sorry." His voice is quiet, almost small.

"I know, Verias."

"I just need you to see that none of this was your fault. Even if you had chosen to be fleshbound, serving Nerefin is a noble goal. One that surely went wrong, but still." He sits up, steadier than he was.

"That's such a Nerefinian way of seeing it, Verias. I was born here, but I never got along with my mother. I learned most of my values from my father, and that's not how Abserians think. I still knew killing was wrong. I was human before I was Bound. The memory was there. Not having a soul doesn't absolve me. Being sad about it doesn't make me no longer guilty for hurting you. Being broken isn't a pass to do anything I want."

"It's not. But you were forced into being fleshbound. They would have tortured or killed you if you hadn't killed those people. You had no choice." Verias's voice has grown desperate.

"Verias, I know you want me to be innocent because that makes you innocent. We were both forced into doing terrible things. But we did have a choice. We could have died instead of hurting other people, but we didn't. We paid for our survival in blood, and you have to face that fact."

Verias pulls his hand out of hers, furious. It's in the hollowed-out pits of his eyes and the set of his shoulders.

"I tried," he says, and Kin's stomach rolls, acid boiling in her gut. She stands to flee, but there's nowhere to go. "I tried to burst my war machine and let the battle take me, Kin, and when Reshon was done choking me half to death he watched me even closer! *I tried! And so did you!*"

"I don't know what you're talking about. I never tried to die."

"Yes, you did. You tested Lessa at every turn, hoping she'd get rid of you. You—"

"I was trying to show her she didn't control me." The words come out torn to pieces.

"You're fooling yourself if you don't think that was just as self-destructive as anything I've done; you're just fleshbound and don't have the scars. So you can stop acting like you're so strong and noble for facing down the truth. You're just as afraid of it as I am."

"Then why would you make a deal with Reshon? Why would you put yourself in danger like that?" She's so sick she could vomit.

"I thought it was worth it," he says. Kin turns away. There's nothing else she can do, knowing how much he'd been willing to give up for her. She wants to run from him and never come back, never have to look into his face and see herself reflected back.

"I'm sorry." It's so hard to say that Kin's throat aches. She hates him for always being right about her, and hates herself for always being wrong about herself. "I lied to you. When I told you about what happened at Felver's house."

"I . . . wish I could say I didn't know. It didn't really add up," Verias says. Kin wants to turn around and slap him for being continually honest when she'd much rather he lie.

"Merit is right. I am slipping."

"I don't think you're slipping," Verias says. "I think you've become someone different from who you were back then."

"That's so. I'm still sorry."

"You don't have to be. If you weren't ready, you didn't need to tell me the end," Verias says.

"I want to tell you the end. It just hasn't happened yet."

CHAPTER THIRTY-TWO

IT'S HARD TO KNOW THE TIME WITH NO WINDOWS TO LET IN the sun. Verias sleeps hard, and doesn't want to move when he does finally wake. In the pitch black of the cellar, he dips into the Wellspring to create a droplet of light that makes a slow, feathery path to the floor. Kin lies on the ground, dead asleep, with her boots for a pillow. Her eyes are deeply shadowed, her hair tangled.

Verias steps over her as gingerly as possible to tiptoe to the angled doors. She locked them, of course, which means that for Verias to even know what time of day it is, he'll have to find the key. When he looks back at Kin, he realizes she holds it loosely in her cupped palm, the back of her hand against the floor. Verias bends to take it, and Kin grabs his wrist in an iron grip, her other hand drawing a knife in the blink of an eye.

"Stars, Verias," she breathes. "You can't scare me like that." She lets her head fall back onto her boots. "Did you light candles?"

"Just a little magic trick."

"Well, be careful." She hasn't let go of Verias's arm, her hand shaking. "Someone might sense it and come to investigate. Why were you taking the key?"

"I wanted to see what time it is. It's so dark, it could be midnight or noon."

"Mm." Kin lets him go, her hand falling open so Verias can

take the key. She closes her eyes, relieved, her breath still coming fast.

"Should we leave Sestera?" Verias asks as he unlocks the door. The best course of action at this point is probably to avoid mentioning Kin's anxiety.

The rain outside has stopped, sun streaming into the cellar with a glorious burst of fresh air that feels scrubbed clean overnight. It's mid-morning, not yet the full heat of day, but Verias is sure he'll be happy for the cool of the cellar come afternoon. If they're still in Sestera.

"Kin?"

"No. We'll stay here for a while." Kin sits up, stretching.

"In the cellar?" Verias asks. He leaves the cellar doors open while he lights a few candles. They'll go through dozens at this rate.

"Yes. For a few days, while you recover your strength and I get accustomed to . . . this." She gestures vaguely at her body. "They likely won't be letting anyone out of the Mouth, either, otherwise people could just leave the Honey Quarter and go to another gate. We'll have to find another way out, and we're not in any state to fight."

"If we're staying in Sestera, I think I ought to go back to the homepalace. I don't know how, but it has to happen."

"What? Why?"

"With your soul and me gone missing, they'll be sure I was involved and hunt us down. If I make an appearance, I'll look less guilty," Verias says.

"I don't know about all that. Besides, you're still Merit's target as far as we know. You don't want to get any closer to them than you have to, especially since they turned on us. The good news is that if we can't get to the Deep Quarter, they'll have just as much trouble getting to us. Anyway, Lessa wouldn't set foot in the Honey Quarter even if it wasn't under a sanitary cordon.

This is our chance to rest without looking over our shoulders."

"I don't know. Reshon said I was leaking magic."

"How is that possible?" Kin asks. Her gaze is sharp, piercing him with arrows of anxiety. What if they're hunting him right now? What if they find Kin's mother and hurt her? Kin's right, this is too dangerous.

"I don't know. Have you noticed anything? I feel . . . I don't know. I can't say what's normal any longer."

"Neither can I," Kin says. "Verias, do you think your eye has anything to do with it?"

Verias unconsciously touches his face. He hasn't thought about the growing spot in his eye in ages. It hasn't seemed important, and it isn't affecting his sight in any way. But it has grown since meeting Kin. It might be related to their link, though Verias has no idea what that has to do with his leaking magic. For the first time in months, he wishes he could speak to his father. Between him and Gavian, they've seen everything, and they would likely know what to do.

Thinking of Gavian makes his heart sink. Gavian insisted that the safeguard is the only thing that could save Verias from disaster, before he made further discussion of the subject impossible. Verias has to get to the Wellspring soon, if for no other reason than to extinguish the beacon inside him.

"You're not fit to travel, Verias. You need more rest." Kin must be reading his mind. "But we'll have to be ready to leave at all times," Kin says. Verias groans.

"Maybe I could make some breakfast before we pack up?" he suggests, not very hopeful.

"No firewood," Kin says.

"Damn. No magic allowed, I suppose."

"Of course not. There are some sausages in the cupboard. Some cheese and apples, too."

Verias has been dreaming of eggs, but the sausages are tasty.

He's never lived in a city before, and has serious concerns about the sanitary cordon as far as supplies go. What happens when all the food is gone? What happens when the merchants and peddlers want out of the city? The situation is precarious at best, and he catches himself digging at a scab above his eyebrow just thinking about it. He hasn't seen a single Healer since the cordon flags went up. Where are they?

"Hello?" a soft voice says from the door. A snap of instinctive magic surges into Verias, but Kin is faster, at the bottom step in an instant with knives at the ready. Her back to Verias, she tenses, but Verias can't see who's there.

"What are you doing here, Mother?" Kin asks.

"What am I doing here? I thought you were dead, Kindred!"

Kin backs away from the shallow stairs, putting up her knives, and an older woman spills down into the basement to hug her. Kin appears to be in shock, not returning the embrace. When her mother pulls away, it's to look Kindred up and down at arm's length, like one might assess someone who's been ill for a long time. Verias senses a wisp of magic, eyes snapping between Kin and her mother. Kin never mentioned her mother having magic, and when Kin returns his curious look with a blank one, he's sure she doesn't know.

"You've built a whole little home down here. What for?" Kin's mother asks.

"I don't want to get into it, Mother. How did you get through the Mouth?"

"I went to the Sanitary Council, of course. Either they forgot my face or they're desperate enough for help that they decided to forget how much they hate me. Who's this?" Kin's mother asks. Verias thinks it highly unlikely that anyone would forget her face; though her skin is pale rather than brown, she looks quite like Kin. Beauty like that is something a person remembers.

"This is Verias, Mother. Verias, this is my mother Sola Tris- sel. Are you moving back into the house?"

"No. Well, yes, but I'll be using it as a hospital. I'm not sure how long; you know how red rose plague can keep a person in bed for weeks. Do you know any healing, Verias? I can tell you're very strong—"

"Mother, you can't create a hospital here. There are people looking for us," Kin interrupts.

"What have you done this time?" Mistress Trissel asks. Ve- rias feels uncomfortably like a goat watching a wolf stalk a weaker member of the herd, and for once Kin isn't the predator.

"I haven't done anything, Mother! I—"

"There are people after me," Verias cuts her off. She cuts her eyes at him, but at least an argument hasn't started yet. Or a physical fight. It doesn't seem impossible given the thick tension filling the cellar. "People who seek to control me for my power, who think to use me as a weapon of war."

Mistress Trissel gives Verias an appraising look. For a mo- ment, he fears that she'll say he ought to do his duty for Nerefin and go back to Felver's army. Instead, she frowns.

"The Binders again, no doubt. They love war because prison- ers taken in battle can be made into fleshbound, and the more fleshbound they have, the tighter their control over Nerefin," she says. Kin nods, no longer looking like she's ready to fight.

"We can't let them have him." Kin meets Verias's eyes. De- spite all that's happened, she still wants to protect him, and the thought makes Verias's heart go soft. With the stress of the last few days, that wonderful, welcome feeling has been missing. He misses her stubbornness, her resolve. Mistress Trissel clears her throat, breaking his focus on Kin.

"Well, it's certainly a concern, but I reckon the hospital will help. There will be Healers in and out, and the magic will hide his signature," Mistress Trissel says.

"It might do that, but it might also draw attention to what people thought was an abandoned house," Kin replied.

"Both things are true, but if we stay, perhaps I can learn more healing. Be of help," Verias says. "Just being in the presence of magic can give me an idea of how it works. Please, Kin. This might give me an idea of how to help you. You gave me five days, remember?"

"Rumor has it that many Healers have already been engaged by Lord Felver," says Mistress Trissel. "Either that he's busy quelling some sort of trouble in the lowlands, and he's taken many casualties, or that the plague was brought here by some of his men. Either way, there are few Healers left in Sestera."

"That would explain why the Sanitary Council closed the gates. They know they can't fight it if people outside the Honey Quarter get sick. Better to kill anyone trying to leave than risk the whole city dying." Kin's eyes are somewhere far away when she speaks, and butterflies flutter madly in Verias's stomach. He shouldn't have said anything about her soul, shouldn't have reminded her of her pain.

"I've spoken to other herbalists. There should be more coming in the next few weeks, but I have much work to do, especially educating folk about how to stay safe." Mistress Trissel seems not to notice that Kin is troubled, or that Verias is worried. Without another word, Kin goes to the bed to lie down, her back to Verias and her mother. "Kindred—" Mistress Trissel begins. Verias shakes his head at her, trying to tell her not to push Kin. For a moment, he fears she won't take the hint. "Well, I have a house to clean. I'll come back later, though. I could use some help with the cart."

"We'll help as much as we can," Verias says, though he knows it won't be much.

Mistress Trissel gives him a curt nod before she leaves the cellar. Verias has an urge to follow and speak to her, make her understand, but he can't do that without telling more than Kin would want him to. He sits at the edge of the bed, and is surprised when Kin is the first to speak.

"I'm sorry. I just . . . couldn't." Her voice is muffled by the pillow. "You ever just can't?"

"Kin, those words make absolutely no sense when arranged that way," Verias says.

"Shut up. I was overwhelmed." She shoves at him with one hand, face still buried in the pillow. "It's just like her to be conspicuous when we need to hide."

"We'll be ready to leave. When have you ever not been ready?" Verias catches her hand before she pokes his eye out. "You are acting like an utter maniac."

"My mind is full of terrible thoughts, Verias. I think I am a maniac."

"What terrible thoughts?" Verias asks.

"I couldn't sleep the other night, thinking of hurting you."

"Oh, Kin." It's no wonder she's so upset. "I suppose I'm lucky you're out of your mind, because I am too, and nobody else would tolerate a man made entirely of scabs," Verias says. Kin's laugh is short and flattened out by wool stuffing.

"I think that's a little different, Verias."

"It is. I'm constantly giving into picking. You're strong enough not to act on your thoughts, and even if you did, I wouldn't mind," Verias asks. She rolls over onto her side, looking up at him with tired eyes and making him immediately regret letting the words slip out. His face heats.

"You wouldn't mind if I strangled you while kissing you?" Kin's brows appear to be trying to leave her face and go upstairs to visit her mother. As if thought of her hand at his throat hasn't been in his thoughts, haunting him, for days.

"At least I'd die happy."

"Shut up." Kin buries her face in the pillow, but Verias gets a glimpse of her smile before she does. It's the tiniest sunbeam, the smallest grain of hope. Maybe he can do this. Maybe he can convince her not to destroy her soul.

CHAPTER THIRTY-THREE

KIN AND VERIAS FALL INTO A ROUTINE OVER THE NEXT FEW days in the cellar. They wake late in the morning, moving slowly without sunlight to rouse them, and go up to the house to help Kin's mother with the chores. Once they spend a few hours making the house livable for eventual patients, Kin's mother brings in herbs from her forays into the countryside and complains heartily about the escort of guards who ensure she won't spread the plague by reentering the city through another gate. Kin helps prepare the herbs, and Verias sits nearby, asking questions. Kin is no fool—she knows why he's taken an interest in healing—but having someone to talk to, having her hands busy, keeps her mind occupied. Being distracted is better than thinking about her past or her future, but it also keeps her from watching her back. Risky.

Holding a knife has grown just as dangerous as a failure to remain vigilant in a city full of enemies. The sight of light glinting off one of her mother's finely honed work knives makes memories and sensation rush in. Blood and death and, above all, hate. Stars, how she hates the Binders, Reshon, Lessa, Felver, and every person in Sestera who stood by while Kin was forced to become a monster. She has to put the knife down, reminding herself that it's only a tool, when her hands shake.

Verias never asks what's wrong. When he's with her, he'll cross to her and put a comforting hand on her back. He just lets her breathe in and out, steady herself before she picks up the knife and gets back to work. Still, the day she hurts herself has to come. Kin's mind wanders to thoughts of violence, her hands tremble, her knife slips, and her thumb and forefinger are open and bleeding into calendula blossoms. She grits her teeth over a growl of frustration.

"What's wrong?" Verias asks.

"My hand slipped."

"Here. Let me heal it." He reaches for Kin's hand. "Oh, that's bad."

Magic rushes through Kin, the pain of the cuts knitting together almost as bad as the pain of cutting herself. Or, rather, the pain she ought to have felt. Her only real sensation was surprise that her blade had caught something other than plant material.

"Kin?"

"What?" Kin looks down at Verias.

"I asked you if that's better, but you were somewhere else."

"I'm sorry. It's much better. I've just been feeling . . ." She shrugs away the thought.

"How do you feel?" Verias asks.

"Like a puppet. Sort of . . . moving about without my own purpose. That doesn't make any sense."

"Yes, it does. You're at loose ends." He still holds her cut hand in his, warm and gentle. Kin can't help but remember the way he said he'd die happy with her hand at her throat, and she struggles to control the fear that rises up alongside something softer, less nameable.

"I am."

"What do you want to do with yourself once this is all over?" Verias asks. "Not settle down, certainly." His lips curl.

"After the Wellspring? I thought we would go to Lubria," Kin says. "That's the safest place. And someone there will have need of my services. There's always someone who does."

"I don't mean what *can* you do. I want to know what you wish for."

Kin hesitates. The one thing that has eaten away at her, that sent her back to the Honey Quarter again and again for over a decade, is the home they stand in now. It ached to watch the windows break, the dust settle on floors, the insects eat away at anything they could find. She wants the home she remembered, where her mother grew herbs in window boxes and her father washed the floors with lemon soap on hands and knees every week. Even as they work to make it livable again, Kin knows the place can never be the home she remembers, but it can be *a* home.

"Not that it can ever happen with Mother here, but I want my house back," she says. Verias's expression is comically surprised.

"So you *do* want to settle down." He hasn't let go of her hand.

"I want to rest. I don't know if that's the same thing as settling down."

"Would the Honey Quarter even be restful?" Verias asks. He's right, of course. As peaceful as it is under the sanitary cordon, the Honey Quarter will grow raucous and bustling once the plague ends.

"I don't know. I just know I couldn't stand living out in the country somewhere, like Mother does. That's too quiet. I'm not making any sense."

"You're a woman of contradictions."

"That's poetic of you," Kin says. "It must be frustrating for you, having to deal with me."

"Well, it's certainly never boring."

Kin manages a weak laugh. He's trying to cheer her up, and she appreciates it, but she only has a couple days left before Verias will Bind her. She doesn't want to spend those days pretending to be happy when she isn't. The thought of destroying her soul, of being completely lost in violence, scares her so bad she thinks she might be sick, but she knows of no other way to keep herself safe. She can't trust herself with her soul, so it has to go. At least Verias hasn't let her go, her hand in both of his.

"What is it?" he asks.

The front door squeals open on its rusty hinges before she can answer, and Verias gives her a regretful look as her mother enters the kitchen. Kin starts disposing of the bloodied blossoms, not wanting her mother to notice how out of sorts she is. Like Verias, the woman never stops asking questions, and Kin isn't in the mood to invite them. It's bad enough that she can't help telling Verias everything.

"I have good news and bad news," her mother says. "The good news is that I have bed frames coming today. The bad news is that I won't be able to see to gathering willowbark this afternoon."

"It's too hot for that, anyway," Kin says.

"The heat only means we need it even more. I don't want feverish patients in here burning up without it. I need the two of you to take delivery of the beds."

"We can't. I'd love to help, but unless you want to be scrubbing up blood for the next month . . ." Kin shrugs.

"Maybe we can handle the willowbark?" Verias suggests. Kin shoots him a look, but he's looking at her mother with his hopeful, helpful expression.

"We *could*," she says, attempting to imply that they oughtn't. "But I won't go unless it's after dark, and it's likely there are still guards keeping watch outside the city where Emmala's tunnel lets out," Kin says.

"The King of Thieves doesn't know any other reprobates with smuggler's tunnels?" her mother asks. Kin doesn't know whether to be angrier about the fact that her secret has been thrown in the middle of the room like a sack of turnips, or that her mother is being so condescending about it. Either way her best option is probably to flee and never speak of it again, otherwise she'll kill her mother for spilling her secret, and Verias will kill her for lying.

"Fucking *pardon me*?" Verias asks. Kin doesn't look at him.

"My father and I were both Sestera's King of Thieves. We can discuss it later," she says through her teeth.

"I . . . very well. In any case, I'm stronger now than I was," Verias says. "I doubt a few guards can stop me."

"You have gotten too brave. I'm not fighting my way through that passage for some bark, and neither are you. There are willows on the Fisherman's Quarter side of the river. We can just swim over there and get some, as long as we don't make too much noise. The people who own the docks over there put up barriers so nobody can tie up a boat on their property, and I'd wager the city guard didn't bother putting anyone there to watch."

"You want to swim in that water?" Verias grimaces.

"I'd rather drink from the Embraile than try going back through the tunnel right now." Kin means that it's safer to swim when she has a human soul and is now capable of being stabbed to death. Kin doesn't know how much her mother knows, but it will only complicate things for her to hear about Kin's soul.

"I suppose we might need to use that passage again, and the more we do, the less viable an option it becomes." Verias scratches his beard, clearly elsewhere.

"Well, now that's decided, you two had better go hide in the cellar," Kin's mother says.

Kin suppresses a groan. Once, she had tools to cope with boredom; thievery requires quite a lot of watching and waiting, and the bigger the prize, the more boredom involved. Assassination is often much the same. Now, hiding out in a cellar with nothing to drink and no enchantments to keep her blackest thoughts from bubbling up, the afternoon and evening will be misery.

"You're troubled," Verias says as Kin locks the cellar door.

"Verias, when am I not troubled?"

"You are *showing* that you're troubled lately, and that concerns me," he corrects himself. After Kin pockets the key, she turns to find him frowning at her. It sends a shock of anxiety through her; is he angry that she's been keeping secrets? Her stomach clenches.

"What is it?"

"You don't trust me to fight the way you do," Verias says. He picks at a bit of skin on his lip. "Not surprising, of course. I'm not much of a fighter."

"Verias, I think I ought to tell you something about how the King of Thieves does business. Or how my father and I did," Kin says. Verias sits down on the bed, watching her expectantly. "The King of Thieves is loyal to all. They protect everyone who works for them, which includes physical protection. If the King of Thieves is working a job, they fight for everyone else there. To the last breath. That's their purpose. The thieves who work with them are loyal to the King without fail. I am supposed to be a protector. Understand?"

"Why don't the thieves protect the King?" Verias asks.

"They do. If they open their mouths to speak a word against the King, another thief will make sure they never say anything else. They'll bribe guards or witnesses, make sure nobody else speaks against the King, either." Kin feels a muscle twitch in her temple.

Verias's eyes search her face, the way they always do when he's about to ask a hundred questions. She doesn't want to say the words aloud, and she prays to every star in the sky that he won't make her lie.

"So between us, you're the King," Verias says.

"What? Verias . . ."

"And I'm your loyal subject."

"I was only saying that—"

"Kin, I'm only making fun," Verias says, a smile beginning to play about his lips. Relief rushes through Kin, cool and calming. "I know what you're trying to say, but cannot *believe* you were King of Thieves. Will you tell me all about it? I want to know everything."

"No, I will not. You scared me! I thought you were angry. I'm not talking to you for the rest of the day."

Verias laughs. He knows as well as she does that the day will be dull as dirt, and she'll never keep her word. After a long, slow afternoon and evening, she and Verias are both itching for an hour or two of freedom. When at last Kin opens the cellar doors, letting cool night air fill the stuffy cellar, the stillness of the night is less eerie than the daytime quiet of the sanitary cordon. At least nighttime is supposed to be quiet. As they get closer to the river, the sound of its lazy passage gently ripples the air and fills the nostrils with muddy wet scents. The smell of the river isn't as strong as it is during the day, when Sestera's waste is actively flowing in, polluting the water and air with its stench.

"I never understood how they let this river get so dirty. It's water from your Wellspring, isn't it?" Kin asks. A waterbird calls somewhere nearby before settling down to sleep.

"I don't know. I mean, all water comes from the Wellspring. But well water is different from river water."

"Different how? Just cleaner?"

"It is that. But no, it's just . . . different. Closer, more connected, if that makes sense," says Verias. "How . . . clothed are you planning to be in that?"

"Not very. You can wear trousers till they stand up on their own, and I'm not doing wash until then." Kin starts taking off her boots.

"Enchanting," Verias says, but he follows suit.

Kin takes off everything except her braies, including her knife belt, tucking it all into a little nook in the stone bank where a rock has come loose. Her mother has given her a small basket, into which Kin tucks two sharp work knives and one of her baselards. She catches Verias shaking his head at her, wearing a small smile.

"Not all of us are born with our weapons," she says.

As Kin wades into the murky water with her basket on her head, the thought makes sadness rise inside her, so cold and bitter it might be winter. As a Carrier, poor Verias was born deadly enough that he had to be safeguarded to keep him from hurting people. Kin knows he'd never harm anyone on purpose, and it feels unfair that his abilities were capped before he was even aware of it.

On the other side of the river, a stone wall rises up twice as high as Kin is tall. It might be a good place to enter the Fishers' Quarter if that becomes necessary, but if the plague continues to spread, all of Sestera might end up behind a security cordon. If Kin's mother has anything to do with it, the people of the Honey Quarter will soon be well, and the gates will open. The most important thing right now is willowbark. Kin hands Verias a knife and shows him how to carve the bark away from young branches by the light of his magic.

They work in silence, the occasional breeze whispering through the drooping willow branches. Still, Kin can't shake the sadness that overcame her on the opposite bank, the quiet only adding layer after layer of guilt. Every time she thinks about Verias, she remembers how much he'd been willing to throw away for her. How can she repay him for that? How could she be worthy?

"Something troubles you," Verias said when their basket is full of bark and sticky with thin sap.

"True." Kin has no interest in discussing any more of her worries tonight, and Verias doesn't push her. They swim back across the river, Kin with the laden basket perched atop her head. She wants to float all the way to the sea and forget about everything. Farewell plague, farewell mother. Goodbye to Verias, who she'll miss, but who is a source of constant guilt and frequent confusion. Honor and Amity likely already think she's dead. It would be easy to just slip away, even if the moon, now almost full, is still there to watch and remember. Is there somewhere Kin can go and never see the moon again?

"Kin? Aren't you going to get dressed?" Verias asks. He's caught Kin staring toward the sea, her skin already dried by the river breeze.

She isn't sure how long she's been standing there, can't even remember getting out of the water, but Verias is already dressed, so she hurries to catch up. She really isn't herself; she'd missed having a look while he was mostly naked, missed acting when he said *at least I'd die happy.* They've sort of run up against each other a few times, neither having the courage—or perhaps the energy—to do much more than kiss. It's really a shame. It could have been a lovely escape for a day, or a week, perhaps even a month. At this point it doesn't matter. She refuses to miss something she never had to begin with, especially when there are other things to worry about, like footsteps in the night.

Kin grabs Verias's arm, pulling him against the bank. He doesn't question her, instead twisting his arm to hold her in return. They stand frozen, silent, as the Embraile whispers sleepily by, and listen for boot heels. The feet don't move in perfect time like soldiers, but they certainly belong to guardsmen. Nobody else would be out at night, in such numbers, during the sanitary cordon, and armed by the sound of spear butts striking the ground. People in the Honey Quarter are smarter than that.

"Come out, Kin," says a smooth, familiar voice. "You can't hide from me."

CHAPTER THIRTY-FOUR

"MERIT," KIN WHISPERS. VERIAS NODS, HIS BODY TAUT WITH anxiety but his heart still as stone. "I count six besides them. Can you put up some kind of barrier? It would make things easier."

Merit speaks before Verias can: "I'm sorry, but Reshon made you my new target, Kin, there's no point in trying anything."

Though Verias doesn't know Merit well, he's sure he hears honest regret in the fleshbound's voice. Verias pushes down the guilt that swarms up inside him like a cloud of locusts, having to work hard to access the Wellspring. Magic slots into place around Verias and Kin, and she draws in an audible breath, belting on her knives.

"Are you ready?" she asks at a whisper. Verias shakes his head, his guts roiling. If he wasn't terrified by the prospect of fighting Merit with an Unbound Kin, he'd probably think he was probably dying from some kind of mortal river sickness. Kin gives him the gorgeous, feral grin he's been missing so much. "Drop the light. And try to keep me away from Merit. I want to be taking cuts at guards before I engage with them."

Verias nods, and Kin winks at him before starting to climb up the bank. Verias follows, not wanting to let her get out of the vaguely spherical shape of his enchantment. He nudges at it, trying to make it bigger for Kin's strategy. Crossbow bolts sing through the air as soon as the guards see them, but when the bolts pass through Verias's shield, they catch fire, breaking up into glowing embers and falling to die on the street. One of the city guards tries to put his hand through the barrier and snatches it back, hissing through his teeth.

"You don't have to do this, Merit," Kin says. Merit looks at her with mournful dark eyes. Verias moves to his right, shunting Kin away from Merit. The guards spread out, the oval of light cast by the lanterns they carry splitting into two golden circles.

"Reshon won't give my soul back until you're dead and he's in Reshon's hands." Merit jerks their chin at Verias. "I'm sorry," they say again. Their voice cracks.

"It's we who should be sorry, Merit. We failed, and you got caught up in it," Kin says. "If I survive this, I'll get your soul back. I swear it."

"Don't bother. I can't bear another failure." Merit steps through the magical boundary, a thin skin of searing orange light surrounding them until they emerge on the other side, unharmed. A cold lump of fear, tinged with failure, settles in Verias's stomach as Merit draws their knives, watching Kin expectantly like one might observe a friend considering her next turn at cards. Kin, calm as the Wellspring's waters, mirrors them.

"It's funny." Merit circles Kin, taking up a fighting stance. "How many times have I told you that your apologies were useless with no conscience behind them?"

"A fair few." Kin's smile is humorless, wolfish.

"Kin, don't," Verias says. Kin ignores him. "Please, let's just run."

"There's nowhere to run," Merit says. "Unless you've cut me into bits first."

"Take care of the rest," Kin tells Verias.

Verias wants to obey, but it's nearly impossible to look away. Now that she's no longer Bound, Verias feels as though every look he gets at Kin might be the last, and that makes his stomach boil with fear. It's nearly impossible to focus on magic, and he struggles to shore his wall up as he tries to keep one eye on the guards and the other on Kin and Merit.

Merit makes the first move, a slash that Kin turns away as she backs past Verias. Verias's guts tie in knots; he knows enough about knife play that he can tell Merit is trying to drive Kin back. And it's working, Kin taking half a step back, and another half-step, a full step, never returning a stab or a slash. The sick feeling only gets worse as Verias follows, pushing the bubble out. She isn't fighting. She isn't even trying.

"Kin, fight them!" Verias yells. His magic begins to lose its integrity, pulsing faintly with the waves of nausea trying to roll him under. "I'm losing my hold on this spell!"

"I'm doing my best!" Kin shouts, the last word turning into an angry growl. "Stop distracting me!"

When Verias looks at Kin, he can tell she's hurt by the way she moves. She and Merit move away from him, toward a narrow alley. In the shadows, their shapes meld together into a dark blur. Verias tries to circle the guards, get to Kin, his shield forcing them back with yelps of pain as they're scalded. One drops a lantern, and it explodes into hot shards of glass as the oil burns out all at once. A high scream pierces the dense, damp air, transforming into a shriek of anger.

The other lantern goes out.

"Kin?" Verias calls. His eyes, adjusted as they are to the light, see nothing but shadows, vague shapes. Wellspring's waters, let her be alive. No response. "Kin!"

No response. Verias struggles not to vomit. A hideous gurgle comes from somewhere to his left, and he swallows hard, mind wobbling back and forth between staying in the terror of dark or creating light to see possibly greater horrors.

He opts for light, reaching for the comforting presence of the Wellspring's power, and decides it's less dangerous to have his back turned to the city guard than Merit. A dim purple orb fills the mouth of the alley with its glow. Merit is mercifully bent double, too busy with whatever injury Kin has done them to pay Verias any attention. Verias's relief only lasts a moment; a slender brown hand lies on the rounded cobbles next to Merit's foot. Verias gags, but he manages not to be sick.

"Kin?" He calls again, eyes streaming. She's nowhere to be seen, though her soul sings to him somewhere in the darkness. The only sign that she was ever there is the severed hand.

"She's always been an obnoxiously tricky little bitch." Merit straightens, the stump of their arm tucked tightly into their other armpit to stanch the bleeding. They take a step toward Verias, who backs away.

"Too smart for her own good," he agrees.

"You understand." Merit's voice is strained, weak. On the verge of snapping. Verias takes another step, boots scuffing as the remaining guards back away from him in turn. For the first time since his training with Felver's men, his hand goes to his belt for his knife. Merit gives a hoarse laugh, though Verias isn't sure at what. He pulls his weapon.

"I don't want to hurt you, Verias. You've been very tolerant of me considering the fact that I killed you. It's just that Kin clearly loves you. You're a good hostage. It's nothing personal." Their remaining hand is white-knuckled on their dagger.

At the mention of Kin's name, Verias's senses return to him in a rush, and he lets the light blink out. Guards shout for light, terrified of being caught in the dark with Kin. Verias creeps away, dodging guards by sound alone. Fists clenched painfully, he fills the holes in his shield with chunks of magic, and thanks the Wellspring that the nausea has released him from its clutches.

Verias recognizes the scent of Kin's hair oil before her hand covers his mouth, her other arm snaking around his chest to pull him stumbling back against her body. Even knowing it's Kin, anxiety rises up so strong inside Verias that he's lightheaded. Though he no longer breathes, she stays there for a long moment, as though sensing that a small comfort is needed.

"Count to ten and bring the light back," she whispers, her breath against his ear sending a shudder down the length of Verias's spine.

Kin lets go, the cool of the night air curling around Verias in her absence. He doesn't start counting right away, trying to put up his knife and disoriented by Kin's presence as always. When he does get to ten, he finds himself running up against a barrier, like trying to dig through frozen ground to reach the Wellspring. All of the spells he's ever learned have fled, his barrier has long since crumbled, and Verias silently curses himself for a useless fool as terror rears its head. Why does he have to fail now, when it's most important?

"Slow down!" Kin shouts somewhere to his right, like she knows exactly how fast Verias's brain is going. Wellspring's waters, he's pathetic. Verias pushes down his panic with gritted teeth, hands balled into fists, and the street flashes to searing life.

Kin has vanished again, despite how much brighter this light is this time. There are more guards missing than accounted for by a single inert body laid out on the ground. Merit's eyes find Verias, and their body angles toward him. Their face is ashen and sickly, and Verias wishes he could do something to ease their suffering. It will have to wait. He raises his dagger and tries to make his body as small a target as possible, and Merit falls upon him faster than an eyeblink. Verias manages to turn away a vicious thrust with his free hand, but his back runs up against a wall, Merit advancing as inexorably as a rockslide, raising their knife.

Kin is suddenly between them, raising a spear stolen from

one of the guards. Merit's slash strikes the wooden pole, taking out a massive chip and leaving it weak. Kin snaps the spear over her knee, ducking under a slash that should have slit her throat. Verias tries to get out of the way entirely, and Kin steps into the space he just left. She raises the blunt end of the halved spear, but Merit reverses their grip, and she has to bend backward to stay in one piece.

Verias steps in to grab Merit's injured arm, pulling them away from Kin so she can regain her footing. Merit uses Verias's grip against him, pulling him down to drive their knee into his gut. He doubles over, the magic rushing out of his body in an instant, plunging them all back into darkness once more. Merit's knee smashes into his nose, and Verias trips as he staggers back, falling to one knee that screams in pain when it strikes the hard cobbles.

He scrabbles desperately at the Wellspring's power, trying to bring back the wall, bring back the light. A cry sinks into the walls around him. Kin's voice. Verias doesn't want to make a sound and tell Merit exactly where he is, but a groan escapes him with the struggle of building magic pressure. Light flares bright around him, just in time to see Kin get between him and Merit again. She screams, the sound turning to rage as her arm drops to her side with Merit's knife clean through it. Her left hand brings around the half-spear, and Merit falls with what is unmistakably two horrible thuds. Their head rolls to the side, bouncing on its way.

"Who wants to try me first?" she shrieks at the remaining guards.

Verias tries to bring up the barrier again, feels the pieces crumble, but the guards are already running. Verias's fingers are numb from clenching them into fists, his stomach uncurling like a pill bug under a log.

"Why were they with Merit?" His voice comes out a croak.

"No idea." Kin's voice is terribly pained. She looks down at Merit's severed head, which is glaring up at her from the ground. "Too bad they can't talk like this. We could ask. Merit, blink twice if you were sent with these amateurs."

Merit just scowls at her.

"Oh well." Kin jams the spear into Merit's inert body. "Sorry about this." She picks up Merit's head and tucks it under her arm. "Can't have his head growing back to his body. Come on."

Kin goes back to the bank, where she picks up the basket of willow bark. Verias follows, wiping his nose on his sleeve. As his eyes adjust to the moonlight in the absence of lanterns, he notices that there's only a tiny smudge of blood left behind. His nose feels very, very broken, but at least being dead offers a few positives. Kin's health is the greater worry now, anyway, a dagger still sticking out of her forearm.

"Should I take care of that wound?" Verias asks.

"No. Wait until we get back, or someone might be able to follow your magical trail. Or the blood trail."

"I'm sorry I didn't help, I just panicked, and—"

"It's better that you didn't help. Throwing around fireballs would have been a beacon for anybody looking for us," Kin says. The knots in Verias's stomach loosen just a little bit.

"It was so easy when it was Reshon, back at the inn," he says.

"That's because you hate Reshon. Neither of us wanted to hurt Merit." Kin's voice is weak, frayed at the edges with pain. There's blood on her face, dripping on her shirt. Verias takes the basket from her so she can lean against him with her good arm. "We'll help them. I don't know how, but we will."

They walk the rest of the way in silence. When they get home, they find that Mistress Trissel has left four buckets of water out by the cellar so they can rinse off the river water, but they have the wound to contend with first. The knife has gone between the two bones of Kin's forearm, mercifully clean. Looking at it is nowhere near as bad as Merit's severed hand, or worse, their head, with all its meaty bits just hanging off its stump of a neck. It glares at Verias when Kin props it against the foundation of the house.

"I think I can fix this," Verias says.

"You'd better be able to, or fetch Mother quick. Otherwise I'm likely to bleed out. Hold my arm, will you?" Kin asks. Verias obeys, one hand below her elbow and one around her wrist. Kin grabs the knife hilt and takes quick, short breaths, one, two, three, before she jerks the dagger free. Blood begins to pour from the wound, and Verias works as fast as he can, patching together muscle and nerve, vein and skin. Though his power has increased since being unsafeguarded, it's still far more difficult a job than any he's done for her, less instinctive than working on his own wounds. He can't tell when he's doing something wrong, listening as Kin's breath comes in sobs. She's shaking, barely able to keep her feet, and even after the wound is healed, Kin is unsteady and on the verge of fainting.

"Come. You need to rest," Verias says.

"I want to wash up."

"Stubborn."

Verias has gotten used to her undressing whenever she feels like it just as much as he's grown accustomed to her stubbornness. Kin strips down completely, and Verias pours two buckets of well water over her body, trying to avoid her hair. She shudders as the cold water sluices over her body, rinsing away blood and river water.

Verias himself is beginning to feel drained, but he washes up too—after he sends Kin inside and finds some clean clothes. When he's finished, she's notably not resting, instead sitting up in bed with Chestnut, frowning into the middle distance. Merit's head is nowhere in sight, probably tucked into the cabinet.

"You need rest," Verias says again.

"So do you," Kin says.

It strikes Verias that no matter how angry Kin is—and these days she's frequently angry—and no matter how much he hates the way she plays at being strong when she needs help, she still cares for him. She still risked her life and endured pain to protect him, and what has he done for her? Fumbled every enchantment he tried, and gotten her soul put back in her body when she didn't want it.

Kin holds out her arms, and Verias knows that the only thing he can do to repay her is to offer a little comfort. Her skin, though damp and cool, sends warmth flowing through him. Even if she was just cold and wet and tired, Verias would want nothing more than to hold her, to be near her. Wellspring's waters, he hopes he can give back even a fraction of the safety and peace of mind she gives him. She deserves it, and that fact makes Verias bite his tongue before he can tell her how much he loves her. She doesn't need his foolishness now.

CHAPTER THIRTY-FIVE

THE AIR IN THE CELLAR IS HEAVY, PRACTICALLY RIPPLING like water when someone knocks insistently at the cellar door. It's likely past noon, given how hard she slept, but Kin pulls a pillow over her head and ignores the sound. She knows exactly who's bothering her, and she is in no mood.

"Please tell me this is a nightmare and I can go back to sleep," Verias says.

"You answer it."

"You're on the outside," Verias says. He has a point, but Kin would rather have his knees in her kidneys than get up. She lost quite a bit of blood before Verias healed her, and her face is tender and puffy where Merit slashed her. Kin drags herself out of bed anyway, pulling the sheet off Verias to wrap around her body. He grumbles something that sounds grouchy.

"Wellspring's waters, what in the world happened to your face?" her mother asks as soon as she lays eyes on Kin.

"Nothing."

"Well, you didn't get that swimming the river."

"Nope." With sunlight and fresh air to wake her, Kin is beginning to wonder what her next move ought to be.

"I need my willow bark please, it needs to be laid out to dry or it'll mold. Do you want me to look at that?" Kin's mother asks.

"No, Mother." Kin hands over the basket of bark.

"It'll scar if you don't take care of it."

"I don't care."

Kin's mother looks her up and down like she's never seen Kin in her life. She shrugs and walks off without another word. A heavy sigh builds inside Kin, but she holds her breath. She's too awake now to go back to sleep, though it's all she wants to do. There's too much to worry about for rest. She can rest when she's dead. Stars willing, that will be soon, because Kin can't take much more fighting, much more guilt.

"We should leave for the Wellspring," she says, turning back to Verias. Her breath catches in her throat when she looks at him sitting up in bed. His nose is swollen, maybe broken, and he has two black eyes.

"I don't think we should. With a plague going around, the Wellspring will be utterly overrun with people looking to be healed. Speaking of which, do you want me to heal your face?" he asks. "It looks horrible."

Kin fingers the cut, which makes a neat, aching line from her cheekbone down to her throat. "I really don't care. Besides, you look worse than I feel."

"You don't care now." Verias closes his eyes. The thick, chill presence of magic fills the air, and Kin watches the swelling go down and the bruises lighten. He touches his face, feeling for tender spots. "You might care later."

"Why would I?"

"You're tired, Kin. Sometimes when you're tired, things stop mattering." Verias stands, crossing to her. For once he isn't shy about standing in front of her in just his braies. "Let me fix it. If not for you, then for me. I can be of use if you let me."

"You have been of use," Kin says. He sighs.

"I've been a burden, and then, even though I'm afraid of everything, *I* shouted at *you* for being scared. It was unkind of me, and I'm sorry. I don't think I ever said I was sorry." Verias picks a scab off his lip as he watches Kin, waiting for a response.

Something tense and painful unravels inside Kin. She tried to push him away, even though she knows perfectly well that she needs him. And he stayed with her, despite her constant attempts to destroy anything that makes her even the tiniest bit happy.

"I'm sorry, too. I don't know why I can see good in you, but not in me, when we're so much alike." Kin knows why, her throat bubbling with the burning need to tell him: she always thought herself a monster, from the first feral thoughts that sprouted in her childish mind. She can't remember exactly how it started, but she remembers the cold terror, the need to hide in shame. It's no wonder the shadows called her, no wonder she found a natural talent for creeping through the night. No wonder it was so easy to steal. She'd already done far worse things in her head.

"I suppose I've been living with guilt and a conscience all along. It's too much for a person to bear all at once," Verias says. His gaze grazes her body, exposed by the sheet falling around her elbows. "Kin, you should be burned all over from walking through that barrier yesterday."

Kin looks down. Most of her skin is completely healthy, except for some old scars, a fresh cut along her ribs, and the new brown mark on her arm where Verias's healing has only mostly taken. "It must be the link," she says. She suddenly feels more naked than she ever has in her life, and fights the urge to wrap the sheet more tightly around her body. She's ashamed of her mind, and she refuses to be ashamed of her body, too. She needs one thing about herself that she doesn't hate.

"I can still feel your soul. Hear it, if we're in the same room." Verias's dark eyes are bottomless, locked on hers. "I'm afraid, Kin. What if this connection breaks? What if you die? I'll be alone, in silence, forever."

Though Kin has no awareness of Verias's soul, she finds herself worrying for the future too. It's the first time she's done that in years, if she doesn't count plotting her escape. She doesn't. Getting away from the Binders wasn't so much as a goal or even a plan as it was something to keep her mind occupied through the long nights spent awake, waiting to kill or be punished. Sometimes just waiting for the sun to come up. Stars, she's tired of waiting.

For a while, Kin and Verias just look at each other. Concern is clear in his furrowed brow, and Kin is sick with guilt just for making him worry. She brushes past him but doesn't lie back down. She just wants to keep her back to him and avoid the horrible naked feeling of being *seen* as she really is: scared, in pain, wanting everything she can't have. Happiness, peace. Him. That scares her more than anything else. Kin hasn't had a lover in years, has never been very good at being in love. She's good at *loving*, good at caring about her friends so fiercely that it hurts, just like she cares for Verias. She wishes with all her heart that she could be like him, be *with* him, but Kin doesn't trust herself not to ruin everything.

Verias touches her arm through the sheet. Kin has unconsciously pulled it around her whole body again. "I know you're in pain, Kin. Talk to me. Tell me what hurts."

"I can't," she whispers.

"Kin, please. At least look at me." Verias has a stubborn set to his jaw when she turns back to him. "I know you're afraid, but—"

"I wish you didn't know. I hate the way you know me. I hate the way you look at me." Kin stares at the floor, not wanting Verias to see the tears that sting her eyes, the emotions that are too big for her body to hold for another moment. "Just Bind me again. Please. You don't have to destroy my soul, just keep it with you."

Verias is silent for a time. Though Kin doesn't look up at him, she's sure he's watching at her in that thoughtful way of his.

"You'd trust me with your soul?" he asks.

"Yes," she whispers. He risked everything to get her soul from the Binders. Kin can't trust herself, but she can trust Verias.

"Kin, please look at me." His voice is a whisper so heavy with emotion that it might have been a shout. She meets his eyes, one warm brown and the other endless black. "I am not worthy of carrying your soul for you. Nobody ever will be. That's why I had to get it back to you, no matter the cost."

Kin can barely breathe. He doesn't understand, and he just keeps reminding her that *she* is the one unworthy of *his* trust. Verias's eyes search her face.

"Kin, do you know why I can see through you?" he asks. Kin can only shake her head. "It's because you're not a pane of glass, it's because you're a mirror. You and I are so much alike. The difference is that you've had to harden your heart, wear a mask and armor to protect yourself, because you had nobody to care for you. I did."

"Did you?" Kin asks. His family is one nightmare after another, and he didn't appear to notice until they stooped to kidnapping. Only Verias's brother sounds worth calling family at all, and he's dead.

"In some ways, yes. In others, no. Perhaps I was trying to make up for my own family's failure to see my needs by healing you. I wanted just one person in the world to take care of you, since you aren't interested in doing it for yourself. Because you do see me, and for me, that's a relief. I don't want to watch you pull away from me, Kin. I can't even begin to explain how much it hurts. And that's selfish, I suppose."

Kin wants to tell him why she always ruined her friendships, why she and Honor slowly drifted apart until that last embrace. Why Iyara is dead and why she and Merit can never reclaim the closeness they once had. But speaking the words is impossible. Her mouth opens, and no sound comes out except a single sob that she chokes back like bile.

"I saw your dreams, Kin. I saw what happened when they Bound you."

"Please don't remind me. I just want to forget." The guilt is all-consuming, a fire that threatens to burn her alive. Her tears are searing, her body trying to shake apart.

"It's your secret to keep. I just wanted you to know that I see why you do this."

"You don't." Kin wipes her face on the sheet. "I trusted myself better than I trusted her, and we all paid for it. She paid the greatest price of all of us." It's all Kin can manage.

"Oh, Kin," he whispers. Verias takes her face in both hands, pulling her down to kiss her forehead. "I'm going to see if I can get you some tea. It might comfort you."

Kin almost bursts into tears, so grateful to him for letting it alone, for giving her space to breathe, if only for a few minutes.

Verias makes sure Kin is settled before he dresses and emerges from the dim cellar. For a few moments, he just breathes in the hot, smelly Honey Quarter air and feels the sun on his face. Living underground is becoming stifling. Still, the cellar is preferable to the house; the tension between Kin and Mistress Trissel is worse than sitting in the dark all day, and it can only get worse when the place fills up with sick people.

Mistress Trissel is in the kitchen, laying scraps of willow bark on a rickety-looking wooden rack to dry. It's shocking how like Kin she is, working with precise movements, her back straight and her eyes fixed on what she's doing. Chestnut weaves around her ankles, apparently having decided that the house is preferable to the cellar. Verias clears his throat.

"Has she changed her mind?" Sola asks, not looking up. For a moment, Verias has no idea what she's talking about. He forgot about Kin's face with all the other things to worry about.

"No. I was just hoping you had tea," Verias says.

"I don't, but I have some nice tisanes in the cupboard there. I wouldn't bother, though. She's impossible when she's like this," Sola says.

Verias bothers. The jars of herbs are each labeled with a neat, rounded hand. Peppermint, verbena, chamomile, really everything imaginable, and many Verias doesn't recognize.

"She'll come round eventually," Sola goes on. "She's always struggled with anger."

"What?" Verias feels like he's fallen asleep while Sola had a whole conversation without him.

"She's so angry she can barely speak. You didn't notice?"

"No. Why do you say that?" Verias asks. Kin is tired, slipping into despair, but she doesn't seem angry to Verias's eyes.

"I can just tell. I am her mother, and she hasn't changed at all."

"Mistress—"

"It's Sola," she corrects Verias. Her abruptness is strongly reminiscent of Kin's. This is a woman who will brook as little nonsense as her daughter, and apparently respectful use of a title falls under the category of nonsense.

"I don't think she's been allowed to change," Verias says.

"Can you tell me what happened? It may make things easier for her."

Verias gazes at the tisane labels, not really seeing them. Kin is scared and tired, and she wouldn't like it if he went around spilling all her secrets. He picks up a jar of olive leaves, remembering that calm evening camping, and turns back to Sola, who watches him expectantly. Again Verias can feel magic simmering beneath her surface calm, and curiosity gets the better of him.

"I don't think I should tell you. She's been through a lot, and I wouldn't want to tell you anything she isn't comfortable saying herself. I'd rather talk about you."

"Me?"

"You have magic," Verias says.

Sola's eyes narrow. She's been standing at the table the entire time, but now she sits, leaning back in her chair with her arms crossed. Defensive.

"You're powerful," she says. Verias shrugs. He's always been the weakest in his family, and it makes him uncomfortable to have his newly released power mentioned. "But you shouldn't be able to tell."

"I'm a Carrier. The Binders removed my safeguard. I've never actually heard of—not even read about—another Carrier doing this, so there's no way to know what changes have occurred."

"Hm. What are you thinking?" Sola asks. She's clearly noticed that Verias's voice is distant as he looks over her head. A memory is nagging at him. Perfect sapphire blue flawed by a scrap of glimmering gold.

"She's like you, isn't she?"

"Yes."

"What *are* you?" Verias asks.

Sola sighs. She's doing the same calculations Verias is, wondering whether she should say anything about Kin that Verias doesn't already know. Verias has to know, or his mind won't let him rest for a second until he does. Something is near to connecting in his head, wool about to come together into yarn, an answer to . . . he doesn't even know what.

"Does Kin know?" he asks.

"No. Our gift is ancient, tied to the moon. It's hidden even from us until it's released. Once it is, it's still impossible for anyone" —her eyes narrow— "*almost* anyone to see unless we show it."

"Did your husband know?" Verias hopes that leading her along with questions will draw an answer to the unknown question out of one of them, he doesn't know which.

"Yes. How could he be a father to Kin if he didn't know everything about her?"

Verias doesn't want to think about the argument that will ensue if Kin finds out that her mother has kept something as important as this from her for so long. He wouldn't want to be on the wrong side of Kin's anger for finding out and not telling her, but he isn't sure it's his place to tell her. And yet.

"So why not tell her?" Verias asks.

"Like I said, Kin has trouble with anger. Everything is always about how unfair life is, but changing it isn't in her nature. I feared that she would misuse her gift out of anger."

Verias bites his tongue. Life is exceedingly unfair, and for a girl growing up in the Honey Quarter, it would be clear from the start. With her gentle heart, it must have been a constant source of pain to see other people suffering. She, like her father, has done her best, but still carries the same burden Verias does. The millstone's weight of never feeling adequate rests on both their shoulders, and now that's easier to understand. In her own way, Sola has done as much damage as his own father.

"Don't tell her," Sola says. "It's not your place, and I won't release her power even if she asks, so there's no point."

"Of course it's not my place," Verias says. "But it is yours."

"I just got her back in one piece after I thought she was dead. I'm not risking it."

"Perhaps this is your chance to start over, instead of keeping secrets from her."

"She's keeping secrets from me. I can tell," Sola says. She's just as stubborn as Kin, and it makes Verias want to scream.

"What are you to her, anyway?"

"I'm her best friend," Verias says. Sola watches him, looking very much as if she wants to accuse him of hiding something, but she won't get anything from him if she does. He won't tell Sola that he loves Kin before he tells it to Kin's face. If he ever has the courage to do it at all.

"I suppose you are, at that." She stands and goes back to work, leaving Verias to return to the cellar in silence.

CHAPTER THIRTY-SIX

VERIAS FINDS KIN WITH HER MAP OUT, SITTING ON THE BED with the paper spread over her lap. The sheet she'd wrapped around her body has slipped down again, exposing her soft brown shoulders. For a moment, he just takes in her puffy, cut face, the way she chews her bottom lip as her eyes dart around the map. She doesn't look up while he makes tea, nor does she speak until he hands her a cup and asks where she's thinking of going.

"I haven't the faintest idea. If I'm Merit's target, perhaps now is the time to go to Lubria," Kin says. "They'll always know where I am, but the further we get from them before they're put back together, the better."

"That's so," Verias says. She seems entirely her old self, and Verias doesn't trust it as far as he can spit.

"The problem is that we would have little choice but to go to Estren for a ship, and that's Lord Felver's territory. We'd be walking into a lion's den," Kin says. "And to get to Estren—"

"We need to go through Solemn Gorge," Verias says before she could finish. He sits down with her, looking over her shoulder at the map.

"I suppose I didn't think that plan through very well. We'll have to go elsewhere. Abseris would be safe, but it's so far." Her sigh is felt more than heard, as if she can't admit that she wants to go there. Still, Verias can sense her yearning and understand.

If she can't be here in the city she loves, of course she wants to be in her father's home country. "They'd expect me to go there, anyway."

"Well, last we saw Felver's army, it was closer to Sestera than it was to Estren. It might well be safer in Estren than it is here," Verias says.

"Mm." Kin sips her tea, her thumb tapping the edge of her map. "Mother lives somewhere on the way. Maybe she'll let us stay in her house for a few days. It's not as if she's using it, and we could tend to her garden for her so the weeds don't take over."

Verias watches her as she scans the map. While it's easy to see that Sola has hurt Kin, and that they argue whenever they're in a room together, their relationship is still an anomaly in his mind. With the way Kin talks about her, Verias expected Sola to be like his father: cold, constantly belittling her. That Kin simply assumes her mother would allow them to stay in her home tells Verias that Sola at least cares more about her daughter than she does her honor.

After a while, Kin lets out a long sigh and folds the map, setting it on one of the pillows. Her sudden burst of energy has waned, leaving her curled around her tin teacup.

"I wish I'd been able to kill Reshon when I had the chance," she says. "I don't want to fight Merit again, and I don't like keeping them captive. I don't like that the only solution I can think of is cutting any new growth off of them."

"I don't like it either." The thought makes Verias queasy. "Do you know if there's any way to break the enchantment that connects them to you?"

"You can only end the contract by killing your target, having it passed on to someone else, or getting a new assignment that overrules the first."

"So a fleshbound can't have two targets at once?" Verias

asks.

"No. I don't know why. Maybe it's some form of linking? It makes sense, since your soul is being connected to another person's by an enchantment, but . . . Verias, are you listening?"

Verias's brain is already running away with the idea of linking. It's important, somehow, but he's been thinking about it as something between Binders and their fleshbound; after all, Lessa mentioned that touching a soul would cause a Binder to empathize too much with their fleshbound. But what if Kin and Verias's link formed because he was her target?

"Why would it grow stronger after the contract was passed to Merit?"

"What?" Kin asks. Verias doesn't even notice he's spoken aloud until she says something. He has to stand up, has to pace to make his brain work harder, faster.

"It's something to do with the flaw. The touch. It's hidden, but under extreme stress, perhaps—"

"Verias, you're talking nonsense." Kin catches Verias's hand, sending a rush of life into his veins.

"Kin, what was Reshon doing with Lord Felver?"

"Felver probably had fleshbound." Her thumb skims his knuckles. She must sense the turmoil bubbling up inside Verias like poison. He's sick with it, the room tilting.

"Reshon was my handler, for lack of a better word." He presses his hand to his chest, as if he could feel his soul if he pushes hard enough.

"What flaw are you talking about?" Kin asked. "The one in your eye?"

Verias's hand falls to his side. He'd forgotten about that again—he's rarely looked in a mirror even before they moved into the dank little basement. The dark spot that spread through his iris wasn't there until after joining Felver's army, was it? He can't remember. Though he recalls every battle, the time he spent in Estren, being trained to use the war machines, is a blur of misery. Escape attempts, trying to fade into the shadows of a strange city while Reapers chased him, brutal canings and sleepless nights.

"He Bound me," Verias says.

"He can't have," Kin replies. "You can't send a fleshbound after a fleshbound, remember?"

A tiny knot of tension unravels in Verias's chest, but there are so many other fears inside him that he's still trapped, swaddled in chains.

"He tried. He tried to Bind me, but I can't remember. Why can't I remember?"

Kin's hand presses against the back of his neck, strong and firm and comforting, anchoring him in the present. He's in a whirlpool of nauseous memory, grasping for something too painful, too ephemeral to hold. A deep ache settles behind his inkblot eye, making him press his hand to his temple in search of relief. Reshon tried to take his soul. Something went wrong, something broke, shattered, let something loose.

"It doesn't matter," Kin says. "You're here now. You're with me. You're safe."

"No," Verias croaks. He'll never be safe again, not until he knows for sure what Reshon did to him. "I have to know."

"Shh." Kin strokes the back of his neck, smooths his hair. Her hand is a searing brand against his already feverish skin, but it sends a chill through him. He feels about to shake himself apart.

"You remember your Binding. I saw."

"I do, but I remember everything." Her fingers brushes his jaw, the cellar so quiet that he can hear beard hairs scratching against her calluses. The sound makes him shudder. "Verias . . . if you want to find out, I can do that for you. But you won't like what needs to be done."

Verias and Kin gaze at each other for a long moment. To find and question Reshon, Kin needs to be Bound, otherwise the chances of survival drop precipitously. His deep need to learn what's gone missing from his memory wars with fear of hurting Kin. What's more, Kin might use this as a way to destroy her soul. He can't let that happen, can't bear the thought of perhaps the last person who cares about him thinking of him as little more than an insect. Verias wants her in his life, as his best friend or his lover or any way he can have her. Watching her pull away would be agony.

"I told you, I trust you with my soul. I want you to keep it," Kin says. Verias has to look away. Her trust in him shouldn't be what puts Verias over the edge, but it is. He shatters, panic washing over him in suffocating waves. The room darkens at the edge of his vision, but not like shadow is closing in. It's as if a searing light has burst to life, making everything else seem dimmer by comparison. The only thought in his mind is that one way or another, this is the end of their short stretch of stability. He can't Bind her. He can't live with what happened to him. Everything is falling apart. Everything is falling apart. As usual, he takes the coward's way out. He faints.

Magic fills the cellar, swirling around Kin like a whirlwind, so strong that lights dance before her eyes and her ears pop. The wave tangles her hair, knocks over all their meager possessions, and swings open one of the cabinet doors. Verias crumples like an empty flour sack, and she grabs his shirtfront to keep him from falling to the hard dirt floor. Fear grips Kin's insides like a fist, but she forces herself to remain calm. Her mother is upstairs. She might be able to help.

Kin puts aside her teacup and settles Verias on the bed. She rushes to the door, not bothering to do more than pull the sheet tighter around her body, but her mother still beats her there, bursting inside without knocking.

"What happened?" she asks, wild-eyed and white as a sheet. She pushes past Kin before she gets an answer.

"He panicked. It's a long story. I don't think I should tell you all the details."

"You two and your secrets."

"What?" Kin doesn't know of any secrets Verias has.

"Quiet. I'm concentrating." Her mother closes her eyes, takes a long, deep breath.

"Mother, what secrets?"

"Just clean up." The words are a bark, and Kin jumps.

Kin decides it best to obey; it isn't as if there's anything else she can do. She dresses and picks up her map, which has blown into a corner, and starts setting upright everything that's fallen, shutting the cabinet door where Merit's severed head is wrapped up in as much fabric as Kin could find in their saddle-bags. A tingle of magic sweeps through the room, and out of the corner of her eye, Kin can see her mother kneeling on the floor, completely still, as she stares at Verias.

That is *not* Verias's magic. Kin is intimately familiar with the feel of his work: being deep underwater, not needing or wanting to breathe. This is dry, sandy snow, tingling across the skin. It shivers around Kin's mother, shifting like dunes or drifts. Kin can barely breathe. Her mother has magic, has hidden it from Kin for forty years. Why would she do that, when Kin's father had magic, too? Though he rarely used it, talk of magic had been completely normal in their household. Nothing would have been different, had Kin known. Or perhaps, everything might have been different.

Kin is no fool. The only reason she can think of for her mother to keep her magic a secret is that Kin had been born with the ability, too, and that it had been somehow important to hide that fact from her. She wants to be angry, to hate her mother, but she's too worried about Verias to give it any further thought. Later.

Her mother stands, stiffly turns to Kin as if the movement hurts. Kin swears she can see tears in those sharp eyes.

"Mother, what is it?"

"It reminded me of your father, that's all. When he was ill." Her expression is set, and though Kin's instinct is to brush it off, the sight of Verias unconscious fills her with an uncharacteristic sympathy.

"I know you loved him to the end," she says. They never agreed, but they always loved each other.

"Yes, well. He'll be fine when you wake him. If you do. He's exhausted, and must have just lost control of his magic." She fusses with her long purple skirt. "You should be careful with him, Kindred."

"You think he's hiding something?"

"No." Her hands tighten on the fabric. "He scares me a little, and he should scare you, too."

"I'm not afraid of anyone."

"That's exactly why I'm saying it. I can see how you look at him."

"Mother, do *not* get in my affairs or I'll get in yours," Kin gives her mother a warning look. They can talk about it later, as long as her mother *gives over.*

"I'm very supportive of you settling down, I'm just saying that maybe someone less dangerous—"

"Nobody is settling down, Mother, and you don't get to tell me what to do when you've been lying to me all this time." Though Kin doesn't raise her voice, her mother stands very still, a deer staring down a wolf. Kin's whole body tenses with the familiar pain of being looked at like she's a predator. Though she hasn't been close to her mother in years, it aches like an old wound. "You've been hiding magic from me. Why?"

"For your own good," her mother says.

"How's that?" Kin's voice shatters.

"It's inside you, too. Your father and I feared that your anger would lead you to misuse it."

Kin's hands ache from clenching them into fists. "How can a person misuse a healing ability?" she asks, this time through her teeth.

"Our gift isn't like that of the Healers you know. It's old magic, like your father's was. I can harm as easily as I can heal."

"And you thought that given that gift, I would hurt people? Why would you think that?" Her whole body aches with the effort of holding in the hurt, the anger. Magic like her father's could have been an anchor, could have kept her from falling apart when he died. It could have been enough to fight the Binders.

"You were so focused on learning to fight, so bitter about your lot in life," her mother says, as if reading her thoughts.

"I wanted to learn to fight because I thought I had no other choice. I looked around the Honey Quarter and saw hundreds of desperate people who were willing to do anything. I was bitter because there were people on the other side of the Honey Gate drowning in so much money that they could never spend it all. There still are. Men like Lord Felver, who see people like Verias, people like *you*, as toys. People like the Binders, who live in luxury in their homepalace while I'm in the dungeon being tortured." Tears stream freely down Kin's face. "Why shouldn't I want to tear all that down?"

"I don't know, Kindred. That's why I didn't tell you. I had no reason for you. I still don't. I just knew for sure that I couldn't bear the thought of you hurting someone with a gift I gave you."

Kin laughs. She can't help it. All that effort, and Kin still became a monster more horrible than her mother could have imagined, with no sign that she'll become more human. The world keeps throwing obstacles at her, reasons to fight or die. Her mother's fears can only be assuaged in a world where girls don't dream of becoming King of Thieves because it's the only way they can imagine easing the pain of their neighbors. No such world exists, and it's unlikely to in Kin's lifetime. But she can at least try to make the world fairer for one person, and that person isn't herself.

Kin turns her eyes to Verias's slack face, the fear and worry gone from his features. He looks five years younger in sleep. Her mother might be wrong about many, many things, but she's right about one thing: Kin loves Verias. Maybe in a different life, a kinder world, she would be thinking about settling down with him. Her mother touches her shoulder, and Kin wants to pull away, but there's no one else there to comfort her.

CHAPTER THIRTY-SEVEN

VERIAS LURCHES OUT OF RESTLESS DREAMS AND INTO consciousness with acid in the back of his throat. He's lost, in pure darkness, his nose filled with the scent of earth. Terror wells up, but strong, gentle hands touch his face, bringing him back from the brink of panic. He isn't buried alive; he's in the now-familiar cellar, on a straw mattress, a warm body pressed against his.

"Shh. It's me. It's me," Kin's voice says. Her presence makes Verias feel as if he's stepped back from the edge of a cliff, but his body still aches with tension, his chest still bound by fear as palpable as heavy rope. Whether she can sense his anxiety or has simply guessed, her thumbs stroke his cheeks. "How do you feel?" Her voice shakes, and Verias reaches for her hands. They're unsteady.

"Anxious," he says, not sure whether he's talking about himself or her. "What happened?"

"You lost control of your magic. You had me worried."

"I'm sorry," Verias whispers.

"I know. Let me light a candle."

Kin's weight lifts from the mattress. Flint grinds against steel, and vague yellow light fills the little basement room. A creak of old hinges precedes the scent of evening in the Honey Quarter. The air is always cooler and fresher this time of day, and Verias wants nothing more than to wander the streets just to escape the stuffy basement. When he sits up, he's dizzy and weak.

Kin perches next to him. She doesn't speak, just letting Verias lean his head against her shoulder. City birds chirp outside, and a breeze manages to find its way underground.

"I'm going to find Reshon and question him," Kin says.

"I know."

"I need you to Bind me," she says, and Verias wants to. A wave of self-loathing rises within him. Selfish. He's refused over and over again, because he's afraid for her, and now he's ready to change his mind because he needs something.

"I don't want you to put yourself in danger for my sake. Again, I mean. We should leave Sestera before anything else bad happens," Verias says. Kin sighs, reaching for Verias's hand.

"Stop that." Kin touches his face, thumb brushing his lip, and he realizes he's gnawing at the skin there. There are bits of it on his tongue, and he has to take them out of his mouth with his fingers, face hot with humiliation. He doesn't know how anyone stands being around him. "Verias," Kin says sternly. Verias meets her eyes. "You don't need to be ashamed. I'm not disgusted by it. It hurts me to see you ripping at your skin, but scars don't mean you're ugly. Otherwise I'd be ugly, too." She touches a scar on her chest where her collar has fallen open.

Verias wants to kiss it, feel the raised skin against the tortured flesh of his lips. His whole body is on the verge of shivers, sudden desire trying to take hold of him despite everything else.

"Where did it come from?" he asks.

"I think it was from a fight in a tavern. I don't remember it very well. I used to drink quite a lot before jobs. I was just a baby, really. Sixteen? Seventeen? Young. I was a mean drunk, which was useful. I wanted to be King of Thieves. I had to prove I was the bravest, the smartest. The meanest," Kin says. "It wasn't being mean that eventually made me King. It was being in control."

It was her control that drew him to her in the first place. Before she was Unbound, she always seemed to know exactly what to do. He misses that about her, he realizes, and she's clearly missing her own shattered confidence. Perhaps that's one of many reasons Kin has drawn away from Verias, why she hasn't kissed him in so long that he's forgotten what it feels like.

"Can I make a confession?" he asks. Kin looks at him strangely before she nods. "That night when you put your hand at my throat . . . that was the safest I've ever felt. It was quiet in my head because I knew you were in control."

To his extreme shock, her bark of a laugh is followed by tears spilling down her cheeks.

"It's funny." She wipes her face with the heel of her hand and places that same hand at the juncture of his collar bones. It fills him with warmth. "I kept regretting that. I remembered you being too callow to mistrust me. I could only think of the danger I put you in, the fear I felt, thinking I could kill you in an instant. I didn't ever think that you remembered it differently."

"It was like nothing could touch me." When Verias touches her arm, his fingers find the fresh scar from Merit's knife. It's puffy, healed yet still healing. He brings the mark to his lips, listens as her breath catches, the most beautiful sound he's ever heard.

"Doesn't that hurt you?" Kin pulls her hand away, dragging it along his jaw to raise his chin, forcing him to look at her. Something about that single, innocent act of control sets Verias on fire.

"I don't care," he says. Kin's dark eyes search his face for a moment before her lips are on his, soft and opening for his tongue like a sweet, ripe apricot splitting at the seam. Her hands find their way into his hair, taking two great handfuls in a firm grip. The faint dizziness from his spell returns, making him feel drunk and woozy. Or maybe it's her, stealing away all his senses with her kiss.

"Please do this for me," she whispers against his mouth. "Let me give you that peace of mind again. Otherwise you'll always have questions about Reshon. Let me help you," Kin says.

"I can't."

"Take my soul. It's yours," Kin says. Verias tries to look away, but she holds him still with her hands still tangled in his hair, forcing him to gaze into those deep, dark eyes. "Don't say you're unworthy. I've chosen you because I trust you. It's yours. I'm yours."

With those words, his last defenses crumble. "And I'm yours, Kin. Always. I'll guard your soul with my life."

Something warm blossoms inside Kin, something that frightens her with its tenderness. How can she protect herself when a feeling that soft can make a home inside her hollowed-out chest? But with Verias, she doesn't have to protect herself alone. He's not just offering to protect her soul, but with that one word, *always*, he's offering to shield her heart with his. Nothing can take away the pain of her past, but perhaps, if she lets Verias protect her as she protects him, Kin can have someone who understands. Perhaps Merit was wrong. Perhaps she and Verias can be stronger together.

"Lie down." Verias kneels on the floor so she can obey. He brushes the hair from her face before pressing a gentle hand to her forehead. "There is a chance this could go bad. I've never done this."

"I'm not worried. I trust you," she says.

Verias smiles sadly at her. "Oh, Kin. Hold my hand. I'll be quick."

Maybe Kin should be scared. Her first Binding was the worst day of her life, without question, but she never does learn. She closes her eyes, magic piling on top of her, and grits her teeth in preparation for the pain. For a moment, Kin hopes that Verias's Binding will hurt less than Lessa's.

The agony is exquisite, far more finely honed than her first Binding. Instead of a crushing pain, it feels as if her entire body is shot through with needles. Her last breath burns in her lungs as she holds it behind her clenched teeth; she doesn't dare let it out or it will surely turn to a howl loud enough to echo through the empty streets.

The pain doesn't stop, but instead slowly fades as Verias works the conscience spells to ease her tortured mind. Kin's breath eases out with a low groan, and for a long time, she can focus on nothing but trying to breathe again. It takes ages for Kin to even notice that Verias is stroking her hair, kissing her tear-streaked cheeks. He holds her soul clutched to his chest, as if it's the most valuable thing in the world. It glimmers faintly, like the warning coloration of some venomous insect.

"I'm sorry. I'm sorry," Verias chants. "I don't know what happened. I almost lost control of it. I'm sorry."

This time Kin doesn't bother to tell him that he apologizes too much. She's too glad it's over, too tired to speak. Too relieved to care about anything else. Though her arms are weak as carded wool, she wraps them around Verias's neck in search of comfort. He holds her tight, kissing her hair until she grows too tired and has to lie back.

"Can you mark Reshon for me? Make him my target?" Kin asks.

"This part doesn't hurt, does it?" he asks. "I've seen it. I think I know what to do, but—"

"It doesn't hurt."

It almost feels good when Verias's magic washes over her again. It's like the reverse of having someone lay a warm blanket over her body in winter; a sheet of cool relief falls over Kin, calling her to her purpose. Magic hums in her brain, dragging her toward the homepalace, where she can feel Reshon going about his horrible business. Preparing to take Verias back to Bind him for unknown ends.

Kin lets out a long sigh, her anxiety soothed by the knowledge that she can do something, anything, to make it all right. Verias touches her face, his hands soft against her skin. Unworn by weapons and gentle enough to cradle her soul.

"Kin, I want to try something else. A counterspell to keep you safe."

"I trust you," she says again. Magic pierces her body once more, the pain shallow this time. She can breathe, can feel the magic sifting into place around her. It fades slowly, filling her with something Kin has never felt, a tingling like too much sun on her face.

"There. You're safe. They can't hurt you any longer."

Warm droplets fall upon Kin's face, one, two, three. The last falls upon her lips, salty on her tongue. When she opens her eyes, Verias has turned away, not wanting her to see him weep.

CHAPTER THIRTY-EIGHT

VERIAS CAN SEE THE CHANGE IN KIN ALMOST IMMEDIATELY. By the next day, she's back to her old self, plotting and planning without the cloud of guilt hanging over her head. He carries her soul in his pocket, occasionally touching it to make sure it's still there. It's like keeping a just-hatched baby bird with him, checking to see it's still breathing and peeping and hungry.

If it's possible, she's more gorgeous than ever. Perhaps it's only because every time their eyes meet, hers are filled with a softness he's never seen in them before. When he touches her, she leans into him instead of pulling away, her smile easy and frequent. It's a fight for Verias to keep his hands off her while they're helping her mother put sheets on beds and boil up medicines, and it must be obvious. Sola keeps frowning at him as if warning him not to waste time.

Still, Kin and Verias eventually have no choice but to hide in the cellar. As Kin swings the doors shut, she pauses, cocking her ear to the alley above. A stab of anxiety pierces him before he realizes she's not listening for intruders, but tilting her body toward the homepalace.

"Reshon?" he asks.

"Something felt strange. But he's still there, doing whatever horrible things he's been up to since you Bound me."

"Being handsome and terrible, probably," Verias tries to keep his tone light, but Kin gives him a sharp look.

"He's definitely both, but I don't want to talk about him." Kin locks the doors and puts the key in her pocket.

"Actually, let's. You said you made a joke to Reshon ages ago," Verias says. "You refused to tell me what it was."

"I asked him if he was going to threaten to stab me and stick his cock in the hole." Kin shrugs.

"Excuse me?"

"It's something men have said to me in the past." She's so casual that Verias almost thinks she's making a joke in extraordinarily poor taste.

"That's the most horrible thing I've ever heard," Verias says.

"People who want to sleep with fleshbound have . . . interesting tastes. You become accustomed to them." Kin sits on the bed, stretching her long legs out in front of her.

"Wait. Wait, have you—"

"No, I most certainly have not!" she snaps, uncharacteristically prudish.

"I'm not judging you, I'm just saying that if you *could* it would certainly be interesting to try," Verias says.

"What's wrong with you?"

"Nothing! Why does that sound like an accusation?"

"This is an unexpected side of you," Kin says. Verias can't help but laugh at her surprise.

"What about me makes you think I don't have intellectual curiosity?" he asks.

"I just didn't think that curiosity extended to such things," Kin says. Verias laughs even harder at her choice of words. "Shut up or I'll stab you and put your *own* cock in the hole."

"Horrifying." Verias drops down next to her. "You are very scary."

"Don't tease." She puts her arm around his shoulders and presses a kiss to his forehead. It's all the invitation he needs to pull her down to kiss her. She makes a surprised little sound in

308

the back of her throat that turns into a laugh as Kin straddles his lap.

Her weight is at once comforting and bittersweet; Verias wishes he still breathed and could feel her pressing the air from his lungs. His hands steal beneath her shirt, searching out her plump, heavy breasts and the soft, inviting curve of her stomach. Kin's kiss turns rough and hungry, her tongue searching out his, her hands tangled firmly in his hair. Wellspring's waters, she's so incredibly strong and yet so soft.

Kin breaks away to tear off her shirt and trousers, standing above him in only her braies. Verias kisses her stomach and thick, muscular thighs, runs his fingers over the curve of her glorious ass. She laughs again, tilts his chin up.

"You'd do anything for it, wouldn't you?" she asks. He nods, too overcome to speak to tell her he'll crawl on his belly for her. "I told you already. I'm yours. All of me."

Kin allows Verias to lay her down in the pillows, lets him run his hands over her body. He grazes her nipples, listens for her gasp. She shimmies out of her braies, utterly uncapable of shame or shyness, and spreads her legs for him, inviting him to skim two fingers over her cunt, feel the wetness there. He lifts his fingers to his lips, letting the taste of her fill his mouth, rush to his head. If all the other ways he's touched her didn't make him hard, this should have, but being dead is even worse than he thought.

"Do you like the taste of it?" Kin's voice is velvet in his ear.

Verias doesn't speak, not wanting to ruin the moment with death. He slides down between her open legs, kisses her inner thighs, the skin slick and hot. She shifts beneath his lips, letting out a languid sigh. Her life energy buzzes in his head, her soul a sweet hum against his. He laps the wetness from her silken cunt, revels in the taste and scent of her. Kin moans as he traces circles around her most sensitive spot, listens for her breath to catch when he finds the right rhythm.

It's when Verias suckles at her swollen pearl that Kin gasps. He keeps going, urged on by her little whimpers, the startled, hoarse cry when he rakes his teeth over her. Kin grabs two great handfuls of hair, rolling her hips to put his lips and tongue just where she wants them. She tenses, fresh wetness running down his chin, and shudders once, twice, before she goes limp, her hands falling away.

"Stars, Verias," she murmurs, the last word dissolving into a gentle laugh. "Here." Kin pulls Verias up to unlace his trousers.

"Don't bother. I'm too dead for it." He moves her hands away. As usual, she's naked while he's fully clothed.

"Oh, fuck." Kin's face is clearly disappointed, and Verias winces with a chill stab of guilt. "I was going to make you cry."

He laughs, the guilt melting away, and lies down beside her. "Were you?"

"I still could, if you're feeling adventurous."

"Adventurous how?" Verias asks, a bit of anxiety making his teeth clench. Silly. She'd never do anything he doesn't want.

"Have you done it in the ass before?" Kin asks.

"Either a few times or none, depending on whose ass."

"Yours is the ass at play here," she says, smirking at her own joke.

"Then never."

"I thought you said anyone will do." That odd moment at the tailor's shop seems a thousand years ago, and it's a surprise that she'd remember it at all.

"Yes, well, you can imagine that my options were limited in Solemn Gorge. It's not like I was here running through everyone in Sestera," Verias says.

"I really do recommend it," she says.

"I don't think I would even if I could."

"Oh, Verias." Her eyes are soft as she smiles at him. Kin

brushes a lock of hair from his face and kisses his forehead. "You are so lucky I'm here to be a bad influence on you. Clothes off," she says.

He stands to obey, watches her cross to the washstand while he strips off his shirt and unbelts his chausses. She picks up the little pot of greasy ointment that he always forgets to put on his scabs, and scoops out a great blob that she puts on the back of her hand, warming it with her fingers. He catches a little thrill of nerves that isn't at all unpleasant.

"Hurry up, I want to ruin your life," she says, folding herself up to sit cross-legged at the foot of the bed, still fully naked and shameless as always. It gives Verias quite a lot to look at, and for a moment he just stands staring at her. "Verias," Kin says, her voice soft but firm. "You can say no if you want to."

He definitely doesn't want that. He finishes undressing and follows her gesture to sit at the end of the bed. He feels horribly exposed, every scab, scar, and pockmark visible, his belly an uncomfortably present fold, but Kin looks at him like he's the most beautiful thing she's ever seen. For a moment she rests her uninjured cheek against the inside of his thigh, smiling so softly that Verias is sure she's forgotten her promises to make him cry and ruin his life.

"Lie back," she says, and her voice drops to a whisper. "Relax."

Verias obeys. It's strange and miraculous to feel the anxiety flow out of his body when he knows that Kin is there to take control, to keep him safe. When her soft lips brush his inner thigh, a moment of anxiety catches him, but it fades almost as fast as it came.

Kin's lips and tongue send shivers through Verias, but the sensation is tempered by the knowledge that he's physically incapable of becoming hard. He isn't sure this will work at all, but he can enjoy the attention, the novel pleasure of her finger circling a place he's never been teased before. Verias accidentally lets out a small, surprised moan, and Kin chuckles low in the back of her throat.

"Ready?" she asks.

"Yes." He wants more, wants to satisfy his curiosity and his growing desire, though he fears he'll have to visit the Wellspring before he can ever finish what Kin has started.

Her finger slides inside, giving a gentle feeling of fullness that's unlike anything Verias has ever experienced. Kin's lips brush his inner thigh, his balls, and for a moment, he's overwhelmed by the sensation. But soon Verias wants more, letting a groan of need escape before he can stop himself.

Kin pushes deeper, finding a place Verias hadn't known to exist. Buzzing pressure builds up inside him, spreading through his whole body. Slow, lapping waves like the tide coming in and out of the Embraile, reaching their nadir when Kin pauses now and then to slick her finger again before she goes back to work. Each time she presses against that sensitive spot, Verias soars higher, closer and closer to a release building deep within.

"Kin, please . . ." He doesn't know what he's asking for. Harder, faster, *something*, anything to break the tension.

"Patience, love. Patience."

Verias has none, his emotions rubbed raw by all that's happened, by mounting pleasure and frustration, by that one word: *love*. He tightens involuntarily around her slowly teasing finger, not a drop of shame left in his body. His need is a hot coal in his belly, spreading fire until it washes over him in waves that just kept coming, until stars burst in front of his eyes and he has to ask Kin to stop.

The shudders rocking Verias's body calm, until it's only his hands that shake. He's in a warm haze, barely able to notice the sound of water being poured from a ewer, soft fabric against his stomach when Kin cleans hot stickiness from his skin. She pulls him into her arms, and he finds himself so utterly spent that he simply melts into them, so comfortable and happy that nothing matters but her.

CHAPTER THIRTY-NINE

THERE'S ALWAYS A QUESTION, THE MORNING AFTER TAKING someone to bed, of whether things will be different or awkward, which is why Kin prefers to vanish into the night, leaving no trace but the occasional pair of braies or a stray stocking. There was, of course, the time she abandoned an entire pair of trousers, but she usually pretends that never happened.

Verias is a bit quieter than usual while they eat breakfast on the cellar steps, trying to get a little fresh air before they lock themselves in again. Chestnut is visiting, washing his face in the doorway and paying Kin little mind. There are voices upstairs, and somebody with a hard, dry cough. Kin remembers that cough, the nausea and delirium, the misery of it all, and struggles to finish her cheese and toast.

"Oh *no*," Verias says. Kin looks up from her sad, cold breakfast, waiting for him to explain, but he just stares through her, a look of horror spreading across his face.

"What is it?" she finally asks.

"I forgot about Merit," he says. Kin bursts out laughing. "Wellspring's waters, where did you put them? They had to have heard everything last night."

"Don't worry, I took precautions. I bundled them into a few shirts and a blanket so they wouldn't hear any of our plans. It works just as well for fucking noises."

"Thank goodness." Verias's shoulders relax. The coughing

315

from the house slows, ceases. "I can't help but feel bad for them all wrapped up in there like that."

"Merit is just lucky I didn't make good on my promise to piss in their mouth after I cut their head off." Kin tosses her bread crust into the alley for the birds. It's stale anyway.

"After all that talk of apologies?" Verias asks.

"It's the principle of the thing, Verias. I have to keep my promises or my word isn't worth anything," Kin says.

Verias snorts, but falls silent. He finishes his own breakfast and reaches up to pet Chestnut, frowning. Something is clearly bothering him, and it isn't just post-fucking awkwardness. Kin is by no means as good at reading people as Verias is—most of the time he just looks anxious to her—but she knows that it's Reshon he's thinking about. She touches his knee, and he jumps, startling Chestnut, who runs into the house, ears back and tail fluffed out.

"Tell me what troubles you," Kin says.

Verias gazes at her for a long time, an intensity in his sad dark eyes like she's never seen before. Not even the night before, when they'd thrown everything else aside for a few sweet hours.

"I'm afraid I won't be strong enough for what's to come," he says. Kin squeezes his hand.

"You are so much stronger than you think, Verias. And when you can't be strong, I'll be strong for you."

"What's your plan?" he asks.

So trusting. It occurs to Kin that he gave himself over to her completely long before last night. She wishes she could go back in time and slap herself for not noticing, for being so caught up in pain that nothing else mattered. Stars, he's so beautiful, inside and out. She wants to kiss every little scar on his face, to show him how much his trust means to her. Instead, Kin stands and hauls him up, tips his chin up with her thumb. Kin barely brushes his lips with hers, not wanting to hurt him; his lower lip is shredded, puffy.

"Unfortunately for all of us, it's time to talk to Merit."

Kin has never actually seen what happens to a fleshbound who's been beheaded, but she'd expected a sort of tiny doll's body growing on the stump of the neck. When Kin takes them from the cupboard, Merit has instead grown a fleshy lump of a neck and one shoulder with some of a chest. They still can't talk, of course, because while their glob of flesh likely has portions of lung inside, they have no diaphragm to control the air. How Verias talks when he doesn't breathe is a mystery for another time.

"We need your help, Merit." Kin places them on the washstand, propped up with a towel. Merit scowls at her. "Blink once for yes and twice for no."

"They're likely wondering how many blinks for 'fuck yourself with your own knife.'" Verias puts in.

"That's three blinks," Kin says. Merit helpfully blinks three times to let her know that they understand. "Merit, listen. You probably noticed that Verias Bound me again. I mean to find and capture Reshon. I also mean to keep my promise and get your soul back, so I need you to cooperate. Does he keep your soul with him?" she asks.

Two blinks. Unfortunate. Kin wasn't exactly *hoping* it would be that easy, but she hadn't completely ruled out the possibility that Reshon would consider it safer to keep Merit's soul with him. He hasn't underestimated Kin yet, which is a shame. Kin has many fond memories of defeating those who have done so in the past.

"If we want to get their soul, we'll have to break into the Vault," Verias puts in. "Go back to . . . well, not the original plan. That was much more subtle. It's likely we'll have to put a hole in the Vault to get in at this point."

"Mm." Kin doesn't want him to see the wild glee that bubbles up inside her at the thought of doing what she wanted from the start: destroying as much of the homepalace as possible in one fell swoop. Stars, if she could kill Lessa . . . it's almost enough to send a shiver down her spine. Merit is glaring at her, as if they can see into her mind. "You don't think it's possible," she says.

Two blinks.

"Do you think we have any better chance if you're able to help?" Verias asks.

"Verias, don't ask them that."

One blink.

"Ugh."

"What?" Verias asks.

"They've always been like this." And Iyara had always agreed with them, much to Kin's annoyance. "They fancy themself more rational than me."

"Well . . ."

Kin rounds on Verias. He watches her with a blandly smug smile on his face. "What exactly is that supposed to mean?" she asks.

"I'm quite sure you felt a little tingle at the thought of blowing a hole in the Vault of Souls," Verias said.

"Just a little one," Kin says grudgingly. He's too smart, too curious, *and* too perceptive for his own good. She's going to murder him.

"Perhaps having someone level-headed along might help?"

"Oh, *please*. They're no more rational than I am," Kin says. "They beat me half to death after Iyara died, or would have if I could die."

Merit very deliberately blinks three times. Kin wants to take them off the washstand and kick them into the alley with the trash. Whether the vivid image is one of the nightmarish thoughts that like to intrude on her brain is a matter of opinion at this point. She usually doesn't mind Merit as much as they hate her, but they're doing a good job of making the feeling mutual.

"You go fuck yourself. Do we want to risk them betraying us?" Kin asks Verias.

"I don't know. They could certainly be useful, but there's the obvious problem of them having tried to kill me."

"And me. Though in fairness, I also tried to kill you. I say we're better off hiding them somewhere and giving them their soul after we've stolen it. I'll ask Mother to keep an eye on them. It's not as if they'll go anywhere for a while."

Kin unlocks the cellar doors and goes up to the house, where the kitchen is searing hot, water constantly on the boil to treat patients with tisanes and poultices. All the windows in the house are thrown open to entice a breeze, though the air from outside isn't much better than inside. The stink of last night's chamber pots, at least, is a healthy, normal stink. The musky, slightly putrid scent of sickness introduces a wrongness to the house, which Kin can't help but think is a sign that she'll never get her home back. It's probably foolish to think that she could.

Kin waits in the sweltering kitchen for her mother to come back from the front room; Kin can hear her talking to patients in her low, soothing voice. An intense envy wells up inside her, bearing a memory along on its swells. She was young, sick with red rose plague just as these patients are. Her mother had been too busy ministering to the other sick people to have any time to care for Kin. Kin's father was the one to soothe her fears and wash her ravaged skin, to blot her forehead with a cool, damp rag. She buried those keenly painful, lonely memories years ago, and struggles to push them back down. Why had her father gone and died when he'd always been the one to care for her and nurture her?

"What are you doing up here in daylight?" Kin's mother

319

asks. She holds a basin in her hands, filled with damp rags.

"Verias and I have business to attend to."

"Under the sanitary cordon?" she asks, arching an eyebrow.

"Don't worry. We shouldn't come in contact with another person," Kin says. It's only half a lie; she'll surely run into humans, but they're Binders, and she doesn't plan to leave any Binders she sees alive.

"Hmph." Kin's mother drops her basin on the work table and takes a kettle off the stove to pour boiling water over the rags inside.

"I need you to watch Merit while I'm gone."

"Merit? They're here?" She looks sharply up at Kin.

"They are, but they aren't well." Understatement of the year. Understatement of the century.

"Do they need care? Is it red rose plague?"

"No, Mother. They're fleshbound." It seems best not to mention her own Binding. "But I want to return their soul. They deserve to have it back."

"You mean you're going to steal it," Kin's mother says. "You never learn. This is just like what happened with Iyara."

"You don't know what happened to Iyara." Kin stiffens, guilt shuddering through her, followed by panic. If Verias's spells have failed, she's trapped with the memory, old pain and old regret.

"I know what rumors said. That you tried to steal from Lord Felver, and when you failed, you took Merit and Iyara down with you." She shaves soap into her basin with a knife as she speaks, utterly calm.

Kin takes a long, deep breath to steady herself. She doesn't want to argue, or she'll be distracted. All she wants to do was argue, but there's nothing she can say to the contrary. The rumors are true. Kin *did* fail in her one duty as the King of Thieves: to protect her people when they worked. She stood in Felver's bedchamber, half-naked and bleeding, and ratted Merit and Iyara out. All because she was fool enough to believe a lord in his silks, with his smooth-voiced lies, when he said that the only way to save her best friend was to tell the truth.

"I only want to help Verias and Merit," Kin said. And get revenge, but her mother doesn't need to know that.

"What were you trying to steal back then, Kin?" Her mother looks up from the wash. She's pale, dark shadows under her eyes from working so hard. If Kin knows her mother, she's also likely sleeping poorly. Kin bites her lip. Even if she hates her mother—she doesn't, she's only slow to heal, frozen in time— Kin knows that many others in the Honey Quarter depend on people like her mother to help treat those who likely have no other option. She has to be healthy.

"Don't worry yourself about it, Mother. You need to rest a little. I have money. Do you need me to hire you an assistant?"

"I'm quite well," she replies. "I'll watch over Merit, but Kin . . . be careful. I've just gotten you back. I don't want to lose you again so soon."

For a while, Kin can't speak. She recalls being sick all those decades ago, how she'd been too young and too scared to notice how tired her mother must have been, how hopeless she must have felt losing patients, even with all the magic in the world.

"I'll be careful," Kin says, and turns to leave.

"And Kin? Look after Verias, too," her mother says. Kin turns back.

"I thought you were afraid of him."

"I am, but when you lose someone, you lose a little piece of yourself. I know losing Iyara must have shattered you. The two of you grew up like sisters. Neither of us could bear it if you lost somebody else."

"I will, Mother. And just in case I don't come back, I'll put the money is in the cellar stovepipe. For when you need it."

Kin's mother shifts her feet. It's clear she wants to hug Kin, but she's been around sick people all day, and doesn't know how Kin will react. Though Kin is by no means the hugging type, her mother's openness softens her. Now that she's Bound again, there's no catching plague. She embraces her mother.

It's painfully awkward. Her mother is sweaty from working all day, and her hands are dirty and slick with soap, so she can't really return the embrace. But she lets out a long, shaky sigh, and Kin is glad to release a little tension.

"What did she say?" Verias asks when Kin heads back downstairs.

"She'll look after them."

Kin doesn't want to talk about what happened. Her mother's sudden desire to exchange affection feels strange and fragile. Half of Kin's heart wants to push her away—she wanted distance for so many years, so why should Kin give her anything else?—but the other half of her heart is still that of a hopeful child, lying awake at night, feverishly watching the line of yellow light beneath the door. Hoping that her mother would return from the heartbreaking work of caring for the sick, the dying, and the dead, to parent her.

"Do you think she'd be able to heal them once we have their soul in hand?" Verias asks.

"No. She's too tired. Working too hard. We'll either have to find someone else or drag them along, wherever we go."

"Presumably through the tunnel," Verias says. "I don't know of any other way out of the city, do you?"

"By boat is the only other way, but we'd have to go through the tunnel to get to the Fishers' Quarter to buy or steal one. Or climb that bank by the willows."

"No matter what we do, we're certainly in for a fight," Verias says.

"We should rest until tonight. We'll go after dark." Kin

reaches for Verias's hand. Their eyes meet, and for a moment, Kin hopes. Outside, it begins to rain.

CHAPTER FORTY

KIN KEENLY MISSES SHADOW ON THE WAY TO EMMALA'S tavern. Rain is absolutely bucketing down, and the tavern is closed, all its windows dark except the one in the attic room where Emmala sleeps. Kin wants to make sure Emmala is well, not in any trouble after the Sanitary Council found her secret way out of the city, but there are only so many hours in the night during high summer. A long, dark winter night would be much better for making trouble.

Kin leaves Verias at the gate and slips through, sidestepping puddles to keep her footsteps silent as she ghosts into the stable. Much as she enjoys Verias's company, it's good to be alone for a moment or two after days of being stuck in a cellar. The dry, dark stable is empty, the smells of horse and straw still strong. No city guards, which puts Kin on edge, but she still calls Verias inside.

Boards have been hammered over the hidden door, and a chain looped between the bars to two opposing stalls with no break in the links. They'd brought a sorcerer in just to seal it off. Kin looks around for a tool to open a link, but finds none. It would be easy to break off the bars in the stalls, but Kin doesn't want to destroy Emmala's property. Having no business and possibly a fine for smuggling is bad enough without having to replace things.

"Verias?" she says. "Can you cut this?"

"Of course." Verias waves her away and pulls the chain taut.

Her body shudders with magic as he draws it in. A shearing blade of blue-white cuts through the air and slices the chain, which falls to the ground with a din of clattering links. Kin hoped that her ability to sense Verias's magic would fade when he Bound her, but nothing about the Binding worked out as planned; she's still stuck with stomach-churning guilt and reminders of her father whenever Verias uses magic. If anything, her ability to sense his work seems even stronger now.

Kin grabs the first board blocking their path and wrenches it down. The wood is unsanded and rough, but she's strong and frustrated at how unfair everything is, and her fingers are callused. Verias's magic shivers behind her, but Kin carries on, tearing away boards and throwing them to the side until she can open the hidden door. When she turns to Verias, he's looking at her with that thoughtful expression.

"What?" Kin asks.

"I always thought you were so strong because you were fleshbound," Verias says. "But you held your own against Merit."

"It's not the Binding. I spent years running around on rooftops and getting in fights before then."

Which is why Kin had been planning to retire from active thievery. A person can only take so much damage before they have to stop.

"Sounds horrible." A ball of light appears over Verias's right shoulder, lighting the entrance to the tunnel.

"So does sitting around all day reading," Kin says.

"I am *offended*. What's your ideal day like, then?" Verias asks as Kin pulls the door shut behind them.

Kin stops in her tracks. She doesn't know. She's been living in misery for so long that the idea of an ideal day isn't even a fantasy. It just doesn't exist for her. She would gladly go back to drunkenly stealing ladies' jewelry boxes over what she's been forced to do as a fleshbound, even if she hadn't been happy with that life in years.

She barely remembers why she became a thief. Was it her father, who she'd loved with everything she had? Was it looking around the Honey Quarter and wanting to put some of the ill-gotten gains of the wealthy into her neighbors' hands? Was it her mother, who had always wanted to hold Kin back, who clearly feared the anger and pain that Kin had held inside her entire life? Perhaps it was all of it, the perfect circumstances to create someone who saw no other choice but to steal.

Tears begin to prickle her eyes. She wishes she could go back and wipe out everything that has happened because she followed in her father's footsteps. If she could just hide the things her mother hadn't been able to understand, maybe she would be someone different. Someone better.

Verias takes Kin's hand, not saying anything. He just lets her be angry and sad and regretful, handing her a handkerchief when the tears flow so heavy that she has no idea how she has any left. The only thing she doesn't regret is that no other journey could have led her to meet someone who actually understands what it's like to be feared, to have urges that frighten even her.

Kin is merely damp instead of soaked by the time they reach the end of the tunnel. She presses her ear to the door to listen for guards on the other side. Nothing. In fact, the silence is eerie; she's gone through this passage dozens of times, and even at night there's insects or wind or *something*. She meets Verias's eyes, not wanting to speak. He gives her a curt nod, and an aura of magic surrounds him, sending a shiver down her spine like a cascade of goose down. Kin draws one of her knives.

She pushes at the door, but it doesn't budge. It must be barred shut on the other side. After putting up her knife, Kin tries pushing with both hands, then her shoulder. It just makes the joint ache.

"They must have bricked it shut," Kin says

"Good news, if I can get through it. It means there's likely nobody on the other side," Verias says.

"If. We need you at full strength for this."

"Just take my hand. It should help."

Kin reaches for Verias's hand. He sighs, closing his eyes, and Kin watches him relax, his shoulders dropping, his grip loosening. The light that drifts over his shoulder goes out, but the faint glow that surrounds him allows Kin to watch as he works, his face carved out by shadows. Tendrils of light filter up from the earth, drawing up from some deeply buried arm of the Wellspring. Pyramidal blocks of magic settle around them, shivering with energy.

This is wildly different to watch than her father's magic, which showered down from the stars like rain or tiny little meteors. Kin glances up at the earthen ceiling, wondering if her father could have accessed that power from beneath the dirt. She wonders if her mother's hidden ability can be seen. Fresh anger flows into her, stronger than before. She tries to force it away, but it refuses to let her go, burning her from the inside out. Kin closes her eyes, trying to block Verias's magic from view in hopes that she can calm herself. She takes deep breaths, tries to work the tension out of her jaw, but she's trapped in it.

"Kin. Kin, stop!" Verias snaps. He tries to pull his hand away, but Kin's fingers are cramped and aching, and she can't make herself let go. "Kin, let go."

"I can't. What's happening?" A fleshbound shouldn't have be able to feel this kind of fear. She shouldn't freeze, shouldn't feel her heart slamming against her breastbone and the tingling in her fingertips. She shouldn't be able to feel this foreign force inside her body.

"You're pulling it away from me.," Verias's voice goes flat. He's terrified too, it's all going wrong, it's all ending. "I need you to let go, Kin."

"I can't," she says again. She's sick to her stomach, her skin burning.

"You can do this, Kin." The effort it takes to speak gently is clear in Verias's tone. "You can let go."

Verias's soft, gentle voice is a balm, soothing away the tiniest bit of dread. For a moment or two, Kin breathes easily, but her chest tightens again. He reaches for her with his other hand, pulling her into an embrace. She should feel trapped by him, but instead she wishes she could just burrow into his chest and live there. To plant herself like a seed, to be soft and grow.

"Good. Good," Verias whispers into her ear. His breath sends a shiver down her spine, and sudden, unexpected desire blossoms inside her. Her breath catches, and the searing fire creeping into her bones is gone. The tunnel lights up bright as day, a thunderous sound tearing through the air.

The abandoned barn has blown out like an overfilled bladder, stale straw drifting down onto their heads. Verias is shaking, or Kin is shaking, or both of them are, she isn't sure. She's empty, starved for something she can't name, like she's been sick for weeks and just now feels her stomach is strong enough to eat. The full moon hangs above them, hovering in impatient wait for Kin to reach out for it. Instead, she clings to Verias.

"That was terrifying," she says. The thought of fighting after such a struggle is exhausting, but at the same time, anything else in the world would be easier than what she just did.

"We have to move," Verias says. "Someone will have sensed that. My family, if they're still nearby, or the Binders."

"Or my mother, and she's beside herself right now."

"Or her. I don't think Sola is capable of being beside herself; you certainly aren't."

"Sola? You've gotten cozy with her." Kin climbs through the slanting door, helping Verias behind her.

"She barked at me when I tried to call her Mistress."

Kin doesn't respond, too busy taking in the destruction around them. Boards and bricks and dirt are scattered fifty paces away. Did she do that, or did Verias? Her head spins with the thought. She doesn't *want* magic, not now. She would have accepted it as a child, as a way to do something good. She might even have taken it as an adult, before she was Bound. Here and now, magic is a useful tool for other people, but it has caused her too much pain to want to feel it running through her veins, to feel herself burning alive.

"Come," Verias says. "We only have so much time."

A light has come on in the farmhouse, and the old farmer will be out asking questions any moment now. Kin and Verias steal into the darkness and back toward Sestera.

Verias watches Kin warily as they walk, waiting for something else to go wrong. What happened shouldn't be possible. The Wellspring is as infinite as the air in the sky; nobody can take someone else's magic any more than someone can breathe another person's air. There's just so much of it that more rushes in to replace it.

It has to be something to do with the magic inside Kin, sleeping until this moment. Verias hadn't even thought about it when he Bound her, for she had been Bound once before with no magical effects that anybody noticed. That's why it got away from him, became twisty and hard to control and caused Kin more pain than it should have. Still, Sola had said that the power had to be released or it could never be used.

It must be the link, but Verias can't work out how. He'll have to experiment to riddle it out, and at this point, he simply does not have the time. They're traveling with all their belongings, just in case they have to get out of Sestera before the sun rises. That would surely break Kin's heart, but there's nothing to be done for it.

"Kin—"

"Shh!" she hisses, cutting him off with an arm across his chest. "Do you hear that?"

Verias stops to listen. They're nearing the main road, and a mournful nightbird is calling in a hedgerow. One or two crickets chirp irregularly around them, and rain patters down, but otherwise, the night is silent. He strains his ears, stomach tight.

"Music," Kin whispers. "This way."

She creeps toward the hedgerow, drawing Verias along with a hand on his doublet like he wouldn't follow otherwise. He isn't sure he wants to. Anything that puts Kin on edge is deadly dangerous. As they draw closer to the hedgerow, huge shapes loom in the darkness, blotting out the weak light of the stars and filling Verias with a sick, familiar dread that makes him want to vomit. He'd never expected to see the unholy things again, and his whole body itches with the urge to burn them to ash.

"Felver," Kin whispers. "That's his banner."

Verias's eyes are already on the banners at the edge of the war camp, but he can't see them well enough to make them out. It doesn't matter. His mind is racing already, terror skittering around in the back of his brain. Felver has come for him. Why else would he bring a whole army to Sestera? It makes no sense otherwise. It still makes no sense. Verias is one man. He isn't that important.

"The plague is his chance to take Sestera," Kin says.

"What? Why would he want to take Sestera?" Verias asks.

"Why wouldn't he? He already has his boot heel on half of Nerefin, and Sestera would surely win him the rest," Kin says.

"But wouldn't the other nobles stop him? It isn't as though

Nerefin has a king. There's no single person he can kill and assume power," Verias says.

"It might have a king by morning. Why would they try to fight him for a plague-ridden city? They've likely fled elsewhere by now, anyway. The rich always flee when things like this happen. We need to grab a soldier and question them. They probably won't know the full plan, but they can at least confirm my suspicions." She doesn't look at Verias as she speaks, instead scanning the hedgerow for a gap. "Stay here."

"Oh, go fuck yourself," Verias says. Her head whips around. "I'm going with you. Despite the fact that it appears I've been spending too much time with you already."

"Ha. Come along, then."

Kin ghosts alongside the hedge, appearing to fade in and out of the shadows. If Verias hadn't spent so much time with her lurking at the corners of his vision, he wouldn't be able to see her at all. She finds a place to sneak through the hedgerow, and Verias immediately regrets going with her. Even in the shadows cast by the full moon falling against the hedgerow, he feels exposed, the war machines rearing up into the blue-black sky like something out of a nightmare.

His stomach churning, Verias slips along behind Kin from shadow to shadow. Soon, Verias can make out individual voices of guards watching the perimeter of the camp. The smells of cookfires and horses fill the air, mixed with a wisp of sour wine. It's all too familiar, too much. The urge to destroy it all rears up inside him again, and Verias has to remind himself that an army is too much to burn by himself.

"That one there," Kin says. She points to a large form backlit by an orange fire, a spear leaning against their shoulder. "That one's tired or tipsy, see how he's swaying? We need to find an opening in the hedge that's close enough to shove him through."

Verias nods, though he isn't at all sure that Kin sees it. They feel amongst the thick leaves for a gap, but eventually Kin has to cut a few branches away, tossing them into the ditch. Nobody will see until the sun rises, anyway.

There's precious little place to hide, and Kin and Verias are forced to squat down on the other side of the road, keeping an eye-straining watch on the guard until he glances away. Kin moves like a snake, sneaking up next to the guard to grab him by the throat in a now-familiar choke. Verias hurries behind, jaw clenched so hard he sees stars, to snatch the spear out of the guard's hand and keep him from running Kin through. In moments, the man has gone limp, and together they drag him off the road.

"Can I have your handkerchief again?" Kin asks. Verias hands it over, still damp with tears or rain, and she shoves it into the soldier's slack mouth. It takes her a few harsh slaps to rouse him, enough that for a moment, Verias fears he's dead.

The soldier tries to scream, his voice muffled by the wad of fabric in his mouth, but Kin pulls out a knife and he falls quiet under her silent threat. His throat works, veins and tendons standing out against the skin, and Verias experiences a pang of sympathy against his will.

"I'm going to let you speak, and you are going to tell us why Lord Felver has brought an army to Sestera," Kin says. The man nods, and Kin pulls the handkerchief from his mouth.

"He heard about the plague." His voice is gravelly but steady. "Thought it'd be a good time to take the city, I reckon."

"Any other armies coming to help him?" Kin asks. The man shakes his head.

"I don't think so."

"How do you plan to get inside the gates?"

"I don't know. I just know my unit's meant to burn the Honey Quarter to ash," says the soldier.

Verias doesn't see Kin's hand tighten on her knife hilt, but he hears leather creak. He senses more than sees her mind working, her goals shifting, and fear like he's never known surged up inside him. She's Bound, he reminds himself, and can't die, but it doesn't comfort him at all. She'll destroy herself for Sestera, for the innocent people in the Honey Quarter. She's already done it once before.

"We have to warn the city guard," he says. He has to keep her from trying to fight the whole army herself. He has to protect her from herself at any cost.

"Too slow. We have to stop him, here and now."

"Him personally? How are you going to get to him in all that?" Verias gestures to the encampment at large.

"How do you think I got to you?" Kin asks in return. It was a silly question, yes. But there's a frantic energy around her, even in the dark. He'll try any argument.

"Why didn't you try to kill him when they sent you for me?" Verias asks.

"I didn't have my soul. I couldn't risk them adding more time. They would have known it was me even if I got away clean."

"And what about now?"

"I'm already a fugitive. You can only get so wet. Come on, Verias, we don't have time for all this talk," Kin says.

Verias has to admit, revenge is tempting. Felver was as much to blame for Verias's suffering as Reshon. Still, he needs to know what Reshon did, and why. They need to get Merit's soul back.

"There's too much that needs doing in Sestera," Verias says. "I'll make you a deal. I'll sabotage the war machines and then we'll get out of here, and we can come back later. I'll even make Felver your target."

For the space of several heartbeats—or what Verias remembers as that span, now that his heart no longer beats—Kin doesn't speak. The silence and heat of the night are suffocating.

"We'll have to bring this one with us," she says. "We can't let him go, and we can't leave him tied up here to starve if nobody finds him. So come quiet, or I won't be quite so thoughtful," Kin tells the soldier.

"I'll walk," he says.

"Good. Let's go."

Verias wishes he could breathe a sigh of relief, let the tension out somehow. He shrugs his shoulders instead. No chance of convincing Kin not to go with him, so they stuff the guard through the hole in the hedgerow and head toward the camp. Going back makes it feel like the world is a music box running in reverse, anxiety building in Verias's gut as he follows Kin around the perimeter, avoiding guards on their way to the black masses of war machines that blot out the stars.

Acid rises in Verias's throat when they get close enough to smell the hideous machines. Wood, oil, blood. Screams in his ears. The urge to run competes with an unexpected, shivering desire to climb inside one of the war machines, to turn all the destruction that Felver and Reshon squeezed out of him back onto them. He could destroy the homepalace with one of them, if only he still had the collar that bound him to his machine.

"Wellspring's waters," he whispers, shocked by his own thoughts. Kin responds only by grabbing his arm. Her grip is so tight that he looks at her, follows her shocked gaze to the steady light of a lantern passing between the war machines. A familiar voice, loud and commanding, cuts through the thick air of the summer night. A flash of pale blue and black is visible between spidery wooden legs, and in the space of an eyeblink, chaos blooms in the night.

CHAPTER FORTY-ONE

KIN IS ALREADY TEN STEPS AWAY BEFORE THE CAPTURED guard yells something she can't hear over the rush of magic in her ears. Whether Verias is gathering the power of the Wellspring to help her or stop her is unknown, and doesn't matter at all. Nothing can stop her from killing Felver. He gave her to the Binders, he lied to her, he used and tormented Verias. No target given to her with magic has ever drawn her as powerfully as Felver does.

Felver's guards move to surround him, but Kin's eyes are already fixed on him. The square face, older than it was the night it all fell apart. The eyes, exactly the same pale blue as the shade on his banners. The voice, deep and resonant, of a man born for grand speeches, for passing judgment over the guilty, with never a care for his own sins. Her knives are drawn, bound for Felver's throat and chest. She'll take no chances.

"You!" Felver's eyes lock on Kin's as she enters the sphere of light that surrounds him. There's anger in his voice, a steel that pierces the veil of time and makes fear rise in Kin, and her body stops without her permission.

"You're dead. You're dead for what you did to him and Iyara," Kin says aloud, to remind herself that there's no turning back now.

"I don't even know who you're talking about. You should feel lucky that I remember you." Felver is trying to anger her with his dismissiveness, trying to force her to make a mistake. "Kill her."

Boulders of magic tumble through the night. The nearest war machine comes apart, a massive snapdragon spraying seeds of magic across the camp. The blast throws Kin to one side, pain blossoming in her face and arm as she lets her body go limp. She rolls, surging to her feet at the soonest opportunity. Her ears ring. Somewhere nearby, somebody moans in pain. A shriek of frustration builds in Kin's chest, breaking loose as she scans the area. Felver is gone.

"Kin, run!" Verias's voice comes from the darkness. "Hurry!"

A sickly tingle of magic alerts Kin to a Reaper's lightning bolt just before it sizzles over her head. Thank the stars Verias Bound her again, because she doesn't stumble, pelting through the camp-turned-battlefield and dodging chunks of metal and wood embedded in the ground by the force of the explosion. Another blast roars behind her, a wall of air slamming into her back, and lightning screams through the night.

Kin grabs Verias as she sprints past, and he stumbles a few paces before coming into step with her. The voices behind them fade, until all she can hear is her own breathing and their feet pounding toward Sestera.

Kin chances a look behind them and nearly trips. Nobody is following them. She stops, listening for footsteps or hoofbeats.

"Why aren't they following us?" she asks.

"They know we're headed to the city." Verias's voice is strained. "They're mobilizing the army so they can get to Sestera before the city guard can do the same."

Kin's stomach drops. They should have just slunk away from the camp, instead of making themselves known to Felver. Now the only thing they can do to save the people of Sestera is to make sure they're prepared for the attack to come. Kin starts to walk, the last remnants of her final meal before being Bound trying to exit her body one way or another. Her mother. Emmala. Even Honor and Amity, safe as they might seem in the Wool-workers' Quarter, are in danger. As for the Honey Quarter, Kin simply does not know. Nobody but the actual denizens of the Honey Quarter care about that part of the city.

Kin wracks her brains for anything that might help. The homes of the Honey Quarter are uniquely flammable, often with floors covered in rushes, and thatched or wooden roofs where other homes have tile. Some are even roofed in oiled canvas, or windowed with paper. Felver has to know that the plague and everything else will burn to nothing in hours.

The only possible solution is to seek out the help of other no-bles and hope they come in time to end a probable siege, if they come at all. Felver's army is the largest in Nerefin, and who would fight him without assurance that they would not fight alone? If they have warning enough, the Binders might lend their magical skill and their fleshbound to the city. Someone has to know better than Kin. She can't be the only thing standing be-tween her city and destruction. She prays to the stars it's so.

The gates, as expected, are locked for the night. Kin's original plan was to tell the guards that she's on orders from the Binders, and to grease a few palms. It's always worked in the past, though it's always her last option. It lets Lessa know that she's in the city, and that was the last thing Kin wants most nights. Tonight she doesn't care. Lessa and the others can have her, as long as the guard knows what's coming from just an hour away.

"It's an emergency," Kin says to the man who opens the spy-hole. "Lord Felver's army is nearby, preparing to lay siege to the city."

The guard just stares at her.

Kin wishes their captive hadn't escaped back at the camp. "I do *not* have time to argue with you. Let us in."

"It's just that we've had some people get out of the Honey

Quarter and try to come in through this gate," says the guard. "You look like you came out of the Honey Quarter."

"I'm fleshbound, and this is my Binder." It's strange to say, no matter how true it is. "We were on a mission, bound for the homepalace when we came across the war camp."

"I wouldn't recommend trying to stop us," Verias says. The way his voice goes too bland under stress makes him sound deadly serious. Kin just hopes the guards aren't smart enough to know that Kin would never let him risk breaking down the gate. Not with what's coming.

"Thought I felt magic," the guard says. "I have to talk to my captain."

He slams the spyhole shut, and jogging footsteps can be heard moving away from the gate. Kin gazes up at the ballistae that line the city wall. Stars, let them be ready. Every muscle in her body is tight and on the verge of shaking, pure determination the only thing keeping her from collapsing into a heap of terrified shivers. Verias reaches for her, but she hisses at him through her teeth. She might shatter if he touches her, or worse, someone might notice that they aren't acting like a fleshbound and Binder ought to act.

The manway swings open, and a guard captain gestures Kin and Verias through with their prisoner.

"You're free to return to the homepalace," says the captain.

"We're staying," Verias says, acting the part she should have let him play from the beginning. He's in charge, not Kin. "Will you be sending scouts?" he asks.

"Of course. The Security Council is being called as we speak."

"Good. Someone needs to tell the homepalace," Verias says.

"Can't you send that one?" The captain nods at Kin. Verias's eyes narrow.

"She stays with me." Verias doesn't look at Kin when he says it, but it feels as though he's wrapped her in a comforting embrace. Sestera isn't quite doomed. She has her city guard, and she has the most powerful sorcerer in Nerefin. She has Kin.

Verias tries not to slouch in his chair, but it's difficult. His body is exhausted with anxiety and the hour and a thousand other things, but at the same time his mind races, still trying to work out why his magic was so affected by Kin's touch. It makes no sense, and it feels like someone is picking at the back of his brain with their fingernails, nagging and nagging until he can think of nothing else. If this comes to a fight—and that seems likely—being too close to Kin might compromise his abilities. Even after she disappeared in the darkness, he could still feel her pull on his power as he blew that war machine to pieces.

What happened since the last time Verias did magic near, not to, Kin? Since their fight with Merit, he's Bound her, he's tried to deaden her conscience (with nothing from Kin to indicate whether it worked), he's set her to hunting Reshon. It had to be one of those events that sparked whatever is happening, but which? The Binding was difficult, and he'd hurt her, but she's been Bound before. All of those spells have been done on her before.

Wait, no. There was something else . . .

"It's the counterspell," he blurts.

"What?"

"That strange magic effect: it's the counterspell." Verias drops his voice to a whisper. The guard captain has left them alone in a small room—possibly one used for interrogations—but someone might be listening at the door. "I wanted to make you impervious to Binders' spells, not thinking about the fact that I Bound you. I thought that perhaps it was to do with the inclusion in your soul, the magic buried deep within you. But

341

it's not you that's changed, it's *me*."

"What inclusion?" Kin whispers. "What are you talking about?"

"The first time I saw your soul in the Vault, I noticed a flaw, a speck of gold. Lessa thought it might be why you were so hard to control. It wasn't until I asked your mother about her magic that I knew what—"

"You knew she had magic?" Kin asks.

"It wasn't very obvious, and I don't think anyone else would notice; she says it's hidden, different."

"You asked her about it? Why didn't you say something?" Kin's voice rises.

"I . . . I didn't think it was my place to interfere."

"You're supposed to be my closest friend, my confidant, and you thought telling me would be interfering?" Kin asks, the anger in her voice making Verias draw away. He's so wrapped up in the excitement of discovery that he forgot that Sola was keeping secrets. That he was keeping secrets for her.

"I just thought that it was better to hear it from her."

"That's the problem, Verias, you don't know her. She was never going to tell me. I only found out because she would never, *ever* let anyone suffer when she could do something about it. Well, anyone except me."

Verias reaches for her hand. It's instinct driven by the audible pain in her voice. She pulls away, and Verias's heart drops into his stomach. He wishes he never asked Sola about her magic, wishes he could have ignored the curiosity that always seems to get him in trouble.

"I'm sorry," he says.

"I'm sure you are," Kin says. Her voice is so cold that he flinches, but there's nothing he can say or do, because she stiffens, turning her head away. Toward the homepalace. Verias knows what she's going to say before she speaks. "He's moving.

Where's he going in the middle of the night?"

Verias snaps upright.

"To let Felver in," he says. It makes perfect sense; why else would Reshon pretend to be a Reaper while possibly trying to Bind Verias? Why else would he lurk around Sestera, manipulating fleshbound and outright stealing from the Binders when he could have just turned Verias in? He's been using them to weaken the homepalace by stringing them along. What else has he done? What else has he interfered with?

"We have to stop him," Kin says.

"No. Think about it. With the attack, this is the perfect time to break into the homepalace," Verias says. "I can take Merit's soul back. I could free all the fleshbound."

"Not unless they all lined up to have their souls put back in," Kin says. "Besides, what's the point of being freed if they all just die in the streets?"

"If we split up, I can break in during the confusion. We couldn't have planned this better. The guard has already sent a message to the homepalace to tell them that the city is about to be attacked, so it's going to be in chaos. You can take care of Reshon."

"Wait . . . he's moving north." Kin cocks her head. "Why would he be going to that gate?"

"I don't know. Kin, you have to go."

"Just be safe, Verias. That place is a pit of snakes, and Lessa will kill you given the chance," Kin says.

"She'll have to work hard for it."

"Good. Good." Kin crosses to the door, pauses. "We'll talk when this is over, Verias."

Nausea churns up in the back of Verias's throat, but he nods. "Meet me at the East Gate."

"I'll find you." She rushes out of the room.

Verias wants to believe that they'll both survive this, fleshbound and dead or not. He wants to believe that she'll still care for him afterward, but dread has swaddled him in its thick, suffocating arms. He should've told her he loves her, just so she'd know. It's too late now: he can feel her fading into the distance, sprinting toward Reshon.

He too has to move, making his way out of the guardhouse and into the markets, dark and dead. The cobblestones hump out of the darkness to try to trip Verias, but he stays on his feet, running as hard as he can. The streets feel uncommonly empty, especially when he cuts through the Golden Quarter, where many of the rich have their homes. Not even servants or animals move, and Verias knows that Kin is right. The nobles and the other wealthy have fled the city. Though he's terrified, he's comfortable in his certainty that splitting up was the right thing to do. They can't risk Reshon letting Felver in before the Binders and the city guard are mustered, nor can they let this opportunity to set things right pass.

As he nears the homepalace, Verias senses magic and slips into an alleyway. Kin would be proud of his instincts, that he doesn't simply run. Instead, he listens. Voices follow the tell-tale tingle, but he can't make out much. They're speaking too softly, their voices a susurration like the rushing of the Wellspring below Verias's feet. There's no question of who they are, surrounded as they are by the glow of magic. There are only eight of them, out of many dozens in the homepalace, but eight Binders are nothing to scoff at.

Something stirs the air behind Verias, and he turns to find a knife at his throat. It's held by a man with pale skin that nearly glows in the moonlight, and hair that's blood-red in the dark. Fleshbound, Verias has no doubt.

"Watch yourself," he whispers. "Dangerous out tonight."

"Worse outside the walls," Verias says. The fleshbound smirks at him, apparently amused, before he vanishes into the night. Has Verias seen that man at the homepalace? As he waits for the streets to fall silent again, he remembers that face: it was the man he witnessed being Bound, screaming. A shudder runs through Verias. After all he's seen, the Binding was the worst. How he'd been able to put aside the memory to Bind Kin, he doesn't care to examine. He doesn't think he'd like the answer.

Kin's anger is easy to shove down when Reshon hums in the back of her head, begging her to find him and slit his throat. She can't tell whether she hates Reshon personally for what he'd done to Verias, for being a Binder, or if she's just generally angry. Either way, she is not above treating him roughly in her questioning. She's glad that Verias, gentle-hearted as he is, won't be there when she rearranges Reshon's face.

She runs along the parapets of the great city wall to get to the Woolworkers' Quarter faster, avoiding the urge to stop and warn Honor of what's to come. Though Kin has no idea how it has come to pass, Reshon is now the most important thing. If she stops him from opening the gate, she'll buy more time to alert what's left of her friends and family. Nothing can be allowed to stop her.

Kin can feel him drawing close, running or maybe riding a horse, as if he knows his time is short. If Kin thought for even a second about Reshon's motives—besides catching Verias—she would have known. Binders have no true loyalty except to the homepalace, and Kin fears that mercenary mindset will allow the city to fall. Reshon allying himself—or worse, every Binder in Sestera—with Felver will leave them safe when the city falls. *If* the city falls, Kin reminds herself, pushing harder, faster.

Soon the wide cobbled street leading to the gate comes into view, and Kin spots a figure on horseback, trotting toward the gate. Kin is a good hand with throwing a knife, even ones as long as her baselards, but she can't risk killing Reshon. She can attempt to kill the horse instead, but a fall from a horse is always dangerous even if she has the heart. Her old instincts take hold, her eyes dart between rooftops of their own volition, and Kin leaps. First the right foot between the wall's merlons, air whistling in her ears, left foot to the peak of the roof, right to the eyebrow window, little slip, heart in her throat, no time to pause. Left-right-left down toward the eave, both feet on the roof of the one-story shed below, broken tile, swooping stomach and hard cobbles.

Kin rolls, smashing her bad elbow on an upturned cobblestone before she's on her feet, grabbing for Reshon's ankle with one hand. His saddle slips as she yanks at him—stars bless this horse if he's the type to blow up when you saddle—and Kin has Reshon on the ground, her knife pressed to his throat. But he feels wrong, slender and slipping out of her arms so fast that Kin can barely grab a handful of robes.

"Lessa!" she snaps when she sees the hateful little woman's face. It doesn't make sense. Kin's fleshbound senses tell her that this is her target, that this is Reshon. "What kind of trick is this?"

"You don't think Binders *know* when they've been marked for death?" Lessa sneers. "I didn't think you'd fall for it, but here you are. Where is Everis, or whatever his real name is? Not with you?"

Kin's heart crumbles into her guts. This is all a distraction. Reshon is likely on his way to the East Gate, and Verias . . . he'll have to fend for himself. She has to catch Reshon. Once again, Lessa has taken everything from her, and Kin doesn't have the time for revenge. She shoves Lessa to the ground and does what she's always been best at: she steals Lessa's horse.

CHAPTER FORTY-TWO

THE HOMEPALACE IS ALIVE THAT WARM, WET NIGHT, golden lamplight pouring from nearly every window on the front face of the main hall. Relief moans through Verias, drawn up short in an instant. They're preparing to defend the city. They'll be alert, ready for an attack, and Verias is going to break in alone. He can't just burst in, not that he'd planned to. He doesn't have a plan of any kind, and he needs one fast, his feet still carrying him toward the homepalace.

Verias goes through the front doors to the entryway where Lessa often stands. Nobody waits there to speak to a Binder, nor does anyone greet or stop him. However, the grand doors leading deeper are faintly aglow with magic. Locked. That would keep a less determined man out, he supposes, but that man would have to have any amount of respect for the social contract put forth by the erection of walls. Walls have little meaning to a sorcerer, and in a building full of people actively using magic, Verias will likely go unnoticed.

He draws from the Wellspring, lets just enough power sigh into him. With no Kin to siphon off the energy, everything is normal again. Thinking of her brings a pang of regret, but he shoves it aside, sharp arrowheads of magic working in concert with tumbling blocks that slice through mortar and push aside stone. The work creates enough heat that it smells like a blazing hearth missing the softening influence of woodsmoke. Verias's skin feels dry and tight as he crouches to pass through the small opening he's made.

Verias hurries up the north wing, trying to keep his footfalls as quiet as Kin's. Rich wool carpets line the floors, deadening the sound of his boots, but there's nowhere to hide if he comes across a Binder. All he can do in that case is act casual, like he belongs there. Like his guts aren't all in a knot, his head full of magic and imagined ways he could die. All the Binders he's seen in the homepalace wear robes like the ancient wizards in the library frescoes, putting on airs with which Carriers aren't bothered. A fight is on its way, no matter what he does. All he can do is put it off as long as possible, save his strength for the Vault and the enchantments that surely protect it.

Voices come from nearby, arguing heatedly about something Verias can't understand with all the cross-talk. Panic surges up, nearly letting the tightly controlled nausea that tickles the back of his throat overwhelm him. He's almost to the end of the north wing, where the Dean's Hall corners and an open door leads to stairs to the next floor. Instinct tells him to hide, just hide and hope nobody sees him, but Verias tells instinct to shut its cowardly mouth. He runs, sprinting into the door and flattening himself against the wall, praying to the Wellspring that nobody has noticed him. A metallic taste clings to the back of his throat.

The argument grows louder, and Verias is able to pick out the Dean's voice. He's saying something about Felver, but that's all Verias gets before the group hurries around the bend, their voices fading. Verias peeks out into the corridor, sees several retreating backs. He only watches for a moment before he takes the stairs two by two.

Verias starts back down the Dean's Hall, passing around the courtyard and once again edging against the wall to take a look down the corridor that holds the Vault. Just as the last time he visited, nobody stands guard. The Binders rely instead on the many enchantments that fill the corridor with palpable magic, like sand burying him under is tingling weight. This is not a situation that calls for subtlety; it will be too difficult to distinguish each spell and pick it apart, like trying to untangle a basket of yarn that a litter of kittens has gotten into. The only way to fix the tangle is to use scissors.

Verias doesn't simply allow the Wellspring's power to fill him. He pulls it in, a siphon sucking at its infinite power as hard as he can. It pushes into his organs, strains against the cage of his ribs, ripples through every muscle. Pure white light fills his vision, blanking the homepalace out and making his head feel like it's about to explode like an overripe pumpkin. It's enough. It has to be enough, or he'll surely die within the next few moments.

Pain cuts through the Wellspring's waters like searing hot steel, and Verias releases it all in a single swipe, a headsman's ax coming down on the Binders' enchantments. Pain turns to agony, and he slumps to one knee, half-leaning against the wall.

"I knew you'd come back for her soul," the Dean's voice says.

Verias's heart would've stopped if Merit hadn't done the job ages ago. He's brought Kin's soul back to the Binders without even thinking. He has the advantage—the Dean somehow thinks it's still in the Vault—but there's a slow, steady leak of thick, old blood from a wound in his stomach that would have cut him in two if the Dean hadn't paused in killing him to gloat. If the pain makes Verias faint, anyone can find where he keeps Kin's soul in the inner pocket of his doublet, as close to the skin as possible. They'll control her again, hurt her again. Verias would rather die than let that happen, but he has nowhere to hide it, no way to defend it with the wound filling his brain with pain. Every attempt to reach the Wellspring leaves him weaker, the slow leak of his life energy turning to a steady flow.

"Do you think us such fools that we wouldn't see why you were so interested in linking after Reshon told us you were in league with Jole?" the Dean asks. Verias fumbles in his pocket for Kin's soul. "Or do you think yourself so clever that your plan was too perfect to fail?"

Verias can feel the Wellspring's power pushing against his back. Even if he survives his wound, the Dean will keep cutting until there isn't a scrap of life left in Verias's body. He does the only thing he can think to do: takes three deep breaths, braces himself, and shoves the glowing orb of Kin's soul into the hole in his own body.

The first sign that something's wrong is Lessa's horse screaming like a mad thing. The second sign is that he throws Kin, sending her crashing to the cobblestones with a hideous crack inside her neck, followed by pain that suffuses her entire body like boiling water. The third, and probably worst sign, is that when Kin manages to get to her feet, she's completely surrounded by the eerie glow of magic. Like something has broken deeper inside her than just neck bones, letting loose something she doesn't want or need.

She ignores it.

What else can she do? She has to stop Reshon, and by the time she gets to the gate, he's standing among the bodies of fallen guards, blood and magic everywhere. She shouts his name, watches him turn with a cruel grin. He thinks he can hurt her, but Verias has protected her. As Reshon steps toward her, Kin draws her knives out of habit, but pushes them back into their sheaths. She has to do this with fists to find the answers Verias needs.

"I thought he'd be with you," Reshon says. Magic flows around him, an avalanche of broken glass tumbling through the air. Enough power that he doesn't appear to notice that Kin is filled with just as much, but with Binders, things are never as they appear. She has to be careful. "I don't know why I would. He's a coward. I suppose I expected him to hide behind his pet monster."

Kin circles him, fists held ready. A blood choke. That remains her most reliable tactic when it comes to humans who she doesn't intend to kill. One or two hard hits in the guts—liver or kidneys always hurts them bad—get him on the ground, then choke him unconscious and wait for Verias to come back and question him.

"Only a true monster would think that Verias fighting against being made into a war machine is cowardice." If Kin keeps him talking, he might be too busy being smug to notice that his magic parts when she walks through it, glancing off her skin like falling leaves.

"Ah, yes. That old argument. Only a true monster would make a monster. I've heard that far too many times to care when it comes from the mouth of a killer." Bits of magic begin to piece together around him, a mosaic of energy. "He Bound you again, didn't he? What does that make him?"

"Better than you at your own art. You tried to Bind him, and you failed," Kin says. Magic snaps off, rushing toward her, and Kin steps aside.

"He was flawed. Worse even than you, according to Lessa. By the way, why didn't she just smear you across the pavement?" Reshon asks.

He jerks, putting it together, and forgotten magic shatters over Kin like a bottle in a tavern brawl. She lunges at him, taking her chance to knock him to the ground. His hand dives for his belt, but Kin isn't about to let him get a weapon to hand. She knows how good he is. She hasn't forgotten the pain of the knife tip lodged in her rib, the feel of her own blood filling her guts.

Reshon has to live. He doesn't have to be unharmed. His wrist snaps like a twig in her grip, and she snatches his knife out of its scabbard, throwing it out of his reach.

"What did you do to him?" she asks. The words come out through her clenched teeth, magic straining at it bonds.

"I just tried to Bind him. That's all." Reshon's power pushes against hers. No, not hers. Verias's. She must be stealing from him again, putting him in danger. That's what happened the last time the Wellspring's energy filled her. She has to let it go, but she doesn't know how, can't remember how Verias made it go away.

"What about his memories?" Kin asks.

"What? I don't know what you're talking about! Please don't kill me, I'm begging you—"

Kin grabs Reshon by his shirtfront and bashes him hard against the cobbles to shut him up. "He's missing time. Tell me what happened."

"I don't know, I swear it. The enchantments backfired, almost killed both of us. There might be bits of them still inside him, inside both of us. There's no way to know."

Kin rolls him onto his belly, sitting on his back, and wraps her arms round his neck. Whether she'll allow him to live she hasn't yet decided. It turns out that after being a killer for so many years, it's a hard habit to break. His struggles weaken, one last wall of magic rises, and Kin is thrown from his body like a huge bubble popped beneath her. Her stomach rises into her throat as she watches the sky pass, then the ground, instinct tucking her arms and legs in tight. Kin knows how to fall. From rooftops, from her station. Shards of enchantment drive into her, emptying her of all the magic she'd held a moment before, and she knows that this is the hardest fall she'll ever take. The one from Verias's arms into the abyss.

Verias is dead.

CHAPTER FORTY-THREE

SESTERA TREMBLES.

Kin lies still. Everything burns, a thousand tiny cuts open and weeping. Every grain of power has gone out of her, almost down to the last spark of her own life. It would be easy to rest. It would be easy to sleep. But the moon peers down with expectant light so bright that she can see it pink through her eyelids. Kin has never in her life done anything the easy way anyway, and she isn't about to start now. The manway hangs half-open, broken by the force of uncontrolled power, but the gate remains in place. Every bit of her skin hurts, every hair on her head sears at her scalp, every joint aches, but she stands. She puts one foot in front of the other, plodding toward the open manway as Reshon whimpers in fear and pain, crawling away.

This is what she's for. To push her body past its limits, to ignore its screamed warnings and draw her knives and do what's necessary. To be what humans can never be, to endure what they can never endure.

"He tried to open the gate," a voice croaks. One of the bodies. Still alive.

"I know," Kin says. She doesn't meet the guard captain's eyes where he sits half-upright against the gate. Her gaze will only frighten him. "Can you make it to the alarm bell?"

"How long do I have?" he asks.

"Not long, by the sound of it." Voices, marching boots, hoofbeats. Something larger and more sinister, a deep, resonant thrum that shivers Kin's guts. "I'll buy you as much time as I can."

Kin picks up the manway door, but it's useless, its steel straps blown out and its boards split. She glances around, looking for anything to seal the gap. She can smell the army's torches now, feel the roaring voices in her bones. She goes to the guardhouse and rips the door from its hinges to prop up against the gate, to bear down against it with all her strength while the guard captain struggles to his feet, face contorted in agony.

The first body strikes the door, pushing against her. Then a second. The balance of the door shifts around its axis as more hands press against it. Kin digs in her heels, caught in the furrows between cobblestones, feels the bottoms tear off her boots before she's overwhelmed by the strength of more and more people pressing against the feeble barrier. Kin has to throw the door aside, dancing backward with a small amount of precious time bought. Now she has nothing but her knives, her strength, her wits, and the small gap that only lets soldiers in two by two.

One-two, one-two they fall, dead or dying or maybe simply in too much agony to continue. Kin doesn't care. The pain is gone, evaporated like so much Wellspring water as she does the only thing she knows how to do, her mind replaced by complete blankness. Verias is dead. There's nobody left but Kin, and if she falls, so too will all of Sestera. All of it, that is, except the Binders who have turned on their city. That isn't Kin's concern. They can get what's coming to them later.

She's slowing. Wide spearheads sever muscle and tendon, making it more and more difficult to move. Blood obscures her vision, a red veil covering the world. The bell tolls above the guardhouse, and others answer around Sestera. Kin's back is to the first cross-street, paces and paces from the Merchants' Gate, when she finally loses her footing, hamstrung by a spearhead that stays stuck in her calf when she goes down to one knee. A great cheer goes up as she finally crumples. If she had the strength, she'd laugh, but instead she spirals into a blessed state of half consciousness as she's trampled. She feels nothing. She is nothing, until the smell of smoke fills her nostrils and brings her back to the urgent need of the city. The army has long since passed her by, burning as they go, with Felver at its head. He has to die.

"Get up," Kin tells herself out loud. The words come out wet and broken, accompanied by shards of tooth. She has to fight. She has to help. Do something, anything. "Get up. *Get up!*"

She pushes to her knees. She has more than one broken finger. Faces and fingers are easiest to break. Toes are a little better inside her boots. Too many bruises to count, most organs probably a paste, except the ones enclosed in the shattered cage of her ribs. They're so mangled that Kin isn't sure they even hurt. Her torso is just hot and soft and swollen.

Kin falls the first few times she tries to stand, but she manages to hold herself up against the side of a building. Her body is trying to right itself, things shifting and crawling inside her like thousands of beetles trying to . . . what? Get to a meeting of beetles. The beetle council. Brain is damaged inside her skull, not working right, but still focused on the smell of smoke. Move.

First find an easy-to-climb building then roof to roof to roof listening for battlesounds until Kin realizes her ears are full of blood and cleans them out with a scrap of fabric from her shirt. Better. Worse. Screams and steel against shield. They're still in the Merchants' Quarter, hacking away at a line of city guards. Not a single fleshbound or Binder in sight. Kin takes stock of her body again, how much she can do. Her knives . . . not at her belt. Shit. Rondel is still there, utility knife, boot knife, it's not all bad news.

A shudder wracks Kin, and she thinks Sestera is shaking

again, but something draws her eyes to the Deep Quarter. The sun is rising behind her, casting her shadow directly toward the homepalace. Above the shops and warehouses and homes, in the mauvey-gray sky, a rainbow of light dances for a few moments before going dark. Kin holds her breath, watching, hoping, until stars pop in front of her eyes. It must be her imagination. Verias is dead, and the Binders won't fight for Sestera.

Kin sets her teeth, scanning the crowd. They're closing in on the Merchants' Gate, pushing the guards back and back. The guards will be crushed against the walls of the Merchants' Quarter and slaughtered before they can even decide to surrender, open the gate, and allow Felver and his men to enter the city center. The best thing Kin can do at this point is find Felver and bleed him out so that the army will at least have to retreat and regroup, if not give up entirely.

Horses. He'll be horsed, surrounded by his personal guard and banners, nowhere near danger. There, black and pale blue fluttering in the brand new morning sun. A dozen guards, keeping him safe as he listens to a woman leaning half out of her saddle to speak to him. Kin has the advantage: they won't expect her to come from above. As long as she gets her rondel in his neck on the first try, he'll be dead within a minute, and Kin will end up with so many swords through her that she'll resemble a porcupine. She doesn't care. This, too, is vengeance.

Three roofs forward, following her stretched-out shadow as bits of rib crawl back to their rightful places to begin the healing process. Two roofs northward, flexing her fingers. Pain isn't too bad. She can grip a knife hilt. She stares down at him, listens for the voice that dismissed Verias and ordered her death just hours ago.

Kin almost laughs. There, holding his black dustcloak around his shoulders, is the cloak pin encrusted with onyx and aquamarine that Kin tried to steal so many years ago. Her shattered fin-

gers itch with the old thief's instincts, but she curls one into a
fist and the other around her knife hilt. This is bigger than selling jewels to give money to families in the Honey Quarter. This
is about all of Sestera. This is about one of the parasites that
make the King of Thieves a necessary evil in the first place.

She soars, the world slowing almost to a stop. Wind in her
ears, horse smell, shouts, the resistance of muscle and sinew
against steel blade. Giddy release and dull pain as she strikes
the ground and leaps to her feet. A scream of victory tears itself
from Kin's throat as Felver first slumps in his saddle, then falls
to the cobblestones. Felver's personal guard freezes, and for a
moment there's nothing in the world but a dozen sets of eyes
and her skin and the hot stink of blood sticky on her knife hand.

Kin bolts before they can recover from their shock, running
as hard as she can, though she can never outrun a horse with
her ruined calf still screaming. And there's the sword blade,
singing through her ribs and into her heart. It tries to beat once
more before giving in, and Kin lets her legs do the same, crum-
pling her into a ball in a gutter. At least it's a Merchants' Quarter
gutter, so it's clean enough. Someone nudges her with the toe of
their boot, and seems satisfied that she's dead.

It's been a long time since Kin has been reckless enough for
her heart to stop. She forgot how peaceful it is. Though the city
guard and Felver's army are all thunder and boots and hooves
as they surge against each other, the inside of her head is utterly
quiet, her eyes closed against the sunrise, all the pieces of her
bones rearranged and her soft parts lying in repose. The sounds
of fighting pass her by, and Sestera falls into blessed silence. The
edges of Felver's cloak pin bite into Kin's palm, pinpoints of
sensation tethering her to consciousness with a thread thought:
she won. She got revenge for Iyara, for Merit. For Verias. Nothing else matters.

Voices. Someone rolls her over, puts an ear to her chest. She instinctively shoves them away, the work of sitting up compressing everything in her torso. One hard, horrible heartbeat cuts through Kin's chest. Another. Another, and it's off and running, pounding hard. Her breath sears her throat, memory cascades over her, and she lets out a bloody cough before she can make any words come.

"The homepalace," she slurs. The city guard stares at her. "What happened at the homepalace?"

"It blew up," says the guard.

"Fuck." Tears streaming down now, wobbling to her feet. Kin can't run any more, only hobble toward the Merchants' Gate, stepping over bodies and shoving aside people who try to grab her until she's overwhelmed, too weak to fight off four at once.

"Hold still!" someone yells at her.

"The battle's over," somebody else says. "You don't have to fight any more. We won." The speaker is blurry, and Kin reaches up to touch her own face, finding one eye swollen completely shut and the other almost as bad. "Let us heal you."

"Hurry" is all Kin could say before magic spears through her, shudders coursing over her as flesh knits and organs resume their jobs, hot infection burning away before it can take hold. Her head clears, her vision sharpens, and she wipes blood from her face with a shaking hand. The pair of Healers and the city guards who have held her still let go, and everything makes more sense than it did a moment before. What was she doing? Verias. "Thank you. My mother can help. She's in the Honey Quarter. In the sickhouse there."

"We can't—"

Kin is already pushing past the exhausted Healers, running for the Deep Quarter. She needs to get to Verias. Maybe the link will work, maybe it can save him if she's close enough to touch. The gates are open, people stumbling out with wide eyes in ashen faces. A few robed figures pass with blood on their clothes, and Kin wishes she could stop to spit in their faces, but she doesn't have time.

Huge chunks of masonry lie in the street, and a few warehouses are smashed in by stones or iron window sashes. The main hall of the homepalace is crumbling, listing against the south hall. Contrary to what the city guard said, the south hall is almost completely intact. It's the Dean's Hall that's an empty shell, still glowing faintly with residual magic. That's where Verias will be, if there's anything left. If any hope remains.

Kin clambers over piles of intact stone that turn into shards and then gravel and dust. The Vault of Souls remains mostly intact, steel warped and stone scorched, the great door off its hinges from the crash through what appears to be multiple floors. Magic tingles across Kin's skin, and the door smashes open, sending up a cloud of choking white stone dust.

Out staggers Verias, bloody and battered, hands clutched against his belly. Kin makes a sound she's never heard from herself before, a kind of wordless, crow-like caw that escapes of its own accord. She can't tell which one of them starts running first, falling into each other, each too tired to hold themselves up without the other's help.

"You're hurt, let me heal you—" Verias pulls away, eyes running up and down her body, trying to decide what to fix first.

"The Healers fixed me," she lies, knowing she still has painful healing to do. "Verias, you're bleeding—"

"Not mine. Mostly. Killed the Dean." Verias coughs out a harsh, humorless laugh.

"You got Merit's soul?"

"Yes. Yes. Kin, I'm so sorry for coming here with your soul. They could have taken it back." Tears run out of his eyes, cutting white veins through dark blood.

"Do you still have it?" Kin takes his shoulders as firmly as she can manage. Her fingers were whole again, but she's so tired.

"Yes, but—"

"Then I don't care. I should be the one to apologize. I lost Reshon. There was magic, I don't know what happened, but the manway was open and that was more important." Kin wishes she didn't care if he's angry with her, but she cares. She cares so much that her heart feels like it might stop again.

"I don't care. You're alive. That's all I need." His voice shatters.

"Verias." Kin cups his face in her filthy hands, suffused with a relief stronger than any she's ever experienced. If this isn't the time, there isn't a time to say it. "I love you. Should have said it ages ago, before all this could happen."

"I love you. That's all I could think about when we split up. I was so scared I wouldn't see you again." When he kisses her, his mouth tastes like old, rotten blood, but she doesn't care. They hold each other, the rising sun turning the stone dust into pink-gold clouds around them.

CHAPTER FORTY-FOUR

FOR MANY DAYS, KIN IS CONFINED TO THE CELLAR OF THE sickhouse, too exhausted and in too much pain to stop Verias from fussing over her. Her mother fusses, too, to a frankly irritating degree. Kin is sure that it's to make up for being absent during the last plague, and resigns herself to it. It would be unkind to tell her to go away, but at a certain point, Kin's mother simply does not have the time for such foolishness while helping with the injured and caring for the sick. More than once, Verias has to help Sola into bed at night because she's worked herself to exhaustion, and Kin regrets having too many bone chips floating around her abdomen to help. She doesn't complain, of course. What good would it do?

Like Kin, Merit is expert at silence, speaking little even after they've healed enough to do so. While Verias is quite comfortable with Kin's silence (after all, they've spent weeks together in small spaces where they couldn't turn around without knocking elbows), he's wary around Merit, picking at his face all the time. The tension is nigh unbearable, but Kin forces herself to ignore it. Merit looks at her wistfully from time to time, but that's because she is carrying their soul for them, not because they're ready to do murder.

Kin is more concerned with the city guard, who have decided she's a hero and keep coming to the house despite the plague. She supposes she *is* a hero, to them. But it feels to her as if she hasn't done enough, has never and will never do enough. For a while, she allows Verias to chase them away and tell them she's too badly injured to see them, but eventually she has to stop putting them off. They want her to fix things, and she simply has to tell them she doesn't know how. She doesn't know who gets rid of Felver's sons. She doesn't know what to do with the hulking corpse of the war machine disabled by ballistas and abandoned outside the city, or the many plague-lost dead. She doesn't know what to do with the Binders or fleshbound who remain, and she doesn't want them to be her responsibility.

There is, at least, one thing she knows what to do with. Merit, finally whole again, approaches her while Verias is above, helping her mother, and the guards have finally let her be for the day.

"It's time for me to go," Merit says. They hold out one slender hand.

"Are you sure you want this?" Kin asks. She knows what it'll be like for them, and she can't imagine bearing it alone. It feels like the only thing that's kept her alive is Verias.

"Yes."

"Where will you go?" Kin doesn't want to watch it all crash over them, doesn't want to see what Verias saw when it happened to her.

"Away" is all Merit says. Kin nods. Even with the home-palace gone, Sestera is a hard place to stay after all that has happened.

She reaches into her pocket for their soul, more than just skin-warm. It holds a heat of its own, almost uncomfortable. Like holding a too-hot teacup. For a moment, she and Merit both look at it, settled perfectly into the hollow of her palm, as if it might move of its own accord, vanish and leave Merit wanting forever. They reach out, the seemingly solid stone melting into their fingertips. They let out a long, pained sigh, their face appearing older, more tired. After a moment, they look up at Kin with eyes sadder by fathoms than they had been a moment before.

"Thank you for keeping your promise, Kin," they say.

"Keep one for me, will you? Stay alive."

"I'll do my best." With that, Merit turns and leaves the cellar. Kin stands frozen a moment before she ascends the stairs to watch their familiar form vanish around a corner. That's it, then. Both of her oldest friends are lost to her.

"Kin?" Verias emerges from the house, sleeves rolled up and hands and forearms red from scrubbing. When Kin meets his eyes, he seems to know what's happened. He puts his arm around her waist, pulling her into his side. Kin can sense her soul pulsing inside him, and can't suppress a shudder.

"That feels strange," she says. "I truly mean it when I say I can't believe you stuffed my soul inside your own body."

"I wanted to keep it close to my heart," he says.

"Don't lie. I know you were just trying to hide it," says Kin.

Verias laughs. "It's closer to my liver than my heart, anyway."

"Your liver is on your right side. It's more like your spleen."

"I suppose you would know."

"Reckon so." Kin touches his side, feels the long scar that her mother sealed shut around Kin's soul.

"Any word on Lessa or Reshon from the guards?"

"None. It might be up to us once the plague passes."

"I'd rather it be up to us," Verias says. "I suppose we could have used Merit, but . . ." He shrugs.

"They killed you dead?"

"Accurate."

"We have more important things to worry about for now, anyway." The pain in Verias's voice is obvious. Closure is a long way off, if it exists at all, and Kin doesn't know how to comfort him. Kin kisses his temple. She's grown good at waiting, and he can do the same. They can get through the wait together.

The structure that protects the Wellspring is huge but humble, a massive, unadorned cube that will blot out the dawn come morning. It's built of plain stone, ringed by a low, rambling wall that does little more than keep goatherds from entering when their herds sniff out the tough grass and shrubs within. Verias can feel the intense power emanating from beneath the earth, trying to bubble through him and reach the air.

The inside of the Wellspring is clean and sparse, an entry hall not unlike that of the homepalace, holding a few people waiting to be admitted to the holy space beyond. The Carriers who tend the Wellspring pass Kin and Verias as they wait, going about their daily work. All are safeguarded, their power muted. Verias feels a sudden prick of fear. Will they turn him away when they notice what he is? He has to ball his hands into fists to keep from picking at his face. Kin, noticing his anxiety, puts a calming hand on his arm.

At last, one of the Carriers greets Verias without so much as narrowing her eyes. She leads them to a corridor, then to a plain study, where a plump, elderly woman sits behind a small desk. Her hair is cut short like many others he's seen, sacrificed to practicality to dedicate every possible hour to the Wellspring.

"Well," she says. "You've lost your life energy, have you?"

"Yes?" Verias is so surprised that he can say little else. None of his family had noticed without being told.

"And you've removed your safeguard."

"It was an emergency." Verias's stomach clenches.

"I'm not judging you, dear. I just need all the details. It can be dangerous to dip in the Wellspring at your full power."

"I'm supposed to go *into* the Wellspring?" Verias asks.

"Yes," the Carrier says brightly. "Have you bathed recently?"

"But . . . it's holy." His brain is a step behind the conversation.

"Of course it is. That's why I'm asking when you last bathed."

"Two days ago, perhaps?" Verias guesses. They've been traveling for nearly a week, and he can't possibly put a toe in the Wellspring like that.

"Then I shall have Resta prepare you a bath. Both of you, if you'd like."

"Yes, please."

Kin says nothing throughout the process, quietly holding Verias's hand and listening. She's equally silent in the bathing room, which resembles the one at Honor's boarding house. Verias doesn't know what troubles her, but he doesn't interrupt her thoughts. He has enough worries of his own.

After they're clean, Resta, the woman who greeted them, brings them to the inner sanctum of the Wellspring. It's a building within a building, little more than a well house, the stone ancient and worn by the elements in the centuries before the larger shelter was built. The elderly Carrier waits there, holding a key on a long silver chain.

"She can't come with you," she says. "A soulless person will become trapped inside."

Verias touches his belly, where Kin's soul remains tucked away, safe from any who might use it against her. It's taken a long time to grow used to something hard and foreign inside his body, but anybody who wants it will have to cut him open. He turns to Kin, who gives him an encouraging smile. He kisses her cheek and leaves her behind to enter the well house. The Carrier unlocks the door, passing inside behind him.

A few small oil lamps light the room, which has only a pace of floor before a circle of stairs descends down to the Wellspring itself. The water is dark and still, the scent of wet stone filling the space, which is very clearly bigger inside than it was outside.

"Remove your clothing," says the Carrier.

Much as he wants to argue, Verias obeys, a flush rising in his cheeks. He places his clothes in a neat pile in the corner, where a few towels are folded. He walks down the shallow stairs, cool and damp against the soles of his feet. The magic from the Wellspring is so strong that his whole body shakes with the effort of controlling it. He wants to hold his breath, to keep it all inside.

The lack of a bottom is alarming, the water icy cold, though it's only the beginning of autumn. His head bobs back to the surface, and he floats there, treading water, waiting for the magic. Nothing happens. He's surrounded, cradled, but there's no great event or revelation.

"That's enough," the Carrier says, and Verias swims out of the Wellspring. She hands him one of the towels, and he dries off and dresses. "Are you ready?"

"What?" Verias pauses at the door, thoroughly confused.

"I hope so." She gives him a little shove, and he stumbles through the doorway.

A searing flash of light consumes Verias's vision, pain piercing his chest. Energy rushes into him, filling a hole he'd forgotten was there. When his vision clears, Kin and the two Carriers are watching him closely, all three surrounded by a pale aura that fades as he blinks his eyes to clear them. Kin hits him like a wagonload of bricks, lifting him off his feet with her hug. He can do nothing but laugh, filling his lungs with sweet air over and over again.

They're politely ushered out of the inner sanctum and given directions to the town less than an hour's ride away. Kin leaves Felver's cloak pin with the Carriers as payment for their help.

To settle at an inn in the afternoon is a rare treat due to Kin's own stubbornness. She rarely stops traveling before dark, because why waste an hour of light when she has a mission to complete? But with no mission and nowhere to be (if only for today), Kin finds herself standing at the window in their room, her teacup forgotten in her hand. The sun is setting earlier and earlier, and she worries. Sestera has to hunker down for the long winter, build her strength, because she still has enemies.

Kin drinks down the last of her tea and turns to Verias where he sits on the bed. He's bent over a book, as always. She puts her cup down on the tea table and runs her fingers down the exposed nape of Verias's neck, feels him shiver. Despite his death, his hair has just kept growing, long enough that he frequently knots it around itself to keep it from falling in his face while he reads. Kin tilts up his chin, and his hand falls from his lips, where he's been worrying at a bit of skin.

"You're bleeding," she says. His face reddens.

"I wasn't thinking."

"That's obvious. Otherwise you wouldn't have a book open right now. You're alive again, silly. You have more important things to worry about."

A small smile spreads across Verias's face, and he tosses aside his book. Before he can reach for her, Kin's hands are in his soft hair, the taste of blood metallic and sweet on her tongue. When she breaks away, he looks a mess—grey-flecked hair askew, scarlet on his lip, eyes hot with desire—and Kin wants him more than ever, wants to drive him mad and leave him utterly ruined. It's been so long since that night in the cellar, so many late nights trying to tend the sick and help the city guard. Time to fix what's broken, but none for each other.

Kin blots Verias's mouth with her sleeve, watches the need in his eyes soften ever so slightly. With one hand tangled in his hair and the other pressed to his chest, she kisses him again, too gently to break the cut open again. When his returning kisses grow too forceful, she draws him away by his hair, listens to his breath catch. An answering heat grows inside Kin, making her hands unsteady.

"Do you like that?" she asks, trying to buy herself a moment to take hold of herself.

"Yes," Verias hisses. Kin keeps her grip on his hair, coaxing him to his feet with a gentle tug.

His eyes slip shut as Kin unbuttons his shirt, and a soft gasp escapes him as she draws her fingers over his bare skin. Goose-bumps rise behind her touch. He shivers, so easy to tease, his reactions kindling her desire. She slides her hand down his side, brushes the outside of his thigh and brings her fingers back up between his legs. Kin grazes his trouser laces, tucks two fingers inside the waistband and hears the little sound of need in the back of his throat.

"Take your clothes off." Kin releases her grip on his hair.

Verias strips off his open shirt, bends to remove his boots and stockings with unsteady hands. She can't remember if she's ever thought how good his legs are. She's seen him naked, but there's a definite difference between his body after death and during life.

Kin closes her eyes for a moment, trying to slow the pounding of her heart. When she opens them, he steps toward her, but Kin stops him with a firm hand on his chest. He's so tense, heart fluttering under her palm, that she thinks he might shatter if she touches him wrong. She bends to lay a single soft kiss against his throat, feels him shudder against her.

Kin moves behind him, unlaces her blouse. Verias shivers when she takes it off, letting the fabric brush his skin, and press-es lightly against his back. As she twines her fingers into his, the scent of his skin makes her lightheaded: sweat and soap with a whisper of leather tack and horse. Teasing him will eventually come back on her, but she can control herself. She's an expert at it.

"Sit down." Kin tells Verias, and he obeys, perching on the edge of the bed as his eyes skim over her body with unabashed hunger. She puts her foot up on his bare thigh. "Unlace my boots. All the way."

Verias's usually deft fingers are clumsy as he does as he's told, pulling the laces out with metallic little clicks of aglet against eyelet. He pulls off her boot, peels down her stocking. Kin allows him to caress the line of her calf before she places her left foot on his right thigh. His hands are steadier this time, bolder. If she takes off her trousers, he'll be impossible to control. As much as she wants him, the game is too fun, and she doesn't want it to end just yet.

Kin climbs into Verias's lap to push him back into the mattress. Their lips meet, Verias's hands against her back, running down to cup her ass as his tongue explores her mouth. She lets him play for a while, his fingers straying to her breasts. Her nipples ache at his touch, pleasure streaking from her chest, down through her belly, between her legs. Instinct grinds Kin's hips against his, and she has to stop herself, has to stop him. She reaches for Verias's wrists, pressing his arms into the bedspread. Verias's chest heaves as he looks up at her, eyes searching her face.

"Is it too much?" she asks. He shakes his head. Kin kisses him with the lightest touch of her lips, pulls away, leans back down to brush her lips along the line of his jaw. She can't resist tasting him, running her tongue along his carotid artery. She finds the small scar Merit left behind and sinks her teeth into his throat.

Verias moans, his hips rising up against hers. She can barely breathe, the taste of his skin filling her senses. Even through her clothes, the feel of his hard cock against her cunt makes her heart flutter in her chest like a frightened bird, and she has to pull away, kissing her way down his body until she's on her knees on the floor. Verias makes a desperate, wordless sound of desire when her lips and the tip of her nose brush against his cock. She tastes the beads of enticing salt that have formed on the gentle curve of hard flesh, wets the head with her tongue. Kin dips his cock into her mouth, her throat, the sounds he makes sending aching daggers of need into her cunt.

"Kin, please."

She groans in response. She can't help it, on fire with desire for him. Kin stands, stripping off her breeches. Her braies are soaked through, her body screaming for him. Kin climbs back on top of him, pressing her wet cunt against his cock. He hisses through his teeth, eyes closed, face screwed up as if in agony. She stays still, letting him recover a little before she begins to rock back and forth, bending to kiss him again, his moans vibrating in her chest and the head of his cock teasing her most sensitive parts. She has to stop for herself as much as for him, her forehead pressed against his as they catch their breath.

"Wellspring's waters," Verias murmurs. "You're trying to kill me."

"You'll survive," Kin says, pressing a hand to his throat. His cock pulses against her, and she laughs. "Just don't finish before me, or I'll make you suffer."

Kin reaches down to guide Verias inside her, listens for his ragged gasp. The hot stretch in her cunt is so sweet that she can't hold back a moan. His hands go to her thighs, bitten-down nails looking for purchase. She tightens her grip on his tender throat each time she rolls her hips against his, driving him deeper. Her other hand travels down to touch the hard, swollen pearl between her legs, searing heat spreading down her legs, up her stomach and back.

"Please, Kin, I'm so close." Verias's hands move to her ass, squeezing hard as he spreads her open, rising to meet her. Kin's climax hits like a bolt of lightning, racing to the tips of her fingers and toes, the top of her head. Lights pop behind her closed eyelids, her back aching with the strain of every muscle in her body tensing at once. Her cry tears at her throat, and as soon as she gives one last thrust, he pulls her off his cock. Verias reaches down to stroke himself, his seed spurting out over his hand. Kin takes him by the wrist, lifting his hand to her mouth to lick it clean. A smile spreads across his placid face, eyes closed as he tried to catch his breath.

Kin dropped onto her back, pulling Verias in to lie against her breast. In his own yielding way, he's brought her a moment of peace, and she's grateful. She kisses his forehead, and he throws an arm around her, soft as milk. They drowse as the sun sets, blanketing the room in velvet darkness. The sound of Verias's breathing is perhaps the most beautiful thing Kin has ever heard. She presses her fingers to the side of his throat just to feel his heartbeat, just to be thankful that she'd hesitated all those months ago.

THE END

AN ENDNOTE ON MENTAL HEALTH

Verias and Kin both have obsessive-compulsive disorder (OCD). For the sake of immersion and exploration of what OCD is like for people who are undiagnosed, I haven't named the disorder in the text, but as someone who has OCD and who went undiagnosed for many years, it's important to me that it be discussed here.

Like Verias, I have dermatillomania/excoriation disorder, and have spent the greater part of my life with varying degrees of facial scarring. Like Kin, I experience intrusive thoughts. And like both our lovers, I'm often left with overwhelming shame and guilt, as well as the equally OCD-fueled belief that this is all somehow my fault: if I were a better person, I wouldn't be punished with these thoughts or the marginalization of being mentally ill. For Kin and Verias, being able to talk about these feelings is part of the process of healing from past guilt, shame, and mistreatment.

If you share these OCD traits with them and with me, I want you to be seen. I want you to feel known and cared for, and seek help when you need it. I want you to heal when you have the chance, even if, like the three of us, you have setbacks.

ACKNOWLEDGEMENTS

This book would not exist without the Chipped Cup Collective crew, who encouraged me to try self-publishing and made the whole task seem much less scary. I appreciate all of you so much. I also have to thank Scream Town (as always) for being the absolute best and supporting me through all my wild schemes. Rachel and Laura, thank you for reading this book and screaming at me when Kin and Verias hadn't kissed yet. Sorry for the slow burn! I only kind of meant to torture you.

Thank you to Dan for listening to me throughout all the moaning phases of this book, of which there were many.

To my family members, I love you, and I hope you didn't read this. Sorry about the butt stuff (not actually sorry).

ABOUT THE AUTHOR

A.Z. Louise is an author, poet, and artistic nuisance living in a cheese lover's paradise. In their spare time, they are a collector of fountain pens, impractical hobbies, and useless facts, all of which they are guilty of inserting into their written works. Links to those works can be found at azlouise.com

Robot Dinosaur Press features queer, inclusive science fiction, fantasy, and horror books from a collective of global authors. For an introduction to our work, sign up to our newsletter at robotdinosaurpress.com/newsletter and receive a free anthology of short stories by RDP authors.

www.ingramcontent.com/pod-product-compliance
Lightning Source LLC
Chambersburg PA
CBHW020511260626
47156CB00006B/1961